Theatre, Culture and Temperance Reform in Nineteenth-Century America

Nineteenth-century America witnessed a full-blown campaign against alcohol and, for most of the century, temperance reform was a national cause. As an integral part of the various temperance movements, a new form of theatrical literature and performance developed, both professional and amateur, to help spread the message. John Frick examines the role of temperance drama in the overall scheme of American nineteenth-century theatre, taking examples from both mainstream productions and amateur theatricals. Frick also compares the American genre to its British counterpart.

JOHN W. FRICK is Associate Professor of Drama at the University of Virginia. He is author of *New York's First Theatrical Center: The Rialto at Union Square*, co-editor of *The Directory of Historic American Theatres* and *Theatrical Directors: A Biographical Dictionary* and is a contributing author to *The Cambridge History of American Theatre* (1999). He has published numerous articles and reviews in, among others, *The Drama Review*, *Theatre Journal*, *The Journal of American Drama and Theatre* and *The New England Theatre Journal*. He has worked Off-Off Broadway as a dramaturg and as a stage manager with theatre and dance companies in New York.

Theatre, Culture and Temperance Reform in Nineteenth-Century America

JOHN W. FRICK

University of Virginia

CAMBRIDGE
UNIVERSITY PRESS

PUBLISHED BY THE PRESS SYNDICATE OF THE UNIVERSITY OF CAMBRIDGE
The Pitt Building, Trumpington Street, Cambridge CB2 1RP, United Kingdom

CAMBRIDGE UNIVERSITY PRESS
The Edinburgh Building, Cambridge, CB2 2RU, UK
40 West 20th Street, New York, NY 10011–4211, USA
477 Williamstown Road, Port Melbourne, VIC 3207, Australia
Ruiz de Alarcón 13, 28014 Madrid, Spain
Dock House, The Waterfront, Cape Town 8001, South Africa

http://www.cambridge.org

© John W. Frick 2003

First published 2003

Printed in the United Kingdom at the University Press, Cambridge

Typeface Adobe Caslon 10.5/13 pt.   *System* LATEX 2ε [TB]

A catalogue record for this book is available from the British Library

ISBN 0 521 81778 1 hardback

For Marsha

Contents

Illustrations

Acknowledgements

This book had its genesis a number of years ago as a study of the relationship between the culture of New York's Bowery area and working-class theatre. During my early research, however, I continually uncovered playtexts that dealt with the issue of intemperance – scripts that, unlike *The Drunkard* and *Ten Nights in a Bar-room*, the two temperance dramas with which I was already familiar, were never produced in mainstream theatres and hence were virtually unknown. As the number of these "lost" plays grew as I researched, I became increasingly interested in the link between the nineteenth-century theatre and temperance reform. Before a month of my research leave had elapsed, the subject of my research had shifted to temperance dramaturgy and production.

At each twist or turn in my research, I was assisted by a number of people and institutions who not only fulfilled their responsibilities as librarians or scholars, but took an active interest in my topic as well. I therefore wish to thank the following for their assistance in my research and preparation of this book: Fredric Woodbridge Wilson, Annette Fern, Julia Collins, David Bartholomew and the staff of the Harvard Theatre Collection; Marty Jacobs and Marguerite Lavin at the Museum of the City of New York; Mike Plunkett, Edward Gaynor and Heather Moore at the Special Collections, Alderman Library, University of Virginia; the staff of the Billy Rose Theatre Collection, New York Public Library at Lincoln Center; Mary-Jo Kline and staff at the Kirk Temperance Collection, Brown University; the staff of the Black Temperance Collection, New York Public Library; Tom Lisanti, the New York Public Library; Mary Ann Chach and the staff, Shubert Archive; Sarah Cuthill, J. C. Elsworth and the staff of the Theatre Collection, Bristol (UK) University; Erica Nordmeier, The Bancroft Library, University of California, Berkeley; Andrew Kirk and the staff at the Theatre Archive, Theatre Museum (London); Kathryn Johnson,

Manuscript Division, British Library; the staffs of Humanities Reading
Room, the Manuscript and Rare Books Divisions, the British Library;
Diane Hansen, Historical Society of Oak Park and River Forest (Illinois);
Elmer Haile and Christie Alexander at the Baltimore County Histori-
cal Society; the staffs of the Chelsea and Kensington Libraries, London;
the staff at British Library Newspaper Archive, Colindale, London; and
William K. Beatty, the Willard Memorial Library. In addition, I wish to
thank the following individuals for their advice, assistance and/or encour-
agement: Patrick O'Neill, Ann Louise Ferguson, Stephen Burge Johnson,
Felicia Londré, Andrea Nouryeh, Bob Chapel, Richard Warner, Lavahn
Hoh, Dorothy Chansky, Jim Baumohl, Lisa Merrill and Janine Wyman.
I also wish to acknowledge an intellectual debt to a number of scholars whose
work has influenced mine. They are: Bruce McConachie, Rosemarie Bank,
Karen Halttunen, David Reynolds, Eric Lott, Steven Mintz, Peter Bailey,
Lisa Merrill, David Carlyon, Paul Boyer, John Fiske, Richard Hofstadter,
Robert Wiebe, Stuart Hall and Raymond Williams. In the area of temper-
ance reform, I was guided by the work of Jack Blocker, Joseph Gusfield, Ian
Tyrrell, W. J. Rorabaugh, Thomas Pegram, Mark Edward Lender, James
Kirby Martin, Leonard Blumberg and Jon Miller.

I am indebted to the National Endowment for the Humanities and the
HGC Foundation for grants in support of my research; to the University of
Virginia for a Sesquicentennial Fellowship; and to the Houghton Library
at Harvard for the Stanley J. Karhl Fellowship that enabled me to spend an
entire summer conducting research at Harvard.

Special thanks are reserved for David Mayer, Jon Miller and Stephen
Vallillo, who read the typescript or portions of the typescript and offered
suggestions for improvement; for Don B. Wilmeth and Brooks McNamara,
my long-time mentors, whose advice and inspiration have been invaluable
to me over the years; and Victoria Cooper at Cambridge University Press,
who guided this project for the last year or so. And, my most fervent thanks
are due to my wife, Marsha, who joined me on the sometimes tortuous road
from initial conceptualization to publication.

Portions of this book have previously appeared in the *Journal of American
Drama and Theatre*, the *New England Theatre Journal*, the *Social History of
Alcohol Review*, *Southern Theater*, the *Cambridge History of American Theatre*
and *Performing Arts Resources*.

Introduction: a complex causality of neglect

> Historical documents are not really the shards of lost memories, which, when read, innocently re-present the past. They are elaborately constructed representations, fused memories retold with understandings and intentions specific to the time of retelling.
>
> Carroll Smith-Rosenberg, "Misprisoning Pamela"

In the first half of the nineteenth century, no single issue – not even the abolition of slavery – had a greater capacity for arousing the American passion than did the cause of temperance.[1] Throughout the country, in cities and in rural areas alike, people listened to their ministers vehemently denounce the evils of intemperance from the pulpit; enthusiastically attended meetings of the American Temperance Society, the Washingtonians, the Sons of Temperance and the Martha Washington Society; eagerly signed the Teetotal Pledge; and endeavored in their private lives to obtain what Jed Dannenbaum calls "worldly redemption" through abstinence from alcoholic beverages. Viewed from current historical perspective, the temperance movement was the first large-scale American reform movement of the nineteenth century, one that represented a "struggle for purity at [both] the individual and societal levels," and an issue deeply "embedded in the struggle... of the middle classes to enunciate the dominant life style in America."[2]

Although presently acknowledged as a foundation of all nineteenth-century reform and one of the principal building blocks of the American middle class, in the public mind temperance reform has been most often equated with Neal Dow and the Maine Laws, vigilantism and the widely publicized attacks on the saloon by Carrie Nation and her followers, the "unreasonable" constrictions of Prohibition, and the self-interested maneuverings of a fanatical minority characterized by its obsession with moral perfectionism, social control, class-conscious repressiveness and coercive methods. On an individual level, the typical temperance activist came to be regarded as a "dour, cadaverous, puritanical" zealot – an extremist, "anti-democratic do-gooder" dedicated to meddling in other people's private affairs and to dictating everyone's morality.

While temperance activism was chronicled by the reformers themselves practically from its inception, until relatively recently scholarly investigation of temperance agitation was generally neglected by serious academics and was regarded as being of secondary importance when compared to abolitionism and even women's rights agitation, movements which in their own time were more limited and attracted less public attention than did temperance.[3] All too many American historians – the group routinely charged with conducting rigorous analyses of past events, institutions, constructions – regarded temperance reform as a near-marginal movement; one "on the periphery of major political events, [one] not clearly related to economic or political aims of classes in the economy."[4] Hence, it was not an especially attractive subject for concerted attention and analytical studies by impartial scholars were generally absent from the literature on temperance reform.

Fortunately, during the latter decades of the twentieth century, this "oversight" was rectified by the historical community as temperance reform has been thoughtfully and carefully reconsidered, revalued and afforded the respect it deserves. Major studies by Norman Clark, Jack Blocker, Jed Dannenbaum, Joseph Gusfield, W. J. Rorabaugh, Ian Tyrrell, Mark Edward Lender, James Kirby Martin, Thomas Pegram and others have documented the significant role of temperance reform in the rise of the American middle class, the protection of the nuclear family, the reinforcement of traditional family values and nineteenth-century reform (abolitionism, women's rights, public health, prison reform, etc.) in general.

Although scholars have been filling in the gaps in the history of American temperance reform, the same cannot be said for theatre historians and the myriad temperance entertainments which disseminated temperance imperatives and supported the anti-liquor cause, for (with a handful of notable exceptions) temperance narratives are invariably omitted from theatre history texts and literature anthologies. The problem here is threefold: (1) in American studies and American literature studies, theatre has been virtually excluded from the canon and from college syllabi; (2) within theatre studies itself, the overall significance of the nineteenth-century theatre and drama – melodrama in particular – has been routinely undervalued, even dismissed; (3) even those theatre historians who do recognize the value of nineteenth-century entertainments tend to regard temperance dramas as marginal to both temperance activism and the theatre.

As Susan Harris Smith has aptly noted in a 1989 article in *American Quarterly* and her recent book, *American Drama: The Bastard Art*, prose and poetry have traditionally dominated the "hierarchy of genres" in university literature courses to the extent that dramatic texts are conspicuously absent from most of the major literature anthologies, and when they are included, they are most often of foreign origin, with Beckett, Brecht, Wilde and Shakespeare the most frequent inclusions. The situation is thus critical in the case of "native-written" (i.e., American) dramas, which Smith feels hover "on the periphery" of literature studies. To illustrate her contention, she points to the first edition of *The Norton Anthology of American Literature* (1994), which contained no playtexts at all, and to *The New York Review of Books* which does not employ a critic to review plays.[5] This, it seems, is symptomatic of the fact that playtexts are rarely afforded legitimacy as literary works. It is almost as if the drama had never existed and, as a result, in the literary sphere, at least, American expressive culture remains a house divided and incomplete.

In a published response to Smith in *American Quarterly*, Joyce Flynn, who teaches in the history and literature concentration at Harvard, further examined the causality for plays being excluded from the canon. In addition to the standard root causes for the dismissal of American drama listed by Smith – the "culturally dominant Puritan distaste for and suspicion of the theatre...a persistent, unwavering allegiance to European models, slavish Anglophilia, and a predilection for heightened language" – Flynn points to widespread, endemic "negative associations involving ethnicity and class."[6] Agreeing with David Grimsted's notion that the indigenous dramatic art of the nineteenth century constituted "echoes of the historically voiceless" and hence was clearly popular in both its production and its reception, Flynn advances the theory that since the theatre was the "habitual sphere of outsiders in American culture...both literary and academic America have shared an aversion to the too-close scrutiny of art forms created in cooperation with democratic audiences."[7] In the case of melodrama, this has meant that "nineteenth- and twentieth-century literary evaluation...has all too often measured the genre in terms of prejudicial assumptions about its audience, thereby introducing social and political values into a critical methodology often considered by its practitioners to operate objectively."[8]

It is hardly fair, however, to castigate literature scholars for their "elitist vilifications" of nineteenth-century American dramaturgy when theatre historians exhibit similar attitudes and a similar blind spot. In a particularly cogent and comprehensive essay, Thomas Postlewait outlines and examines the now-familiar binarism that occurs when nineteenth-century melodrama and twentieth-century realism are compared.[9] Although, as Postlewait contends, historically melodrama and realism developed during roughly the same time period, although realistic elements exist in melodrama, and although melodramatic elements are found in realistic dramas, melodrama and the nineteenth-century theatre are commonly regarded as constituting a "pre-history" for the more aesthetically advanced, modern realism to follow. In historical accounts that hint at some sort of aesthetic or artistic Darwinism, "nineteenth-century melodrama, spreading throughout the nation, is seen not only as a simpler (earlier, cruder, incomplete, or primary) form but also as a pervasive presence that limits or resists the development of realism, which must fight for its niche."[10] Viewed in the context of a cultural hierarchy which came to regard realism as the goal sought – the end product in an evolutionary process that stressed objective truth and intellectual honesty rather than romantic exaggeration – it is hardly surprising that melodrama is routinely depicted as being "frivolous and simple," whereas realism is characterized as "serious and complex."[11]

This is just one of many misapprehensions plaguing the constructive study of melodrama. Equally troubling is the belief that melodrama and realism are, or should be, adversarial. As Postlewait summarizes it, both forms: "responded to and were shaped by similar socio-political conditions in the modern industrial and imperial age of nationalism, capitalism, population explosion, urban growth, rapid change, technological advancements, massive migrations and resettlements, ethnic conflict, enslavement, massacres, revolutionary movements, authoritarian controls, and terrible wars. Here in these complex conditions both art forms found their many topics and themes."[12] In making this claim, Postlewait is supported by an unlikely ally, historian Arthur Schlesinger, who wrote that historically "realism and idealism [i.e., melodrama] were not enemies but allies, and . . . together they defined the morality of social change."[13] Thus, not only did melodrama and realism emerge and develop at approximately the same time, but they dealt with many of the same social issues, albeit the melodrama presented those issues symbolically.

Still, Postlewait warns, in order to maintain a discourse and "discuss melodramatic and realistic drama, we require generic definitions," even though such categories are "an abiding problem for critics and historians."[14] In generating a definition of melodrama, current scholars remain indebted to the pioneering work of Peter Brooks and David Grimsted, who laid the foundation upon which subsequent study of the genre has been based. To Brooks and Grimsted, melodrama, as "a mode of conception and expression," is a heightened and hyperbolic drama characterized by high emotionalism, stark ethical conflict, polar concepts of good and evil, allegorical characterization and a hierarchy of truths presented in such a way that ideals become truisms. In the melodramatic structure, characters are placed at "the point of intersection of primal ethical forces" with the resultant tension generated by the constant threat of catastrophe – catastrophe that would result not only in individual disaster, but, by extension, in the collapse of an entire ethical system. Thus, in the moral tug-of-war between the representatives of salvation and damnation – a struggle exteriorized and played out in concentrated and heightened form – the spiritual destiny of society and universe was invariably put to the test. This "spiritual reality" has caused students of the genre to conclude that melodrama, more than other forms, "embodies the root impulse of drama" and deserves to be regarded as, "not only a moralistic drama, but as the drama of morality."[15]

During the last decade, another generation of scholars has expanded and elaborated upon Brooks' and Grimsted's conceptions of melodrama and has advanced our understanding of the genre. In separate papers at a Melodrama Conference, held at the Institute of Education, London in 1992, Jim Davis and Michael Hays advanced convincing arguments regarding the cultural importance of melodrama. Davis maintained that it "operates powerfully on the level of myth and allegory"; while Hays claimed for melodrama "a newly discovered subversive essence, a 'melodramatic' core that made it not only a genre coequal with tragedy and comedy, but the very marker of a disruptive, modern mode of consciousness and representation."[16]

In the United States, theatre and cultural historians Bruce McConachie, Rosemarie Bank, Jeffrey Mason and Elaine Hadley have published equally significant studies of the genre and the theatre(s) that housed it.[17] Bank has written on theatre culture, the ways peoples staged themselves, and has afforded us different ways of reading the social documents (melodramas included) they left behind them; Mason has examined the ways in which melodrama functioned in the construction of a national ideology and certain cultural myths; Hadley has identified in nineteenth-century culture what she terms the "melodramatic mode," which "reaffirmed the familial, hierarchal, and public grounds for ethical behavior and identity that characterized models of social exchange and organization"; while McConachie's scholarship, which chronicles the development of American melodrama and theatre from 1820 to 1870, has dispelled the misapprehension that the genre is monolithic in form and usage. In his studies, he has shown that the genre is considerably more variable than most believed previously and, in the process, has created what amounts to a typology that accounts for differences within the genre – a typology that includes sensation melodramas, apocalyptic melodramas, moral reform melodramas, fairy-tale melodramas, domestic melodramas and gothic melodramas. To these, British historian Michael Booth would add the nautical melodrama, a form of the genre that fell between gothic and domestic melodrama and converted the melodrama from the supernatural to the domestic.[18]

Regardless of "type," there is a consensus that from its inception the melodrama has been utilized as an "affective vehicle." With its symbolical characterization, its either/or morality, its didactic rhetoric and its resolutions that reward hard work and virtue, the melodrama was the perfect fictional system for making sense of everyday experience. Given its emotionality and affective structure, when pitched to a popular audience that was struggling with the daily hardships of life, it was easily radicalized and readily "served as a crucial space in which the cultural, political, and economic exigencies of the century were played out and transformed into public discourses about issues ranging from the gender-specific dimensions of individual station and behavior to the role and status of the 'nation' in local as well as imperial terms."[19]

Yet sadly, despite admonitions that in assessing the relative contributions of melodrama and realism to the understanding and correction of social ills, "we make a categorical and historical mistake when we attempt to fix their identities ... as if each had a controlling genetic code," and seemingly ignoring the work of Brooks, Grimsted, McConachie, Bank, Postlewait and the current generation of scholars that has revealed the depth and complexity of melodrama, the stereotypes persist and the genre is still significantly undervalued.[20] To many, melodrama still is what was written and produced while Americans waited for O'Neill.

Beginning as a critical response to both the old melodrama and the new realism around the beginning of the century, the stereotypical characterization of melodrama quickly assumed the position of historical orthodoxy, as assertions in a recent book on twentieth-century drama testify: "Melodrama invokes [visions of] shallow or excessive emotional effects. The American drama is, for all practical purposes, the twentieth-century American drama [i.e., realism]."[21] Such a binary is not only fallacious, but ironic as well, for in representing melodrama as an "evil" that must be overcome by "good" (realism), advocates of realism adopted the moral polarity of melodrama, the very form they were in the process of repudiating.[22]

The list of realism's defenders (and melodrama's detractors) is a long and distinguished one that includes such notables as William Dean Howells, Henry James, George Beiswanger, Sheldon Cheney, John Gassner and Eric Bentley. While individual differences as to the nature of realism may have existed between them, all agreed to one degree or another with art critic Leo Stein when he stated that "realism means the spirit of *fact* predominant, and the sheer acceptance of reality" (italics mine).[23] Furthermore, since they occupied the "bully pulpit" in the world of dramatic and/or literary criticism at a point in history when the two "adversarial" forms – melodrama and realism – were struggling, they possessed the authority to decide the debate and hence theirs became the dominant opinion. This, to Postlewait, was a critical factor in the melodrama/realism rift, for it meant that subsequent generations of scholars "have allowed the advocates for realism to determine many of the key terms and issues in our historical surveys."[24]

Part of the problem, it seems, can be traced to the erroneous belief that the ideology of nineteenth-century drama in general was "retrograde" and essentially conservative. Theatre historians have always been reluctant to pinpoint the beginnings of progressive thought in the American theatre, and downright loath to locate it in nineteenth-century drama. Most, like critic/historian John Gassner, summarizing American theatre history from Royall Tyler's *The Contrast* (1787) to the dramaturgy of Eugene O'Neill, Elmer Rice, Clifford Odets, Irwin Shaw and other "serious" playwrights and the politically committed theatre of the 1930s, maintain that, while nineteenth-century American dramatists might have been sensitive to social problems, their innate sobriety, their penchant for moral reform and their optimism about the country's future disposed them toward "sentimentality and congenial resolutions" to complex social problems.[25] From this observation – that the vestigial Victorianism of American social and intellectual life discouraged playwrights from embracing a European-style realism – it is but a short hop to the seemingly standard conclusions that the nineteenth-century American theatre was somehow ideologically neutral, that dramaturgy before O'Neill, Rice, Odets, Irwin Shaw and their contemporaries contained no social imperatives, made no social impact, was of no cultural consequence, was certainly not progressive.[26]

The latter term, "progressive," evokes images of Teddy Roosevelt, the Bull Moose Party, muckrakers, the "Age of Reform" and other ideas and events in the late nineteenth and early twentieth centuries; yet progressive thinking, as scholars from Richard Hofstadter to Raymond Williams tell us, had earlier, broader and less politicized meanings. As Williams has pointed out in his ever-useful *Keywords*, the term "progressive," like its opposite "conservative," is a stereotype, is difficult to define because it has a complex history behind it and as both an attitude and as historical pattern is rather vague and not altogether cohesive or consistent. Its use to designate political positions and/or parties dates from the political and industrial revolutions of the eighteenth century and became widely accepted late in the nineteenth century. Prior to that, however, the "idea of progress, as a law of history," was used to denote (1) a set of attitudes that encouraged "a mood of hope" and advocated a social "going forward" (i.e., progress); and (2) "a discoverable historical pattern...[closely associated with] the ideas of civilization and improvement."[27]

Historians of American reform, most notably Hofstadter, Warren Susman and Arthur Schlesinger, have situated the roots of reform and progressive thought in Puritan teachings and beliefs and have postulated that from Puritan times onward, human progress has been equated with moral progress. Susman traced early reformist attitudes to Puritan beliefs in self-restraint and control over appetites and emotions, their strong sense of community and earthly order and their strict code of ethics and morality; while, to Schlesinger, "the core of Puritanism, once the theological husks are peeled away, was intense moral zeal both for one's own salvation and for that of the community."[28] Ironically, it was this latter desire that led to one of the most troubling aspects of nineteenth-century reform: reformers' persistent efforts at the social control of others.

Activists' attempts at controlling the thoughts and behavior of others are particularly vexing to historians of reform, for the conventional picture of the social reformer is one of a person working altruistically to afford others both moral salvation and economic possibilities, to free, in Eric Goldman's words, "the avenues of opportunity."[29] Instead, progressive re-formers frequently did just the opposite, aggressively imposing their mores and standards of conduct upon others and, by so doing, actually restricted the avenues of opportunity. Evidence exists that indicates that even the earliest patriarchal reformers had a stake in controlling the behavior of others, especially their subordinates. While in retrospect such attempts might be considered unprogressive, given that those guilty of social control were by-and-large Christian, liberal and devoted to the welfare of others, they were, Steven Mintz tells us, also understandable since, like all people, reformers were prone to contradictions and inconsistencies in both thought and deed. Thus, Mintz continues, they "were often blind to the more coercive, pater-nalistic aspects and the class and ethnic biases of their reform program[s]."[30]

Given its shifting meaning(s), applying the term "progressive" to historical studies is not without hazards. To complicate matters, what people regard as progressive today may well become hegemonic a few years hence. In *Marxism and Literature*, cultural critic Raymond Williams has accounted for such cultural transformations and interrelations between movements and tendencies through a theory he calls "epochal analysis." Allowing for variations, Williams identified a cultural process wherein movements or tendencies first appear as "emergent," the phase where new meanings, values, practices and relationships are created; in time, these meanings, values, practices and relationships become "dominant"; and ultimately, although they may continue to exist and even function in culture, they fade from dominance and become "residual."[31] Employing Williams' epochal analysis, it is not difficult to envision how an ideological position considered radical in its emergent phase can become hegemonic in its dominant phase. In the case of woman suffrage and the equality of the sexes, to cite just one example, what we now consider common and orthodox was once so radical and extreme as to be thought of as impossible and unthinkable.

Applied to the study of temperance ideology and practices, Williams' theory affords equal insight. Taking just one aspect of nineteenth-century temperance strategy – "moral suasion" – epochal analysis allows the historian to track its historical journey from its entrance into the public consciousness in the 1830s (its emergent phase) to dominance in the 1840s and eventually to residual status in the 1850s as coercive tactics like prohibition gained ascendance. The notion of a residual ideology – one that is dormant but still present – also helps explain the return of moral suasion, in the form of Alcoholics Anonymous, to dominance following the repeal of Prohibition.

Contradictions, ambiguities and hazards notwithstanding, in the study of nineteenth-century reform movements the concept of progressivism, interpreted broadly as "a sense that Americans could intervene in both nature and society to shape a more moral, a more Protestant society," as an "idea of progress, as a law of history," is essential.[32] It is therefore in this larger, Christian/humanist sense – progressivism as "a broad impulse toward criticism and change [that was manifested in] a growing enthusiasm of middle-class people for social and economic reform" – that I use the term, progressive, and it is this very usage that Gassner overlooks in his criticism.[33]

Recent historiography has provided evidence that Gassner's contention, which was presaged by the writings of Walter Prichard Eaton, Arthur Hobson Quinn, Joseph Wood Krutch and others and which has been echoed by historians after him, is problematical in two additional regards. First, it relies upon an either/or mentality. Playtexts were viewed either as revolutionary social protests or as being totally devoid of social content. No middle ground was allowable. Yet, in fact, many plays, especially those written in the late nineteenth and early twentieth centuries, occupied just such a middle ground or transitional space, moving toward the full social protest drama of the 1930s, but still rooted in the "local color realism" of the nineteenth century and dependent upon earlier conventions, values, ideology.[34]

Second, as recorded in *Dramatic Soundings: Evaluations and Retractions Culled from 30 Years of Dramatic Criticism*, Gassner's implications that social reform and moral reform were somehow mutually exclusive of one another fly in the face of a mountain of evidence that demonstrates that, in America as early as the 1820s, moral reform was the foundation upon which social reform rested and the majority of the early social reformers were theologically trained religious leaders. Hence, evolving from common roots in American religion, for many years social and moral reforms were, for all practical purposes, virtually indistinguishable. In this context, such revered nineteenth-century long-running box office hits as *Uncle Tom's Cabin*, *The Drunkard* and *Ten Nights in a Bar-room*, were thus both moral *and* social treatises – and clearly reformist in both intent and effect.

Such oversights, coupled with current assumptions that these plays were merely commodifications of issues prominent in the public consciousness at the time, have contributed to the historical devaluation of important reformist dramas. In the histories, these and other nineteenth-century reformist plays are routinely regarded as anomalies – as entrepreneurial exploitations of ideological issues – rather than as genuine attempts to effect social change. The implication was (and is) that nineteenth-century theatre artists were more interested in reaping profits from the dramatization of what were, at the time the plays were mounted, critical social issues, than they were in exposing and eradicating the social problems these plays examined.

Similar oversights and misapprehensions have plagued scholarship on the temperance-related entertainments and recreational activities that introduced and disseminated an anti-liquor message to a significant proportion of an eager and receptive public. While general and theatre histories may contain references to or brief treatments of the use of theatrical means to advance the temperance cause, there is just a handful of journal articles, a chapter in a book on theatre and the myth of America, one complete dissertation and a portion of a second on the topic.[35] This relative dearth of scholarship is particularly disturbing, since nowhere was the fervor of temperance agitation and the persistence and pervasiveness of the issue more evident than in the myriad theatricalized temperance presentations that ranged from parades and picnics aimed at attracting large numbers of workers and their families, to concerts and lectures provided for a more exclusive, upwardly mobile, middle-class audience, as well as a plethora of theatrical activities intended for a cross-section of the populace.

One of the central obstacles to the full valuation of temperance entertainments seems to be the belief that "even though antebellum temperance drama expressed reform doctrine faithfully, the movement scorned the plays and relegated them, through resolute neglect, to a marginal position."[36] The assumption here is that since temperance dramas are seldom mentioned in temperance society records and were frequently ignored or even repudiated by early temperance organizations, they played little or no role in the reform of intemperance, and had little impact upon the American populace. Equally damaging to the serious study of temperance drama is the belief that because early efforts to eradicate drunkenness had achieved a degree of success, American intemperance had been largely eliminated by the 1840s, and hence temperance dramas that followed, "no matter what the intent of their creators and supporters, rather than helping to change attitudes to a significant degree, were instead affirming a vision that had already come true."[37]

These contentions, in addition to failing to take into account the cyclical nature of American temperance reform and changing post-1840 population demographics that created new generations of the intemperate, are also predicated upon the notion that antebellum reformers were a monolithic group – from the same or similar backgrounds, having identical objectives, employing the same methods – and that attitudes and tactics remained unchanged throughout the history of nineteenth-century temperance reform.[38] While this may have been true to some extent during the early years of temperance reform when most of the prominent leaders were from within the church, by the 1840s, the decade during which temperance entertainment blossomed, a major segment of the American temperance movement(s) had been secularized and no longer were traditional religious moralists the only (or even the dominant) force in temperance activism. As historian/literary critic David Reynolds, examining the emphasis and imagery in nineteenth-century writing, has observed, writers of reform literature, the drama included, displayed a high degree of ethical fluidity, which rendered them readily divisible into discrete groups: "conventional reformers" who avoided "excessive sensationalism and always emphasize[d] the means by which vice [could] be circumvented or remedied"; and "subversive reformers" who, although they publicly claimed to be as interested in the morality of reform as were their more rationalist brethren, were in fact more intrigued by "the grisly, sometimes perverse results of vice, such as shattered homes, sadomasochistic violence, eroticism, nightmare visions, and the disillusioning collapse of romantic ideals."[39] As Reynolds outlines the emergence of the subversive reformer: "Between 1800 and 1850 reform literature was increasingly exploited by popular authors and lecturers who ostensibly aimed to correct human behavior but whose texts show that they were actually engaged in exploring [the dark side of human nature] and even in airing misanthropic or skeptical ideas [and who, in fact] peddle[d] blood and violence under the guise of morality."[40] While strict moralists might have deplored this tendency, which was firmly entrenched by the 1840s, they were nevertheless unable to deny the public stature and influence of such "immoral reformers" as George Lippard, George Thompson, John B. Gough, Mason Locke Weems and T. S. Arthur, the latter a noted writer of temperance melodramas. More significantly, all were regarded by the nineteenth-century American public as leaders in reform efforts.

Philosophically, the appropriation of the nineteenth-century melodrama and other sensationalist drama for the advancement of the temperance cause was predicated upon the age-old belief that the theatre, by presumably holding "a mirror up to nature," could serve instructive purposes and hence inculcate a particular complex of values. Such didactic use of the American stage was hardly revolutionary, for, as Russell Nye aptly observed, "despite their prejudices, even the Calvinist colonists were willing to use [the theatre] for moral purposes, the model...being that 'great expositor of human nature' and 'virtue's friend,' William Shakespeare."[41] As the nineteenth century progressed, the idea of theatre as a "moral educator" acquired influential proponents: playwright and theatre manager William Dunlap sought, both through his writings and his practices, to transform the stage into "a great engine for social good"; Walt Whitman postulated that everyone could profit morally from a visit to a "well-regulated" theatre; and Mark Twain, in a more whimsical vein, quipped that nine-tenths of the population learned morality in the nation's theatres, not its churches.

These sentiments (and rhetoric), applied specifically to temperance drama, were echoed in other sectors of society: by the Honorable Mr. Park, who characterized *The Drunkard* as that "great moral engine, which has been the means of adding thousands to the ranks of reformed men" in an address to the Massachusetts Senate in 1844; by a writer for the *Spirit of the Times* who wrote, "we know of nothing more conducive to the cause of Temperance than the spectacle [i.e., *The Drunkard*] at the Bowery"; by publicity for *The Drunkard's Daughter* which stated that the play was "the strongest propaganda for prohibition yet written in any language anywhere"; in a program note for *Ten Nights in a Bar-room* when it was mounted at the Theatre Royal, Spring Garden, Halifax, Nova Scotia, June 9, 1866 that claimed that the play had "been witnessed by over 100,000 persons – heads of families, members of Churches, all interested in the propagation of the great Doctrine of Temperance, having borne testimony to the excellent effect produced by the life-like delineations of FOLLY, MISERY, MADNESS, & CRIME caused by the brutal, disgusting and demoralizing vice of drunkenness"; and, on occasion, by the nation's temperance societies themselves.[42] Shortly after *The Drunkard* appeared in Boston in 1844, for example, local newspapers reported that the Friends of Temperance had rallied to *The Drunkard*, which they deemed "the most powerful play ever written"; the Boston Museum offered two dramas, *The First & Last Pledge* and *One Cup More, or the Doom of the Drunkard*, "in conjunction w/a Grand Total Abstinence Celebration at Tremont Temple & on Boston Commons" in 1845; and one temperance association, the National Temperance Society, maintained its own publishing house to print and distribute temperance literature, music, and dramas like *True Wealth: A Temperance Drama in Four Scenes* (1889), *A Temperance Picnic with the Old Woman Who Lived in a Shoe* (1888), *A Bitter Dose* (1879), *No King in America* (1888) and *A Talk on Temperance* (1879), a temperance dialogue.[43]

This study, in an attempt to reclaim what has been termed our unused past, that portion of our national history that has remained either undocumented or misapprehended, will demonstrate that the nineteenth-century temperance drama was born of the intersection of temperance motives and ideology with progressive trends in literature and the arts.[44] In the process, it will examine the nature of nineteenth-century temperance entertainments, the particular cultural forces that spawned them and the temperance activists who utilized them to disseminate anti-liquor imperatives, for although never officially incorporated into the lexicon of tactical weapons of the various temperance organizations, in the hands of individual activists and local societies temperance entertainments nevertheless proved, in actual fact, to have been one of the most potent propaganda devices and recruitment tools available to reformers. In this context, this study will regard temperance entertainments to have played an invaluable role in the overall appeal of temperance advocates eager to reach a large, and in many cases, uneducated audience. It will thus position temperance entertainments within the bounds of temperance activism and not on the margins. To ensure a full understanding of the scope, nature and impact of nineteenth-century temperance entertainments, both the so-called mainstream, commercial productions and those alternative presentations that were staged in less conspicuous, non-commercial venues like temperance halls, Sunday schools and church meeting rooms, will be studied. Where documentation exists, special attention will be paid to audience response and attitudes toward both the performance witnessed and the message received.

Because this book is intended for theatre artists and scholars and cultural historians alike, many of whom may know little about the history of American temperance reform, the first chapter will be devoted to a summary and an interpretation of research conducted by social and cultural historians into the nature of American drinking habits during the nineteenth century and the various reform efforts created to curb and control them. This survey of temperance history, rather than being tangential to the study of temperance entertainment, is instead regarded as essential to the reader's comprehending the threat intemperance posed to the average American during the nineteenth century, the extent of the measures taken to eradicate this pernicious social ill and the central role theatre played in temperance reform. To emphasize the widespread appeal and impact of temperance – its capacity to cut across gender, racial and ethnic populations – special treatment of the role and influence of women, African-Americans and the Irish, facets of the overall temperance picture frequently omitted from the histories, will be included.

In order to place temperance drama within a larger tradition – moral reform drama – chapter 2 will examine the ways in which the antebellum theatre manifested general reformist tendencies and then specifically how dramatic representations were employed as temperance propaganda. Initial emphasis will be upon the city as site of social ills and the belief commonly held early in the nineteenth century that the modern city should somehow replicate the moral order of the colonial village; and then the nineteenth-century temperance drama will be examined in this context – as the most ubiquitous and progressive of the moral reform dramas of the era.

Subsequent chapters will trace, in chronological sequence, the advent and development of the American temperance drama from its inception in the 1830s to its demise early in the twentieth century and its fluctuating significance as it was adopted by cultures at various stages of evolution,

from those newly emerging to those in decline. In chapter 3, I acknowledge the presence and impact (both positive and negative) of the British
temperance drama. This treatment of British antecedents will concentrate
upon the emergence of the domestic melodrama represented principally by
the works of Douglas Jerrold, George Cruikshank, T. P. Taylor and George
Dibdin Pitt, and will challenge the assumption, common in previous scholarship on the temperance drama, that the genre is somehow monolithic
in its structure, philosophy and reception. This study will therefore re-
veal and examine cultural factors which contributed to the development
of British temperance dramas imported into this country before the Civil
War; parallels between British teetotalism and similar reforms in America;
the impact upon homegrown (i.e., American) temperance entertainments;
and possible reasons British dramas were not well received in the United
States.

Chapter 4 is a detailed treatment of American temperance melodramas
such as *The Drunkard*, *Ten Nights in a Bar-room*, *Little Katy; or Hot Corn*,
The Drunkard's Warning and other plays that were staged in America's commercial theatres and the temperance advocates (W. H. Smith, Rev. John
Pierpont, T. S. Arthur, P. T. Barnum and others) who wrote and/or staged
them. The time period covered by this chapter – the 1840s to the Civil
War – was arguably the high-water mark for the temperance drama in that,
as a commercial, urban phenomenon, it was at its most visible and, in the
opinion of some observers, had the most impact on the largest audiences.[45]
The plays examined in this chapter are doubly significant because, as Jack
Blocker has illustrated, the period in which these plays were written and
produced corresponded to the end of one temperance cycle and the beginning of another and consequently encapsulated in these texts is evidence
of the dramatic shift from the philosophy of moral suasion popular in the
1830s and early 1840s to the more coercive reform of the 1850s.

Chapter 5 will move the temperance drama out of the eastern cities
into the hinterlands and will "travel" geographically, tracing nomadic touring productions of *The Drunkard*, *Ten Nights in a Bar-room* and other
"mainstream" dramas throughout America's heartland; discussing temperance plays and songs intended specifically for amateur production in rural
local venues like temperance halls, opera houses, churches and schools; and
ending its cross-country odyssey on the west coast, examining temperance
activities at San Francisco's Dashaway (temperance) Hall and the Baldwin
Theatre, the site of the premiere of David Belasco's *Drink*, one of several American adaptations of Zola's novel *L'Assommoir*. This chapter will

also analyze the influence of the Woman's Christian Temperance Union (WCTU) upon temperance dramaturgy and women's growing prominence in both temperance activism and temperance dramaturgy.

While temperance entertainment was very much a nineteenth-century phenomenon and lost both favor and influence before 1900, it nevertheless persisted well into the twentieth century. Therefore, in an Epilogue (chapter 6), I offer an examination of the slippage in and departure from accepted temperance norms and the changes or "shifts" that occurred in the nature and uses of temperance dramas as the nineteenth century progressed. During the waning years of the nineteenth century and the early years of the twentieth, as temperance reform transmogrified into a more coercive, overtly political and increasingly unpopular endeavor, many playwrights wavered in their support of temperance reform, which resulted in a number of plays written during the era that vacillated in their stance on temperance. In addition to those playtexts that remained faithful to temperance ideology and those that were ambiguous in their temperance position, this chapter will also focus upon plays, from *Rip Van Winkle* to *Harvey*, that were seemingly anti-temperance in their "messages" and those that, while claiming to be pro-temperance, nevertheless subverted temperance ideology. This chapter will also include discussion of the temperance film, an art form whose life was cut short by the passage of the 18th Amendment. The final section of the book will be devoted to an Appendix of known (some extant; some not) nineteenth-century temperance plays.

As an interpretive study, *Theatre, Culture and Temperance Reform in Nineteenth-Century America* is not intended to be an exhaustive survey of the individual plays that constituted the nineteenth-century temperance canon; rather, the plays included have been selected because they illustrate various stages or facets of temperance ideology and/or production.[46] With few exceptions, the dramas examined are those that dealt directly with intemperance, supported recognized temperance positions, and therefore can be considered the semi-official dramas of temperance reform (i.e., temperance dramas). While inebriation was admittedly a prominent dramatic device – a significant plot complication or a conventional marker of moral decay – in such well-known nineteenth-century plays as *The Old Homestead*, *The Octoroon*, *Under the Gaslight*, and even *Uncle Tom's Cabin*, the temperance drama per se had as its principal focus the social, moral and personal consequences of intemperance and as its goals, whether implied or directly stated, the support of temperance efforts and the eradication of the "pernicious evil" of drink. This study, while acknowledging the presence of intemperance as a dramatic device in many nineteenth-century melodramas, will focus upon those plays that actively militated against drunkenness.

In an essay titled "Deconstructing the Popular," theorist Stuart Hall proposed that "'cultural change' is a polite euphemism for the process by which some cultural forms and practices are driven out of the centre of popular life, actively marginalized. Rather than simply 'falling into disuse' through the Long March to modernization, things are actively pushed aside, so that something else can take their place."[47] Throughout the nineteenth century, as anti-drink reform grew in scope and influence, one variation of the temperance impulse or another, each constituting a discrete cultural moment, pushed its way to the center of American thought, only to be shoved to the margins by yet another strain of the same impulse. The ebb and flow of the countless transformations, fluctuations and negotiations that constituted the history of temperance reform were recorded in America's novels, serials, tracts and pamphlets; and in its theatres. This study, then, is a chronicle and interpretation of the efforts of countless nineteenth-century theatre-makers and what they signified both in their own time and to contemporary historians.

I

"He drank from the poisoned cup": temperance reform in nineteenth-century America

God, if there is a hell on earth it is that experienced by the wife of a drunkard.
Diary of Jayne Chancellor Payne, June 4, 1843

In the history of the world the doctrine of Reform had never such scope as at the present hour.
Ralph Waldo Emerson, "Man the Reformer"

As the nineteenth century entered its second twenty-five years, intemperance and efforts to reform it, the subject of so many novels, dramas, short stories, newspaper serials and tracts to follow, was on nearly everyone's mind and tongue, and practically everyone charged with providing moral and/or political leadership seemingly participated in a discourse that moved increasingly toward the full-scale condemnation of drinking. Emblematic of this, a young Abraham Lincoln, in a temperance address in Springfield, Illinois, declared that "the demon of intemperance ever seems to have delighted in sucking the blood of genius and of generosity"; Horace Greeley inveighed against intemperance, both verbally and in print, imploring respectable men to "go on Sundays to church rather than to the grog-shop"; and the Rev. David Pickering, Pastor of the First Universalist Church, Providence, Rhode Island, in an attempt to warn his congregation about the pernicious habit of drinking, went so far as to publish a list of the "necessary effects of intemperance." Intemperance, according to Pickering's pamphlet, was "destructive to habits of industry and of health; was productive of poverty; impaired the intellectual powers; 'unfit[ed]' a man for both the duties and enjoyments of social life; led to other vices [i.e., gambling, stealing]; led to falsehood; and, extinguished the finest and tenderest sensibilities of the human heart."[1] Likewise, by the time of Lincoln's address, the remedy for drinking – temperance reform – was as common a topic of discussion as the problem itself, temperance activists were attaining celebrity status, lurid temperance narratives were selling thousands of copies in novel form and attracting large audiences to playhouses, and temperance activity in one form or another was virtually ubiquitous in American society. By the mid 1840s, there were, according to author Bayard Rust Hall, temperance hotels; temperance saloons; temperance picnics; "temperance Negro operas; temperance theaters; temperance eating houses, and temperance everything."[2]

Such activism and public interest, common by the early 1840s, however, was virtually unknown just a quarter of a century earlier. Prior to the 1820s, there was no perceived need for such reform nor for the literary and dramatic activities that disseminated the temperance message nor was there the necessity of proclamations like Lincoln's or Greeley's. In colonial and early republican society, the consumption of alcohol was pervasive, respectable and deeply ingrained, crossing regional, gender and class lines, and drinking was generally regarded as an integral part of daily family life and as essential to routine social, commercial and political intercourse. In eighteenth-century America, alcohol in the form of beer or hard cider (wine or brandy in the homes of the wealthy) was consumed at daily meals by each member of the average family, children included, and home brewing was one of the routine duties of the colonial housewife. Brewing was done several times each week, so a visit to a neighbor invariably involved a sampling of a freshly prepared beverage from the bottle reserved especially for guests. As William Cobbett, a British traveler to the United States early in the nineteenth century, noted "you cannot go into hardly any man's house without being asked to drink wine, or even spirits, even *in the morning*."[3]

When illness struck the family, a common prescription was a healthy "tug on the jug," because alcohol was believed to be, not only a relief for pain and an anesthetic, but a cure for colds and fever, dyspepsia, various inflammations, snakebite, "frosted" toes, broken legs and a host of other maladies. It was also believed to possess medicinal properties to both relieve tension and reduce depression. Even following childbirth, both newborn and mother were supplied with ample doses of rum, brandy or gin in the form of a toddy or punch. And, whiskey and rum were considered to possess restorative capabilities necessary to sustain men at work in the fields or the shop. Thus, in its earliest manifestation, most drinking took place in or around the home, as did much of the production of the beverages consumed, and the consumption of intoxicating beverages was thoroughly integrated into the average colonist's daily life.[4]

In the consumption of liquor, the church reinforced family and medical norms regarding alcohol. Wine was incorporated into the services of the Anglican and Puritan churches, and weddings, wakes, funerals, baptisms, ministerial ordinations and other church activities were routinely occasions for drinking. At a 1678 funeral of a prominent Puritan in Boston, mourners consumed over fifty gallons of wine, while at the funeral of a minister in Ipswich just a few years later, those in attendance drank two barrels of cider and a barrel of wine. And it wasn't just the laity who imbibed. At an ordination in 1810, Lyman Beecher observed that "drinking was apparently universal among the clergy" in attendance and it was not uncommon for ministers to be reprimanded for "drunkenness and riotous conduct."[5] While intoxication was universally considered sinful – the direct result of Satan's presence – most clergy agreed with Puritan leader Increase Mather's opinion that liquor itself was "the Good Creature of God" and that moderate consumption was allowable.[6] The ecclesiastical stance was therefore that habitual drunkenness was to be deplored and discouraged, but "routine" drinking was within church norms and expectations. Tolerance for alcohol use was so entrenched in church practice, in fact, that the Reverend John Marsh, an early temperance leader, recalled another clergyman who was branded a "pest and a blackguard" after he moralized about the excessive drinking in his church.[7]

Liquor played an equally important role in America's social intercourse and was present in abundance practically everywhere men gathered, playing a central role in men's relations with other men. Town meetings were seldom held without heavy consumption of alcohol by participants and spectators alike and court sessions frequently were "wet"; communal activities like clearing the common fields or raising the town church necessitated a cask of liquor for the citizenry; barn raisings required that the farmer who was to benefit from his neighbors' labor set aside several barrels of rum or cider for work breaks; militia musters, an important aspect of pre-republican life, often degenerated into drinking bouts and drunken revels; and at auctions, drinks were served to anyone who made a bid.[8] Liquor at social gatherings was so ubiquitous, in fact, that wine was served at early meetings of the Massachusetts Society for the Suppression of Intemperance, one of America's first temperance organizations.[9]

Intemperance was also integrated into political practices early in America's history. Local elections were often considered occasions for drinking to excess, for it was generally acknowledged that the winners would be determined by which candidates could provide the most free liquor to the electorate. While contemporary readers may regard this practice and the prospect of the nation's leaders being selected by drunkards as reprehensible, it is important to note that when Col. George Washington was seeking a seat in the House of Burgesses in 1758, he spent a total of thirty-seven pounds on election expenses, with thirty-four pounds of this designated for the purchase of liquor for those coming to the polls.[10]

Drinking was also fully ingrained in America's daily commercial life. Business deals were commonly consummated and sealed over drinks in the local tavern and seventeenth- and eighteenth-century employers, both in the village and on the farm, provided liquor for their apprentices and hired hands. In an era before distinct delineations between work-time and leisure-time and when work was still task-oriented, rather than time-oriented, it was considered "traditional" to imbibe during breaks, a practice reinforced by the common belief that alcohol was a stimulus to labor and a means of reviving strength after exertion.

The cultural centrality of liquor was reflected in the prominent stature afforded the tavern or public house, whose significance, according to social historian Ian Tyrrell, "lay in its service as a utility institution in a society lacking a complex structure of more specialized institutions."[11] A central focus of village life and, along with the church, invariably one of the first buildings erected, the local tavern was initially opened as a stopover where travelers could find food, libation and lodging. So essential were the services of the village inn to the comfort of travelers and the economic well-being of the village, in fact, that authorities reserved for themselves the power to order localities without a suitable public house to erect one.[12] While some of the early taverns were clean, well-appointed, comfortable establishments fit for "gentlemen," many were crude, rough-hewn places equipped with a handful of tables, stools and a plank bar. Regardless of their degree of refinement, however, colonial taverns were among the earliest gathering places for American males and one of the only regular sites of drinking outside of the home.

Gradually, over time, the local tavern's function as a refuge for travelers declined, while simultaneously its role as the center of community life grew. The tavern served, not only as a center of commerce where bartering took place and deals were finalized over a drink and as the village's principal conduit to the outside world, but as a polling place and the site of town meetings, auctions, lotteries and militia musters. After militia drills, worship services, town meetings and court trials (assuming that they were not actually held in the tavern), men repaired to the local inn to "refresh themselves," to swap stories and to discuss politics and current events.[13] In some villages, taverns were erected adjacent to churches so that the congregation could adjourn for drink and socializing after Sunday services. Additionally, the tavern served as the communications hub of the village with notices of local interest being posted, letters received held for the citizenry and newspapers brought in by coach made available to patrons, and it was the logical staging site for such entertainments as boxing matches, bearbaiting, cockfighting and gambling.

Furthermore, because all men were believed to be "equal before the bottle," because it was widely believed in colonial male culture that "to be drunk was to be free" and because taverns had traditionally served as recruiting stations for the Continental army and informal headquarters and staging grounds for rebellion, the public house became a symbol of the egalitarianism Americans prized so highly and a vital institution in the "political culture of America."[14] As David Conroy has observed, in pre-Revolutionary times, the tavern was "a public stage upon which men, and sometimes women, spoke and acted in ways that sometimes tested – and ultimately challenged – the authority of their rulers and social superiors."[15]

Understandably, within the hierarchical social structure of the colonial era, established elites were quick to recognize the potential for social chaos should the taverns slip beyond their control. While colonial inns were routinely maintained by citizens of "good moral character" who, it was expected, would run "well-regulated, orderly and respectable" establishments, and even though a 1606 law passed by Parliament made drunkenness a crime, authorities nevertheless sought additional (i.e., legal) means to control the distribution of liquor. In practically all states, public houses were required to be licensed, unlicensed sellers were outlawed and, adopting a facet of the English licensing system, dealers were prohibited from selling liquor to certain segments of the population; while Massachusetts, according to a seventeenth-century statute, went so far as to require that only church members and property owners be eligible to be licensed and, even when day-to-day operation of the taverns was delegated to hired help, the publican remained subservient to upper-class wishes. Thus, according to temperance historian W. J. Rorabaugh, in the early years of the Republic the upper classes were able to effectively monitor drinking by controlling the taverns.[16]

The licensing of drinking establishments ensured that alcohol consumption would take place within a social structure that was "limited and controlled," and inebriation, when it occurred, was generally regarded as an anomaly, not as a significant threat to society.[17] As a result, in colonial

America there was a general lack of anxiety about drinking problems and, compared to middle-class efforts to institute and enforce social controls over working-class drinking and the resultant angry division of antebellum society into lower-class "wets" and middle-class "drys" that all too frequently characterized alcohol reform of the mid nineteenth century and later, class tensions were, for the most part, nonexistent. Colonial and early republican attitudes toward drinking remained laissez-faire; hence they were less confrontational, with efforts to control the consumption of alcohol restricted to the licensing of taverns. Intemperate apprentices and tippling farmhands could easily be punished by their masters, who were expected, according to custom and common law, to control their subordinates; children who showed symptoms of drinking to excess could be disciplined by their parents; and the "village drunk" was easily managed by the town constable.

Institutional controls notwithstanding, then, "the controlled drinking of the American colonies was largely a result of a social order in which an elite of religious, economic, and political leadership was able to develop social codes of conduct that were influential at most levels of society."[18] As Rorabaugh has noted, "the upper classes were able to monitor drinking and to impose restraints...due to the hierarchical nature of colonial society."[19] Accepting the orthodoxy of the era that opinions travel upwards, manners downward, America's elites viewed themselves as "the central point of departure for the diffusion of improvement in both ideas and behavior" and consequently presumed that paternalistically projecting a public image of moderation would serve as an adequate substitute for more formal constraints on the liquor consumption of both their peers and their inferiors.[20] Thus, through a network of both formal and informal social controls, intemperance in colonial America was kept in check and the distribution of alcoholic beverages, a "legitimate and useful trade that furthered [the average citizen's] welfare and happiness," was allowed not only to exist, but to thrive.[21]

During the first decades of the nineteenth century, however, traditional norms governing alcohol consumption came under siege and deference for America's elites and the complex system of social controls that they had instituted to regulate intemperance in colonial America was undermined, or more precisely, overthrown, by what some have characterized as an uncultured and uneducated mass of farmers and mechanics. Viewed from a historical perspective, "the American Revolution was a great solvent working to dissolve the rigid class and status structure of colonial society."[22] As America moved aggressively and inexorably toward the fervent egalitarianism of the

Jacksonian era, drunkenness as an act of liberation, the seeds of which had been planted in the pre-Revolutionary tavern, became a common feature of male culture; alcohol as a reinforcing agent of the bonds between free white men became even more ubiquitous than it had been in colonial times; and what remained of patrician norms governing drinking became insufficient to control intemperance.

The breakdown of upper-class social control was compounded and exacerbated by a whiskey glut in the 1820s that brought the price of distilled beverages within reach of every American. During the Revolutionary War, the importation of both rum and molasses from the West Indies was virtually eliminated by the British blockade of American ports, with one result being an increase in the distilling of whiskey to fill both military and civilian demand for liquor. Grain was so plentiful that farmers were unable to either consume it themselves or to sell it in its original form. However, when distilled, three gallons of highly marketable whiskey could be made from a single bushel of surplus corn. For western farmers, prior to the completion of the Erie Canal in 1825, it was considerably easier and more profitable to transport whiskey to the east than it was to transport the grain from which it was distilled. In addition, the boom in road building following the revolution not only made liquor easier to ship, but a proliferation of new taverns (many unlicensed) along these roads made alcoholic beverages even more accessible and further reinforced the male subculture that revolved around drinking. Thus, at a time when alternatives to liquor were few (coffee and tea were too expensive for the average citizen to drink regularly and both water and milk were widely thought to be common sources of disease), when liquor was more accessible outside of the home and when a poorly paid laborer or farm worker who earned a dollar a day could afford whiskey priced at twenty-five to fifty cents per gallon and could obtain it with little effort, annual per capita consumption of distilled spirits soared by 1820 to over five gallons, nearly triple that of today's. Tacitly condoned by the laissez-faire attitudes of the remaining aristocracy, no longer checked by social controls and now subject to market forces that provided cheap, plentiful whiskey, America was rapidly becoming, as the Greene and Delaware Moral Society declared, "a nation of drunkards."

Simultaneously, long-established perceptions of drinking were changing as the "hearty, carefree, freewheeling, benign" drinking habits of the yeoman-artisan republic that had been monitored and controlled by the upper classes had eroded to such a degree that public drunkenness became commonplace and came to be associated with human misery, social disorder and crime. Between 1790 and 1820 – a transitional period in the drinking habits of Americans – intemperance was becoming recognized as the principal contributing factor in wife-beatings, murders, incest involving a child and her drunken father, neglect and abandonment of families, assaults, lewd behavior, sexual promiscuity, increased indebtedness and idleness.[23] And even if crime and public disgrace were not the results of intemperance, as the ideology of separate spheres gained ascendance during the century and with less alcohol being produced in the home, men were increasingly forced to seek drinking places outside the home. As a consequence, the local bar became "a competitor for the family cash that was increasingly necessary for survival in a commodity economy."[24] As the republic moved into a new century, therefore, Increase Mather's "Good Creature of God" had already begun to be transformed into the "demon rum" of early temperance reformers as Americans, uneasy about their and the country's future, increasingly came to view intemperance as a significant threat to public order and came to recognize alcohol's capacity to, in the words of Roxbury (Massachusetts) lawyer Henry Warren, "unleash terrible passions on society."[25]

Such social decay, "poverty and misery, crimes and infamy, diseases and death" had actually been prophesied as early as 1784 by Dr. Benjamin Rush, a signer of the Declaration of Independence, pioneer in American medicine, and early reformer. In a tract titled *An Inquiry into the Effects of Spirituous Liquors on the Human Body and Mind*, Rush directly and aggressively challenged the orthodoxy of the era regarding alcohol consumption, not only by denying many of the commonly accepted benefits of drinking, such as its capacity to protect against extremes of weather or as a restorative after hard labor, but by intimating that one form of alcohol – the distilled beverage – was addictive for everyone who drank it.[26] While he continued to assert that beer, cider and wine (the so-called "wholesome" drinks) promoted good health and well-being, Rush unequivocally maintained that consumption of distilled beverages undermined a drinker's constitution and resulted directly in "physical, mental and moral destruction," even if the drinker did not drink to intoxication.[27] While Rush's notion of addiction was certainly far from a modern concept of addiction, he nevertheless convinced many readers that distilled liquor was a "substance of irresistible attraction and powerful effect, capable of overcoming human will" and that "like the demoniac mentioned in the New-Testament, [it conveyed] into the soul a host of vices and crimes."[28] By the end of the eighteenth century, Rush's findings and opinions had infiltrated mainstream public thought and were influencing attitudes toward drinking. Given his prestige in American society, his

Figure 1. The Black Valley Railroad

reputation as a scientist, the logic and rationality of his arguments and the widespread dissemination of his findings, it is hardly surprising that Rush's voice would be one of the strongest and most persuasive in early temperance reform efforts and over 170,000 copies of his *Inquiry*, in pamphlet form, would be printed and distributed by mid-century.

Rush's success at popularizing his theories and attracting educated Americans to his views notwithstanding, his influence was just one factor in the emergence of a concerted effort to curb Americans' intemperance. The first temperance movement was born during a confluence of social developments that included not only the breakdown of patrician social controls and the market revolution that made distilled liquor widely available, but the emergence of new social problems spawned by the precipitous and uncontrolled growth of American cities (as outlined in chapter 2) and the effects of the Second Great Awakening, which social historians agree wrought radical changes in moral attitudes and outlook and had a profound impact on social reform during the first half of the nineteenth century. Between 1790 and 1820, the mass of revivals that swept the country not only generated an energy that easily translated into benevolence and service to mankind, but they introduced Americans to dynamic preachers like Charles Grandison Finney, Lyman Beecher, Timothy Dwight and Nathaniel Taylor, all of whom rejected Calvinist notions of "man's ineradicable depravity" in favor of a more optimistic outlook that allowed for the reclamation of sinners and social deviants and hence contributed to a mindset conducive to reformist activism.[29] Considering that a significant percentage of the converts to religion during this period were young, it is hardly surprising that this generation, which came of age in the 1820s, should form the nucleus of reform societies as well as the foundation of a middle class predicated upon a nexus of values that combined evangelical morality and the principles of free enterprise.

"From men so schooled in the thought and practice of evangelical revivalism," Ian Tyrrell points out, "came the architects of temperance reform, the religious leadership that founded the American Society for the Promotion of Temperance" (later known as the American Temperance Society or simply as the ATS) in 1826.[30] Although not the first voluntary society dedicated specifically to the correction of intemperance, the ATS was the first effort to do so on a national scale and, even in its earliest years, it was the hub of a national temperance movement.[31] From the outset, the ATS philosophy of temperance reform differentiated it from earlier efforts that concentrated upon encouraging the moderate use of all alcoholic beverages. Organized by an aggressive group of evangelical clergymen and inspired by Lyman Beecher's claim that "the daily use of ardent spirits [i.e., distilled beverages], in any form, or in any degree, is intemperance" and his call for the public display of statistics reflecting the prevalence of alcoholism and its resultant social disruption, the ATS both advocated total abstinence from whiskey and related drink and created a strategy, an organization and a well-organized system of finance to disseminate their new approach.[32]

Since fourteen of the original sixteen ATS directors were members of the American Tract Society, it follows that they would adopt the printed word as their principal weapon and, following the example of their predecessors, that they would flood the country with millions of pamphlets. Tracts were cheap to produce, could be directed at specific target audiences like women or children and could be produced quickly to respond to special occurrences like the cholera epidemic of 1832 when temperance activists publicized the fact that most of those who perished were drinkers. The distribution of tracts was followed by itinerant speakers (mostly paid) who reinforced the message of the pamphlets with personal testimony and then solicited contributions from their audience and local sponsors. The combined propaganda/fundraising appearances ensured, not only the dissemination of the abstinence imperative, but full ATS coffers as well. More open and more democratic than its predecessors like the Massachusetts Society for the Suppression of Intemperance, the ATS attracted and enlisted both individuals and local societies, bringing to its membership people who routinely were barred from the earlier, more "exclusive" temperance organizations. The inclusiveness of the ATS was reflected in their financial ledgers that showed that over two-thirds of the members contributed five dollars or less to the cause. Through their efforts to make temperance activism more accessible, the ATS "became one of the most successful reform movements in American history, whether measured by the decline of drinking in the near term or by the inculcation of temperance values in the long term."[33]

Tactically, the ATS approach was predicated upon two convictions: first, rather than an attempt to reclaim habitual drunkards, their goal, like that of Benjamin Rush, was to convince those individuals who were already temperate to sign the pledge and abstain from distilled drink. The ATS believed that if they targeted the young and the temperate, once the current generation of alcoholics died, the nation would be considerably "dryer," since there would be no new drunks to replace them. As Justin Edwards, the society's tactical leader maintained, "as all who are *intemperate* will soon be dead, the earth will be eased of an amazing evil."[34] Second, the ATS leadership adopted moral suasion as its principal tool for encouraging men to sign the pledge. In lieu of more coercive techniques, moral suasion relied

SIGNING THE PLEDGE

Figure 2. Signing the Pledge

upon informal persuasion, the pressures of public opinion, moral example, the fear of loss of independence and the creation of alternative institutions (e.g., temperance hotels) to encourage men to remain temperate and join the ATS cause. The necessity of promoting the morality of abstinence is often cited as one reason the ATS welcomed women into their movement.

In the 1830s, perhaps spurred on by their earlier success in reducing alcohol consumption during the early years of the century and perfectionist visions that emerged during the Second Great Awakening, activists adopted a new goal – requiring everyone interested in temperance to sign a new pledge, the "teetotal" pledge, that required the signer to swear off all alcohol including beer, wine and cider as well as distilled beverages. Spearheaded by a new national organization, the American Temperance Union, founded in 1836, activists sought to reform the drinking habits of everyone who imbibed and thus targeted drunkards and moderate drinkers alike. In their efforts, the temperance community was supported and bolstered by new scientific findings (most notably those of chemist William Brande) that both distillation and fermentation created alcohol and that intoxication could therefore result from consuming beer, wine and cider. Thus, the colonial belief that distillation alone resulted in alcohol was proven to be erroneous. Armed with this information, temperance activists brought all liquor under scrutiny and directed their moral suasion efforts at the eradication of fermented as well as distilled beverages.

Intemperance, however, was more than an issue of morality or medicine. At a time when the country was in the midst of both social and economic upheaval, it was seen both as a significant threat to existing public order and as a major impediment to progress and modernization – to the transformation from a rural, cooperative, agrarian society to an urban, industrialized, competitive one. It was also viewed as an impediment to the emergence and cultural advancement of the middle class. According to reformers and entrepreneurs alike, social progress demanded the adoption of an entirely new nexus of values – one that stressed self-mastery, industry, thrift, self-denial and sobriety – as well as the eradication of traditional attitudes and behavior patterns that might be construed as obstacles to change. Heading the list of obstacles to economic prosperity and social progress was the widespread public drunkenness that threatened to subvert the moral integrity and internal disciplines of the middle-class world and to stifle the economic expansion that, at the time, seemed imminent.[35]

In this context, it requires no "great unmasking" to discover the self-interest associated with the entrepreneurial class' attraction to temperance reform.[36] With the breakdown of the colonial shop/farm economic model in which apprentices and farmhands worked side by side with their masters and often lived on the work site, laborers in the increasingly industrialized America of the first half of the nineteenth century became independent of their employers during their leisure hours and increasingly sought companionship and entertainment in the countless bars that dotted the urban landscape. The results of late nights spent drinking included increased absence from the job, accidents, inefficiency caused by workers' exhaustion and, not infrequently, drunkenness on the job. In a workplace that employed hundreds of nameless, faceless workers, factory owners, desperate to maintain order and productivity and eager to reduce absenteeism and accidents, actively and quite publicly supported temperance societies. Thus, efforts to extend temperance reform to the working classes reflected more than the classism and nativism of the era; they demonstrated the economic interests of the entrepreneurial class as well. And it was this shift of focus, from the "respectable" classes to all classes, as well as the fragmentation of the first temperance movement, that indicated that American temperance reform had completed its first cycle and was on the verge of its second.

To historian Jack Blocker, American temperance reform was hardly a single, continuous movement that progressed in the shape of a tragic arc from the uncontrolled drinking of the 1820s through the triumph of Prohibition to ultimate defeat with its repeal; but rather was a series of interlocking cycles, each with its own goals and tactics. "Although the various movements [were] united by the goal of control over drinking," Blocker maintains, "they [were] distinguished by the specific constellations of historic forces that impelled men and women at different times to choose temperance as a solution to what they perceived as a problem in their own lives or in the lives of others. Each movement was different as well because of the lessons temperance reformers drew from the remembered experience of their predecessors."[37]

While reformers' targets and intent may have shifted (or, more accurately, been expanded) by the early 1840s, temperance remained the "most persistent issue in American local and state politics" and in the public consciousness.[38] As Joseph Gusfield theorizes, "issues of moral reform are [often ways] through which a cultural group acts to preserve, defend, or enhance the dominance and prestige of its own style of living within the total society."[39] Influenced by revivalist activity and touted by religious and secular leaders alike, the non-drinking man became the model of respectability and the relationship between temperance and social status – a relationship aggressively promoted and reinforced by anti-liquor activists from 1830 to 1930 – was established. The rationale was simple: moral, abstinent men made better workers, husbands, fathers, leaders, borrowers, citizens; and, those who possessed the will power and strength of character to undertake a program of self-improvement could be trusted to accomplish whatever they undertook. Thus, membership in a temperance organization was "both a sign of commitment to middle-class values and a step in the process of changing a life style."[40] Once an example of "fidelity to saintly virtues," sobriety assumed a significant symbolic, secular dimension as well, having become a necessary aspect of good character and middle-class status, and a touchstone of middle-class respectability.

As the century progressed, the dominance of middle-class norms governing drinking and the targeting of working-class habits became more apparent and increasingly the identification of alcohol consumption with social status was reinforced. According to Gusfield, whose research on the relationship between abstinence and status remains instructive,

> the quest for self improvement implies a gap between those who remain dissolute and those who have achieved respectability [through signing the teetotal pledge]. The incoming group thus widens the status gap between it and the natives. If the lowly Irish and Germans were the drinkers and drunkards of the community, it was more necessary than ever that the aspirant to middle-class membership not risk the possibility that he might be classed with the immigrants.[41]

Such thinking – a mindset encouraged and disseminated by rabid nativists – increased social pressure on habitual drinkers, especially those from the lower classes. The term "rummies" (later, "wets") and the negative moral connotations that accompanied it, for example, became associated with the working classes; while later in temperance reform, "drys" was a label most often applied to someone respectable and middle class. As Christine Stansell observed in reference to evangelical reformers in *City of Women: Sex and Class in New York 1789–1860*, there is a clear link between rhetoric and class intervention. "The language of virtue and vice, traditionally laden with social connotations," according to Stansell, "became for . . . evangelicals a code of class, which described their own mission of social domination in the language of ethical mandate."[42] Applied more broadly, to secular as well as to evangelical reformers and to temperance advocacy in particular, class came to be understood in moral terms. Having begun early in the century as a "vague impatience" with the intractable crudities and excesses of the working classes, the efforts of mid-century middle-class temperance advocates to reform those beneath them ultimately grew into a full-fledged assault on the mores of working people and immigrants.

As immigration brought new generations of drunkards to American cities and the working classes became more prominent and visible, the goals of some temperance proponents actively shifted from preserving the temperate middle class to reforming the intemperate working classes, many new activists joined the war against alcohol, and temperance reform moved toward increased democratization, becoming for the first time open to those who most needed it: diehard drunkards. It was this shift in focus – from moderate drinkers and the already temperate to heavy drinkers and groups previously excluded from temperance reform – that, even more than the collapse of earlier temperance movements, signaled the end of America's first phase of temperance activism.

The shift from a national, but restricted movement to a more inclusive movement began in 1840 when six artisans – a tailor, a carpenter, a coach maker, a silversmith, a wheelwright and a blacksmith – met at Chase's Tavern in Baltimore and, according to legend, having been profoundly moved by a temperance lecturer at a nearby meeting, decided to organize a temperance society dedicated to the reformation of drinkers of their own class.[43] Naming their society after George Washington, who had delivered the country from British oppression, the original Washingtonians began a campaign of moral suasion that they believed could deliver lower middle-class and working-class drinkers from the oppression of intemperance.

Beginning with the reformation of Baltimore as its principal goal, the Washingtonian movement soon branched out to other cities and by 1842 not only had 11 percent of Baltimore's free population over ten joined the society, but similar numbers were being recorded in New York, Philadelphia, other major northern cities and the west.[44]

As historians of temperance movements are quick to point out, the Washingtonian appeal to the lower middle class and working classes was hardly the first attempt to do so nor was their inflammatory reformist rhetoric necessarily new. During the Panic of 1837, artisans whose livelihood was threatened by the growing power of their employers, had banded together for mutual protection into beneficial societies. While the initial motivation for such organizations was economic protection, not the eradication of drink, it is nevertheless understandable that a temperance imperative would have been included, since it was believed that intemperance in times of depression would be invariably catastrophic to the drinker, his family and ultimately to the unity and solidarity of the beneficial society.

Regardless of whether the Washingtonians were true pioneers in working-class temperance reform or not, their immediate success was undeniable and was due to discoveries and techniques that were to become standards of temperance reform for generations to come. The new movement attempted to reclaim chronic drunkards, previously considered irrevocably lost by its predecessors, and drew from the lower middle and working classes. These segments of society had been largely ignored by earlier temperance societies, but in the 1840s, activists were becoming increasingly convinced that the doctrine of personal self-control was the means to social mobility. Furthermore, the Washingtonian appeal was to the drinker's emotions rather than to his reason. Consequently, the intemperate were addressed directly and in person, not simply provided with tracts to read on their own, and, assuming that the most recalcitrant drunkards might not come to their meetings voluntarily, the Washingtonians sent missionaries into the bowels of America's cities in search of those most in need of saving. Furthermore, the Washingtonians, experienced in the bachelor subculture of the bar room and aware of the temptations it offered, worked assiduously to provide environments and entertainments to supplant and rival those of the tavern. Realizing that drunkards and their families might require financial and material aid in order to restore order to their lives, the Washingtonians offered that assistance as well.

Possibly, however, the Washingtonians' greatest assets were their accessibility and their egalitarian nature. Whereas earlier temperance societies met infrequently and the membership sat passively listening to a featured speaker, Washingtonian meetings were held each week and any rank-and-file member could (and often did) speak. And it was the speeches by habitual drinkers or those who had just recently signed the teetotal pledge – the now-famous Washingtonian "experience speeches" – that both defined the society and attracted the public's attention to it.[45] Modeled upon the success of such speeches in the English working-class teetotal movement of the 1830s and predicated upon the assumption that working-class men would invariably resist the admonitions and the censorious moralizing of their social superiors, the Washingtonians enlisted men of their own class – reclaimed drunkards who understood the situations and feelings of those currently enslaved by alcohol – to narrate their own sufferings and to publicly embody the possibility of becoming temperate. Thus, the experience speech became the central and most publicized activity of the Washingtonian meeting.[46]

As described by Timothy Shay Arthur (in *Six Nights with the Washingtonians*, 1848) and others, the drama of the Washingtonian meeting began routinely with the society President's announcing, after the preliminaries were concluded, that the next "hour or so would be spent in the recital of their experiences by such members of the society as felt inclined to speak."[47] This announcement was followed by a heightened sense of expectation and excitement as a series of speakers took the floor, each to describe in lurid and painful detail his taking the first fateful drink; his neglect and abuse of his wife and children; his loss of position, family and respectability; his precipitous decline to a degraded state in one of any number of "skid rows"; his reaching the nadir of existence, frequently characterized by the onset of the DT's; his eventual discovery of the "miracle" of the pledge and his subsequent signing it; and finally, his rapid reclamation and reunion with his family and community. Delivered in a vivid, dramatic, emotional style, the "intensified sensationalism" of the Washingtonian experience speech rendered it a true "charismatic situation" – one that exhibited all the characteristics of folk theatre and domestic melodrama and one that ensured its appropriation as both a literary and dramatic model.[48]

Before the first year of the Washingtonians' existence was over, the inherent theatricality of their experience speech had attracted thousands to a life free of alcohol, and, having realized early that a riveting and theatricalized narrative delivered by a histrionic speaker was their best weapon, they had a number of exhilarating and inspirational "professional" speakers criss-crossing the country, recounting the horrors of drink and recruiting new society members.

Throughout the 1840s, then, despite considerable resistance from lower-class "roughs" and concerted efforts to subvert temperance organization by the liquor industry and its political allies, temperance activity proliferated among groups previously excluded with the result that thousands of artisans and craftsmen joined the Washingtonians and other fraternal societies. During roughly the same time period, Irish, German and African-American temperance societies were established; the role of women in temperance reform was expanded; and temperance activity in the South accelerated. Involvement of these previously excluded groups meant that by the end of the decade temperance activism affected a significant percentage of the American population.

Since the earliest days of temperance reform, women had been involved in activism, albeit in subordinate roles. From its beginnings, the ATS included them and was, as historians have recorded, "one of the first American voluntary organizations to attract large numbers of women," with 35 to 60 percent of local societies comprised of females. As the century progressed, women became even more prominent in temperance associations, ultimately establishing and administering their own organizations.[49]

Female inclusion in temperance associations was only logical, considering the havoc a drunkard could wreak upon his family and cultural perceptions regarding women's moral superiority. Jed Dannenbaum observes:

> Female influence within the domestic sphere was the key to the success of the moral suasion efforts that dominated temperance reform activity after 1830. In her role as the ultimate moral authority of the family, a woman could inculcate strict temperance ideals in her children, refuse to serve alcoholic beverages to guests, abandon their use as ingredients in cooking, maintain so attractive a home and fireside that male family members would not be tempted to seek the conviviality of the saloon, and urge sons, husbands, fathers, brothers and suitors either to adopt or to maintain teetotal pledges.[50]

Although arguably as much myth as reality, the power of woman's moral influence as partial solution to intemperance was written into countless temperance novels and into dramas like *Aunt Dinah's Pledge* (1850) by Harry Seymour, Charles Morton's *Three Years in a Man-trap* (1877), *The Drunkard's Warning* by Charles Taylor and *Saved, or Woman's Influence* by Edwin Tardy. In Tardy's drama, this view is succinctly stated by the heroine, Ellen Mortimer: "'Tis said a woman's influence rightly wielded can accomplish seeming impossibilities, trusting to the spirit of truth for aid, and counsel, no means shall I leave unturned, to save, and win him back to himself, his country and his God."[51]

In the 1840s, such views were immensely popular and women's involvement in temperance activities increased with the Washingtonian emphasis upon moral suasion as the path to national temperance and with the advent of social and economic forces and pressures that urged frugality and personal self-control as the means to, not only family stability, but upward mobility. In these efforts women became the natural allies to the factory owner and the shop foremen whose livelihoods relied upon a sober and reliable work force. As Ruth Alexander notes, the Washingtonians especially had "revealed a deep absorption in the affairs of the home and the conviction that the use of alcohol was inimical to family happiness" and economic well-being.[52]

To support and advance the Washingtonian cause, separate Martha Washington societies designed to "provide food and used clothing for reformed inebriates and their families, both to give relief and to supply the head of the household with a respectable appearance so that he might 'seek employment with any hope of success'," sprang up along side the male associations.[53] Comprised mainly of wives of artisans, throughout the 1840s the Martha Washingtons searched the streets and alleys for those in need of their services and visited countless homes to offer aid to those families ravaged by alcohol abuse and to invite embattled wives to meetings where, in their own experience speeches, they might recount the horrors of a life with a drunken spouse. While these activities in their own right were crucial to the ultimate success of temperance efforts during the 1840s, according to historians of women's rights activism, female involvement in and leadership of organizations such as the Martha Washingtons and its successor, The Daughters of Temperance, provided women invaluable experience in public speaking, founding and administering social organizations, and editing the pamphlets, newspapers and journals necessary for disseminating reformist ideology. As Ruth Bordin points out, "women found in temperance the most congenial cause through which to increase their involvement in public life...It was in the temperance movement that large numbers of women were politicized, and it was through temperance that they experienced wider spheres of public activity in the nineteenth century."[54] And, in fact, such noted women's rights activists as Amelia Bloomer, Elizabeth Cady Stanton and Susan B. Anthony learned their organizational, leadership and oratorical skills within the temperance movements at mid-century. Such a degree of activity has led Blocker, Tyrrell and other temperance historians to conclude that temperance was unmistakably the largest and most attractive reform movement to nineteenth-century women and a significant "weapon with which women could shape their own consciousness and distinctive aspirations."[55]

Like women, African-Americans were involved in temperance almost from its outset and, like women, their involvement and efforts historically have been overlooked, presumably because, having been prevented from joining white societies, they formed their own societies that have yet to be studied. At first, drinking among African-Americans was carefully controlled by colonial governments or slave masters who, although they permitted and even furnished alcoholic beverages to their laborers, restricted its use. Nevertheless, over time alcohol abuse became a problem among both freed blacks and slaves. Many slave owners, having discovered that making their slaves dependent upon the bottle rendered them more subservient, increased daily liquor rations thereby ensuring additional social control over their slaves; and, increased intemperance.

African-Americans responded to the threats of intemperance much as did white reformers. As early as 1788 liquor was branded an evil, causing the Free African Society of Philadelphia to refuse membership to drinkers, and in 1829 African-Americans formed their first temperance organization, the New Haven Temperance Society of the People of Color. Two years later, following the lead of these organizations, two hundred African-Americans in Baltimore founded a temperance society that practiced the established methods of moral suasion and staunchly contended that adopting "temperance and moral reform would prove the worthiness of black character and thus serve as a weapon against" racism.[56]

From the outset, African-American temperance societies resembled their white counterparts in accepting the distinction between distilled and brewed beverages; in employing moral suasion as its principal approach; in eventually espousing total abstinence as the only goal; and in adopting slavery as a metaphor for alcoholism. If the latter was a persuasive argument in white temperance ideology, it was doubly effective in African-American temperance efforts. "By rejecting all alcohol, [organizations like the New England Colored Temperance Society] not only sought to establish [African-Americans'] personal integrity but they saw themselves as promoting the interests of the larger black community by offering practical and symbolic resistance to the forces of racism and slavery."[57]

By the 1840s, abolitionism and African-American temperance activism had become intertwined and inseparable, with famous abolitionists like Frederick Douglass preaching temperance while they spoke against slavery. Having signed the pledge at the behest of Father Theobald Mathew, whom he met while touring and speaking in England and Scotland in 1845–46, Douglass strengthened the anti-slavery foundation of temperance and, with statements like "in order to make a man a slave, it is necessary to silence or *drown* his mind," he focused public attention on liquor's function as a tool of social control.[58]

During the 1840s, African-American temperance activism declined, curtailed in part by violence that targeted African-American societies like the Moyamensing Temperance Society (of Philadelphia) whose 1842 parade was attacked by racist thugs, and by an emerging black nationalism that challenged both abolitionism and temperance reform by providing an alternative to living under oppressive conditions. Their decline notwithstanding, African-American temperance efforts succeeded in persuading large numbers of blacks to sign the pledge, provided black temperance leaders valuable experience in organization and leadership that would serve as a foundation for subsequent reform efforts and must in retrospect be considered to have been a significant and integral aspect of Americans' attempt to eradicate drunkenness in antebellum times.

While temperance reform among the 1.5 million Irish immigrants would not be recognized as a major, organized moral force until after the Civil War, and Irish temperance societies like the Catholic Total Abstinence Union, a federation of local societies usually situated in individual parishes, would not be founded until the 1870s, attempts to control drinking were present during the antebellum era in the form of Hibernian Temperance Societies. Dislocated from their native land, customs and institutions, Irish men, although they lived in America, nevertheless continued to think of themselves as Irish and, driven by poverty and loneliness, organized themselves into bachelor groups whose principal activity was the drinking of whiskey. Shortly after immigrant communities were established in America's major cities, taverns, which served not only as places where "countrymen could gather together in fraternal association," but as informal labor exchanges and refuges from the elements for the unemployed, sprang up in Irish neighborhoods. Confused by the customs of a new country, frustrated by their inability to find work, the target of constant nativist hostility, and raised in a culture in which drinking was common and encouraged, Irish men, the majority of whom were young, were easily seduced into drunkenness. With intemperance tearing Irish families apart, propelling Irish youths into poverty, crime and prostitution, and serving as a significant barrier to their assimilation into mainstream culture, it is hardly surprising that parish priests would embrace temperance efforts and would attempt to establish local temperance unions.

Their efforts were aided greatly in 1849 by the arrival and subsequent tour by the Irish temperance advocate Father Theobald Mathew. The founder of the Cork Total Abstinence Society in 1838, Mathew was a tireless campaigner and by the mid-1840s had induced nearly five million people in Ireland and England to sign the total abstinence pledge. Spurred by his success in England and Ireland, Mathew hoped to disseminate his message in the United States, but was discouraged by anti-Catholic riots in Philadelphia in 1844. In 1849, Mathew was invited to visit America by the predominantly Protestant American Temperance Union and, during a two-year tour that took him to New York, Boston, Philadelphia, Washington and more than 300 smaller cities in twenty-five states, he persuaded over 600,000 people to sign the total abstinence pledge.[59] Of equal importance, his presence provided encouragement to local parish priests who fought the temperance battle in Irish neighborhoods on a daily basis and served as the inspiration for the Catholic Total Abstinence Union to follow. From the 1850s onward, "Catholic participation in the temperance movement, given impetus by Father Mathew's antebellum ministry, [became] a larger phenomenon than most historians have realized."[60] Unfortunately, however, while Catholic reform efforts may have reduced the incidence of intemperance in the Irish-American community, it did virtually nothing to eradicate the "drunken Paddy" stereotype that continued to plague Irish-Americans and fuel nativist attacks for the remainder of the century.

To historians and Irish-Americans alike, the drunken Paddy stereotype was (and still is) problematical. As outsiders to American culture, the first Irish to arrive in the United States, "like immigrants who would later take their place on the bottom rung of the socioeconomic ladder...represented much of what upstanding American society abhorred. The Irish were Celts, not Anglo-Saxons; Papist, not Protestants...They were communal in a land of vaunted individualist achievers; drinkers at the dawn of the American temperance movement[s]."[61] This last tendency, their "love of their glass," which admittedly many Irish-Americans regarded as a badge of their ethnic identity, was viewed by native-born, Protestant Americans as proof of their lack of character and was thought to typify *all* who came from Ireland; yet drunken Paddy was as much fiction as he was fact. According to scientific studies, although more than 85 percent of Irish-Americans drank some form of liquor, the incidence of severe alcohol problems in the Irish-American community was actually somewhat less than that among Slavic or English populations and "the overwhelming majority of men and women of Irish decent [were] no more alcoholic than Italians [were] members of the Mafia."[62] Truth, however, had little impact upon the characterization of the Irish-American as drunken Paddy, which became an urban myth that quickly spread beyond its big-city roots to the culture in general and served to fuel both nativist hatreds and Irish-Americans' perceptions of themselves well into the twentieth century.

Drinking patterns and temperance efforts in the American South are likewise problematical. To date, scholarship remains divided on the prevalence and strength of temperance activism in the South. Some scholars of the issue believe that southern temperance reform lagged behind that in the northeastern states, largely because "the connection between abolition and abstinence weakened the temperance crusade in the South, especially after southern subscribers to northern temperance periodicals received unsolicited antislavery literature [and because] of the absence of the urban, middle class, which supplied the backbone of northern temperance support."[63] However, others, focusing specifically upon southern temperance efforts, found that temperance organization in the South ostensibly mirrored northern developments, that southern temperance activism evolved through the same phases as did the northern crusade and that southern ideology and arguments differed little from their northern counterparts.[64] Further, the latter disputed the popular myths regarding reform efforts in the South – that national "isms" could not survive outside of the northeast and that the South was not sufficiently urbanized to sustain an ongoing temperance movement – by pointing to the success of temperance efforts in what has been described as the "urban perimeter" comprised of Charleston, New Orleans, Richmond, Baltimore, Mobile, Louisville and later Houston, Galveston and Atlanta.

According to separate studies by Blocker, Stanley K. Schultz and Douglas W. Carlson, temperance societies began to appear throughout the South during the 1820s and "by 1831 such societies could be found in every southern state but Louisiana ... In 1831 there were 339 local organizations in the South, 15 percent of the national total."[65] Some of these societies were strictly local organizations, some were chapters of state temperance associations, while still others were affiliated with national societies like the American Temperance Society and the American Temperance Union. As Schultz notes, by the mid-1830s, "every urban center apparently had its local society; many counties throughout the southern states contained a society centered in the largest town; [and] rural and parish organizations copied the constitutions of their urban counterparts."[66]

The slower pace of urbanization in the South and the link between abolitionism and temperance reform notwithstanding, it is only logical that anti-liquor ideology and organization should have become culturally and politically potent given the prominent role alcohol played in both southern culture and economics and the problems that resulted from intemperance. Supplied by a whiskey industry that was one of the most lucrative trades in the South, plantation life integrated ample quantities of liquor into its daily routine, drinking became an essential ingredient in the hunting/fishing culture of the South and even the institution of slavery came to depend upon the steady supply of alcohol to field workers, both as reward and as social control. While excessive drinking occurred among white southerners of all classes – the rich abused their mint juleps, while poor whites feasted liberally on home-brewed moonshine – alcoholism among African-Americans, both slave and freedman, was a particular concern. With many urban bars routinely serving blacks to the point of inebriation, the specter of drunken African-Americans roaming the streets of southern cities presented a serious challenge to both white authority and the general public safety. Not surprisingly, in such a climate in which drinking was either encouraged or tacitly supported yet was perceived as a threat to social order, southern clergy, slave owners, business owners and members of the "respectable" middle class rallied to the newly formed temperance societies during the 1820s, the 1830s and into the Washingtonian era. Not even the ingrained paternalism of southern culture was able to curtail temperance activity, as women in significant numbers joined the cause, often in numbers equal to male activists. Thus, while southern temperance may have been "a movement in miniature" when compared to its northern counterpart, it was nevertheless a vital and recognizable movement and hardly the disorganized, marginal endeavor some have described.

By the Civil War, then, the anti-liquor ranks included members of all classes, genders and most major ethnic groups, and temperance reform could be classified, for the first time, as inclusive of nearly all segments of the American populace. This more inclusive, democratic approach to temperance reform coalesced first in the Washingtonian movement and then its successor, the Sons of Temperance, which some historians consider little more than a further institutionalization of the Washingtonian impulse. Organized as a series of fraternal lodges, the Sons of Temperance and their sister organization, the Daughters of Temperance, provided support services to those who had signed the pledge, thus offering additional safeguards against the backsliding that had plagued the Washingtonians. Furthermore, they adopted a policy of secrecy to remove, or at least reduce, public exposure and resulting scandal should backsliding occur.[67] Of equal importance, the Sons of Temperance also succeeded in accommodating the goals of both temperance "regulars" and former Washingtonians, thereby solidifying a movement that, before their intervention, was fragmenting. Consequently, even with the demise of the Washingtonians in 1844, temperance reform remained open to any American who wished to sign the pledge and join a temperance society, and it was during this second, egalitarian phase that temperance entertainments became prominent tools for disseminating temperance ideology.

At roughly the same time that the efforts of the Sons of Temperance, the Good Templars and similar fraternal societies resulted in a reform that was becoming more inclusive and egalitarian, one segment of temperance activism was also becoming more extreme. Beginning with the no-licensing campaigns of the 1830s, in which local authorities refused to issue licenses to sell liquor to everyone who applied for one, and with visions of a "dry" utopia, coercive attempts to outlaw the sale of alcoholic beverages culminated in 1851 in America's first attempt at full-scale prohibition.

The foundation for the 1851 statute, called the Maine Law, had actually been laid five years earlier. In 1846, Neal Dow, then Mayor of Portland, Maine, and President of the Maine Temperance Union, backed by a coalition of temperance groups, had passed a local ordinance that outlawed the sale of alcohol in Portland. Dow's efforts, which met with vigorous opposition from liquor interests and were shunned and never enforced by timid local officials fearful of the adverse economic ramifications of prohibition, failed; nevertheless, the 1846 local law became the model for the Maine Law passed five years later. His local interests having been frustrated, Dow reorganized his political support, appealed to the state legislature to pass a law that would prohibit the manufacture and sale of liquor statewide and was rewarded with a law that provided penalties stiff enough to discourage its opponents from defying it. Dow's legislation prohibited the manufacture of liquor in the state, severely limited the sale of alcoholic beverages for medicinal use, allowed for searches of properties where liquor was believed to be stored, permitted the seizure of any alcohol found and suggested stiff penalties for transgressors.

Since it targeted "the specter of pauperism and urban crime" and seemingly articulated middle-class respectability, property interests and growing class divisions in America in the early 1850s, prohibition proved to be increasingly attractive to state legislatures beyond Maine. Between 1852 and 1855, twelve other northern states (Massachusetts, Connecticut, Rhode Island, Vermont, New Hampshire, New York, Delaware, Indiana, Minnesota,

Michigan, Iowa and Nebraska) passed prohibition laws, while legislation resembling the Maine Law failed by a narrow margin in Ohio, Pennsylvania, Illinois and Wisconsin.[68]

Not surprisingly, spurred by the widespread passage of prohibition legislation in a short period of time, the liquor industry, drinkers and ethnic groups whose lifestyles incorporated the consumption of alcohol, hastily organized opposition to temperance, founded their own societies, amassed large financial war chests and triggered outbreaks of violence such as the Lager Beer Riot that broke out in 1855 after the Know-Nothing mayor of Chicago closed bars on Sundays. To astute cultural observers, the widening gulf between "drys" and "wets" was to be expected for, although temperance activism had made significant progress curbing intemperance, it had also severely exacerbated ethnic and class antagonisms. While by mid-century, temperance efforts had been generally embraced by the middle class, within the working classes it was still an alternative culture – one that all too frequently divided neighbor from neighbor and worker from workmate.[69] If nativists, evangelical reformers and a portion of the newly empowered middle class deemed the working classes, especially the Irish, as morally worthless and persecuted them for it, the very under classes they criticized, in turn, vigorously resisted their reform efforts and vehemently rejected reformers as "undemocratic, meddlesome folks, always prying into other people's business."[70]

Such a backlash was hardly unwarranted, for in their zeal to redeem the under classes by eradicating intemperance, the root cause of poverty and desolation in reformers' minds, mid-nineteenth-century activists invariably overlooked what Charles Dickens and other cultural observers had publicly acknowledged: that while intemperance could conceivably be the cause of poverty, the converse was equally true; poverty just as frequently could be a contributing cause of alcoholism. Despite mounting evidence of environmental influences upon drinking patterns among the poor, however, reformers were either unable or unwilling to acknowledge these complex sociological factors, and inexplicably "the more exaggerated the alcohol problem became, the more its solution was oversimplified" and the more pronounced the tension between classes became.[71] As Peter Bailey has summarized the case: "temperance reformers were attacked by working-class critics for attributing solely to intemperance the evils which came from the general squalor and meanness of the urban environment – evils which could only be remedied by more comprehensive reforms than restrictions on [drinking and] and the availability of drink."[72]

While the connections between drinking and the misery of slum living may have been overlooked by reformers, they were painfully evident to
ghetto dwellers themselves, as evidenced by the words of one woman in
New York's Five Points who, when asked why she drank, replied tersely,
"if you lived in this place would you ask for whiskey [or] milk?"[73] Given
the hideous social conditions of America's slums and the denizens' attitudes
toward them, it is only logical that even when class tensions and resistance to moral reform efforts were not overt, they were stirring just below
the surface in working-class neighborhoods and, as a consequence, temperance efforts would be met with either skepticism or outright hostility.
When combined with anti-temperance campaigns organized by the liquor
industry, such working-class resistance constituted a formidable barrier to
long-term reform. Ultimately, however, it was not the vigorous efforts by
drinkers and the liquor interests that eventually doomed prohibition, but
rather it was America's growing focus upon the problems of slavery and the
Republican party's avoidance of politically divisive issues like nativism that
led to the decline in coercive measures. As a consequence, by the advent
of the Civil War, prohibition had been repealed in four of the Maine Law
states and there was minimal enforcement in the others.

Since the adoption of Maine Laws required legislation and hence a vote,
temperance in the 1850s quickly became more politicized and campaign-
ing for prohibition became politically expedient. In this political climate,
women, who had been gaining authority in the temperance movements of
the 1840s but were without the vote, were forced temporarily to the sidelines.
With temperance activists abandoning the time-honored moral suasion in
favor of legislation as their principal tool, women were rendered nearly useless to temperance societies. It was this relative political powerlessness, in
the opinion of Jed Dannenbaum and others, that increased "the desire of
temperance women to wield direct power in the fight for prohibition [and]
encouraged some to embrace the cause of female suffrage, the most radical
feminist demand of the nineteenth century since it constituted the greatest and most direct challenge to the male monopoly of the public arena."[74]
From the late 1850s on, women were to play an increasingly prominent role
in temperance activism, often dominating the movement, and the issues of
temperance and woman suffrage were henceforth inextricably linked.

The Maine Law era was also marked by sexual boycotts, during which
sexual favors were withheld from men until they signed the pledge, and
the first episodes of temperance vigilantism, a phenomenon that would
be made famous by Carrie Nation in the late 1890s. Characteristic of the

growing militancy of women, between 1853 and 1859 bands of weapon-wielding women in communities throughout the nation stormed bar rooms, terrorized patrons and tavern keepers and destroyed stocks of liquor. Reflective of a social system that denied them legal recourse to address their concerns, women by the dozens took extra-legal measures to protect their families and their men from the "demon rum" they perceived was destroying the fabric of their lives and endangering their and their children's safety. Intriguingly, the female vigilantism of the 1850s, although "indecorous, illegal and violent," attracted widespread male support, largely because it was perceived as a defense of home and hearth.[75]

During the Civil War, with men away at the front and the Maine Laws repealed, women assumed prominent roles in American temperance reform. Although they would once again have to share authority with men after the war, women during the 1860s experienced the challenges of leadership and in the post-war years were on the verge of dominating temperance activism. Since its earliest days, even though one-third to one-half of the temperance society membership was female, the various reform movements had been organized and led by men. This changed radically in 1873–74 with the founding of the Women's Crusade, a movement exclusively *by* and *for* women and the largest effort at social protest by women to date in the century. Through the Crusade's efforts, which were a direct response to a sharp post-war increase in the number of bar rooms and a precipitous rise in drinking, thousands of women, heretofore uninvolved in temperance reform yet convinced of the threat to their homes and families, were recruited to the cause. Taking a cue from the female temperance vigilantes of the 1850s, the Crusade "adopted as its principal tactic a public march by groups of women that ranged in numbers from a handful to several hundred. At each liquor outlet the Crusaders attempted, through prayer and song, arguments and pleas, to persuade or coerce dealers to abandon their business."[76] The Crusade, although short-lived, nevertheless marked the advent of "a new period of development, organization, and expansion for the temperance movement, one that led directly to the formation of the WCTU and that led indirectly to the victory of national prohibition nearly a half-century later."[77]

If the late nineteenth century was the golden age of the saloon, as Jon Kingsdale, Jack Blocker and others maintain, it was also arguably the golden age of female influence in temperance matters. While the Women's Crusade was admittedly a poorly organized albeit a "short, sharp demonstration of the intense threat that middle-class women felt from the expansion of the

retail liquor industry in the early 1870s and the powerlessness they experienced in the face of government inaction to curb the drink trade," the
Woman's Christian Temperance Union (WCTU) that succeeded it was
a concerted, concentrated and calculated attempt to afford women entrée
into political affairs, to empower them, to "bring temperance reform and
women's activism into the political mainstream."[78] Almost immediately
upon its formation, the WCTU abandoned impromptu, informal, direct-
action tactics like street demonstrations and raids on bar rooms in favor of
less confrontational but more politically effective means like urging temperance education in public schools, organizing local unions according to
congressional districts, and lobbying local, state and federal legislatures for
passage of laws curbing alcohol production and distribution. Using political
tactics that would become commonplace in the twentieth century, "long
before women had the vote, the Woman's Christian Temperance Union
effectively used political influence and developed a range of sophisticated
weapons – testifying before Congressional committees, lobbying the members of legislative bodies, writing legislation, or hiring a paid professional
lobbyist in Washington – to achieve political, primarily legislative, aims."[79]
By the early 1890s, with over 150,000 members nationally and chapters
in every state, territory, major city and an extraordinary number of local
communities, the WCTU was the largest women's organization in United
States history to date. Furthermore, it had created a mass appeal and a mass
political "base for their participation in reformist causes, as a sophisticated
avenue for political action, as a support for demanding the ballot, and as a
vehicle for supporting a wide range of charitable activities."[80]

   In the 1890s, with the founding of the Anti-Saloon League of America
(ASL), American temperance reform became considerably more militant
and moved closer to the goal that earlier had been espoused by only the
most extremist elements of the movement – national prohibition. Founded
in 1895 in the wake of earlier failures of the WCTU and the Prohibition
Party to gain political support for prohibition that was deemed the only
antidote to a growing liquor industry and the proliferation of saloons in the
1880s and 1890s, the ASL, comprised of a new generation of temperance
activists armed with new strategies, initiated the vision that led directly to
the passage of the Eighteenth Amendment.[81]

   Founded at a point in America's development when the saloon was perceived as being beyond social controls, when the emergence of the cabaret
and café lifestyle was attracting public attention and the work ethic was
being degraded, the Anti-Saloon League was particularly effective because

it reflected "the dominant themes of a modernizing America – bureaucracy, expertise, and professionalism [and because it] opportunistically employed the techniques of the emerging organizational society to overcome the partisan political tangles that had obstructed prohibition initiatives in the past."[82] Founded as a single-issue pressure group, and one with widespread grassroots appeal, the ASL supported any political candidate, regardless of party, who publicly advocated prohibition. Applied on both the local and national levels and in primary and general elections, the practical politics of the ASL led to the Webb–Kenyon Act of 1913 that restricted the shipment of liquor between states, to a pro-prohibition congress in 1916 and to national prohibition three years later with the ratification of the Eighteenth Amendment and the enactment of the Volstead Act by which prohibition could be enforced.

Following the popular repudiation of the Eighteenth Amendment in 1933, however, prohibition (and with it temperance reform) came to be regarded as a national embarrassment – a misguided, overzealous attempt to legislate morality on a previously unimagined level. A generation later, Richard Hofstadter would dismiss it as "a 'pseudo-reform' perpetrated on the nation by the cranky remnants of the rural, evangelical culture" of an earlier era and historians to follow began the characterization of prohibitionists, and by extension *all* temperance reformers, as rabid moralists and cultural meddlers.[83]

The humiliation of repeal notwithstanding, throughout the nineteenth century, temperance reform "had reflected the hopeful expectations and anxieties of a rapidly changing society."[84] In its century-long history, it had run the gamut of expectations from moderation to abstinence to legally enforced prohibition and methods from gentle suasion to harsh coercion. Viewed from a comparative perspective, temperance reform had been an optimistic, progressive series of movements that served not only as the means of combating the social evils caused by intemperance, but as the model for other social reforms and political organizations and as a training ground for social activists in general. It had been, in legend and in fact, the reform that had defined and shaped the century.

2

"Nine-tenths of all kindness": literature, the theatre and the spirit of reform

It is almost fair and just to aver (although it is profanity) that nine-tenths of all the kindness and forbearance and Christian charity and generosity in the hearts of the American people today, got there by being filtered down from their fountain-head, the gospel of Christ, through dramas and tragedies and comedies on the stage, and through the despised novel and the Christmas story and through the thousand and one lessons, suggestions, and narratives of generous deeds that stir the pulses, and exalt and augment the nobility of the nation day by day from the teeming columns of ten thousand newspapers, and NOT from the drowsy pulpit!

Mark Twain, *Contributions to the Galaxy*

IN HIS CLASSIC STUDY OF THE REFORM IMPULSE IN AMERICA, *The American as Reformer* (1950), Arthur Schlesinger rendered a service, generally unacknowledged, that has subsequently proven invaluable to later historians: while outlining the nature, extent and limits of American reform, he inextricably linked overt reformist measures and activities, not only to the ideas (i.e., the ideology) that spawned those activities and to the "vagaries and eccentricities" of the reformers who implemented the various measures, but to those literary professionals who wrote about social ills and efforts to eradicate them. Among the myriad disparate events, texts, pronouncements and figures that, in their totality, constituted nineteenth-century reform, Schlesinger seemed most intrigued by the contributions, whether voluntary or involuntary, of some of America's most prominent literary figures. Their perceptive minds, in his opinion, "react[ed] readily to human injustice, and [their] pens, tipped with moral sensitivity, often carr[ied] conviction where the professional agitator batter[ed] against stone walls."[1] In this regard, writing for Schlesinger was, to borrow a phrase from literary historian Stephen Railton, "a public gesture, not...a private act."[2]

Whereas author as reformer (and I include playwrights in this classification) was admittedly a minor theme in Schlesinger's total *œuvre*, it has since been developed into a more central focus of studies by later generations of cultural historians, most notably David Reynolds, Raymond Williams, Warren Susman and, to a lesser degree, Carroll Smith-Rosenberg, Michael Denning, Karen Halttunen and David Brion Davis, whose recent work has carved out a privileged place for writers within the history of nineteenth-century American reform.

A related idea, the notion that reformist activism and reformist literary endeavors were not merely compatible and complementary, but rather were inevitable manifestations of the same impulse – the deep-rooted belief in the perfectibility of man – was advanced a decade later by one of Schlesinger's contemporaries, Henry Steele Commager. Commager noted that reform in the era of transcendentalism reflected "a dominant and pervasive view of the nature of Man and the relation of Man to Nature and to God," one designed to harmonize man with the proper moral order.[3] It also demonstrated, to him, Americans' fervent desire for moral and ideological continuity. Above all, antebellum reform reflected the beliefs that, since man was innately divine and perfectible (a view that had been generally accepted since the Enlightenment), it was inconceivable that he or she should be constrained by slavery of any kind, be it to another human being, to liquor, to Mammon's currency, to sex, or to the innumerable vices that plagued mankind. To both progressive activists and their literary spokespersons, then, reform was emblematic of Americans' collective conviction that neither society's ills nor its sinners were intractable.[4]

While antebellum reform may have sprung from visions of a more perfect future and a millenialist sense of possibilities, it also had roots in Americans' deep-seated fears of cultural chaos, widespread violence, the threatened disintegration of the nuclear family and ever-widening divisions between classes.[5] America, early in the nineteenth century, was in the midst of a period of unprecedented expansion and cultural transformation, as the rural character of the nation, which had defined the Republic, began to yield to explosive urban growth. Not surprisingly, such social upheaval was reflected in the American mindset: a mindset dominated as much by anxiety as by hope. As Steven Mintz views it, the disintegration of the older patriarchal, hierarchical social order spawned fears that the Republican experiment would "degenerate into anarchy, that self-seeking individualism would erode traditional morality, that commercialism would undermine national ideals."[6]

To progressive thinkers, the solution to such threats lay in reform societies and movements that were designed as much to paternalistically shape character and regulate behavior (i.e., social control) as they were to embody the humanitarian impulse to redeem and rehabilitate victims of social change.[7] Although first manifested in American evangelism before the end of the eighteenth century, reform in the decades before the Civil War became increasingly more secularized, more organized into voluntary societies, more narrowly defined by the tactics employed and more specific in the vices it targeted for elimination.

While reformers might have disagreed upon the means to their respective ends and upon the specific vices that needed containment or eradication, there was a clear consensus as to what cultural concern was central in their demonology – namely, that America's burgeoning urban centers represented the most serious moral challenge the nation had yet encountered. Faced with the specter of moral and social collapse, as early as the 1820s Americans projected upon the city their blame for the disintegration of the earlier patriarchal, preurban social order that had ensured traditional morality and social stability, as well as their deep-seated anxieties about the by-products of industrialization and urbanization: immigration, violence, intemperance, the breakdown of the American family, crime, unemployment, deepening class divisions, a commercialism that threatened to destroy Republican ideals and the decay of rural life.[8] So serious was the threat of the industrial city, in fact, that Paul Boyer, in one of the most provocative statements in his book, *Urban Masses and Moral Order In America*, asserts unequivocally that urbanization served as a potent catalyst for social action and that "common to almost all . . . reformers was the conviction – explicit or implicit – that the city, although obviously different from the village in its external, physical aspects, should nevertheless replicate the moral order of the village."[9]

Boyer's claim creates a dilemma for historians, since it seems to imply that forward-looking, progressive reformers needed to look to the past and adopt conservative means in order to solve contemporary social problems. Such reservations, however, are born of our own desire for historical "neatness," not from a flaw in Boyer's historiography, for human history shows us that neither progressives, nor conservatives, nor moderates have remained totally consistent in either thought or action. The pages of history are filled with stories of Federalists with Republican beliefs, abolitionists who were anti-women's rights, abstainers who opposed temperance reform. So prevalent, in fact, is this ideological admixture in human thought and behavior, that

Raymond Williams has coined a special term – "progressive conservatism" – to account for it.[10] Nor was Williams the first to recognize the tension between progressive goals and conservative values and means. Early in the nineteenth century, Emerson identified it, noting that "our history has always been a struggle between ... Conservatism and ... Innovation, between Memory and Hope."[11] Viewed in this context, it is understandable that in an era before reformers acknowledged "the inevitability of the city" and attempted to devise reforms specifically tailored to combating city problems, urban social ills would be viewed strictly as moral challenges, challenges that could only be solved by invoking the dominant morality of the time – rural morality.

Almost from the outset, Americans recognized that modern city culture was radically different from that of agricultural America. The city landscape was littered with commercial enterprises and offerings considered antithetical to rural life (bars, brothels, theatres, gambling dens, hotels, billiard parlors, sporting palaces) and "city types" (streetwalkers, three-card monte players, beggars, ragpickers, hot corn girls, pickpockets, youthful thugs and the like) that were totally foreign to the nation's "countrymen." In the city, traditional social and recreational patterns had been significantly restructured. Leisure-time had been effectively divorced from work-time; public amusements had become an integral part of commercial culture; and socializing with a crowd (what one observer labeled a tumultuous encounter of everybody with everyone) had ostensibly supplanted socializing with a small circle of friends. As Gunther Barth summarizes the prevailing Republican perception of urban life in *City People: The Rise of Modern City Culture in Nineteenth-Century America*:

> At times, urbanization and industrialization seemed to [rural Americans] the roots of all evil. From their perspective ... the new forms of urban life that both supported, such as reading a newspaper on Sunday or spending a salary on clothes, were just one more sign of the erosion of thrift and piety, prudence and self-reliance, those attributes of rural life that they considered the basis of the nation's social integrity, economic stability, and political wisdom.[12]

Consequently, by the end of the Republican era, the dangers and sins of the city, and most particularly of New York, were legion and legendary, and even reformers as aggressive and dedicated as the Rev. Charles Grandison Finney and Lyman Beecher were beginning to question whether America's cities might be restored to moral stability.

Those reformers who remained undaunted by the magnitude of the task they faced certainly did not lack vices to attack. Bands of young toughs prowled the streets of America's major cities, brutalizing anyone they encountered, and, in more organized fashion, gangs with colorful names like the Bowery B'hoys, the Dead Rabbits, the Roach Guards, the Plug Uglies and the Shirt Tails likewise roamed the city, seeking to rob, beat, or fight with countryman and city-dweller alike.[13] Prostitutes, an integral facet of the male consumer world of entertainment and services, and, in the case of New York, one of the principal reasons for its reputation as the "carnal showcase of the western world," routinely advertised their wares in guidebooks to the city and in its newspapers, and conducted business openly in the lobbies of the city's best hotels and in the third tiers of first-class theatres. Brothels on New York's West Side, along the East River and in the Five Points near Paradise Square, were among New York's best-known attractions; while streetwalkers in droves plied their trade on Broadway, the Bowery and lesser thoroughfares.[14] City slums, with colorful names like Corlears Hook, Dutch Hill and Five Points, gained national notoriety and were immortalized in dime novels, plays and various exposés. So too were some of the denizens of these ghettos – the rag pickers, matchsellers, beggars, sewing girls, "street Arabs" and miscellaneous "wretched urchins" – who gained immortality when converted into fictional characters. One, a fictive hot corn girl named Katy, was the central figure in a serialized exposé by Solon Robinson first published in the *New York Tribune* in 1853, published as a novel the following year, and then adapted into one of the most successful temperance plays of the century.

As *Little Katy* and other plays and novels testified, intemperance flourished in the urban climate, due largely to a greater availability of liquor and a more laissez-faire attitude toward use of leisure-time. By 1830, New York alone had one bar for every fifty persons over the age of fifteen, and just one decade later, drunks were seen on nearly every main thoroughfare at all hours of the day, prompting former New York Mayor Philip Hone to complain about drinkers "making [the] night hideous by yells of disgusting inebriety" and to credit alcoholism with contributing to the general depravity and lack of morals in his city.[15]

Added to the litany of New York's menacing, loathsome aspects, street crime, like prostitution, was one of the most public of its ills and one that prompted Walt Whitman to conclude that by the 1840s the city was one of the most crime-ridden and dangerous cities in all of Christendom. Stabbings, muggings, dognapping, purse snatching, watch-stuffing, pickpocketing and "pocketbook dropping" were common occurrences on city streets. According to New York court records, reported crimes quadrupled in the years between 1814 and 1834, while the city's population doubled and Whitman warned his readers that: "There are hundreds – thousands – of infernal rascals among our floating population who will sneak up behind you, or pretend drunkenness and run against you, or inquire the way, or the hour, and snatch your watch, or take you unawares ... knock you on the head, and rob you before you can even cry out."[16] In his advice to the uninitiated, Whitman was especially diligent to point out that every major city was a "countryman trap," and to warn against making acquaintances with strangers on the street. Any friendly stranger, Whitman cautioned, might swindle the countryman as soon as he could get into his confidence. And, indeed the con man/countryman scenario became part of the lore of the big city, written into countless newspaper serials, novels, advice manuals and dramas like Benjamin Baker's *A Glance at New York*, which begins with a "bumpkin," just arrived in New York, being swindled out of a silver watch and ten dollars and then being victimized by a "pocketbook dropper."[17]

In retrospect, city slicker/countryman tensions suggested far more than simply the degree of social decay and the existence of an urban pecking order; they revealed a significant fault line along which Jacksonian America was dividing, as urban and rural cultures grew further apart. Although the America of the early years of the nineteenth century had begun to move to the city, it nevertheless had been born in the country and Americans, both rural and urban, retained "a sentimental attachment to rural living and ... a series of notions about rural people and rural life ... a kind of homage that Americans have paid to the fancied innocence of their origins."[18] Throughout the eighteenth century, Americans had been taught that rural life and farming were somehow sacred and that the yeoman farmer was the model citizen because of his solid work ethic, his democratic spirit and his independence. Thus, in the early years of the Republic, "most articulate people [were] drawn to the noncommercial, non pecuniary, self-sufficient aspect of farm life. It was an *ideal*."[19] This ideal, which came to be known as the "agrarian myth," was, according to Richard Hofstadter, almost universally accepted by 1820 and amounted to nothing less than a form of "rural fundamentalism." And, Hofstadter continues, as young men raised on America's farms migrated to its cities in increasing numbers, the entire culture became more nostalgic about its rural past.[20]

Like most myths, the agrarian myth has been the subject of intellectual scrutiny, and has been successfully debunked by many. Warren Susman questioned the continued superiority of rural life, noting that throughout the nineteenth century, the cities siphoned off the "superior people," leaving only the "inferior" in the country. Max Weber, citing the demands and effects of modern capitalism, stated unequivocally that rural society could not exist separate from urban society. Hofstadter himself admitted that, while the farmer may have given lip service to agrarian morality, in his business dealings he acted like a big-city entrepreneur. And, in possibly the most dismissive attack upon the agrarian myth, anthropologist Clifford Geertz wrote: "The notion that one can find the essence of national societies, civilizations, great religions, or whatever summed up and simplified in so-called typical small towns and villages is palpable nonsense. What one finds in small towns and villages is (alas) small-town or village life."[21]

Attacks upon the agrarian myth notwithstanding, it nevertheless persisted outside of intellectual culture, and informed all of American thought – high, low and middle-brow. Thus, while there was a consensus that the modern city was a parasitical growth on the country and was responsible for a breakdown of the relative homogeneity of American culture, there was an equally strong and enduring conviction that the yeoman farmer, whose life was pure and idyllic, should remain the ideal citizen. And, all of these factors – the schism between urban and rural cultures; the philosophy of primitivism that lent theoretical weight to the yeoman farmer's natural superiority; and the portrait of the wicked, modern city that enslaved and destroyed thousands of young men who were involuntarily made the victims of crime, drink, loose women and reckless speculation – provided ample grist for the literary mill.

While such accounts were admittedly only a fragment of the total urban reality, well before mid-century the wicked city had nevertheless become an abstraction, a moral paradigm that informed the folklore, literature, popular press, drama and the discourse of the era. No longer could the city be regarded strictly as a reconfiguration of physical space; but rather it became a representative environment as social and theatre historian Rosemarie Bank and others have reconceived it.[22] And, whether consciously or unconsciously, this construct – the wicked-city theme – was employed and often exploited by intellectuals, literary figures and reformers alike, who capitalized upon commonly shared suspicions that the modern city represented social upheaval, moral collapse and the end of the Republican experiment. This tendency, which crested in the 1850s and exploited the strong current of hostility to the city prevalent throughout American society, influenced urban moral and social control efforts for succeeding decades.

Authors who exercised their moral sensitivity and either warned the uninitiated against the dangers of the city or exploited the "evil city" motif for profit and titillation ranged from small-town clergy, writers of advice manuals for young men, conservative social critics and authors of "women's melodramas" – the so-called "conventional" reformers whose writings were sincere efforts to promote traditional morality and neutralize the omnipresent menace of city – to sensationalists, opportunists and the subversive reformers. The latter capitalized upon Americans' fears that the decadence of America's cities represented social collapse on a heretofore unimagined national scale, and seemingly took delight in depicting the nineteenth-century city as a "modern 'Sodom' populated by depraved aristocrats engaged in nefarious doings in labyrinthine dens of iniquity."[23] Not surprisingly, the texts they created to disseminate their various perspectives were equally varied and included sensationalist penny press like the *New York Herald* and the *National Police Gazette*; dime novels; pamphlet novels; guidebooks and other nonfiction that offered a simple and "terror-free" way of introducing the uninitiated to the ways of the city; "city-mysteries" novels; and melodramas. The latter two were considered to have been the most extreme and overtly dramatic portrayals of the "sins of the city."

City-mysteries novels were cheap stories, commercially produced and widely distributed to working-class readers, that appeared in the wake of the penny press and European city-mysteries novels like Eugène Sue's *Les Mystères de Paris* and G. W. M. Reynold's *The Mysteries of London*. Written by popular (and frequently notorious) writers like E. Z. C. Judson, who wrote under the pseudonym, Ned Buntline, and others, such novels took readers deep within the bowels of the city, penetrating and invading the nocturnal, urban subcultures in order to expose all the vice of the city, to "lay open its festering sores," so that the socially conscious might take the necessary steps to eradicate the ills. In the hands of these and other authors, many social texts suddenly "lost their semiotic equivalences and became colored by a radical infusion of the imaginative. [In this process], popular reform literature moved from staid, rational tracts on the remedies of vice to sensational, often highly metaphorical exposés of the perverse results of vice," and came to represent what Michael Denning regards as the paradoxical union of sensational fiction and radical politics.[24]

If the 1840s was the decade of the city-mysteries narrative in novel form, as some claim, the 1850s was its heyday in the theatre. Introduced in 1848 by Frank Chanfrau's legendary character, Mose, the Bowery B'hoy, in

H. P. Grattan's adaptation of Buntline's *Mysteries and Miseries of New York*, the genre quickly became a favorite vehicle of some of the leading figures on the New York stage. In 1857, E. L. Davenport portrayed Father Abraham, the lead character in Thaddeus Mehan's exposé, *Modern Insanity; or Fashion and Forgery*, which was staged at the American; G. L. Fox appeared in *Life in Brooklyn, Its Lights and Shades – Virtues and Vices* in the same year; at the National in 1858, Burdette Howe played in his own drama, *The Mysteries and Crimes of New York and Brooklyn*; and Chanfrau continued to revive and appear in *Rosina Meadows, The Village Maiden*, a play that, in type, fell somewhere between the city-mysteries drama and women's melodrama. Perhaps the best known and most popular of the genre, however, was Thomas de Walden's *The Upper Ten and Lower Twenty*, which was played at Burton's Theatre, with Burton in the lead role of Christopher Crookpath. A trusting husband who is deceived by a faithless wife and his best friend (described in one review as "a smooth and oily deceiver"), Crookpath falls from middle-class respectability and becomes, as the stage directions dictate, "an inebriate lunatic." In this debauched state, he takes the audience on a walking tour (or more precisely, a crawling tour) of New York's most degraded and degrading locales.

While ostensibly a melodrama of villainy and deception – one that also contained a strong temperance imperative – *The Upper Ten and Lower Twenty* nevertheless portrayed, quite graphically and unabashedly, the bizarre and nightmarish horrors and the savage struggles of the big city. Like his fellow subversive reformers, de Walden de-emphasized measures to eradicate vice, focusing instead upon its more grisly manifestations and not infrequently becoming fascinated with explorations of the dark forces of the human psyche and subrational fantasies.[25] Using didactic rhetoric as a cloak for their own obsessions with tabooed subjects, subversive reformers like de Walden introduced into the literature of the time (both dramatic and non-dramatic) a moral ambiguity and a pessimistic fatalism that would come to characterize a later, more realistic type of playtext. Thus, despite the "impurity" of subversive reformers' motives and perhaps lacking the deterministic force of Taine's milieu, modern city culture, teeming as it was with vice and temptation, was represented both in print and on the stage as a corrupt and corrupting environment; one in which countless young men and women met their ruin in the early years of the nineteenth century, and it was this ambiguous, largely fictive representation, appropriated into the common culture, that shaped perceptions of the modern city for decades to follow.

The nineteenth-century moral reform melodrama, in both its foci and its world view, was equally reflective of progressive thought at the time as its showier competitor, the city-mysteries play. Both the antebellum reformer and progressive melodramatist conceived of a universe in which there existed a hierarchy of truths that were to be accepted absolutely; both playwright and reformer were directed in their endeavors by an evangelical-mindedness that sought moral explanations for social problems and espoused moralistic solutions; both believed that the best means toward their respective ends was through a gentle moral suasion; and both constructed their imperatives based upon the assumption that man is, in truth, perfectible. As scholars of melodrama from Peter Brooks and David Grimsted to Bruce McConachie and Rosemarie Bank have successfully argued, melodrama advances a portrait of life, not as it necessarily is, but rather as it should be – life idealized. The source of melodrama's much-touted optimism and its Horatio Alger quality derives, in fact, from its internalization of the notion of humankind's perfectibility. As a consequence, the message it (and antebellum reform movements, as well) disseminated was that through hard work and "right-thinking" any man could "make himself over," a transformation that was possible both in moral and socio-economic terms.

During the middle years of the nineteenth century, practically any intersection of urban with rural values reflected the cultural tensions and fears these two disparate value systems represented. In the so-called "women's melodrama," popular during the 1840s and most frequently written under the auspices of the American Female Moral Reform Society, for example, the archetypal leading figures were not only women; they were also rural. At the center of the melodrama was an innocent, young farm girl, described in natural terms, as a delicate flower, a plant rooted in the country, endowed with the love and pride of purity.[26] Into the American Eden where she blissfully resided came the lecherous, sophisticated male. Urban and sexual, he was the

> antithesis of the pure and family-rooted daughter...He invaded the female family circle, ripping the flower-like daughter from [her roots,] and carrying her off to the city...The young woman's final ruin took place in a town or city governed by commercial values...beyond women's sphere...places of absolute sexual powerlessness and danger for the rural daughter.[27]

As routinely constructed, the women's melodrama, a highly ritualized narrative, castigated the attractions of the city and reinforced the correctness

and necessity of rural morality; while at the same time it reflected antebellum women's concern with sexual matters and confirmed the primacy of the
American family and woman's role as its moral bedrock.

A similar pattern – the ruination of a rural youth in the big city – permeated the less overtly polemical mainstream dramas of the era; but in these
cases the imperiled youth was most frequently male, the expected progeni-
tor of the next generation of Americans.[28] In plays like *The Drunkard* and
The Old Homestead, the youthful protagonist fled his rural birthplace to the
city, where his moral flaws were magnified; he fell in with con men, sharpers
and painted women bent upon his ruination; frequented bars, theatres and
gambling dens; took up drinking; and ultimately fell into total degradation
and dissipation. If this pattern were not reversed, most frequently by the intervention of an "outsider" from the country, the story had just one end: the
body of the youth would be discovered floating face-down in the East River.
In both of the above-mentioned dramas, the youth was rescued at the last
minute and taken to the country to be restored to moral and physical health.
By mid-century, the wicked city theme was so ingrained in the American
psyche that even a title, *Under the Gaslight* (1867) – gaslight being a coded
term used to invoke a complex set of urban impressions, all depicting the
seamier side of the big city after sunset – could alert theatre audiences that
the play they were about to see contained scenes set in some dangerous, "off
limits" portions of the urban landscape and would be peopled by nefarious
"city types."

While city-mysteries plays and other melodramas set in the wicked city
functioned as open or mixed texts, providing "an especially democratic meeting place for numerous idioms and voices" that advanced reformist values
indirectly, with their more radical social notions often veiled by the conservative urge to return to the traditional morality of the colonial village,
other plays espoused progressive imperatives more directly. By the second
half of the nineteenth century, reformist playwrights had extended their
efforts beyond generalized indictments of the evils of America's industrialized urban centers to target specific social ills. Abolitionism and racial
issues, for example, were examined in a series of progressive plays. *The
Escape; or A Leap to Freedom* (1858) was an indictment of slavery written by
an escaped slave, William Wells Brown; *Ossawattomie Brown; or, the In-
surrection at Harper's Ferry*, by Mrs. J. C. Swayze, glorified John Brown's
attack on Harper's Ferry; J. T. Trowbridge castigated the Fugitive Slave Law
in *Neighbor Jackwood* (1857); there were three separate adaptations (1856) of
Harriet Beecher Stowe's novel *Dred* and even more adaptations of her classic
novel, *Uncle Tom's Cabin*.[29]

THE FATE OF HUNDREDS OF YOUNG MEN.

1. LEAVING HOME FOR NEW YORK.   2. IN A FASHIONABLE SALOON AMONGST THE WAITER GIRLS—THE ROAD TO RUIN.   3. DRINKING WITH "THE FANCY"— IN THE HANDS OF GAMBLERS.   4. MURDERED AND ROBBED BY HIS "FANCY" COMPANIONS.   5. HIS BODY FOUND BY THE HARBOR POLICE.

Figure 3. Secrets of the Great City

Based upon what was arguably the most progressive single text of the century, the George Aiken adaptation of Beecher Stowe's "Great American Novel" remains the prime example of the nineteenth-century moral reform melodrama.[30] Described by one cultural critic as a "passionate record of the metaphysical and social tensions of antebellum America, [the novel and the plays it spawned] dramatiz[ed] the dialectic between doubt and faith, between rebellion and submission...that had governed American reform for decades...[and aired] almost every conceivable doubt or cynical reflection prompted by the slavery issue."[31]

If *Uncle Tom's Cabin* was the definitive reformist play, temperance dramas and entertainments were clearly the dominant type of progressive text. While the more traditional temperance activists routinely shunned the theatre, the more sensationalist reformers gravitated to theatrical activities for many of the very reasons their more conventional brethren recoiled from them: they were directed principally at the senses; they appealed to the emotions rather than to reason; and, they were perceived by many as being potentially subversive. As a means of disseminating their message to a sizable and diverse audience and attracting potential converts to the cause, temperance reformers produced or endorsed an astonishing variety of performative activities – conventions, dances, meetings (many reflecting the evangelical roots of the movement), picnics, concerts, balls, boating excursions, festivals, lectures, recitations and tent shows – and phrased their imperatives in a wide range of vehicles. These included temperance articles, pamphlets, poems, novels, "illustrated temperance cards," short stories, minstrel sketches, dialogues, drawings (some, like Currier and Ives' "The Drunkard's Progress" and George Cruikshank's "The Bottle" and "The Drunkard's Children," in the serial-graphic mode), plays, skits, "illustrated juvenile tracts" (comic books), songs and broadsides, all designed to convey temperance ideology. In addition to these "standard" vehicles, there were unique, isolated forms such as temperance flags that graphically depicted the drunkard's final trip to the poorhouse, a temperance version of the "Star-Spangled Banner," and later in the century, more complex forms: a magic-lantern depiction of Timothy Shay Arthur's novel *Ten Nights in a Bar-room* that traveled the Chautauqua circuit in the 1880s and 1890s to accompany readings of the novel, and various "transmogrified" versions of *The Drunkard*. The latter included one production in which "a parade of a thousand children [marched] across the stage singing temperance songs; another featured a quadrille of forty-eight dancers; and [a third] in California... exhibited a panorama covering 3,000 square feet of canvas."[32]

Of all the weapons in the temperance arsenal, however, none was more potent than the drama that was unrivaled in its capacity to "touch the feelings with electric quickness," to intensify identification between fictional characters and spectators, to depict graphically the horrors and degradation of intemperance in a style one critic dubbed "lurid waxworks realism," and to "scripturelike...show drunkards their sinful ways and to lead them to a life of sobriety that would herald financial and social prosperity."[33] Prior to its introduction into their tactical lexicon, temperance advocates had been forced to rely heavily upon the written word (treatises, pamphlets, tracts, broadsides), as well as upon sermons and lectures to small assemblages. Following the advent of the Washingtonians and the expansion of their target audience, however, reformers were forced to reassess their methods for mobilizing public opinion and to reshape their strategies in order to confront the realities of an emerging mass and multicultural society. The search for new techniques of mass communication led temperance activists to experiment with the use of music and theatre as organs of propaganda.

While in actual practice the temperance drama exhibited a wide range of variations (*The Drama of the Earth* is patterned upon an epic poem, *The Poisoned Darkys* resembles a minstrel hall sketch, *The Drunkard's Daughter* is little more than a static dialogue between participants and *On to Victory* is self-described as a "temperance cantata in one scene for the little ones," to cite just four examples), the vehicle of choice of most temperance playwrights was the nineteenth-century melodrama already popular on American stages. Having emerged shortly after the French Revolution as a medium for the progressive social ideals of the era (democracy, the rights of man, Rousseauism), the melodrama "provided an emotional equivalent to the 'common sense' philosophy of the period" and "served as a crucial space in which the cultural, political, [moral], and economic exigencies of the century were played out and transformed into public discourses."[34] While the melodrama could be employed to espouse any cause or ideological position – from the most radical to the most conservative – in the hands of antebellum temperance writers, the melodrama served as a progressive genre for a progressive ideology.

Melodrama, however, offered temperance reformers more than simply its relentless brand of didacticism. Faced with the challenge of creating a robust and vivid means of communicating with a mass audience, a significant percentage of which was illiterate and ignorant of artistic conventions, temperance activists heeded the words of the Reverend John Marsh, who staunchly maintained that intemperance had "no rational defense and [would] not be reasoned with. It must be met by a different weapon."[35] With Marsh's and similar statements ringing in their ears and disturbed by audiences that sat impassively through sermons, lectures and other logical arguments, temperance advocates of the 1840s chose to substitute emotional and psychological appeals for the rational arguments stressed by earlier generations of reformers. To many, this meant adopting the kind of message-bearing instrument that "spoke to the heart" – the moral reform melodrama.

Temperance melodramas achieved much of their emotional impact from introducing audience members to characters who were similar to themselves, whose daily lives mirrored theirs, whose aspirations and fears resembled theirs, and whose plight, given one imprudent decision, might conceivably become theirs. When mechanic Richard Thornley in T. P. Taylor's *The Bottle*, for example, took his "fatal first drink" and then forced his wife to join him, working-class men, moderate and heavy drinkers alike, may well have recalled a similar scenario in their own pasts or at least envisioned themselves committing the same acts. And when the Thornley family was evicted because the principal provider had been fired and couldn't pay the rent, when Thornley's son Joe was apprenticed to a life of crime to support his father's habit, when Thornley in "a state of furious drunkenness, kill[ed] his wife with the instrument of all their misery," an empty liquor bottle, and was exiled to an asylum to die an agonizing death, the same men were presumably forced to envision the eventual and, according to the temperance notion of causality, inevitable consequences of their own intemperance. And, with each retelling of the story, temperance imagery and ideology were reinforced.

While plays like *The Bottle*, *Hot Corn*, *Three Years in a Man-Trap* and *Another Glass* featured a predominantly working-class dramatis personae and were directed at an audience of mechanics and artisans, middle-class spectators saw their views on temperance reinforced from the stage by plays that warned of the consequences of even a moment of weakness. Given the dual goals of the temperance reform in the 1840s – preserving abstinence among the middle and upper classes as well as seeking converts from among workers – the depiction of the "fall of a noble house" was as common on stage as the destruction of a working-class family and the setting of a temperance melodrama was as likely to be the drawing room of a brownstone on Union Square as a two-room apartment on New York's Lower East Side. Thus, while Thornley and his family were perishing at the Bowery, patrons of the nation's lecture halls and museums witnessed the decline of college-educated Edward Middleton from a position of a respected land owner to lowly drunkard wandering through New York's notorious Five Points district in *The Drunkard*, or accompanied Vernon, the aristocratic alcoholic of Douglas Jerrold's *Fifteen Years of a Drunkard's Life*, on a boozy fifteen-year odyssey during which he gambled away his savings, his home and his wife's estate.

To Bruce McConachie, these and other temperance dramas were, in essence, allegories. Their rigid cause–effect logic, the "clockwork inevitability" of their outcomes, their abstract typology of characterization embodying "abstract categories of moral behavior" and the mechanistic rigidity of their action and rhetoric, like that of all allegories, combined to create "a didactic universality which drives out all contradiction and ambiguity by excluding the historically specific and psychologically complex."[36] The end result, McConachie continues, is a theatre that "implicitly bullies its audience into believing that there is only one correct interpretation; either you get the point or you don't."[37] In this scheme, Thornley becomes an everyman, susceptible to the perils of alcohol. His first drink starts the deadly causal chain of events that leads to the inevitable outcome – the destruction of his entire family – and the audience is "driven" to one inescapable conclusion: to drink is to invite total disaster. Given these characteristics, it is little wonder that others have been tempted to brand the moral reform melodrama the morality play of the nineteenth century.

To increase the emotional impact of their dramas and to heighten the audience's sense of moral outrage, temperance playwrights, both in England and in America, bolstered their cases by parading across the stage an endless series of pathetic visual images designed to stir audience compassion and, hopefully, action. Spectators at performances of T. H. Reynoldson's *The Drunkard's Children* were subjected to the vision of Mary Reckless, unable to live with the stigma of her father's "crime," committing "self-murder" by jumping from London Bridge; at the end of Edwin Tardy's drama, *Saved, or a Woman's Influence*, they encountered a once-respected intellectual lying in the mud after a prolonged bender, reduced, in his own words, to "a common street loafer – a gutter drunkard – a mark for the ribald jest of each passerby"; while at *Three Years in a Man-trap* they looked on in horror as Maggie Lloyd, driven to madness by the guilt caused by her father's rum selling, ran into the cold, damp streets to catch pneumonia and die.

For their most poignant and evocative images, however, temperance dramatists invariably turned to the most innocent and vulnerable victims of the bottle – small children. While an occasional reformer may have claimed that "little can be known of the suffering and mortification of the children of intemperate parents," most temperance playwrights knew and were more than willing to illustrate that suffering and mortification on the stage. Invariably, the drunkard's child was shown, emaciated and dressed in rags, waiting in a squalid apartment for his or her drunkard father to return home ("Mama, will father soon be home?") or quaking in fear and antici- pation of the beating and verbal abuse that would certainly be forthcoming upon the drunkard's return ("my father's a drunkard and beat me today").

The plight of the temperance child was perhaps best exemplified by the title character of Charles W. Taylor's *Little Katy, or the Hot Corn Girl*, one of the most popular plays of the 1850s. Originating in 1853 as a serialized exposé of New York slum life in Horace Greeley's *New York Tribune* and published as a novel the following year by Solon Robinson, author of the original *Tribune* articles and a temperance activist, *Hot Corn* told the story of a "poor and miserable" corn seller on the Bowery, who fell asleep on the street; was robbed while she slept; upon her return home, was severely beaten by her drunkard mother for not having sold all of her corn; and subsequently died from the injuries inflicted by her mother.[38] While the social issues of poverty, alcoholism and child abuse were pushed to the foreground by the play's "documentary" style, Little Katy herself served as the archetypal temperance child who, despite her own suffering, endeavored through personal purity and force of character to redeem an alcoholic parent. Faced with imminent death, Katy forgave her mother for her cruelty and issued a final plea for her redemption, imploring "Mother – don't – drink – anymore – mother – good b — ." The narration that followed stated simply, "but before the word was finished, there was another angel added to the heavenly host."[39] As testimony to both the power of Robinson's story and of the temperance message it contained, during the 1853–54 season, three separate versions of the play (by H. J. Conway for Barnum's American Museum, Taylor's adaptation at Purdy's National Theatre and a third version by an unnamed author at the Bowery) were mounted in New York, where they rivaled *Uncle Tom's Cabin* in popularity, and the death scene of the National Theatre production of *Hot Corn*, with Cordelia Howard in the title role, was as gut-wrenching as its counterpart in the George Aiken stage adaptation of the Harriet Beecher Stowe classic.

As effective as pathetic images like Little Katy's death scene may have been, seldom did they equal the raw intensity of the delirium tremens scene, the temperance melodrama's obligatory "sensation scene." As described by physicians, delirium tremens or the DT's, a disorder that afflicts heavy drinkers following a binge, "begins with a period of irritation and anxiety,

IN THE MONSTER'S CLUTCHES.
Body and Brain on Fire.

Figure 4. In the Monster's Clutches

frequently accompanied by muscle spasms called 'the shakes.' There ensues a period of paranoid hallucination, during which the subject reports being chased by people or animals."[40] In one documented account of the DT's, the drinker reported that "the road appeared to be full of serpents of all sorts and sizes; some of them were very large and appeared to be thirty feet or more in length . . . I took pains to stamp on some of the largest, when I heard a multitude of voices saying, 'Damn the creature, see, he stamps on us, kill him, damn him, kill him' and I soon found that they were not confined to a very slow motion for instead of crawling along the ground they were now all flying about in every direction."[41]

Not surprisingly, considering the emotional extremes inherent in such "a terrifying testimonial to the hellish darkness of intemperance," the theatrical potential of delirium tremens proved irresistible to playwrights who sought spectacular effects that would frighten the intemperate into abstinence. When performed to its fullest by actors the caliber of "Drunkard" Clarke or E. W. Wynkoop, a former bartender who presumably had ample personal experience with the phenomenon, the delirium tremens scene probably convinced more people to sign the pledge than did all of the temperance tracts ever written.

In its theatricalization of delirium tremens and other alcohol-related traumas, the temperance melodrama was actually presaged in the early 1840s by the Washingtonian "experience speech." Lacking in subtleties, often blasphemous and almost always grossly exaggerated, "the polarities of [the] before-and-after stories were stark, following the melodramatic conventions of the day, contrasting the shadow of inebriation with the sunshine of sobriety."[42] Lack of polish notwithstanding, when compared to the printed literature that had been the principal means of publicizing temperance ideology prior to 1840 and that had unavoidably distanced temperance spokesmen from their audience, the experience speech carried tremendous dramatic force and served as a model for the more complex melodramas that followed.

If the "confessional" nature of the experience speech was recognizable in temperance melodrama, so too was the structural similarity between the experience speech and the drama. While the plots of a small percentage of temperance dramas (*Fifteen Years of a Drunkard's Life*, *The Drunkard's Children* and *The Bottle* among them) were essentially linear, proceeding inexorably from the "first glass of that fatal poison" to catastrophic conclusions in which entire families were obliterated, the majority, like the experience speeches that pre-dated them, were circular in structure, taking the shape of what Jeffrey Mason characterizes as an inverted arc.[43] Like *The Drunkard*, that pictured Mary and Edward Middleton in "peace, purity and happiness" following their nuptials and before "that horrid drink had done its work," most temperance melodramas began with scenes of domestic tranquility and well-being, visually illustrating how much the protagonist risked sacrificing because of his intemperance. Following the introduction of the bottle or the revelation of the protagonist's intemperance, frequently a focal point of the first act, the drunkard began a downward spiral during which he was "ripe for any deed, however wild." In the scenes that followed, the drunkard, unable to hold a job and economically disenfranchised, was pictured gambling, embezzling, stealing from his former employer, swearing, and/or brutalizing his family, all unmistakable signs of the drunkard's moral deterioration and activities guaranteed to further divorce him from respectable society.

The drunkard's personal nadir was usually signaled by a crisis during which he contemplated suicide, experienced the death of a loved one or had a premonition of their death and/or experienced the DT's. Frequently, such scenes of degradation were played out in infamous urban settings like New York's notorious Five Points area or Boston's Dock Square – locales readily recognizable to those familiar with city-mysteries narratives. It was generally at the lowest point in the drunkard's fall that the temperance spokesman was introduced. Occasionally, the temperance representative was a close friend of the protagonist or a co-worker who had been present since the beginning of the drama; but, just as frequently, the reformer was a stranger introduced into the plot at the last minute to effect a solution, much in the manner of the classic deus ex machina.[44] In the denouement, the drunkard, with the guidance of the temperance spokesman, finally recognized the ramifications of his drinking, signed the pledge and, in the final moments of the drama, was "reconciled to sobriety." The immediate benefits of signing the pledge were visually reinforced by representing the reformed drunkard restored to health, surrounded by his loving family and often materially rewarded by promotion at work or increased public recognition and status.

Such a plot structure was by no means the invention of temperance melodramatists, for, as Bruce McConachie observes: "Central to neoplatonic belief, from Plotinus onward, is the notion that cosmic reality is circular; that all things emanate from a primal unity, achieve separation and differentiation, and then reconverge into 'the One,' their initial point of departure."[45] While hardly classical, the circularity of the temperance melodrama, when it did occur, nevertheless established a unity or harmony at its outset; progressed through disunity or discord as the drunkard abandoned or abused his family and sank into degradation and despair; and finally restored the drunkard and his family to a state of harmony or well-being upon his renunciation of the bottle and return to stability and respectability.

By the mid-1840s, the impetus for American playwrights to restore the drunkard to sobriety proved so strong that even malefactors as dastardly as Little Katy's mother were eligible for redemption and reinstatement into society, if they were willing to sign the pledge. Politically, such redemptionist tendencies positioned the temperance melodrama squarely in the mainstream of assimilative temperance reform and aligned it with the dominant recruitment strategy of the 1840s – moral suasion. Rather than viewing the drinker as someone who had rejected hegemonic middle-class values and an intractable deviant to be punished, reformers considered the drunkard "one of them to be reclaimed," someone who knew and accepted the established public morality, and who felt guilty about breaching it. Compared to the more coercive, "outer-directed" strategies of temperance agitation that emerged late in the decade and later manifested themselves in the Maine Laws of the 1850s and later as Prohibition, assimilative reform phrased its appeals more as invitations than as demands.

If assimilation was the goal of most antebellum reformers, "the favored instrument of reform was a sentimental 'moral suasion' that appealed to the drinker's spiritual, domestic, and economic self-interest."[46] By the late 1830s and early 1840s, temperance leaders (especially the Washingtonians) were rapidly becoming convinced that if the habitual drinker were approached with sympathy rather than with moral indignation, and, if he were presented a model for his life that was both attainable and attractive, he could be rescued. In this context, the temperance melodrama, which projected an ideal world where characters forged their own destinies and where the distribution of rewards and punishments was governed by a strict code of poetic justice, illustrated what "could be," if only the drinker would give up the bottle, and what "ought to be," as long as the teetotaller remained abstinent.[47]

As both an instructive instrument in its own lifetime and a cultural record in ours, the temperance melodrama was (and is) an extremely valuable document. Functioning as a "social barometer," the genre reflected and enunciated, not only the dominant values of the era, but the tensions, cultural ambiguities and fears that plagued Americans in the decades immediately preceding the Civil War. In the midst of the social and economic chaos of antebellum America, fear for the integrity of the nuclear family was especially prominent on reformers' lists of concerns. As the ideology of separate spheres for men and women gained ascendance, especially in America's cities, men of all classes were encouraged to seek recreation outside of the home and, in the process, were increasingly drawn to the entertainments and male companionship offered by the myriad bar rooms that dotted the urban landscape. For temperance leaders, the prospect of males spending a greater percentage of their leisure time in bar rooms created a disturbing domestic scenario for if, as reformers predicted, the family provider were to spend most of his weekly earnings on liquor and bar room entertainments, the family in turn would be deprived of the money that "was increasingly necessary for survival in a commodity economy"; and if, they maintained, fathers continued to be lured out of the home to the local bar, children would be deprived of the parental support and guidance to which they were naturally entitled.[48] More serious than the issues of poverty and neglect, however, was the likelihood that if the husband/father were to return home in a drunken state, wife-beating, incest, family desertion and assaults on children would ensue.

Confronted with a problem of growing proportions and potentially catastrophic consequences, temperance playwrights responded to the perceived crisis by dramatically representing the threat "on the boards," characterizing intemperance as the "fiendish destroyer of the American family" and portraying liquor as the principal competitor for the weekly paycheck. Through their efforts, countless Americans were introduced to the neglected, battered, abandoned and murdered families of drunkards, and the plaintive question, "Mama, will father soon be home?" became one of the most frequently heard lines on the nation's stages. On rare occasions, such as in the final scene of *Three Years in a Man-trap*, following the drunkard's reclamation, the answer was "Yes, darling. It is nearly seven o'clock and he is never late now"; but more frequently, the reply was a quiet, resigned, "No, dear. I'm afraid not." Considering the frequency of the latter response, it is little wonder that children like Mary Morgan in *Ten Nights in a Bar-room* felt it necessary to follow their fathers to the bar room and to plead with them to return home. The urgency and the desperation of generations of American children can be heard in Mary's pleas:

MARY: [Outside R.] Father! Father! Where is my father?
            Enter MARY R. – runs to MORGAN.
      Oh! I've found you at last! Now won't you come home with me?
MORGAN: Blessings on thee, my little one! Darkly shadowed is the sky that
      hangs gloomily over thy young head.
MARY: Come, father, mother has been waiting a long time, and I left her
      crying so sadly. Now do come home, and make us all so happy.
[The well-known song, "Father, dear Father, Come Home with Me Now,"
      may be introduced with effect][49]

Although few historians would dispute the fact that during the first half of the nineteenth century countless families were decimated by alcoholism, the true import of the threat to America's families and to its youth, according to social historians, has been routinely understated. During the first decades of the century, the country, in Karen Halttunen's opinion, was in the midst of a "critical period when its character was not yet formed" and was experiencing severe anxieties about its future. Faced with what they perceived as serious threats to the Republican experiment and to the ultimate survival of the nation, "Americans came to believe that [their] only chance for survival lay in the character of the rising generation." As a result, increased attention was paid to the raising of the young, the country was literally flooded with conduct manuals written expressly to advise the nation's youth how to best safeguard their moral character and Americans in general became more vigilant in their efforts to protect the next generation, and, in their minds, the country's future. In this context, the threat that intemperance posed to children transcended the status of a common social ill and became a "symbolic expression of deeper fears about the direction of American society."[50]

In both the nineteenth-century temperance drama and the world that it mirrored, whenever children were victimized by "the curse of drink," invariably their mothers were victimized as well. Although, during the 1840s and 1850s, small vocal bands of women, distressed by the widespread suffering caused by male intemperance, became politically active, joining the Martha Washingtons (the female branch of the Washingtonians), participating in early prohibition efforts, staging sexual boycotts and engaging in isolated vigilante attacks on bar rooms, the majority of American wives remained silent – totally dependent upon their husbands for their welfare, their security and for economic support. Common law granted the husband the sole right to all family income, including his wife's, and placed all property rights in his hands, while inheritance practices dictated that properties be routinely transferred to male heirs rather than to widows. To complicate matters, in an era when legal divorce was available in only a few states, when occupational opportunities for women outside the home were practically nonexistent and when desertion was unthinkable, wives were virtually trapped in marriage unless they were willing to risk social stigma and economic ruin.

Bound by such grim economic realities and social constrictions, antebellum drunkards' wives "were expected to bear their lot, and to use the superior moral influence that the culture attributed to women to try to reform the drinking husband."[51] Reflecting this pattern, the dramatic literature of the era written by both men and women was filled with silent, suffering wives who, like Mary Middleton in *The Drunkard*, did menial work to support their families while they patiently awaited their husbands' reformation, or like Nettie Glenn in *Three Years in a Man-trap*, attempted "to reason with him when he [was] sober...to be all smiles and cheerfullness, to make his little home so bright that he will find himself happier there than in the false glitter of the bar-room."[52] Women's suffering, in reality and on the stage, however, was by no means restricted to waiting patiently for their men to return from the grog shop; in countless plays they were subjected to vicious beatings by their drunken husbands, and in several cases (*The Bottle* and *Fifteen Years of a Drunkard's Life*, to cite two) they were murdered. With few exceptions, dramatic literature reinforced one message: a lone woman whose sole weapon was her "moral authority" was virtually powerless against the combined forces of the liquor industry, her husband's coterie of bar-room companions and the drunkard himself.

From its inception, temperance literature identified one additional victim of alcohol abuse, the drinker himself. Following the lead of Benjamin Rush, who believed that distilled spirits were habit-forming for certain weak-willed individuals, the more progressive reformers in the 1820s and 1830s began to acknowledge liquor's addictive power and to characterize alcoholism as a "disease" that the drinker was unable to control. These reformers, while they still maintained that drinkers remained morally responsible for their decisions and held that drunkenness was a sin against both God and society, nevertheless were forced to admit that, although a man may be moral and well-intentioned, human will power was frequently frail and often insufficient protection against the temptations to which man was exposed. The danger of drinking, reformers theorized, arose at the point when the weak were paired with the "poison" that they were incapable of resisting and that had the power to "enslave" them.

Beginning in the 1840s, temperance drama actively promoted this conception of alcoholism by commonly depicting the drunkard as a man of moral, albeit weak, character. In their before-the-bottle scenes, playwrights were careful to stress that, except for the predisposition to drink, the protagonist was an "honest, industrious fellow" who was "full of good qualities." Mary Gray in Thomas Morton's *Another Glass*, for example, claims that her husband, Martin, "is full of good qualities...if only he would but leave off that horrid drink..."; Louisa, the wife of a drunkard in C. W. Taylor's *The Drunkard's Warning*, states that her husband was once "kind, affable, generous and true...but in an unguarded hour he clasped the envenomed bowl,

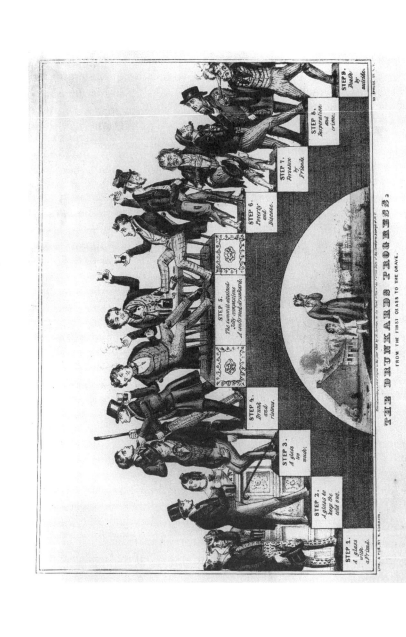

Figure 5. The Drunkard's Progress: From the First Glass to the Grave

reveled in its fallacious charm, & sunk at last degraded beneath its withering influence"; while the authors of *The Drunkard* wrote an entire scene devoted exclusively to demonstrating Edward Middleton's moral attributes.[53] In rebuttal to Lawyer Cribbs' suggestion that he evict an aged widow and her daughter from Middleton property, Middleton responded: "Mr. Cribbs, I cannot think of depriving them of a home, dear to them as the apple of their eyes – to send them forth from the flowers which they have reared, the vines which they have trained in their course – a place endeared to them by tender domestic recollections, and past remembrances of purity and religion."[54] Presumably, the playwrights hoped that the audience would retain a favorable opinion of Middleton's overall character and, despite his having deserted his family and having degenerated to an "enslaved and wretched state," would ultimately judge him to be "a weak man to be pitied rather than a bad man to be detested."[55] Tactically, such an ethic, avoiding as it did the moral damnation of the intemperate, reinforced and promoted the Washingtonian brand of assimilative reform that envisioned and encouraged the reclamation of drunkards.

By characterizing drunkards as "voluntary slaves" and admonishing the temperate and the intemperate alike that drunkenness led inevitably to a loss of personal autonomy, antebellum temperance reformers gave added resonance to the temperance appeal of the 1820s and 1830s. Not only did the various tracts, circulars and orations resound with warnings about loss of independence, but popular entertainments and other mass temperance activities publicized the admonition as well. It was a common practice, for example, to refer to the abstinence pledge as a second Declaration of Independence, to substitute "Prince Alcohol" for George III in versions of the Declaration intended for public reading, or to stage mass signings of the pledge as part of Fourth of July celebrations. The symbolism inherent in linking these events is obvious: antebellum reformers viewed the war against intemperance as an analog to the war against the British and envisioned the battle against intemperance as requiring as much courage and virtue as the Revolution.

For their part, temperance dramatists stressed the theme of voluntary slavery in practically every script they wrote. Typical of this tendency, playwright Nellie Bradley, in the first act of *Marry No Man if He Drinks*, declared through her raisonneurs, Laura and Nellie, that all of the "young men" in the play, although moderate drinkers at the time, were in "imminent danger, for this insidious habit [drinking] will increase and become more powerful, until its victims are drawn down into a vortex of degradation and shame, bringing ruin on themselves, and sorrow and misery to kindred and friends."[56] When, by the middle acts, the men had still not reformed, Laura grimly concluded that unless they abandoned drinking, it would "make slaves of them all." This sequence alluded, not only to the power of liquor to enslave, but to the progressive nature of the alcoholism that, if left unchecked, according to nineteenth-century thinking, led directly from the "first sip of that fatal substance" at a social gathering or at home to the eventual discovery of the drunkard's bloated body floating face down in the river.

Exploiting Americans' near-paranoiac fear of enslavement, zealous ante-bellum temperance leaders began to speak and write in apocalyptic terms of intemperance toppling "the temple of civil and political freedom" and bring-ing "destruction and misery... on the land," and to brand liquor interests as "highly conspiratorial" with their "tentacles" in every American house-hold. Similar strains of paranoia in antebellum society have been identified (in separate studies) by Richard Hofstadter, Bruce McConachie, Karen Halttunen, Judith McArthur and others in cultural phenomena as varied as advice manuals for youth, apocalyptic melodramas, the spread of slavery and mainstream politics. Described by Hofstadter, the central image in the "paranoid style" of thinking is

> a vast and sinister conspiracy, a gigantic and yet subtle machinery of in-fluence set in motion to undermine and destroy... a nation, a culture, a way of life... The enemy is clearly delineated; he is a perfect model of malice, a kind of amoral superman: sinister, ubiquitous, powerful, cruel... (and) since the enemy is thought of as being totally evil and totally un-appeasable, he must be totally eliminated...[57]

In its scope, intent and degree of danger, the coalition of liquor manu-facturers and their distributors was characterized by reformers as just such "a perfect model of malice" – conspirators who, for personal gain, were bent upon robbing men of their personal liberties and, in the process, subvert-ing the Republican experiment. Temperance leaders, while they may have disagreed upon goals, strategies and constituencies, were therefore in full agreement upon the central figures in their demonology, which included the distiller, the tavern owner, the bartender, even the corner grocer who sold liquor to his neighbors. Although reformers held all liquor manu-facturers and distributors equally culpable in theory, temperance literature (particularly the drama) concentrated upon the most accessible conspira-tor, the local bar owner, who was branded a "trafficer in human souls and blood" by the American Temperance Society and singled out as a target for reformers' wrath. The bar owner was regarded as especially insidious because, like Simon Slade, landlord of the Sickle and Sheaf Inn and a former mill owner in *Ten Nights in a Bar-room*, and entrepreneur Tom Lloyd, the bar owner in *Three Years in a Man-trap*, he lent an aura of middle-class respectability to the sale of alcohol, steadfastly maintaining that he was guilty of nothing more than being a hardworking businessman. Given his prominent position in temperance demonology, it is little wonder that, in keeping with the melodramatic convention of poetic justice (and temperance notions of vengeance), the tavern owner suffered a punishment commensurate with his crime. Glum, a bar owner in *Three Years in a Man-trap*, was viciously beaten to death by an old drunkard who had been patronizing his bar for years; Slade was clubbed into oblivion with a whiskey bottle by his own son; and Lloyd began to drink, his business failed, his daughter died, he was imprisoned for a variety of crimes and died in his cell during a siege of the DT's.

Viewed retrospectively, the temperance drama, in its century of existence, dealt with practically every issue of importance to the temperance cause. These included: the dangers of family and social drinking; total abstinence versus moderation; the value of temperance societies; legal means of restricting the production and distribution of alcoholic beverages; the negative influence of "bad company" and the "bachelor culture" of the bar room upon American working men; the physical abuse of women and children by the drunken head of household; the economic destruction of the drunkard's family; and even the dangers of drinking cider.[58]

As effective as such propaganda may have been in focusing public attention on the social consequences of intemperance and the evils of the liquor industry, activists learned quickly that proselytizing and sermonizing were not sufficient to "penetrate the lives" of drinkers or to effect significant changes in Americans' use of leisure-time, nor was temperance propaganda wholly effective in breaking the ties between traditional forms of recreation and drinking. Since colonial times, grog shops had served as social centers for local males, providing not only liquor, but facilities and opportunities for gambling, singing, cockfighting, boxing and other sports. As Jon Kingsdale notes, many men "thought of and treated the corner bar room as their own private club rather than as a public institution. They used it as a mailing address; leaving and picking up messages, and meeting friends there; depositing money with, or borrowing from, the tavern-keeper. [They] played cards, musical instruments and games, ate, sang and even slept there."[59] Later recreation centers – theatres, bowling alleys, billiard parlors – likewise

served liquor and cultivated a "clubhouse" atmosphere, often becoming recognized more for the quality of their bars than for the principal entertainments or sporting facilities they advertised. In an era before organized sports
and city parks, these institutions served as the hubs of male recreation.

Since early temperance activists had little direct exposure to the tavern, the bowling alley or the billiard room, they remained largely unaware
of the prominent position these institutions occupied in the nineteenth-
century "bachelor subculture," nor could they envision how men, once they
had signed the pledge, might survive in a culture in which drinking and
recreation were closely interrelated. It was the Washingtonians who, having
emerged themselves from the bar rooms, were the first to suggest "suitable
means of enjoyment and improvement of the leisure hours." Rather than
suppress amusements, the Washingtonians proposed instead an "alternative
world of recreation," a system of alternative amusements by which they
attempted to either recreate or supplant tavern life. Their early attempts
at providing "rational recreation" resulted first in the creation of reading
rooms and the sponsorship of hymn sings and poetry readings, all aimed at
"the improvement of mental culture" and all described as rather "dour" endeavors; but, evidently aware that more "exuberant" entertainments would
be required to keep the temperate interested, temperance balls, concerts,
parades, theatricals and Fourth of July celebrations were added to the list of
amusements "divorced from drink." By the end of their second year of existence, Washingtonian alternative amusements, such as a temperance concert
in New York in December 1842, were attracting audiences in the thousands
and were successfully competing with those associated with "King Alcohol."

Many of the most successful temperance dramas were thus written for
venues other than commercial theatres. Of the hundreds of temperance dramas written during the nineteenth century, just a handful (*The Drunkard*,
Ten Nights in a Bar-room, *The Bottle* and *Hot Corn* among them) succeeded
on Broadway, the Bowery or in the major museums. The remainder, like
George M. Baker's *The Temperance Drama: A Series of Dramas, Comedies
and Farces for Temperance Exhibitions and Home and School Entertainment*,
were created expressly for groups like "Divisions of the Sons of Temperance, Good Templar Lodges, Sections of Cadets, Bands of Hope and other
Temperance Societies" who met in temperance halls, church basements, or
"temperate theatres." Still others, like Effie W. Merriman's *The Drunkard's
Family*, were written to be "acted by children" in school, at home or in
Sunday School. Thus, while companies of *The Drunkard* and *Ten Nights
in a Bar-room*, were competing with city bars and persuading thousands

in major urban centers to sign the pledge, temperance plays were serving additional thousands as alternate amusements in the nation's small towns.

Evolving as they did in the early 1840s at the height of Washingtonian activity and the democratization of alcohol reform, temperance entertainments proved the ideal means of communicating the temperance message of abstinence and hope to a mass audience. Using forms appropriated from the commercial stage and the bars themselves, nineteenth-century reformers created a network of entertainments that not only legitimated the emergent middle-class life-style based upon self-control and self-denial, but disseminated this ideology in a language that was engaging, attractive and accessible to "the people." Seldom brilliant, often crude, nineteenth-century temperance entertainments nevertheless encouraged generations of Americans to shake off the chains of intoxication, to join the substitutive culture of teetotalism and to live a life "unclouded by the demon Alcohol, beneath the free banner" of temperance.[60]

3

"Every odium within one word": early American temperance drama and British prototypes

When the devil saw that he could no longer catch souls fast enough, he turned himself into gin, & since then he has been very successful.

Arthur Moulds, *The Village Bane*

First, the simple glass, with cautious sip
Is held to the honest, guileless lip;
Then the cheerful tumbler, with health to friend,
Is friendship meant, in friendship knows no end;
Then the dram to give a wet to dinner,
Of future failings – false and fair beginner;
Then the full bottle of generous port,
Is needed to give the sinking frame support.
With punch-bowl we midnight vigils keep,
And dissipation sinks in sad, unhealthy sleep.
Next, brandy when we wake, and gin at noon,
And idleness and want attend us soon.
At length, of friends, clothes, money – all bereft,
To die despised, is all the drunkard's left.

George Dibdin Pitt, *The Drunkard's Doom; or, The Last Nail*

THE AMERICAN TEMPERANCE DRAMA BEGAN ITS EXISTENCE quietly and simply, and not, as might be expected, in New York. During the 1825–26 season, *The Forgers*, a "dramatic poem" written in blank verse by John Blake White, sometime playwright and painter, was presented at the Charleston Theatre in Charleston, South Carolina, which, although it was gradually losing its position as one of America's leading theatre cities at the time, was nevertheless still capable of making significant contributions to America's theatre history. Ostensibly a revenge tragedy, which depicts its protagonist, Mordaunt, as the victim of a vengeful former lover who employs liquor as a weapon to bring about the hero's downfall and ultimate suicide, the play illustrates in "vivid and didactic fashion" the evils of both drinking and gambling. After a short run, *The Forgers* disappeared from the Charleston stage and the American dramatic scene altogether.

The Forgers was followed in 1834 by a play titled *The Six Degrees of Crime; or, Wine, Women, Gambling, Theft, Murder and the Scaffold*, a city-mysteries play which illustrated the "riotous" life of a wealthy young man and his ultimate downfall, in the process running "the gamut of immoral activities to which the youth of America might be tempted."[1] Adapted from Theodore Nezel and Benjamin Antier's *Les Six Degrés du Crime* by Frederich Stanhope Hill, playwright and manager at the Warren Theatre in Boston, *Six Degrees of Crime* is commonly regarded by theatre historians as one of the earliest moral reform melodramas, a type of drama Bruce McConachie believes to have been "derived from the traditions of Calvinism and [to have] appealed mostly to native-born workers and lower-strata members of the business class from Protestant backgrounds."[2] Originally rehearsed at New York's Park Theatre and scheduled for opening there, *Six Degrees of Crime* mysteriously opened at the rival Bowery and then went on to achieve a relatively long life on Broadway, largely through the efforts of C. W. Clarke, an actor who specialized in playing the intemperate to the degree that he became known professionally as "Drunkard" Clarke. Under his sponsorship, *Six Degrees of Crime* briefly achieved a measure of success and then traced a downward spiral in popularity from being "an old friend of years ago" when it was re-mounted at the Bowery in 1843 to being used as a "matinee lure" by the National in 1854 to ending its life as a "hoary antiquity" just one year later. Its sad demise notwithstanding, *Six Degrees of Crime* is credited with helping to create the vogue for temperance drama, as well as with illustrating the feasibility of representing social problems and proposing moral solutions on America's stages.

While *The Forgers* and *The Six Degrees of Crime* incorporated the dangers of alcohol abuse into their narratives as secondary issues – as a tool for a villain to use against a victim or as one of a series of urban evils – American audiences would have to wait until 1841, just three years before *The Drunkard* appeared at the Boston Museum, to witness the first drama concerned principally with the long-term impact of alcoholism. In spring of that year, *Fifteen Years of a Drunkard's Life* by British melodramatist Douglas Jerrold opened at the Chatham and although its run, according to George C. D. Odell, was short, its impact was nevertheless significant. In fact, the inveterate chronicler of the New York stage staked out a prestigious place in the history of temperance drama for *Fifteen Years of a Drunkard's Life*, claiming that "obviously this edifying work was a predecessor of *Ten Nights in a Bar-room*, that devastating drama of the near future. Perhaps it was a predecessor of all moral dramas unto our own day."[3]

Jerrold constructed his three-act "domestic drama" by interweaving two discrete, but related narratives: the first centering on an upper middle-class drunkard, Vernon; the second on Copsewood, a yeoman inebriate. Both have become addicted to alcohol before the play begins and despite their pathetic promises and futile attempts to reform, both repeatedly prove that they are incapable of shedding their habit regardless of the consequences. In Act I, audiences are introduced to the two drunkards in the early stages of their habit, as separate scenes show them returning home after a night of drinking and debauchery and, later in the act, spectators witness the economic consequences of their intemperance. Copsewood has lost his family's farm and doomed his father, mother and sister to poverty by "misplacing" the rent money during his drunken escapades; while Vernon meets his financial ruin through gambling while drunk. More significant, perhaps, to the long-term development of the temperance drama, this act also contains the first recitation of everything a drunkard has to lose through his intemperance, an interpolation that was to become a standard feature of temperance drama. Frequently, this litany was provided by the temperance spokesman in the play; in *Fifteen Years of a Drunkard's Life*, however, it was provided by the drunkard himself:

> A tavern life! and with a house like mine, where fortune has profusely showered her dearest blessings – a wife, meek as the dove, and innocent as infancy – friends, with true hearts, and cultivated spirits – books, music, painting, all the arts that give a grace to life and raise man beyond himself – that I should leave this continued, never-tiring round of pure delights, for the brawl and hubbub of a tavern – to argue without instruction, laugh without enjoyment, and at length drown the reasonable man within a wine-cask – oh! let it pass away as a hideous dream, and be no more remembered.[4]

To even the most uneducated and uninitiated nineteenth-century audience member, the contrasting polarity of the life-styles encapsulated in this passage and the dire warning it contained must have been evident.

In Acts II and III, which take place five years and ten years after Act I respectively, the economic disenfranchisement begun in the first act has long since been completed and the audience is shown the moral deterioration that also accompanies intemperance. Both Vernon and Copsewood, now costumed in rags and covered with grime, have been reduced to lives of beggary and crime, condemned to wander the countryside in search of just "one glass more." Their moral bankruptcy and desperation culminate in a burglary of the home where Vernon's wife, Alicia, has been staying; in Vernon's murder of his wife, whom he has failed to recognize in his drunken stupor; and in his own death. Copsewood, in turn, is captured, taken prisoner and led from the stage in disgrace, leaving American audiences without the conventional "happy ending" they expected and routinely received at the end of a melodrama.

If, as Odell contended, *Fifteen Years of a Drunkard's Life* is the true prototype of the nineteenth-century temperance play, it is reasonable to expect that many, if not all, of the identifying characteristics of temperance drama would be in evidence in Jerrold's text; and, in fact, many are present. The text contains dramatic devices — the reliance upon visual representations of the effects of drink through costume and makeup, the depiction of alcoholism as a form of slavery, the portrayal of the drunkard as a "good but weak man," the deleterious impact of intemperance upon women and the inclusion of the stock characters of the villain and the temperance spokesman (Glanville and Franklin respectively) — that were to become standard, if not obligatory, in the temperance drama. In addition, Jerrold dealt with issues such as the compulsive force and the progressive nature of the disease (i.e., the concept of addiction), the rationale for total abstinence and the possibility of controlling the distribution of liquor through licensing laws or prohibition, issues at the heart of temperance ideology.[5] The latter, whether or not drinking should be controlled by legal means, was a debate never resolved by temperance activists in either the United States or Great Britain and remained one of the most contentious and divisive issues addressing temperance reformers and dramatists alike, as was the question of the drunkard's responsibility for his own affliction, yet another subject pioneered in dramatic terms by Jerrold. The impact of Jerrold's text upon later dramatists is perhaps best illustrated (albeit in a rather left-handed manner) by the thematic and structural similarity between it and William W. Pratt's temperance classic, *Ten Nights in a Bar-room*, which according to the authors of *The Revels History of Drama in English*, "borrowed liberally" not only situations but actual lines from its predecessor.[6]

As a reform-minded author, Jerrold, like his close friend Dickens, was responding through the medium he knew best to the radical changes and ruptures occurring in the environment in which the English people, especially the "humbler classes," lived and worked and the correlate hardships that accompanied such transformations. This "condition of England question," as one historian termed it, "made it impossible for any earnest writer [or artist] to hold aloof from the sociological battles, so [as a consequence] the restless philosophy of the period reacted strongly [in] its poetry, history, fiction" and drama.[7] Jerrold, by dramatizing the social, political and personal consequences of intemperance in the early years of the nineteenth century, thus joined fellow authors and artists who focused public attention upon this and similar social ills, thereby inexorably fusing radical politics with artistic representation. As the century progressed, this union of cultural/political concerns and artistic means – a union that would culminate in the emergence of realism, expressionism and other "socially aware movements" – ultimately attained the status of orthodoxy, prompting Raymond Williams and others to conclude that, in Williams' words, "an essential hypothesis in the development of the idea of culture is that the art of a period is closely and necessarily related to the generally prevalent 'way of life,' and further that, in consequence, aesthetic, moral and social judgments are closely interrelated."[8] Advancing this theory a step further, cultural historians after Williams are quick to stress that this cultural reflexivity is most evident in the popular arts – from Yankee plays and minstrelsy to vaudeville and Chaplin films to contemporary movies and rock and roll – which often are among the first cultural manifestations to represent and introduce into the discourse cultural transformations even as they are taking place.

It is no historical accident that Jerrold chose temperance as the subject for one of his earliest dramas. In the England about which he wrote, intemperance had already reached epidemic proportions, destroying entire families, creating havoc in the workplace and causing a host of social disruptions from urban crime and poverty to increased unemployment and homelessness. Mirroring drinking in colonial America, the consumption of alcoholic beverages in England prior to the nineteenth century was a seemingly permanent fixture in traditional social and cultural practices and was commonly perceived as "normal" and even expected. Drink was invariably present in rites and activities involving assertions of manhood, in everyday business dealings and in routine social intercourse. As it was in the average American town, the rural village or neighborhood pub was the center of daily recreational life where the price of a man's drink was the entry-fee to comforts denied to him in his own home, to a sense of community that had disappeared at his place of work and to the latest gossip. And liquor was present at daily meals, at work breaks and common entertainments whether in the private clubs, public houses or the home. With alcohol ubiquitous in practically every aspect of daily life, culture-wide intemperance was unavoidable.[9]

Public drunkenness, already perceived as a significant threat to the moral, social and economic well-being of the country early in the century, was elevated in 1830 to the level of national crisis by the passage of the Beer Act. The act was originally conceived as an attempt to "produce a great change on public opinion and practice" and as a means of controlling intemperance by encouraging drinkers to exchange gin, the drink of choice of many and a known intoxicant, for beer, which at the time was thought to contain no harmful spirits and had consequently gained the reputation of being "the temperance drink." Within five years of the enactment of the new licensing act, however, upwards of 20,000 new drinking places (called jerry shops) opened throughout England, triggering a precipitous and predictable rise in intemperance. The impact of beer houses was compounded by their publicans' practice of providing free drinks as an incentive to patronize their establishments. Spurred by the opening of the new jerry shops, by counter-measures designed by producers and distributors of non-beer beverages to recapture patrons and by a life-style that incorporated excessive drinking into the daily routine, annual liquor consumption nearly doubled between 1825 and 1835, from 3,684,000 to 7,315,000 gallons.[10]

Just as Americans had responded to the explosion of intemperance following the whiskey glut of 1820 and the social disruptions it caused, the Beer Act prompted Britons to take action. Inspired by reports of the efforts and successes of their American counterparts that were brought to them by American seamen, English middle-class temperance activists undertook to first ensure the sobriety of members of their own class and then to reform the "lower orders."[11] Like American temperance movements, English temperance was the creation of the middle class; but unlike America, where temperance remained a middle-class movement throughout its history and the principal means of achieving respectability and even the possibility of upward mobility, British temperance focused mainly upon the working classes.

To mobilize the lower classes, temperance activists adopted as their organizational model, the British local association. This structural concept had been pioneered and popularized years earlier as the way artisans and laborers best worked with one another by the Methodists, who were active in working-class neighborhoods. As historians stress, it is impossible to overestimate the influence of Methodism on, not only temperance reform, but upon all reform involving the working classes. Following the publication of E. P. Thompson's landmark *The Making of the English Working Class*, it became customary to acknowledge that "Methodism and Utilitarianism, taken together, [made] up the dominant ideology of the Industrial Revolution... and [Methodism in particular] contributed greatly to the Puritan character-structure of the nineteenth-century artisan."[12] In an industrial system which demanded self-discipline and subjugation to an outside authority, Methodist teachings that stressed a submissiveness and self-denial comparable with that of even the most zealous Calvinist sect were welcomed by industrialists; while outside the factory, on the moral front, Methodists waged a continuous battle with the jerry shop and the "denizens of Satan's strongholds." Methodism, as Thompson notes, was aggressively "hostile to many traditional English amusements and levities – taverns, fairs, pleasure gardens, any event where there might be a large congregation of people" – which they regarded not only as a nuisance, but as "sources of idleness, brawls, sedition or contagion."[13]

As the eighteenth century ended, reformers had much to reform. If Patrick Colquhoun, who investigated criminal activity just prior to the end of the century, can be believed, *fin-de-siècle* England was rife with crime. According to his findings, in the city of London alone, the criminal class consisted of 50,000 prostitutes, over 5,000 publicans and roughly 10,000 "thieves," the latter category consisting of an assortment of "receivers of stolen property," coiners, gamblers, lottery agents, cheating shopkeepers, riverside scroungers, and colourful characters like Mudlarks, Scufflehunters, Bludgeon Men, Morocco Men, Flash Coachmen, Grubbers, Bear Baiters and Strolling Minstrels. In all, the criminal class composed 115,000 out of a metropolitan population of less than 1,000,000.[14] Needless to say, facing the staggering task of ridding England of so much vice and corruption, reformers welcomed the support and moral passion of the Methodists as well as their teachings of submissiveness to authority and self-control, precepts that would prove especially useful for middle-class temperance activists.

However, a caveat is warranted here. As Brian Harrison is careful to emphasize in his history of the various movements, temperance reform was more than a simple attempt to impose middle-class values and manners on the lower classes. Rather, it was an "encouragement" of working-class self-respect, self-realization and self-help. In a society where class position was determined "from outside," social mobility severely limited and interclass relations proscribed and rigid, temperance afforded the working man the opportunity to at least define himself as "respectable," to remake himself into what Thompson calls the "self-respecting artisan." It is Thompson's self-respecting artisan that Harrison has in mind when he writes that "essential to an understanding of the nineteenth-century temperance question is the...gulf...between the 'rough' and the 'respectable' poor."[15]

In 1832, respectable working men (or those aspiring to respectability) took charge of their own destinies by adopting the most extreme measures used by temperance activists to that date: teetotalism.[16] Under the leadership of Joseph Livesey, a weaver, seven artisans founded the total abstinence movement by which they intended to eradicate intemperance among the working classes through the use of moral suasion. Not satisfied with simply preserving sobriety among those already temperate, Livesey and his companions set about to reclaim diehard drunkards, a stance which immediately caused tension in temperance ranks.

Central to the teetotal campaign were two "extreme" activities which immediately separated the teetotalers from their more moderate temperance colleagues: the public signing of the pledge – a secular conversion experience that some in the movement compared to being baptized in terms of the spiritual renaissance it effected – and the equally public act of narrating the horrors of their lives as drunkards. Drawn from the breast-beating, biographical confessions common in Methodist churches, the teetotal experience speech, delivered by a rank and file member of the movement, enabled the reclaimed alcoholic to both convey the nightmare of drunkenness in crude, abrasive, yet vivid, language, and to portray his actions as if they were virtues of the highest order. Given the similarities between British teetotalers and the American Washingtonians – their shared focus upon reforming inveterate drunkards, their belief in the spiritual renewal that resulted from signing the pledge, their use of the experience speech to "stir the passions" of alcoholics and their sending "missionaries" into working-class neighborhoods – it is likely that the six Baltimore artisans who mobilized American working men to combat intemperance in their communities in the early 1840s were aware of their English predecessors, especially considering that by the 1830s, there was a continuous exchange of ideas between temperance activists of both countries.

With the exception of remaining a working-class movement and the general lack of involvement of women (when compared to the Martha Washingtons, the WCTU and other women's associations in the United States), British temperance reform after mid-century continued to closely resemble its American counterpart. In 1853, just two years after the passage of the Maine Laws, the United Kingdom Alliance was founded in Manchester to coordinate prohibition efforts that were gaining ascendance at the time.

The increased interest in prohibition corresponded to a growing distrust of the principle of self-control that had been espoused by teetotalers and a shift in focus from the drinker to the seller of liquor. While both trends promised success for proponents of legal constraints on the sale and consumption of liquor, their efforts failed and the decline of the prohibitionist movement, as well as a period of relative prosperity and complacence in the 1860s, brought both a reduction of temperance activism and with it an increase in intemperance. Only the severe depression in the early 1870s (which corresponded to the American Panic of 1873) was able to put a brake on drinking and spur renewed interest in temperance reform. Considering that most of the temperance reform efforts just described occurred and the bulk of the temperance dogma was codified after he wrote *Fifteen Years of a Drunkard's Life*, Jerrold's inclusion of teetotal ideology, his belief that all forms of alcohol were equally pernicious, his subtle hints about the necessity of prohibition and his insights into the psyche of the drunkard and the nature of alcohol addiction show him to have been both an uncommonly astute observer of the cultural climate of his times and a harbinger of trends to follow.

By the time that *Fifteen Years of a Drunkard's Life* opened at the Chatham, it was actually thirteen years old, having opened in 1828 at the Coburg Theatre in Southwark, then as now a working-class area on London's South Bank. At the time of its premiere, its author was the house dramatist at the Coburg and was employed by George Bolwell Davidge to churn out the sensational and violent melodramas necessary to the survival of London's minor theatres. Jerrold had begun his playwriting career in 1818 with *The Duelist*, a low comedy, which was initially rejected by the management of the English Opera Company. Retitled *More Frightened than Hurt*, the play was produced successfully at Sadler's Wells in 1821, but recognition eluded Jerrold until 1828 when *Fifteen Years of a Drunkard's Life* and *Ambrose Gwinnett; or, a Sea Side Story*, "both of which can lay claim to being regarded as the first example of developed domestic melodrama," attracted public attention and brought their author a measure of success.[17]

Although his claim to have been the originator of the domestic melodrama was somewhat clouded by J. B. Buckstone's counter-claim that his own *Luke the Laborer* (1826) was in truth the prototype of the genre, no one could contest Jerrold's having written England's first nautical melodrama. *Black-Ey'd Susan* (1829), which he wrote for Robert William Elliston at the Surrey following an acrimonious split with Davidge earlier in the year, was not only the popular and critical success Jerrold had been seeking, but was the first of a variant of melodrama that concentrated on British naval glories and the heroism of the English sailor. During the ensuing decade, Jerrold went on to write plays (*The Devil's Ducat* [1830]; *The Rent Day* [1832]; *Nell Gwynne* [1833]; *The Wedding Gown* [1834]; and *The Painter of Ghent* [1836]), not only for the minors, but for London's patent theatres as well, thus ensuring for himself a prominent place in English melodrama history. "Although he has received comparatively little critical notice," historian Louis James writes, "Jerrold's impact on the early stages of melodrama was at least as great as that of Boucicault in the sixties."[18]

While the success of these works alone is hardly sufficient to substantiate James' claim, other scholars, most notably Raymond Williams, Ernest Reynolds and Victor Emeljanow, have observed that many of Jerrold's plays were significantly more than "mere entertainments"; they were, in fact, "overt investigation[s] of social problems" or, in Jerrold's own words, "dramas with a purpose." In *Problems in Materialism and Culture*, Williams even suggests that not only were plays like *The Rent Day* and *The Factory Girl* (1832) "open attempts to dramatize a new social consciousness," they, like the Sunday papers that were gaining popularity in London in the 1820s and 1830s, combined "sensation, scandal, and radical politics" much in the manner of American subversive reformers' writings.[19] Based upon David Wilke's anti-landlord drawings *Distraining for Rent* and *The Rent Day*, Jerrold's dramatic rendering of the latter drawing was viewed by the playwright's contemporaries as an obvious and overt exploration of "the cross pressures of the period" and as an attempt to plead the cause of the poor and oppressed classes of society. Written and produced at a time when landlord–tenant tensions were nearing a boiling point throughout England, *The Rent Day*'s fiery rhetoric was construed by both sides of the dispute as especially inflammatory. The following diatribe, delivered by a tenant farmer to his landlord's overseer, is typical of Jerrold's writing and particularly revealing of his ideology: "If [the master] must feed the gaming-table, let it not be with money, wrung, like blood, from the wretched. Just tell him, whilst he shuffles the cards, to remember the aching hearts of his distressed tenants." Likewise, Jerrold's *The Factory Girl* drew "with lamentable truth the picture of a weaver's lot, which is to be the slave of the inhuman system of overworking in English factories, and too often a victim of the petty tyranny of those who are placed in authority over him."[20] Even in less overtly political plays like *The Devil's Ducat* (which debuted at London's Adelphi Theatre in 1830, was seen at the Chatham [New York] in November 1840 and became a favorite vehicle for American actor-manager J. W. Wallack), Jerrold attacked social evils, inveighing against materialism, a life-style-based solely upon money and the ethical standards of the businessman.

Jerrold's radicalism was just one manifestation of a growing radicalism in the English drama in general. While many melodramas, even at mid-century, continued to be classified as either escapist or as coercive – "a means of educating and disciplining the lower classes at a moment when their political awareness and activity had grown to the point of threatening the order constructed by their betters in the middle class" – an emergent strain of drama that focused upon the socio-political situation of the lower classes was introducing a distinctive subversive tone and a disruptive mode of consciousness into the theatre.[21]

Early in the nineteenth century, as literary historian Elaine Hadley has noted, melodrama "emerged...as a polemical response to the social, economic, and epistemological changes that characterized the consolidation of market society in the nineteenth century."[22] Just as melodrama (especially Pixérécourt's "Bastille" plays) had become overtly political during the French Revolution, the English domestic melodrama, in response to "the disease of modernism," became increasingly radicalized by its selection of subject matter – the everyday hardships suffered by workers and their families at the hands of landlords, factory owners, the liquor industry, class hostilities, a harsh urban environment and, in some cases, governmental agencies – and by rhetoric designed to foreground and accentuate the grim realities, class hatreds and daily crises routinely encountered by the masses. Featuring peasants, artisans and other "common" men as heroes who were aligned against upper-class oppressors, plays like Jerrold's *The Rent Day* and *The Factory Girl*, J. T. Haines' *The Factory Boy* (1840), and *The Factory Lad* by John Walker (1834) overtly, violently and often realistically expressed anti-aristocrat, anti-employer, anti-landowner and anti-urban sentiments while they simultaneously exposed the era's most serious social ills to public scrutiny. The scenes of *The Factory Lad*, for example, "contain a sharp edge of real experience rather than the fantasy more common to [gothic and nautical melodramas], its speeches bear a striking resemblance to socialist propaganda of the period, and it has an uncompromisingly 'open' ending."[23] In retrospect, this growing polemical nature of the domestic melodrama certainly contributed to critics' opinions that the theatre had never before in its history been more "base and low" than it was during the first fifty years of the nineteenth century and was in large measure responsible for the respectable middle classes' absenting themselves from the theatre until the latter half of the century when the drama became more "gentlemanly" and refined. As Michael Booth summarizes this transformation and the resultant critical response: "It would be fairer to say that drama did not so much 'decline' as, within new social and cultural contexts, radically change its nature."[24]

The early domestic melodrama, with its violent spectacle and focus upon social problems that were represented in a mode designed to highlight their inherent ethical conflicts and inconsistencies, found a natural home in London's minor theatres and a constituency in the city's working classes. Since minor theatres like the Coburg, the Surrey, the Adelphi and the Pavilion were essentially neighborhood theatres that frequently employed a house playwright who would write for a particular audience, they were eminently qualified and eager to represent the harsh realities and domestic "misfortunes of the lower classes" who lived nearby and to depict an idealized alternative life – a life that featured characters of their own class and a code of poetic justice that punished the wicked and guaranteed the ultimate triumph of the virtuous poor. Undeniably escapist on their surface, upon closer examination these melodramas were also "realistic in that [they] presented not only the daily life of London streets and homes, but also a considerable number of serious social problems" that affected the poor.[25] Adopting the new theatres as their own and demanding increasingly sensational melodramas, working-class audiences at the minors quickly asserted their wills upon the management, forced upper- and middle-class patrons to seek other entertainment venues and in the process created new patterns of patronage and taste that ultimately changed the overall nature of the nineteenth-century theatre.

By the time Jerrold began writing for the Coburg (officially the Royal Coburg; later renamed the Royal Victoria; and then the Old Vic), it was already one of the most notorious of the minors, having earned the nickname "the blood tub." Situated on the New Cut in a neighborhood George Sala described as "one of the most unpleasant samples of London you could offer a foreigner," the Coburg drew its audiences from nearby tenements and, just before show time, from the gin palaces and jerry shops surrounding the theatre. Unlike the Surrey, which attracted audiences that routinely included a handful of middle-class spectators "eager to get a peep behind the curtain that conceals the forbidden [and] to catch a glimpse of that naughty world [they] dared not visit in any other way," the Coburg's audiences were uniformly of the "lowest kind," a fact that was not lost on cultural observers who dared to visit the theatre.[26] Their accounts range from the dismissive to the patronizing. Hazlitt compared his venture to the Coburg to finding himself in "a bridewell, a brothel, amidst Jew-boys, pickpockets, prostitutes and mountebanks"; Barton Baker felt that "the audience was the lowest and vilest in London, the scum of Lambeth"; Henry Mayhew, recalling an incident in which a small boy's cry that he could not see was met by a chorus of voices demanding that he be thrown from the top gallery, concluded charitably that the "gallery audience do not seem to be of a gentle nature"; while Charles Mathews offers the following account: "The lower orders rush there in mobs and, in shirt sleeves, applaud frantically, drink ginger beer, munch apples, crack nuts, call the actors by their Christian names, and throw orange peels and apples by way of bouquets."[27] Such accounts, however, colorful as they may have been and derived from first-hand observation, must be read with care, for as Jim Davis tells us, the critics' comments may often "tell us little about what actually happened and more about the attitudes of the investigators."[28] Nevertheless, even when the reviews are tempered somewhat, it is still apparent that the Coburg's audiences were among the meanest and vilest in London at the time.

Given the progressive nature of Jerrold's subject matter – one that resonated in working-class communities – and its opening first at one of London's most popular minor theatres and later at the working-class Chatham in New York, *Fifteen Years of a Drunkard's Life*, by all expectations, should have been a success. Yet the play attracted small and unenthusiastic audiences in both cities. At first glance, it is tempting to presume that since Vernon, the upper-class protagonist, received significantly more stage time than did his working-class counterpart, Copsewood, Jerrold had aroused the audience's resentment; but even a cursory historical survey of temperance drama reveals other plays featuring an upper- or middle-class protagonist (most notably *The Drunkard* and *The Drunkard's Warning*) that achieved relatively long runs.

A plausible explanation is to be found in a comparison of what the nineteenth-century working-class audience expected from the melodrama to what, on occasion, it actually received in the theatre. It is practically axiomatic to state that melodrama, as a "realization," "is a making real of what an audience *wants to believe* is reality. In its simplicity it becomes a truth which is, rather comfortingly, fixed, coherent, reliable."[29] Adopting such statements, it is quite easy to assume that all melodramas conformed to these expectations and somehow remained "pure in form"; yet, in contrast to these "standard notions," Raymond Williams offers an infinitely more sophisticated and informed assessment of the actual state of early nineteenth-century melodrama. In melodrama, he writes:

what [is]...observed is a paradox: the elements of the social and moral consciousness which was to inform serious naturalism went mainly, in England, into the melodrama, which at the same time preserved as the foundation of its conventions, providential notions of the rightings of wrongs, the exposure of villainy, and the triumph or else the apotheosis of innocence. At the same time...the more naturalistic presentation of scenes, characters and actions moved in general away from themes based in a radical consciousness. The result was a muddle.[30]

And it was this very "muddle," in the form of the characters, structure, thematic treatment and overall tone of *Fifteen Years of a Drunkard's Life*, that may have confused or possibly even repulsed audiences at the Coburg and the Chatham.

While playwrights later in the century would find a balance between representing "the real" while satisfying the need for the "ideal" – between "missionary realism" and melodrama – Jerrold could not. Although he sub-titled *Fifteen Years* "a melodrama," in many respects the play violated, even undermined, the melodramatic formula. As Louis James has observed, the play has no hero nor villain. Because both Vernon and Copsewood are drunkards when the play opens, Glanville (the so-called villain) is not the principal embodiment of evil, but someone who simply exploits the pre-existing evil (the bottle) that has already taken its toll. And, since the audience first meets Vernon when he has already fallen from grace, it is denied a glimpse of the heroic qualities the protagonist has sacrificed to drink. Further, the conventional melodramatic conclusion in which rewards and punishments are meted out based upon moral merits and defects, is sub-verted, with good and evil alike perishing at the end much in the manner of the "inconsequential slaughter of Jacobean tragedy."[31] Lastly, in depict-ing alcohol as addictive and the drunkard as incapable of controlling his habit, Jerrold clouds the issue of blame, thereby blurring the ethical po-larity required by melodrama and introducing a grim determinism into his script.

Viewed with these violations of convention in mind, it is likely that in departing from the melodramatic formula and introducing naturalistic elements into his drama, Jerrold was simply too modern for his audiences. It is also likely that Jerrold suspected his modernity, for just four years later, when *The Rent Day* met a similar fate at the box office, he admitted: "The subject of the piece was 'low, distressing.' The truth is, it was not then *la mode* to affect an interest for the 'course and vulgar' details of human life, and the author suffered because he was...years before the fashion."[32]

What is certain, though, is that *Fifteen Years* "exposed the problem of social melodrama – how to reconcile a plot structure, based on the defeat of evil by virtue, with complex issues of character and social condition."[33]

The next temperance drama of note to be mounted in England illustrated just how advanced *Fifteen Years* actually had been. In September 1832, George Dibdin Pitt's *The Drunkard's Doom; Or, The Last Nail* opened at the same theatre, the Coburg, where Jerrold had debuted his play. An intriguing mixture of the old German legend of Peter Klaus, Irving's Rip Van Winkle and Dickens' *A Christmas Carol*, *The Drunkard's Doom* depicts a fantastical Gothic voyage that results in the reformation of a drunkard, Adelich Starke. After his drinking companions fall into a drunken sleep during a night of debauchery, Starke is transported to a hieroglyphic cave where he witnesses an army of fiends making coffins for drunkards. Taken on a tour of the cavern by Olfinger, a being half dwarf, half fiend, Starke is shown the coffins of his drinking companions "gone to their account with all their sins," the casket for his father, who has many years left to live because "he leads a regular life, lives hard, labours hard, and drinks nothing but water" and finally his own coffin. Olfinger then holds up a coffin nail, telling Starke: "The next cup you drink strikes this in, and we shall send the coffin home directly." Thereafter, each time Starke tries to take a drink, Olfinger appears to tap the glass with the last nail. Fearing death should he take even one more drink, Starke reforms and is rewarded with the love of his sweetheart, Agatha, whom he previously had lost because of his drinking.

While its message – abstain or die – was undeniably serious and reputedly "no London playwright laboured [more] industriously at driving home morals" than did Pitt, *The Drunkard's Doom* was nevertheless more a "jolly romantic comedy" than a serious social commentary. Both fantastical and a-historical (it was "not supposed to occur in any particular age"), the play avoided ascribing intemperance to either the individual alcoholic, to the producer/seller, or to cultural forces. Displaying neither the deterministic force of Jerrold's drama nor the ethical tensions of later temperance melodramas, Pitt's play seemed almost light-hearted, even "playful," proving that in the 1830s, "drink could [still] appear on the stage without social implications."[34]

In retrospect, the true successor to Jerrold was not Pitt, nor any other dramatist for that matter, but rather the caricaturist George Cruikshank, best remembered for his illustration of Dickens' work. Near the end of the 1840s, a series of plays based upon two of his serial graphic illustrations of the course and effects of alcoholism – *The Bottle* (1847) and *The Drunkard's*

Children (1848) – appeared on the London stage and both achieved a popularity denied earlier temperance dramas. When *The Bottle* first appeared in print in September 1847, a writer for *Douglas Jerrold's Weekly Paper* predicted that it "will, no doubt, be speedily placed upon the stage. [It] is a perfect domestic drama, in eight acts."[35] Londoners did not have long to wait for the fulfillment of this prophesy, for on October 18 the first dramatization of eight tableaux of *The Bottle* opened, advertised by the City of London Theatre in Norton Folgate as being, not only authorized by Cruikshank, but actually supervised by him in rehearsal.

At first glance, Cruikshank, who at the time *The Bottle* and *The Drunkard's Children* were published, had gained notoriety as a drunkard as well as England's leading political caricaturist, might seem an unlikely candidate to either advocate temperance activism or to influence the course of nineteenth-century theatre; yet, in truth, he was well equipped to do both. As a young man growing up in a culture that tolerated excessive drinking, Cruikshank had gained a reputation as a heavy drinker and bon vivant. However, as the son of an alcoholic whose drinking contributed to his early death, Cruikshank, even while he was drinking, had been attracted to temperance. The resultant ambivalence was evidenced in his drawings during the 1830s and the early 1840s. While his depiction of the gin shop in Dicken's *Sketches by Boz* (1836), "The Battle of A-Gin Court" in the *Comic Almanac* for 1838 and a plate representing Father Mathew as a water pump warning a group of drinkers to "Touch not – Taste not – If you must take anything, take the pledge" in the 1844 *Comic Almanac* demonstrated the illustrator's affection for alcohol, the "Gin-Juggernaut" in his *Sketch Book* (1835), the "Pillars of a Gin Shop" (also in the *Sketch Book*) and his illustrations for John O'Neill's poem *The Drunkard* offered evidence of his growing awareness of drink's pernicious nature and the social ramifications of intemperance.

The resolution to Cruikshank's internal conflict came, according to biographer Blanchard Jerrold, shortly after the completion of *The Bottle*. Eager to gain the widest distribution for his work and equally eager for acceptance by the temperance community, Cruikshank presented the plates to William Cash, then chairman of the National Temperance Society, for his endorsement. Although impressed by the message contained in *The Bottle*, Cash, a Quaker unable to reconcile the harsh warnings of the illustrations with the personal habits of their creator, bluntly asked how Cruikshank could continue drinking while so vividly and passionately representing the "evils of the bottle." This query, says Jerrold, proved to be the impetus Cruikshank needed to sign the pledge and to fully accept teetotalism, a life-style he subsequently adopted with the same fervor – he brought to all of his endeavors.[36]

After abruptly embracing total abstinence, Cruikshank became an active and vocal temperance organizer and lecturer, speaking to audiences himself at venues like London's Exeter Hall, creating pictorial dramas like *The Bottle* and *The Drunkard's Children*, or chairing mass temperance meetings. While *The Bottle* was undoubtedly the most lasting of his contributions to the temperance cause, to Cruikshank the highlight of his activism occurred in 1854 when he chaired a meeting of "Total Abstainers" at Sadler's Wells. As reported in the *Illustrated London News*:

> This popular place of amusement was appropriated to a purpose of a somewhat novel character – for a meeting of 'Total Abstainers'... The Abstainers met in full force – Mr. Cruikshank in the chair. After the Chairman addressed the meeting, with much piquant and incontrovertible truth, an oration was delivered by the great Temperance advocate, J. B. Gough. At the close occurred the incident which Mr. Cruikshank has described with his graphics pencil. It is well known that our Artist is a total abstainer, and naturally he was unwilling to lose so good an opportunity as then offered itself for swelling the stream to which he belonged. Accordingly, he appealed to the audience to come forward and take the pledge. Nor was the appeal made in vain. A rush from box and pit and gallery was the result. A plank bridge was laid across the pit to the stage, along which poured the living tide. A young lady was the first to lead the way; her devotion was rewarded by cheers such as seldom resound in any theatre. Upwards of three hundred followed her example.[37]

Cruikshank was equally acquainted with the theatre of his time and its potential as a device to disseminate propaganda. In their youth, he and his brother, Robert, appeared on stage with their close friend, Edmund Kean, on more than one occasion and, according to one of his biographers, Cruikshank once contemplated a career on the stage. Later in his life, he acted with an amateur company formed by Dickens and coached by William Charles Macready and played the part of Oliver Cobb in Jonson's *Everyman in His Humour* and Doctor Camphor in Kenney's *Love, Law and Physic* at the Theatre Royal, Haymarket, and later, Pedrillo, in *Plot and Counterplot* at the St. James. While his acting career turned out to be sporadic and short-lived, Cruikshank's fascination with the stage never diminished and later manifested itself in the pictorial dramas he drew for various publications. So vivid and theatricalized, in fact, were Cruikshank's "grotesques" that Baudelaire described their essence as "an extravagant violence of gesture

"TOTAL ABSTAINERS'" MEETING IN SADLER'S WELLS THEATRE.—DRAWN BY GEORGE CRUIKSHANK.

Figure 6. Signing the Pledge at Sadler's Wells

and movement, and a kind of explosion, so to speak, within the expression. Each one of his little creatures mimes his part in a frenzy and ferment, like a pantomime-actor."[38]

In Victorian London, where "the distinctions between journalism, [theatre] and literature that seem so obvious to us today were...by no means so clear-cut," such cross-disciplinary representations were common and a single social, cultural, political or artistic impulse might assume many forms.[39] Thus, when Cruikshank's harrowing tale of drunkenness and destruction was retold in eight separate stage versions of *The Bottle*, in several magic lantern shows of his tableaux, in waxworks representations of them, in a penny novel adaptation and in two poems (one by H. P. Grattan and an ode to Cruikshank by Matthew Arnold), all inspired by the serial graphic drawings, few observers at the time were surprised.

The Victorian pictorial drama, a genre that told a story with a social theme and told it in dramatic terms, had descended from the serial graphic mode pioneered nearly a century earlier by Hogarth in his "progress" series. An astute cultural observer motivated by the desire to expose the social ills of his day, Hogarth, by his own admission, set out to chronicle "the customs, manners, fasheons [*sic*], characters, and humours" of mid eighteenth-century London. Hogarth's efforts afforded later generations not only a penetrating glimpse into the moral decay of the era, but into the Georgian social landscape as a whole. Commenting upon reformist tendencies that he found in the *Rake's Progress* and the *Harlot's Progress*, Fielding stressed that "those two works of his...are calculated more to serve the cause of Virtue, and the Preservation of Mankind, than all the Folios of morality which have ever been written."[40] Like the later moral reform melodramas to which they are structurally and thematically related, Hogarth's pictorial dramas show the rake, the harlot and the drinker in the gin shop as flawed, blameworthy creatures; yet, they also characterize them as victims of a corrupt and corrupting social environment, thereby betraying a moral ambiguity which would permeate staged versions throughout the nineteenth century.

Hogarth's second significant contribution to the arts of his time was his recognition of theatricality as a means of both attracting the attention of an audience and conveying his social messages. Hogarth's plates are filled with a myriad of realistic physical details that are endowed with symbolic significance and they are peopled by compelling and inherently dramatic characters like highwaymen, harlots, gamblers, petty thieves, jockeys and actors/actresses.[41] These figures Hogarth arranged into expressive dramatic tableaux, many resembling the gestures and facial expressions found in the acting handbooks of the era. That Hogarth was aware of the theatricality of his designs is evident from the following statement: "My picture was my stage and men and women my actors who were by means of certain Actions and Expressions to Exhibit a dumb shew."[42]

If Hogarth was the father of graphic social criticism, then Cruikshank and David Wilke were clearly his heirs and were among the first illustrators to see their graphic works translated to the London stage. Hogarthian in both their political potency (the years between 1828 and 1832 were years of hardship and violence in Southern England that saw numerous foreclosures and injustices committed by absentee landlords) and in their theatricality, Wilke's *The Rent Day* and *Distraining for Rent*, in particular, were ripe for translation to the stage by a dramatist like Jerrold who shared Wilke's social conscience. Jerrold's appropriation of Wilke's graphic representations as the basis for his play, *The Rent Day*, with the artist's drawing of the same name used at the opening curtain as a tableau and *Distraining for Rent* at the end of the first act as a "final realization," was in fact so effective that one reviewer noted that "the arrangement of the various persons, as the drop fell, was so striking that the audience testified their approbation by three rounds of applause."[43] Another indication of the success of the merger of dramatic dialogue and text with visual tableaux was the speed with which Jerrold's play was either copied literally or imitated. Sadler's Wells mounted *The Rent Day* and *Distraining for Rent: A Domestic Drama* by A. L. Campbell on February 20, 1832, while the Adelphi staged J. B. Buckstone's version shortly thereafter.

Like Wilkie's illustrations, Cruikshank's *The Bottle* proved to be tempting to the minor theatres, to their house playwrights and to Cruikshank himself. During the autumn of 1847, competing theatre managers practically tripped over each other in their efforts to mount a version of Cruikshank's eight tableaux. The playbill for the "official," and hence "most authoritative," version adapted by Thomas Proclus Taylor for the City Theatre declared in type just slightly smaller than that of the title that "the whole of the Tableaux [are] under the Personal Superintendence of MR. GEORGE CRUIKSHANK"; but, while the Cruikshank/Taylor production was the "sanctioned version," it was not to have the field to itself for long. Within days, plays claiming to be faithful adaptations of Cruikshank's pictorial drama opened at the Royal Pavilion on Whitechapel Road, Mile End; at the Standard in Shoreditch; at the Albert Saloon in an adaptation by C. Z. Barnett; and two separate productions of a spin-off by George Dibdin Pitt were mounted simultaneously: one at the Britannia Saloon in Hoxton; the second at the Victoria.[44]

Competition to be the first and/or the "recognized" version of *The Bottle* was so fierce that the Royal Pavilion adaptation actually reached the stage on October 10, before the Cruikshank/Taylor version, and the Victoria posted broadsides announcing Pitt's *Bottle* even before the City Theatre company had finished rehearsals. The Victoria broadside for October 11 announced that at their theatre "will be presented an entirely New Pictorial Drama of Real Life, from CRUIKSHANK's celebrated Work of the same, entitled THE BOTTLE, Embodying CRUIKSHANK's admirable Illustrations in a Series of highly-wrought Dramatic Situations and portraying the course of the Drama in Eight striking Tableaux." Two weeks later the Victoria brazenly claimed Pitt's drama as "not only the BEST VERSION, but BETTER ACTED and BETTER PUT ON THE STAGE than ANY or ALL the many Pieces now being represented at the Various Theatres in London on the same subject. It has had a noble career, a splendid career, and still continues its mighty triumph."[45]

Cruikshank's serial graphic, the source of so much theatrical furor, consisted of eight plates, each a tableau depicting a stage in the drunkard's (artisan Richard Thornley's) progression from relative sobriety and respectability to degradation, madness and early death while simultaneously chronicling the agony accompanying an entire family's ruination, the inexorable consequence of intemperance. The first of Cruikshank's plates, titled "The bottle is brought out for the first time: the husband induces his wife 'just to take a drop,'" shows the Thornley family at the exact moment the instrument of their ultimate destruction is introduced into the home, but before it has taken its toll. As in other pictorial "dramas," the symbolism is in the details. The room itself is well furnished with a grandfather clock gracing one wall; a picture of the village church where the Thornleys were married hangs next to it; the mantle is cluttered with bric-à-brac; a wreath hangs on a door; a rich carpet covers the floor; the kitchen table is adorned with a neat tablecloth and is covered with food; and, a well-stocked cupboard can be seen immediately behind the family. Thornley is shown with the bottle raised in his right hand while his left reaches out to his wife, who is depicted resisting the offer. The eldest daughter stands behind her mother in apparent female opposition to the bottle, while the couple's son and infant daughter happily play on the floor just below their parents' table. All are well dressed, well fed and all are smiling. With the exception of the ominous presence of the bottle, it is a scene of ideal domestic tranquility.

Figure 7a. The Bottle by George Cruikshank

Figure 7b: The Bottle by George Cruikshank

Figure 7c: *The Bottle* by George Cruikshank

Figure 7d: *The Bottle* by George Cruikshank

Figure 7e: The Bottle by George Cruikshank

Figure 7f: The Bottle by George Cruikshank

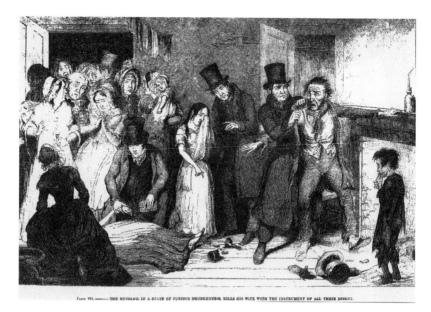

Figure 7g: The Bottle by George Cruikshank

Figure 7h: The Bottle by George Cruikshank

The next plate in the sequence, which shows the effect of "the first drop," is in stark contrast to the first. As described by Blanchard Jerrold: "The sottish husband, with a pipe hanging from his mouth, his handkerchief awry, his clothes in disorder, sits drowsy with drink, his children looking fearingly at him, while the wife is giving a bundle of clothes to the servant girl, to pawn, 'to supply the bottle.' The starved cat is licking an empty platter upon the table; the cupboard door ajar discloses empty shelves"; and the painting of past happiness hanging on the back wall has begun to tilt.[46] Just as audiences got an immediate impression of the essence of a scene in the theatre from its *mise-en-scène*, viewers of Cruikshank's plates instantly sensed what had transpired since the previous illustration and the circumstances of the moment. Subsequent plates likewise conveyed meaning through the employment of Hogarthian devices – a broken porcelain cottage on the mantlepiece; an open coffin against a wall, a poignant and familiar Victorian image; an empty liquor bottle used as a candle holder; a child's broken toy; an old shawl tacked to the window frame with a fork; an empty fireplace – until in the seventh drawing the ultimate symbol of destruction, the bottle, is finally used as a murder weapon and lies broken on the floor in the center of the page. The *mise-en-scène* of the final illustration is equally disturbing; the room in which the family lived and perished, with its one door on the "upstage right" wall, has been dehumanized by the removal of all personal adornments and transformed into the drunkard's jail cell.[47] The final impression, conveyed by the madness reflected in the drunkard's face, is a terrifying testimonial to the hellish darkness of drink and "a very powerful bit of realism."[48]

From his eight tableaux, it is evident that, like Hogarth before him, Cruikshank recognized that while the novel might be the most narrative of forms and painting the most pictorial and static, it followed that the staged drama with its story unfolding through visible enactment held the most expressive potential and was "the site of a complex interplay of narrative and picture."[49] Reduced to simpler terms, terms that circulated widely in the theatre community at the time and to a large extent determined the contemporaneous *mise-en-scène*, "playing a character successfully did not involve a search for coherence and unity but [rather] the creation of a succession of good pictures."[50] Given such thinking, it is perhaps inevitable that dramatists of the era would mine England's periodicals for ready-made plots drafted in graphic form and that Cruikshank's plates portraying "the most powerful of classical subjects, the fall of a noble house, [should be] democratized and rendered in nineteenth-century images, whose center in *The Bottle* is the hearth."⁵¹

While the "art of the serial picture-maker was an art of vivid compression, of putting the stages of action into readable visual situations," as Martin Meisel notes, "the art of the dramatist added to that [the] requirement[s] of time-filling elaboration" and time management.⁵² Consequently, T. P. Taylor's "amplification" of Cruikshank's plates incorporated several comic roles into the basic story; provided Thornley with companions from both the temperance and the drinking communities; created a "real" character for the lead actor to play (instead of simply the passions expressed by Thornley in the plates); and added strong scene cadences leading to the climactic tableaux, each depicting an irreversible loss and each vividly illustrating the centrifugal disposition of the characters. The only exception to this structure – with plates encapsulating the essence of scenes at their conclusion – was Taylor's use of Cruikshank's first drawing as the tableau at the opening curtain. The necessity of providing an interval for audiences was met by dividing the acts between plates three and four and assigning much of the temperance-related dialogue and the drunkard's introspection to Act I, thus allowing the family's destruction to progress unimpeded and to even gather momentum in Act II. From the act break on, the events "are linked into a nearly continuous action, a single epoch that occupies the [entire] act."⁵³ Thematically, Taylor magnifies Thornley's responsibility for bringing the "poisoned apple" into the household, which was treated as a "spontaneous, careless act" in Cruikshank's renderings, by giving his actor lines that show he is aware of the consequences of his actions and is even sorry for them; and, in several instances the playwright (or perhaps Cruikshank as "advisor") directly indicts the cause of all miseries – the public house – an issue developed only tangentially in plate IV.

Despite its similarity to early urban stage realism, *The Bottle*, in all of its many versions, was nevertheless popular with mid nineteenth-century theatregoers, remaining on one or more of London's stages for several months in the era before long runs became common. While familiarity with the play's geography and characters would have increased its popularity with residents of the Norton Folgate section of London and, allowing for their having been repeatedly exposed to more realistic recreations of local environments on stage, *The Bottle* was nevertheless far from the sentimentalized, idealized representation of domesticity people preferred to see in their theatres and, as *Fifteen Years of a Drunkard's Life* had in 1828, might have been expected to alienate audiences. One possible explanation for the

difference in responses, according to Meisel, is that like much of Dickens'
work, *The Bottle*, "although aimed specifically at those drinking classes that
could not afford the vice, commanded a response in classes and subcultures that normally felt themselves superior to temperance melodrama."[54]
A second explanation is offered by Louis James, who suggests that an alternative reason for the play's popularity lies in Taylor's solving the seemingly
irresolvable problem of matching the temperance theme, which is invariably
tinged with an unrelenting sense of determinism, with the melodramatic
expectations of an identifiable villain and an assignment of moral blame.
Instead of the traditional villain, the embodiment of pure evil who precipi-
tates all of the play's misfortunes through his actions, Taylor has provided a
unique solution to the location of evil in his drama. "Instead of using symbolism, outside temptation or social causation, he simply transferred the
mystery of evil to a dark silent object, a bottle."[55] Constantly reintroduced
in each scene – either raised as an invitation to drink, as an object to be
refilled, lying shattered next to a murdered wife, or conspicuously absent in
the final scene/plate – the bottle attained near-character status, in the end
visually embodying all of the evils of intemperance. The bottle itself, the
instrument of the family's destruction, thus became simultaneously melodramatic despoiler and naturalistic symbol, and was credible on both levels.
Consequently, whereas audiences were unable to reconcile Jerrold's mixture
of melodramatic and realistic elements in *Fifteen Years* or to blame Vernon
for his drunkenness, the villainy of the bottle in Taylor's play was readily
recognized. Furthermore, since Thornley's downfall and demise were both
self-induced and deserved – the act of a moral criminal and its eventual
punishment – the Victorian demand for poetic justice was satisfied, while
an unsentimentalized resolution was allowed to remain and its reception was
ensured. Perhaps by this point in England's theatre history, as Jim Davis has
suggested, there was "no reason why a popular audience, used to the rigours
of everyday life and a significant lack of easy resolutions to their problems,
may not have responded with a certain degree of irony or even cynicism to
the benign world view imposed upon them" by pure melodrama.[56]

Alternative adaptations of Cruikshank's plates added little to the history of *The Bottle*. In Pitt's *The Bottle Bane*, the protagonist is attracted
to drink, not by his own desires and weakness, but by the villain of the
piece, Lushington, who after he has ruined the artisan (John Milford)
and his family, attempts to seduce Milford's daughter. Poetic justice is ensured by Milford's arrival at the scene of the seduction "just in time" to
kill Lushington before going mad and dying. Likewise, Barnett, in his

adaptation, attributes the Thornleys' ruination solely to a villain named Graceless, who, like Lushington, dies at the hand of an enraged Thornley. Barnett's play, although never approved by Cruikshank and less popular than its competitors, varied from other versions in several significant respects: the central murder was enacted, not between the scenes as in the other adaptations, but on stage; its structural economy afforded the audience the opportunity to "see the pieces drop into place... and reinforce[d] the sense of a fatal progression"; and following Thornley's death, the end of Cruikshank's narrative, the hero awakes to find that the entire tragedy has been a dream and that he still has a chance to save his family.[57] Presumably, audiences were left to reflect, not only upon the possible consequences of their own drinking, but the opportunity for redemption that Barnett implied still existed.

Although *The Bottle* attained a measure of success in England and enjoyed periodic revivals for more than a decade, neither Taylor's nor Pitt's dramas attracted audiences when mounted in the United States. The initial opening of Taylor's adaptation at the Park Theatre on November 15, 1847, was regarded as a "comparative failure" despite a favorable review in *The Spirit of the Times*. A second production at the Bowery in December of the same year was similarly received even with "Drunkard" Clarke in the role of Richard Thornley, and a third attempt at Barnum's American Museum in January 1849, again starring Clarke, ran for what Odell termed a "harrowing" run. Thereafter, *The Bottle* was revived only sporadically and then only as a vehicle for actor benefits. By the early 1850s, all versions of the play had vanished from the New York stage, with only an occasional production staged in the hinterlands.

The second "translation" of a Cruikshank pictorial temperance drama, *The Drunkard's Children*, was treated even more ignominiously in America, never achieving even a single production; yet in England it surpassed its predecessor in popularity, triggering a period of intense competition between minor theatres, each offering a different version of Cruikshank's story of the fate of the Thornley children. On July 2, 1848, *The Era* announced that "'The Drunkard's Children' illustrating all the plates designed by Mr. George Cruikshank... the entire arrangements under the personal superintendence of Mr. George Cruikshank" would open at the Surrey the following night.[58] When the next issue of *The Era* appeared on July 9, no less than four additional dramatizations of the Cruikshank plates were advertised: J. B. Johnstone's *The Drunkard's Children* at the Royal Pavilion; *Basil and Barbara: The Children of the Bottle, or The Curse Entailed* by

George Dibdin Pitt at the Britannia Saloon; J. Courtney's *Life: Founded on The Drunkard's Children* at the Victoria; and, *The Drunkard's Children, or A Sequel to The Bottle*, adapted by T. P. Taylor for the City of London Theatre. All were scheduled to open within ten days of the original and, as was the practice of the day, each claimed superiority over the others.

The text of the "official" version of *The Drunkard's Children* at the Surrey, although suggested and heavily influenced by Cruikshank himself, was actually written by T. H. Reynoldson, house dramatist for the Surrey, who had experience adapting Hogarth for the stage. Like Taylor in his rendering of *The Bottle*, Reynoldson began the first seven scenes with a Cruikshank tableau "discovered"; but unlike Taylor, Reynoldson added a supplementary tableau at each scene's end. Cruikshank's final plate – the daughter's suicide – like the last illustration in *The Bottle* series, was used at the final curtain.

Considerably less complex than that of its predecessor, the plot begins several years after the final plate of *The Bottle* and focuses upon the lives and fate of the Thornley children, Edward and Emma, described by the artist as "neglected by their parents, educated only in the streets, and [having fallen] into the hands of wretches who live upon the vice of others."[59] Subsequent scenes illustrate their downfall, tracing their movements from the gin shop, the gambling den and the dancing-rooms to various felonious acts and finally to a prison cell where Edward is condemned to live out his remaining days in isolation, and to London Bridge from which Emma, unable to shed her hereditary curse, her soul irrecoverably "seared" and "blasted," jumps to her death. The overall impact of the drama was enhanced by Reynoldson's presenting it as a single unbroken act, thereby preserving "the sense of an inexorable rhythm in the march to destruction," rather than breaking his drama into discrete acts as did all stage renditions of *The Bottle*.[60]

Both on stage and as a text, *The Drunkard's Children* utilized some of the most effective devices temperance melodrama had to offer. The plight of a drunkard's children had been publicized by activists since the earliest days of reform and in fact was the subject of an entire treatise (Number 24 of the *London Temperance Tracts*) which detailed their treatment. According to that tract, in addition to the physical abuse and suffering that resulted from having a drunken father, their fate entailed an inevitable loss of caste, conceivably the worst possible occurrence in Victorian middle-class society and one temperance playwrights employed liberally. Reflecting this, in all of the various versions of *The Drunkard's Children* the Thornley children descended into the gutter, frequenting gin palaces, dance halls and other "dens of sin," before ultimately being consigned to prison and to untimely death.[61] While Edward was imprisoned officially and permanently, Emma was likewise "sentenced," her life reduced to visiting her brother's cell daily. This image, "of the woman visiting in prison the less innocent creature to whom she is tied by blood or affection," Meisel tells us, was "recurrent in the iconography of the age" and was widely utilized by all manner of reformers.[62] Similarly, the river suicide, which ended all but the Johnstone adaptation, was a common feature in nineteenth-century melodrama and had actually been anticipated by *The Bohemians; or, The Rogues of Paris* by Edward Stirling (1843), W. T. Montcreif's *Scamps of London* (1843), Charles Selby's *London by Night* and by Cruikshank himself in *Sketches by Boz*.

Despite its structural attributes, its utility as propaganda and its popularity in England, *The Drunkard's Children* was not without its detractors. Some viewers deplored what they considered a "slaughter of the innocents," while other more ideological critics faulted it for being a chronicle of consequences, not actions. Furthermore, with redemption (Johnstone excepted) never a possibility and the children doomed from the outset, the tension generated by the anticipation and uncertainty of the outcome of *The Bottle* was missing; hence, the play was inherently less dramatic. Possibly the most severe criticism, however, was rendered by Cruikshank's friend Dickens, who, although he thought *The Drunkard's Children* emotionally and morally powerful, nevertheless accused the artist of being reductive in his assessment of the root societal causes of intemperance. Critiquing the play in *The Examiner*, Dickens wrote: "Drunkenness does not begin [in the gin shop]. It has a teeming and reproachful history anterior to that stage; and at the remediable evil in that history, it is the duty of the moralist, if he strike at all, to strike deep and spare not."[63] In this assessment, Dickens reprised a review of *The Bottle* published the previous year: "The philosophy of the thing, as a great lesson, I think is all wrong; because, to be striking, and original too, the drinking should have begun in sorrow, or poverty, or ignorance."[64]

The "catastrophic" melodrama in which entire families perished because of the sins of the drunkard was by no means the only form of the temperance narrative circulating in England at mid-century. By the early 1850s, British audiences had been exposed to a second, more optimistic pattern in the temperance melodrama – one which saw the drunkard reclaimed and reunited with his family by the end of the narrative – that was popular in the United States. Theatergoers were already familiar with *The Drunkard*, written by W. H. Smith and "A Gentleman," a play that was destined to become a classic of the genre, and in 1848, the same year *The Drunkard's*

Children was produced, *Another Glass* by Thomas Morton, a drama which focused not upon the ultimate destruction of the drunkard and his family, but instead upon his reclamation and restoration to moral and societal health and his reintegration into his family, was staged at The Lyceum (21 April).[65] *Another Glass* begins routinely with reports of the drunkards (there are actually two in this play) having returned home intoxicated the night before; contains the "standard" claims that the drunkards were decent men before they began frequenting the pub ("Our husbands have good hearts...but alas! bad companions"); and inevitably spirals downward as the men lose their jobs, physically threaten their wives and attempt to assault their former employer. Their eventual reclamation is only effected when a temperance spokesman, a character that had been employed in *The Drunkard* and that would become a common feature in American temperance drama, intervenes. Since the drunkards in this play are represented as weak, but good, men, however, their redemption is morally, physiologically and socially possible and allowable.

Despite the obvious appeal of the message in both *The Drunkard* and *Another Glass* – that regardless of the seriousness of his drinking, a drunkard has the opportunity for reclamation should he reform – the original pattern of British temperance drama in which the drunkard and his entire family suffered draconian punishments for his transgression, which was pioneered by Jerrold and refined by Cruikshank's adapters, persisted through the 1860s. In *The Village Bane; or, Two High Roads of Life* (186?) by Arthur Moulds (produced at the Temperance Hall, Leicester, with the author in the lead role) the drunkard, unable to reform, perishes, thus reinforcing the unmistakable message that the only end for a drunkard was death; while in a second play by Moulds, *Danesbury House: A Temperance Entertainment* (1862), two of three drunkard sons of a wealthy industrialist drink themselves to death and the family patriarch is murdered by one of them in a drunken rage. Adapted from one of the most popular temperance novels of the era written by Mrs. Henry Wood, whose specialty was temperance fiction, *Danesbury House* espoused an unmistakable abstinence message: the morally strong drink only water, the "safe" liquid.

In addition to its temperance imperative, *Danesbury House* strengthened deterministic tenets by reaffirming "one of the popular beliefs of the period, [that] all the children [in both novel and play] were...products of their environment."[66] The single teetotaling son was the offspring of the patriarch's first wife, an abstainer; while the sons who became drunkards were born to his second wife, a wine drinker who encouraged them likewise

1. Pit and Galleries : An Appreciative Audience.—2. Stalls and Boxes : Burnt-Cork Minstrelsy.—3. The Café : "The Cup which Cheers but not Inebriates."

THE ROYAL VICTORIA COFFEE PALACE AND MUSIC HALL.

Figure 8. The Royal Victoria Coffee Palace and Music Hall

to drink. Intriguingly, Moulds incorporated into his plot another popular trend of the time: the creation of temperance saloons and music halls much like the one created in the 1880s by theatre impresario Emma Cons at the Victoria, the site of Jerrold's *Fifteen Years of a Drunkard's Life* more than sixty years before.

Although it was the original mode of temperance writing, by the last third of the century, the deterministic style that had dominated the early English temperance drama had ostensibly disappeared, either superseded by the American-style melodrama that stressed the reclamation of the drunkard or by early experiments with the urban realism that would ultimately become the accepted mode of dramatic social commentary. Those who clung to the melodramatic mode that advanced and sustained a belief in the alterability of life, the perfectibility of humans and a "benign providence" that ensured poetic justice shifted their emphasis from a "linear moral structure to a circular one [and] from inevitable succession [and] retributive consequences" to the possibility of, not only redemption and restoration to previous status, but to a social and moral status above their previous station.[67] Once they had been exposed to the American model (and English copies), British audiences in the final decades of the nineteenth century, like their American counterparts, repudiated the tough-mindedness of a Cruikshank who could send a man's son to the thieves' kitchen and his daughter to the brothel. In the process, they eventually recoiled from plays like *The Bottle* and *The Drunkard's Children*, plays that *The Era* considered "painful" in their fidelity to nature and which Dickens said "haunt[ed] the remembrance, like an awful reality"; plays which "must have appalled" the American yeoman and have been "too horrible" for public viewing.[68] Just as the exotic and fantastical in the early melodrama had given way to the more "domestic," realistic social exposés of the 1840s and 1850s, the more deterministic temperance narratives gave way in their turn to a more optimistic, suasionist melodrama and, as they had countless times before, "the shared structures in the representative arts helped constitute, not just a common style, but a popular style" – a style in fact so popular and pervasive that it came to represent *all* temperance dramaturgy to those generations that followed.[69]

4

Reform comes to Broadway: temperance on America's mainstream stages

[Intemperance] is the insatiable destroyer of industry marching through the land, rearing poor-houses, and augmenting taxation: night and day, with sleepless activity, squandering property, cutting the sinews of industry, undermining vigor, engendering disease, paralyzing intellect, impairing moral principle, cutting short the date of life, and rolling up a national debt.

> Lyman Beecher, *Six Sermons on the Nature, Occasions, Signs, Evils, and Remedy of Intemperance*

Turning facts into interpreted symbols, the final stage of the historian's craft, becomes the most difficult and is the most intellectually dangerous.

> Warren Susman, *Culture as History*

ON TUESDAY, OCTOBER 8, 1850, READERS OF NEW YORK'S leading newspapers would have found little to arouse their curiosity or passions. In *The Herald*, they would have discovered an announcement of an anti-free school meeting, been informed that Henry Clay was at his home in Lexington, Kentucky, learned of the failure of the tobacco crop in Tennessee and been brought up to date on the latest proceedings of the Common Council; *The Tribune* reported on the anniversary of literary societies at Columbia University, a "false-pretense" swindle that had just come to the attention of the authorities, the return of Dr. E. P. Banning, who was renowned for his lectures on "spinal and kindred disorders" and the previous day's events in local courts; while *The Spirit of the Times* of October 12 (the first edition of the week) featured articles on a man who "butted a bull off of a bridge," a poem about a pretty milkmaid and a story about General Winfield Scott. All three papers' entertainment columns reported that Mme. De Vries was appearing at the Astor Place Opera House, that Tripler's Hall had just opened on Broadway at Bond Street and that the new hall would host Jenny Lind later in the month, that Fellows' Ethiopian Opera

Troupe was being featured at the Olympic, that a panorama of Cuba was available to patrons and that *The Drunkard* continued to be presented at the American Museum each night at "7 ½ o'clock."[1] No mention whatsoever was made of the fact that the previous night the legendary P. T. Barnum had quietly celebrated the 100th consecutive performance of *The Drunkard* at his famous American Museum on lower Broadway. While this event may have passed virtually unnoticed at the time, its significance has not been lost on historians who maintain that Barnum's production of *The Drunkard* heralded the entry of temperance narratives into mainstream theatre and immediately became the standard against which all other temperance dramas were measured. At the same time, it served as the prototype of the long run that was to become a standard practice in the late nineteenth- and twentieth-century commercial theatre.

A more extensive survey of New York's newspapers and Odell's chronicle shows that *The Drunkard* was just one example of the theatricalization of temperance propaganda for, as Odell records, beginning in the 1840s and continuing into the 1850s there was a veritable "outbreak" of temperance entertainments in New York and "everywhere everyone was haranguing on this engrossing topic."[2] Concerts featuring prominent performers of the era were sponsored by the Temperance Society of St. Paul, the Young Men's Washington Temperance Society and the Washington Temperance Benevolent Society at the Lyceum, Hall's Exchange Buildings and the Concert Hall at 406 Broadway; "edifying spectacles – Temperance Dramatic Sketches and Musical Entertainments, 'the aim of which [was] to illustrate the essential benefit of following out the course of prudence'" – were mounted at the Coliseum, which Odell regarded as the precursor of Barnum's lecture room; and Jerrold's *Fifteen Years of a Drunkard's Life* held the stage at the Chatham in the spring of 1841.[3] Of all of these activities, however, by far the most prominent and influential was *The Drunkard*, a play destined to become one of the most popular and best-known temperance dramas of all time.

By the time *The Drunkard* was first seen at Barnum's museum, it had already become prominent in the annals of American theatre history, having run in Boston for 144 (non-consecutive) performances in 1844 and having been featured prominently in temperance rallies in Massachusetts. The play had debuted, not at Barnum's museum, as some historians have asserted, but at another famous museum, Moses Kimball's Boston Museum located at Tremont and Bromfield Streets. Kimball's museum, which opened in 1841 (the same year Barnum bought out John Scudder's "congress of wonders" on

Broadway at Ann Street), was an amalgamation of oddities acquired from the old New England Museum, artifacts from the New York Museum and Nix's Museum of New Haven, and assorted curios from the Columbian Museum on Milk Street near Oliver. The objects displayed were, for the most part, acquired and exhibited because of their capacity to attract crowds, rather than their scientific value. Just as his predecessors (most notably Charles Willson Peale of Philadelphia) had done, Kimball, for reasons both artistic and economic, added theatrical productions to his list of scientific exhibitions, objets d'art and "freak" attractions.

Like other successful impresarios in the museum business at mid-century, Kimball had "mastered the rhetoric of moral elevation, scientific instruction, and cultural refinement in presenting [his] attractions."[4] With experience almost as varied as Barnum's – as a dry goods dealer, a goose quill salesman, a purveyor of "gentlemen's goods" and a publisher – Kimball had developed the business acumen necessary for success in a highly competitive field. His shrewdness was perhaps best demonstrated by his "idea that he might entice more people into his Museum, if he could promise them a platform show with music, 'which the God-fearing folk of Boston could stop to watch or not, as they wished'," and his establishing and maintaining a friendship and business relationship with Barnum.[5] Throughout their careers, the two entrepreneurs regularly traded "hot" exhibits like the Fejee Mermaid, one of the most successful Barnum–Kimball collaborations. According to Andrea Stulman Dennett, "the two men entered into an agreement to share in the expenses and profits of the mermaid, which was to remain the permanent property of Kimball, although it was Barnum's task to create the notoriety."[6]

While Kimball may have been sympathetic to moral reform, producing *The First and Last Pledge*, *One Cup More, or the Doom of the Drunkard*, *The Two Mechanics, or Another Glass*, *The Gambler*, *Uncle Tom's Cabin* and a revival of *Six Degrees of Crime, of Wine Women, Gambling, Theft, and the Scaffold* in the early years of the Boston Museum, its principal temperance advocate was Kimball's stage manager, W. H. Smith, a reformed drunkard and the author (or one of the authors) of *The Drunkard*. Born William Henry Sedley in North Wales, Britain, Smith ran away from home at the age of fourteen to join a troupe of strolling players. After several years of novitiate, during which he adopted the stage name Smith, he was engaged on a regular basis as a walking gentleman at the Theatre Royal, Lancaster, graduating by 1824 to light comedy and juvenile tragedy roles at the Theatre Royal, Glasgow. In 1827, one year before Jerrold's *Fifteen Years of a Drunkard's Life* debuted at the Coburg Theatre, but at a time when temperance had become part of daily discourse in England, Smith emigrated to the United States.

Upon arriving in his adopted country, Smith quickly established himself as a serious and talented actor, accepting roles at Philadelphia's famed Walnut Street Theatre, the Chatham in New York and the National, the Tremont Theatre and the Boston Museum in Boston, playing opposite actors the stature and caliber of Junius Brutus Booth, the elder. According to obituaries published shortly after his death in 1872, Smith was "robust, rosy, stately, with a rich, ringing voice, a merry laugh, and a free and noble courtesy of demeanor; a man of singular refinement and cultivation; a 'very magnetic and delightful reality.'"[7] As an actor, Smith was a diligent student and an extensive reader to whom nearly all lines of business came naturally and his style, as described by a contemporary, was intellectual, truthful and "warm with emotion." In his prime, Smith was regarded by his fellow actors as an excellent musician, boxer, singer and dancer. Early in his stage career, "he was peerless in juvenile business – in his latter days unrivaled in certain lines of 'old men'" and as a swordsman he was regarded as a rival to the elder Booth, generally thought to be the best fencer on the American stage.[8]

In 1842, after a decade and a half as a journeyman, Smith was selected by Kimball to be the stage manager at the Boston Museum, a position he was to hold for the next eighteen years. As stage manager, Smith was "undoubtedly one of the best in the country, bringing to its onerous duties a long and rich experience, thorough knowledge of human nature, [and] calm judgment and a just appreciation of what [would] best adorn the drama…"[9] It was during his tenure as stage manager, for example, that Edwin Booth made his stage debut in 1849 in *Richard III*, Boston audiences were introduced to *Uncle Tom's Cabin*, Lester Wallack played in *Richelieu* (a role that Booth would later claim as his own) and *The Drunkard*, the play that arguably was the Museum's most famous single presentation, appeared in the theatre's repertory. By the time he left the Boston Museum in 1860, its theatre had become as famous as the attractions featured in its exhibition halls and had been immortalized as the birthplace of American temperance drama.

In numerous newspaper accounts of *The Drunkard* (both contemporary and modern) and many anthologies, Smith is credited with being the sole author of the play, as well as with being the first to play the part of Edward Middleton. While there is no dispute of the latter, the issue of authorship has never been resolved. According to legend and to accounts from fellow actors like Harry Watkins, with whom Smith worked on several occasions, the stage manager was a "hard drinking man who signed the pledge of total abstinence" and thereafter dedicated himself to reforming others.[10] In Watkins' opinion, Smith was simply translating his own experience to the stage and was portraying himself when he played Middleton. Considering that the Washingtonians were firmly established in Boston by 1841 and their temperance "message" and methods of canvassing the ranks of known drunkards had literally swept through the city by the end of that year, it is likely that Smith had encountered their spokesmen and was "dry" by the time he assumed the position at the Boston Museum in 1842.

The issue of authorship was clouded shortly after the play was first produced in 1844 by the Introduction to Number 1 of the Boston Museum Edition of *American Acting Dramas* (1847) which stated:

> Many inquiries have been made as to the authorship of 'The Drunkard,' and, as rumor has named a dozen or more persons, some of whom have never troubled themselves to deny their identity in regard to connection with the subject, we give the facts which, if of importance to any but those immediately concerned, are as follows; The proprietor of the Museum (Moses Kimball), ever ready to take the tide on its flood in any matter of general interest, conceiving that a drama might aid the cause of temperance, and prove highly productive for his establishment, engaged a gentleman of known and appreciated literary accomplishment to undertake the task. Unfortunately, his production, though eminently worthy of the gentleman and scholar, was, from want of theatrical experience, merely a story in its dialogue, entirely deficient in stage tact and dramatic effect. Under these circumstances, the manuscript was placed in the hands of Mr. W. H. Smith with the request that he would finish it, and prepare it for the stage. This was done, and the piece produced under his direction.[11]

In variants of this story, the "gentleman" initiated the contact with Kimball, presenting his finished, unsolicited manuscript to Kimball, who then assigned Smith to make it stageworthy; while yet another version has the gentleman entering a playwriting contest sponsored by the Museum.

If such a "gentleman" in fact ever existed and if he did in truth contribute to the scripting of *The Drunkard*, that gentleman most likely was the Rev. John Pierpont, Pastor of the Hollis Street (Unitarian) Church and a prominent Boston reformer. Not only was Pierpont an active and vocal proponent of the "moral dramas" staged at the Boston Museum, but he is credited with bringing Smith to the attention of Kimball when the latter was in need of a stage manager. And, when Pierpont was seen in the audience for *The Drunkard*, it was generally acknowledged that it was not his "first manifestation in things theatrical" and speculation as to the degree of his involvement with its creation was rife.[12] While such evidence is admittedly scant, it has nevertheless been sufficient to convince historians as respected as Henry Steele Commager and David Grimsted to grant Pierpont joint authorship status.[13]

Conjecture as to Pierpont's part in the scripting of *The Drunkard* and theories of joint authorship have attained credibility due largely to Pierpont's vigorous and public reform efforts, many of them unpopular at the time; his reputation as a temperance poet and man of letters; and his dogged determination to effect social change even in the face of widespread, organized opposition. Like one of his idols, Rev. Lyman Beecher, Pierpont used his pulpit to attack slavery, intemperance and other social evils and like Beecher, he refused to temper his remarks or shy away from a fight. As a result, his words were frequently indelicate. Convinced of the righteousness of his causes, his attitude, like that of his fellow reformers, was uncompromising and his assaults on the entrepreneurs who profited from vice (especially intemperance) became a personal crusade, with Pierpont's fulminations often naming brewers and winebibbers by name and castigating them with "an indignant eloquence" in the presence of his entire congregation. At a time when the church elders were renting the Hollis Street Church basement to a rum seller for use as a warehouse and a number of liquor merchants rented pews, few in Pierpont's congregation shared his enthusiasm for temperance reform. In 1838, Pierpont's enemies, both within and outside his church, mounted a concerted effort to oust him from his pulpit.

In an impeachment campaign that came to be known as the "Seven Years War," Pierpont was accused of "entering into *every* exciting topic which the ingenuity of the fanatic . . . could conjure up to distract and disturb the public mind, such as *imprisonment for debt, anti-Masonry, Phrenology, Temperance,* and last of all, *Abolition of Slavery*."[14] In a pamphlet titled "Proceedings of a Meeting of Friends of Rev. John Pierpont and His Reply to the Charges of the Committee of Hollis Street Society," Pierpont, while denying advocacy of phrenology and anti-masonry, responded in characteristic fashion to the committee's charge that he was a temperance spokesman: "*'Temperance?' Guilty, guilty, guilty!* – On this count, gentlemen, I shall make no defense, *nolo Contendere.*"[15] As one biographer noted, Pierpont was so devoted to the temperance cause that he was more than willing to wear the crown of the martyr.

Even more distressing to Pierpont's congregation than his reformist efforts, however, was his attraction to and active participation in the arts. A prolific writer of verse, early in his ministerial career, Pierpont became known throughout Boston as the "temperance poet," although he often published his work anonymously or under the pseudonym "Spurzheim, the Imported Mountebank." In addition to his poetry, in their impeachment effort the Hollis Street Committee charged Pierpont with such anti-clerical activities as "the writing of books"; with attacking an anti-temperance drama, *Departed Spirits, or the Temperance Hoax*, in a poetic sermon; and with contributing a prologue which had been recited from the stage of the Tremont Theatre in 1827. While no actual proof of authorship of the latter existed at the time and the theatre management remained silent on the issue, Pierpont's enemies claimed that the name of the writer, J. Jameson, could be interpreted as J[ohn], son of James [Pierpont] and remained convinced that their minister had written the prologue.[16] In its campaign to discredit Pierpont, the Hollis Street Committee continually foregrounded his close and continued affiliation with the theatre as clear evidence of his lack of fitness for the ministry. Pierpont's rumored association with *The Drunkard* only exacerbated matters.

While the controversy surrounding authorship may have complicated Pierpont's life, it presumably increased public interest in the play, for by the time Barnum decided to stage *The Drunkard* in 1850, it had already achieved national recognition. With Smith in the role of Edward Middleton, George E. "Yankee" Locke as the original landlord, and Adelaide Phillips (later renowned as an opera star) as Julia Middleton, the play had opened at the Boston Museum on February 12, 1844 and during the 1844–45 season had been presented a record 140 times. During roughly the same period, Barnum had developed his museum into America's premiere entertainment venue, in the process bringing about "a major transformation in the function and cultural stature of the nation's proprietary museums" and becoming this country's most famous showman.[17]

Barnum had entered the museum business in 1841 by purchasing Scudder's American Museum on Broadway at Ann Street from the heirs of museum pioneer John Scudder. During the ensuing decade, Barnum not only augmented Scudder's original collection of attractions until it reached an estimated 30,000 exhibits, but he added freaks, novelty performers, baby and animal shows, and stage presentations; while the exterior of his museum was repainted as a giant advertisement for the offerings inside. By the time he purchased Edmund Peale's museum collection in 1849, Barnum had established himself as the dominant figure in the burgeoning American entertainment industry, his enterprise became the model for anyone considering a career in show business and by mid-century "it was already considered unthinkable to visit New York without seeing" the American Museum.[18]

In 1850, the same year he staged *The Drunkard*, Barnum undertook a total renovation of the central features of the American Museum and included in the improvements was the reconstruction of one of the most famous rooms of the building: the Moral Lecture Room. In place of the original Moral Lecture Room, which was described as "narrow, ill-contrived and inconvenient," Barnum built an auditorium intended to emulate rooms in the royal palaces of Europe, which would accommodate three thousand patrons in a parterre, first balcony, gallery and proscenium boxes.[19] The parterre and stage were situated on the second floor of the museum, while entrances to the various seating sections were located on the third, fourth and fifth floors.

When Barnum selected *The Drunkard* as the inaugural drama for his new Moral Lecture Room, no one who knew the impresario was surprised. According to his biographers, by the mid-1840s Barnum had become distressed, not only by the alcoholism of his show business contemporaries, but by his own consumption.[20] His wife, Charity, was convinced that Barnum was deluding himself that his "moderate" drinking was harmless and that her husband was on "the drunkard's path"; but, more significantly, his biographers contend, the showman himself secretly feared that he was losing self-control because of his drinking. By late 1847, Barnum was consuming a full bottle of champagne each day and, as a consequence, was unable to work after noon. In 1848, evidently swayed by a particularly persuasive temperance lecture directed at "moderate" drinkers delivered by Universalist minister Edwin Chapin, Barnum went into his wine cellar and destroyed sixty to seventy bottles of champagne. Shortly thereafter, Barnum sought the Rev. Chapin, asked for a copy of the teetotalers' pledge, signed it and for the remainder of his life, both swore off drink and dedicated himself to the temperance cause.

Having once again taken control of his own life, Barnum undertook the salvation of others with the same zeal he brought to all of his projects. Although he was a frequent temperance lecturer – one of the movement's "podium stars" – and in the 1850s journeyed to Maine and other Maine Law states to publicize the prohibition cause, his greatest contribution to the battle against intemperance was likely the use of his Moral Lecture Room as a pulpit from which to disseminate temperance ideology. Not only did he mount his own anti-liquor dramas like *The Drunkard*, *The Drunkard's Warning* and *The Bottle* and provide copies of the teetotal pledge at the box office for audience members to sign after these shows, but he freely lent his theatre to other temperance groups and provided acts to other temperance theatres like Teetotalers Hall. At the same time that he was presenting temperance plays, in yet another part of his museum, Barnum continued his war against intemperance with a tableau titled *The Drunken Family*, "a wax representation of a family dressed in rags and living in squalor captured gazing upon the face of a dead little boy."[21]

As significant as these pro-temperance offerings might have been, Barnum did not limit his temperance efforts to stage shows and the lending of performers. Adopting the Washingtonian notion of "alternative entertainment venues," he not only banished the conventional theatre bar from his establishment and refused to readmit patrons who had snuck out to neighborhood taverns at intermission, but he created a temperance saloon which provided everything found in the standard pub except liquor. Thus, at a time when other New York theatres at mid-century liberally dispensed liquor both during the shows and at intermission, and liquor was an integral facet of the urban entertainment scene, Barnum turned his entire establishment into an environment totally and publicly "on the temperance plan."[22]

In both his behavior and attitudes, after 1847 Barnum re-created himself according to his new-found morality, incorporated it into his entertainments and, in so doing, became the prototype for a new breed of reformer, a breed which sociologist Howard Becker labels the "moral entrepreneur." The moral entrepreneur, according to Becker, "operates with an absolute ethic; what he sees is truly and totally evil with no qualification. Any means is justified to do away with it."[23] Further, he is a man who, having discovered the commercial value of decency, believes that entertainment and morality are highly compatible and, as a result, actively promotes his moral views through artistic means. As a tactical approach, the moral entrepreneur "master[s] and [then exploits] a rhetoric of cultural refinement and moral elevation to legitimate a new kind of theatre" and then sets out to elevate the morals of the subordinate class by eliminating or at least publicly suppressing those lower-class ideas and behaviors which he deems annoying, wasteful, immoral or even dangerous.[24] To do so, he capitalizes upon existing middle-class precepts that emphasize the development of self-discipline as the means to social progress, which, in turn, justifies his regarding himself as rational and civilized while categorizing the lower classes as emotional, "barbarian," uncontrollable and in need of moral education. In turning his museum to moral purposes, Barnum served as a model for

moral entrepreneurs to follow – from vaudeville impresarios Tony Pastor and
B. F. Keith to Walt Disney.

Arguably the prototype of American temperance melodramas and considered by the British to be paradigmatic of life in antebellum America,
The Drunkard structurally emulated the Washingtonian experience speech,
taking the shape of an inverted arc. In it, the protagonist Edward Middleton
is first introduced to the audience as an educated middle-class landowner
who, although remembered by his neighbors as a bright and good boy when
younger, is now represented as a "dissipated collegian given somewhat to
excess – giddy, wild and reckless."[25] This is the characterization fostered and
disseminated by the play's villain, Lawyer Cribbs, who takes special care
to enumerate Middleton's moral flaws to Mary Wilson, a virginal young
girl whom Cribbs covets sexually and who occupies a cottage owned by
Middleton.

Initially fearful that Middleton intends to evict her from her cottage,
Mary, upon meeting the young man, is nevertheless immediately impressed
by his kindness and is quickly won over by his innate goodness, which is
evident despite his propensity to drink. Before Act I ends, Middleton and
Mary are married and Cribbs, having been robbed of the opportunity to
seduce Mary and harboring a long-standing grudge against the Middleton
family, has already conceived the means of ensuring the couple's destruction.

In the ensuing acts, capitalizing upon Middleton's inability to resist the
bottle, Cribbs lures the young husband away from his home to a series of
taverns where he quickly becomes a drunkard – a truth visually depicted by
the progressive deterioration of his once-elegant clothes and a growth of
beard – and abandons his wife and young daughter, Julia. The precipitous
downward spiral, so well-documented by former drunkards and featured so
prominently in Washingtonian testimonials, has begun, a fact celebrated by
Cribbs, who declares triumphantly: "I know his nature well. He has tasted,
and will not stop now short of madness or oblivion."[26]

Having fled his rural home with its agrarian morality, Middleton's further moral decline is represented geographically, by showing him wandering through some of the most notorious and forbidding areas of the big
city, the only refuge left to drunkards. In the Boston Museum production,
Middleton frequents Boston's Dock Square and "a well-known bar room
on School Street"; while in the New York versions, his moral decline leads
him to the infamous Five Points neighborhood on the city's Lower East
Side.[27] In these decayed and degraded environments, the once respectable
landowner, in the throes of the DT's, is seemingly doomed to die in shame;

Figure 9. Broadside, The Drunkard

however, just as Middleton prepares to end his own life, the Washingtonian representative, Arden Rencelaw, intervenes to prevent the suicide. Then, through the offices of Rencelaw, a reformed drunkard himself, Middleton is convinced to swear off liquor forever, to sign the pledge and to resume his rightful position and duties as husband and father. His reclamation is depicted in a non-verbal final scene described by the following stage directions: "*Interior of Cottage as in Act 1st, Scene 1st. Everything denoting domestic peace and tranquil happiness... [Middleton] plays on flute symphony to 'Home, Sweet Home.' Julia sings the first verse... The [singing] is then taken up by a chorus of villagers behind.*" The play ends with a tableau in which Middleton sits at the kitchen table with his hand on a bible, Mary stands behind him and Julia kneels at her father's feet.[28]

In retrospect, there was an undeniable "historical logic" to *The Drunkard*'s entering the temperance discourse at this time. By 1844, the Washingtonian experience speech, with its roots in the emotionalized and graphic confessions found in eighteenth- and nineteenth-century British Methodist services, had already become widely recognized as a "secular conversion experience," a readily available means to a spiritual rebirth for drunkards. Viewed in light of its incipient religiosity, it is possible, according to theatre historian Jeffrey Mason, to regard *The Drunkard* as an "exegetical representation." Mason reasons: "'Exegesis' connotes explanation or exposition, especially of a text, and the interpretation is more direct and less sophisticated than in the case of formal hermeneutics. The association with scriptural readings is not... misleading, for the temperance plays did serve an exhortatory purpose somewhat similar to that of the circuit minister's sermon."[29] This notion is supported, not only by the "demonstrative" quality of acting required by *The Drunkard* and other temperance dramas, but by the transformation of theatre stages into veritable pulpits by moral entrepreneurs like Kimball and Barnum.[30]

Religious analogs aside, *The Drunkard* contributed significantly to the transformation of temperance narratives from the raw, unmediated emotionalism of the Washingtonian experience speech to the aesthetic realm, a necessary step if the temperance imperative were to reach beyond the Washingtonian hall and appeal to a more middle-class audience. As Terry Eagleton has aptly pointed out, "the aesthetic offer[ed] the middle class a superbly versatile model of their political aspirations, exemplifying new forms of autonomy and self-determination, transforming the relations between law and desire, morality and knowledge, recasting the links between individual and totality, and revising social relations on the basis of custom, affection and sympathy."[31] In this context, operating somewhere between the class culture of the eighteenth century and the mass culture of the late nineteenth, temperance and other moral reform dramas played a vital role in what Joseph Gusfield has termed "status politics" by advancing the notion of abstinence as the principal means to middle-class respectability.

The Drunkard's historical importance, however, was by no means limited to its contribution to the formation of the American middle class and its role in mid-century status politics; the play examined sexual politics of the era as well. Its rhetoric, setting and circumstance, evidenced by the following exchange between Middleton and Cribbs in Act I, all link it inextricably to women's melodrama and, through that genre, to women's issues in general:

> MIDDLETON: Cribbs, do you know this girl has no father?
> CRIBBS: That's it; a very wild flower growing on an open heath.
> MIDDLETON: Have you forgotten that this poor girl has not a brother?
> CRIBBS: A garden without a fence, not a stake standing. You have nothing to do but to step into it...
> MIDDLETON: Leave me old man; begone; your hot lascivious breath cannot mingle with the sweet odor of these essenced wildflowers. Your raven voice will not harmonize with the warblings of these heavenly songsters...[32]

Such natural imagery, the threat of the "sophisticated and powerful" urban male (Cribbs) seeking sexual conquest, the "feminization" of the rural setting and the lack of male protection for a "religious and virtuous" widow and her daughter who was "nurtured in the wilderness," were all routine facets of women's melodrama designed to expose and emphasize the vulnerability of the female home and were common inclusions in women's narratives. Furthermore, as Carroll Smith-Rosenberg has observed, in the women's melodrama of the era "daughter" was a critical term – one which "bespoke middle-class women's identification with working-class women, an identification that had no true parallel in male bourgeois discussions of working-class men because it was based on middle-class women's sense of their own marginality within male economic structures."[33] Consequently, with the employment of a single word, whether consciously or inadvertently, the authors of *The Drunkard* interwove both gender and status politics into their masterwork.

Perhaps even more disturbing than *The Drunkard*'s exposition of women's social and sexual vulnerability, which was a given in women's spheres at mid-century, was the question it raised about women's capacity to exert moral influence over their husbands, also a given in antebellum thought. In fact, it was widely believed that "female influence within the domestic sphere was the key to the success of the moral suasion efforts that dominated temperance reform after 1830. In her role as the ultimate moral authority of the family, a woman could inculcate temperance ideals" in her husband and children.[34] While *The Drunkard* continued to stress the tactical validity of moral suasion if practiced by a male (Rencelaw in this case), it expressed doubts about women's powers of moral suasion. At the critical juncture of Act II, when Middleton is contemplating abandoning his family for the city, Mary proves totally ineffective in dissuading him from leaving. Nor, it is evident, has she dissuaded him from drinking. And, although she moves to a wretched garret in the city to be "near" him, her presence does nothing to prevent his further moral and physical deterioration. Ultimately, it is male intervention, not female moral suasion, that redeems him. Thus, at the very height of suasionist beliefs in the 1840s, *The Drunkard* revealed the limitations of – perhaps even manifested a profound distrust of – the efficacy of woman's moral influence and exposed the inconsistencies and contradictions inherent in both temperance ideology and women's rights activism.

The issue of ideological purity is an interesting one and is certainly one raised by *The Drunkard*. In his cultural study of P. T. Barnum, *E Pluribus Barnum: The Great Showman and US Popular Culture*, Bluford Adams suggests that in the years between its opening at the Boston Museum in 1844 and Barnum's mounting it six years later, the play had traveled a considerable "ideological distance," appealing more to the middle classes at the American Museum than it originally had in Boston. By valorizing the temperance spokesman, Rencelaw, and by demonizing sellers of alcohol, *The Drunkard* "flew in the face of the secular, moral suasionist Washingtonians" and their successor, The Sons of Temperance, by appearing to support both Christian and prohibitionist solutions.[35] On the face of it, such conclusions appear to be consistent with temperance history and are therefore tempting. Prohibitionist initiatives, in the form of the Massachusetts Fifteen-Gallon Law of 1838 and the various no-licensing campaigns in different sections of the country during the late 1830s and 1840s, it is true, were already gathering support and moving toward the full-scale sanctions of the Maine Laws of the 1850s; yet, despite barbs aimed directly at the saloon keeper and lamentations about the existence of alcohol, *The Drunkard* falls considerably short of advocating legal constraints. Instead, Smith and his collaborator are content to rely upon the moral force and persuasion of their spokesman, Rencelaw, to solve the play's central problem: Middleton's drinking. It is equally important to emphasize that the protagonist, Edward Middleton, was not created as a mechanic who was co-opted by the middle class, as Adams intimates, but rather was created as educated and middle class in the first draft of the play and hence was the ideal protagonist to reach the middle-class audience both museum proprietors and temperance advocates alike were attempting to reach and retain. It also significant to note that throughout their short history, the Washingtonians attracted reformers of all stripes, including those with religious convictions.[36] Thus, assuming joint authorship of *The Drunkard*, it is more likely that its internal inconsistencies are due, not to alignment with non-secular or prohibitionist interests as Adams suggests, but rather to the admixture of Pierpont's religious and middle-class sensibilities with Smith's British working-class perspective.

Adam's "misapprehension" of the temperance spokesman Rencelaw's status and his failure to include upper-class activists within Washingtonian ranks is a common one; yet, in truth, during the early 1840s, the movement included hundreds of Rencelaws – wealthy men who joined their fellow Washingtonians and ventured nightly into the city's "mean streets" to seek drunkards for reclamation. While contemporary accounts of Washingtonianism generally mention only its artisan roots and membership, Washingtonianism was welcomed by most upper- and middle-class temperance reformers, and a number of them joined Washingtonian societies and "forged links to existing associations of the older type."[37] Nineteenth-century temperance novelist T. S. Arthur testified to this intermixture of classes by including a story in *Six Nights with the Washingtonians* about a wealthy merchant who, after a prolonged period of drunkenness, signed the Washingtonian pledge; and historians Stuart Blumin and Paul Boyer both stress the increasing complexity of both the community of temperance activists and their motives during the 1840s. Blumin, in fact, notes that not only were wealthy men likely to become Washingtonian "urban-morality foot soldiers," but a number of early individual Washingtonian societies were actually "composed mainly of men who move[d] in a higher class of society than others."[38] Likewise, with a degree of continuity from earlier, more religious temperance organizations, it was to be expected that men with strong religious convictions would be found within the ranks of the Washingtonians. Thus, while the "typical" Washingtonian was likely to be an artisan or mechanic, not a merchant or a philanthropist, and was generally more oriented to secular rather than religious "preaching," men of Rencelaw's social status and religious nature were nevertheless included in the movement and successfully operated within the Washingtonian ideological boundaries. Certainly Barnum identified with the wealthy Rencelaw for, at one time, he considered playing the Washingtonian spokesman himself and, when the play opened at the American Museum, the actor who did play him bore a strong resemblance to Barnum.

Produced by Barnum in 1850, more than five years after the demise of Washingtonianism, but in the heyday of the Sons of Temperance, *The Drunkard* achieved immediate success. By July 8, the date Barnum opened his production, the play had been attracting audiences at the Bowery for nearly a week, as the theatre's advertisement in *The Spirit of the Times* of July 13 testifies: "The Drunkard which has been put upon the stage here most efficiently, and has created a great sensation, continues to be the principal item in the entertainment of the evening...People flock in large numbers to witness the representation of this moral drama."[39] Within weeks, the play had been "duplicated" and mounted at the National Theatre (with Joseph Jefferson as William Dowton), at the Brooklyn Museum and, renamed *One Glass More*, at Niblo's Garden. Advertised as a "moral lesson," *The Drunkard* attracted people who had never before entered a theatre but saw no harm in attending a lesson in morality in a "lecture room." The play was even presented at special matinees for the accommodation of children and "persons unable to be out evenings." As one observer at the time noted: "The general public [is]...cleverly caught by an awful picture of the terrible curse of drink, called 'The Drunkard' which raised the place of the favor of the rigidly moral persons because it preached a harrowing sermon."[40]

By the end of the decade, however, the play that practically single-handedly transformed Barnum's museum from an enterprise that exhibited freaks and curiosities into a site for moral lectures was being dropped from the repertoires of New York's leading theatres. Increasingly, the play was relegated to minor theatres like the Odeon and Seaver's Opera House in Williamsburgh, Brooklyn, or to touring companies. By 1875, *The Drunkard* had ostensibly disappeared from the New York area and, while it lasted on the road until the early years of the twentieth century, its time in the limelight (with the notable exceptions of a Boston Museum production in 1884 which featured Sol Smith Russell as Bill Dowton, William Seymour as Farmer Gates and Annie Clarke as Mary Wilson, and a little-known production by the Federal Theatre Project) had passed. By the time of its "passing," however *The Drunkard* had done more than any other play, with the possible exception of *Uncle Tom's Cabin*, to legitimize the theatre in the eyes of respectable Americans.

A decade after the decline of Washintonianism but before *The Drunkard* slipped from Barnum's Museum, the Bowery and other first-class theatres, the narrative that, when adapted for the stage, was destined to become even more popular nationally appeared as a novel. *Ten Nights in a Bar-room and What I Saw There*, written by the journalist/novelist T. S. Arthur, was published by Lippincott, Grambo and Company and J. W. Bradley in 1854 as a defense of prohibition. Although neither critically nor commercially successful on its release, by the beginning of the Civil War the novel had become a popular classic and when the temperance novel all but disappeared after the war, *Ten Nights in a Bar-room* took on new life in a theatrical adaptation by William W. Pratt. Having opened at New York's National Theatre on August 23, 1858, the play that would eventually eclipse *The Drunkard* in popularity refocused public attention upon Arthur's narrative and reconfirmed his reputation as the "prose laureate of teetotalism" and the "prophet of prohibition."

Arthur was admirably equipped to write a work that significantly advanced both the cause of temperance and the cultural legitimacy of the theatre.[41] By the time he wrote his *magnum opus*, he was recognized nationally as a crusader against, not only drink, but gambling, smoking, mesmerism, materialism, business speculation and was known as an advocate of woman suffrage and socialism. Equally important, Arthur had distinguished himself as a publisher, an editor and an author of everything from propagandistic pamphlets to full-length novels. One of a class of writers called "magazinists" – a group of journalists who, according to de Tocqueville, spoke the language of the middle classes and was heard by them – Arthur attained his literary reputation in the pages of America's leading periodicals. Beginning in the mid-1830s with the editorship of the short-lived *Baltimore Athenaeum*, he subsequently became affiliated with a series of periodicals that catered to popular literary tastes, either as editor (of *The Baltimore Saturday Visitor*, the *Baltimore Book*, *The Baltimore Literary Magazine*, *The Baltimore Merchant*, *Arthur's Ladies' Magazine*, *Arthur's Home Gazette*) or as a writer (in *Godey's Ladies' Magazine*, *The Saturday Courier*, *Graham's Magazine*). In 1841, with a "modest" literary reputation already established, Arthur moved from Baltimore to Philadelphia to reconstitute himself as a writer of temperance and reformist fiction. It was this portion of his career that would bring him immediate fame.

Before leaving Baltimore, Arthur had heard rumors of unusual temperance meetings being held by a new group of temperance activists, the Washingtonians, in a hall on the corner of Lombard and Hanover Streets.

Initially attracted to their meetings because of journalistic curiosity, Arthur quickly became "converted" by their exuberance for saving diehard drunkards and by the passion of their experience speeches. As a consequence, he subsequently returned to attend a total of six successive meetings. These he chronicled first as a series of articles in *The Baltimore Merchant*, then as a series of six pamphlets, and finally in a book, *Six Nights with the Washingtonians: A Series of Original Temperance Tales.*

The latter was the first in a series of successful reformist works that included *The Crystal Fount, for All Seasons* (1850, temperance); *Three Years in a Man-trap* (1872, temperance); *Women to the Rescue: A Story of the New Crusade* (1872, the women and temperance); *Cast Adrift* (1873, an attack on the evils of the lottery); *Danger; or, Wounded in the House of a Friend* (1875, a warning against moderate drinking); *The Bar-Rooms at Brantly; or, The Great Hotel Speculation* (1877, a defense of "temperance coffee houses" and "friendly" inns); *Grappling with the Monster; or, The Curse and Cure of Strong Drink* (1877, temperance); and *Saved as by Fire* (1881, temperance). In all, during his career as a novelist and writer of "tales," Arthur produced over two hundred works and during one decade, the 1840s, he was single-handedly responsible for 6 percent of all the native fiction published in the United States. In his own time, it was said that Arthur accomplished as much for temperance with his pen as John B. Gough did from the speaker's platform.[42]

With *Ten Nights in a Bar-room*, Arthur abandoned the assimilative reform of the Washingtonians – a view of the drunkard as "part of a social system in which the reformer's culture was dominant" – in favor of the coercive reform advocated by Neal Dow and the Maine Law proponents.[43] According to Joseph Gusfield, "coercive reform emerges when the object of reform is seen as an intractable defender of another culture, someone who rejects the reformer's values and really doesn't want to change."[44] Whereas moral suasion implies a symmetrical relationship between the drunkard and his saviors with a direct appeal to both the drinker's reason and emotions, coercion establishes an asymmetrical relationship between reformer and drunkard. Dialogue is unimportant to the coercive reformer; the only thing that matters is the amount of force (especially legal force) he can mobilize to ensure victory.[45] By embracing coercion, Arthur adopted an adversarial relationship to anyone affiliated with liquor or the liquor industry, becoming one of the chief propagandists for prohibition.

While Arthur is remembered as both a prolific and widely read littérateur and an important social reformer, he is seldom remembered as arguably the most influential nineteenth-century proponent of the teachings of the

Swedish theologian and mystic, Emanuel Swedenborg. Arthur had been initially attracted to Swedenborgian "Heavenly Doctrines" in the late 1830s while still living in Baltimore and, shortly after converting to the faith, he became a prominent member of the Church of New Jerusalem, editing church magazines and serving as president of the American New Church Tract and Publication Society.[46] Having been raised in a religious home, Arthur was predisposed to gravitate toward teachings that advocated a collective response to evil and protected the sanctity of the family. Following his conversion to Swedenborgianism, its "good works" principles and world view became the core of his subsequent work.

As summarized by Francis Lauricella:

> The characteristically Swedenborgian note was to postulate a fundamental "correspondence" between spirit and matter. An otherwise dead material world was quickened into life by an infusion of God's love, and the material world progressively subjugated to the spiritual realm. The spiritual influx was available as divine grace to all men and women who chose to accept it . . . Swedenborgianism was psychologically akin to Calvinism in its vivid evocation of hell and hellish agents, "networks of hell," conceived as operative in the spiritual and material realms alike.[47]

To Arthur, surveying antebellum American society, there was no greater nor more effective instrument of Satan than liquor; no greater embodiment of the spirit of evil than the individual, selfish decision to drink regularly and to excess.

Initially, Arthur's response to the spiritual and social disorder caused by intemperance was to postulate that in order to triumph over the instrument of Satan, each man and woman needed daily to reject the selfish impulse to drink. Such thinking and belief in individual battles against the bottle originally led him to the Washingtonians – to their optimistic view of the possibility of reclaiming drunkards through the signing of the teetotal pledge. However, after witnessing the failure of the Washingtonians and the widespread backsliding of many of their members in the mid-1840s, Arthur lost faith in the efficacy of moral suasion as the solution to the evils of drink and was forced to reassess "anti-institutional impulses affirming the spiritual liberation of the individual as the key to redeeming the world."[48]

In the process of reassessing his beliefs, Arthur rejected Emersonian notions of self-reliance and individualism as a means to the perfectibility of man. Man alone, he came to believe in the waning years of the 1840s, was simply incapable of controlling his nature, was incapable of saving himself from the evil that surrounded and ensnared him. Clearly, such thinking was distinctly less optimistic, more deterministic. Perhaps it was this deterministic outlook in an otherwise melodramatic and sentimentalized story that inhibited sales immediately after the novel's publication. In other words, perhaps *Ten Nights in a Bar-room* simply "came too near the dangerous ground of realism to be altogether welcome in [the] story-paper world."[49]

Given the individual's inability to resist the forces "in league with the demon liquor" and his Swedenborgian belief that a man alone didn't possess the inherent strength to save himself, it was inevitable that Arthur would repudiate Washingtonian (and Emersonian) individualism and recognize that the only remaining solution to intemperance, the most pernicious of all evils, lay in collective social action: coercive action.[50] Consequently, after the demise of the Washingtonians, Arthur turned his focus from the individual drunkard toward the human accomplices of the "forces of hell" (liquor manufacturers, tavern keepers, bar tenders) and toward the "earthly strongholds of hellish dominions" (the bar rooms themselves), and ultimately toward the antidote to such evils: prohibition.

To the advocates of prohibition in the late 1840s and 1850s, the tavern owner was the embodiment of Satan hiding behind the principles of American capitalism; while every bartender was "a Simon Legree in a white apron." With the passage of the original Maine Law in 1851 and subsequent Maine Laws in thirteen other states and territories in the early 1850s, prohibitionists successfully moved the issue of intemperance from the private sphere to the public, political arena and, for the first time, demonstrated the possibility of a community solution to alcoholism. Published three years after the passage of prohibition legislation in Maine and at the height of public resistance to its provisions, *Ten Nights in a Bar-room*, the novel, was undisguised propaganda designed as a defense of the Maine Law.

In 1858, at roughly the time that Arthur's novel was beginning to gain popular recognition, his story was translated to stage by William W. Pratt, a New York playwright, actor, temperance lecturer and preacher. After a short stint as a minister, Pratt returned to the theatre to adapt *Ten Nights in a Bar-room* and to place it where it could, in his mind, achieve the most impact – on the stage. Pratt, in the process, changed relatively little of his model. Minor episodes in the novel were omitted and he added a Yankee character, Sample Switchel, and his female love interest for comic relief; but Pratt remained faithful to Arthur's plot, themes and ideology.[51] Furthermore, at critical points of the story, Pratt hedged his bets by excerpting

entire passages from the novel. In his hands, Arthur's basic narrative remained as dark and deterministic as the novel, a veritable "phantasmagoria
of shocking and sensational incidents," one that arguably found its proper
medium on the stage at mid-century.[52]

In his introduction to the John Harvard Library edition of *Ten Nights in
a Bar-room*, Donald A. Koch speculates that not only was there lingering
puritan resistance to novels until the late 1840s and early 1850s, but there was
a similar conservative reluctance to embrace the temperance novel as an accepted form of propaganda. Since the theatre had long since been conceded
to Satan by the puritan-minded, there were no such barriers facing Pratt's
drama, which found a large, receptive audience, especially in rural America
and among those who were not habitual readers. While it is impossible
today to assess how much influence Pratt's drama had upon popularizing
Arthur's novel or to predict what might have happened to the novel had not
the play been written, it is generally conceded by historians that from 1858
on, the general public was unable to distinguish the novel from its stage
adaptation and that the two went hand-in-hand into the history books.

Ten Nights in a Bar-room was clearly the most apocalyptic of Arthur's
works and was the most deterministic American-written temperance narrative to that date. Utilizing a time-sequence device, a series of elapsed
intervals (the ten nights of the title are spaced over a period of ten years)
illustrating the progressive nature of alcoholism, Arthur and, after him
Pratt, exposed their audiences to the devastating effects of alcohol on a
series of characters, some innocent; others evil.[53] Arthur strengthened his
case for prohibition by structuring his work around four murders, each
directly attributable to alcohol. While he previously had shown lives shattered by drink, he had rarely become so extreme as to attribute violent deaths
(i.e., homicides) to alcoholism; yet his Cedarville and its tavern, the Sickle
and Sheaf, are dens of death. Beginning with the death of the drunkard
Joe Morgan's daughter, Mary, felled by a shot glass thrown in anger by
the bar keeper, Simon Slade, the cycle of drink-induced violence continues
until it has consumed Willie Hammond, the promising young son of one
of the town fathers; his mother; Harvey Green, an itinerant gambler; and
the tavern owner himself, a victim of parricide. The latter dies at the hand
of his own son, whose character has been poisoned, the audience is told,
by his growing up in a hellish atmosphere, the bar room. Only Morgan,
the town drunk, is allowed to escape the violent chaos caused by intemperance and the presence of the bar room; but only after the sacrifice of
his guardian angel daughter. By the final scene of the play, audiences had

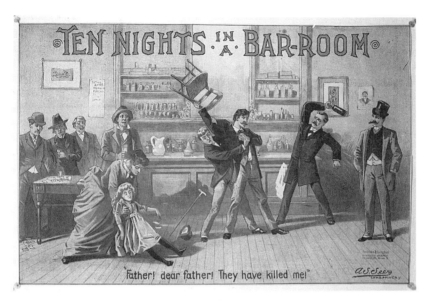

"Father! dear father! They have killed me!"

Figure 10. Poster, The Death of Little Mary in Ten Nights in a Bar-room

been primed to welcome the plea for legalized prohibition, uttered in the novel by Morgan himself, but declaimed from the stage by the temperance spokesman, Romaine:

> You must cut off the fountain, if you would dry up the stream. If we would save the young, the innocent, we must cover them from the tempter, for they can no more resist his assaults than the lamb can resist the wolf. They are helpless if you abandon them to the powers of evil. Let us, then, one and all, resolve this night that the traffic shall cease in Bolton County. A large majority of the people will vote in favor of such a measure.[54]

The rhetoric here is unmistakable. The use of the plural "we" denotes the call to collective action while terms like "majority" and "vote" indicate that the action required, in order to be effective, must inevitably be political.

The pattern of violence in *Ten Nights in a Bar-room* reflected Arthur's Swedenborgianism view of the nature of the redemptive process, a process that required the active expulsion of evil and the human accomplices of evil from society by force. In his masterwork, Arthur turned to the ancient principle that "he who lives by the sword, dies by the sword." In the closing scenes of the novel/play, after consuming the innocent, "the agents of demon liquor [Green, Slade] are killed in a paroxysm of violence amid the chaos that they themselves had unleashed."[55] Like the Thebes of Oedipus and Hamlet's Denmark, Arthur's Cedarville (an equally sick society) is ultimately purged of the toxin that is destroying it by first identifying what is poisoning it and then destroying both the toxin and its agents.

Arthur's Swedenborgian faith also allowed him to untie one of the temperance melodramatist's Gordian Knots – the assignment of blame for intemperance. As Jeffrey Mason has pointed out, since quite often in American-written temperance dramas, "the drunkard was beyond blame, the temperance apologists looked for other scapegoats, and the most convenient one was an abstraction – temptation."[56] Commonly this temptation or free-floating evil in the environment was reified in the form of either a conventional melodramatic villain or occasionally the bottle itself, both external forces. Seldom, if ever, was the drunkard alone directly responsible for his own plight, this despite the prevailing belief within the temperance community that the source of intemperance was man's sinful nature and that drunkenness was a moral failing. Arthur, unlike many of his fellow temperance dramatists, refused to shrink from the assignment of blame for intemperance, claiming that "since the spirits worked through earthly agents whose spiritual quality man could at least dimly discern... the individual retained some control over his own spiritual destiny. [Hence,] the drinker had chosen, often unknowingly, to align himself with the forces of hell."[57] In Arthur's moral code, the drinker was capable of exercising a degree of free will and should, accordingly, be held responsible for his own intemperance.

The conscious, volitional nature of man's compact with the devil, alcohol, was perhaps best illustrated by man's decision to reap financial gain at the expense of others by operating a bar room. Early in *Ten Nights in a Bar-room* (both the novel and the play), a considerable amount of dialogue is devoted to tavern owner Slade's rationalization of his selling a profitable mill in order to open an even more profitable saloon. Reciting a litany of capitalistic benefits, Slade ultimately defends his choice to run a bar by claiming that, as a publican, he is just as respectable as when he was a miller and that his tavern is an economic asset to the neighborhood. By the end of the narrative, however, the author(s) have given the issue of free will a 360-degree twist, arguing that just as man might choose to drink or to maintain a tavern, he might as easily band together with his fellow man to take control of the marketplace and eliminate alcohol from his environment. The latter – the call for collective political action – answers another of Mason's imperatives: that temperance drama be affective, that it offer a social solution to a social problem.

When *Ten Nights in a Bar-room* first opened, Pratt and the management of the National hoped that it would equal or surpass the success of *The Drunkard*'s Broadway run at five theatres simultaneously. Instead, the Arthur/Pratt play had a "modest" run at the National and then disappeared for three years until the Howard Company revived it at the Bowery. The play enjoyed a brief reprieve from obscurity in 1866 when Barnum mounted it at his museum and the following year when it returned to the Bowery. After that, *Ten Nights in a Bar-room* was staged sporadically around the city – at Wood's Museum, Banvard's Opera House and Museum, Koster and Bial's Aquarium, Alberle's Eighth Street Theatre, Proctor's Criterion Theatre (Brooklyn), the Standard Museum (Brooklyn), and the Grand Street Museum (Brooklyn) – until, after a brief reappearance at the National in 1888, "the venerable relic" slipped quietly out of town.

While *Ten Nights in a Bar-room* was still in New York, however, it proved to be an irresistible vehicle for performers seeking a star turn. George E. "Yankee" Locke, the original Sample Switchel at the National, practically made a career of the play, much as "Drunkard" Clarke had of *The Drunkard*, and *Ten Nights in a Bar-room* was a veritable magnet for young actresses seeking to portray the "martyred child." Among some of the most notable actresses to take the role of Mary were Cordelia Howard, who had already perfected the ascension scene through countless performances as Little Eva in *Uncle Tom's Cabin* and Little Katy in *Hot Corn*; Little Jeannie Yeamans (1870); and four years later at the Boston Athenaeum, Little Minnie Maddern (Mrs. Fiske). The most "unusual" performer to appear in the play, however, was the infamous temperance vigilante, Carrie Nation, who went on tour in the role of Mrs. Morgan, smashing bottles with her usual gusto.

Even before it had disappeared from New York, like the myriad "Tom Shows" that, in truncated and bastardized form, brought the Uncle Tom narrative to the hinterlands, versions of *Ten Nights in a Bar-room* were played practically everywhere during the latter years of the nineteenth century: in churches, in tents, in temperance and town halls, in opera houses and on showboats. Frequently, the play was sponsored by the local chapter of the WCTU. Thus, at a time when *The Drunkard* had slipped from the public consciousness, *Ten Nights in a Bar-room* was ubiquitous and anyone growing up in the waning years of the century invariably had a memory of seeing the play.

In addition to the countless "acted" versions of the Arthur/Pratt narrative, during the 1880s and 1890s a number of magic lantern shows also represented the travails of Joe Morgan, Simon Slade and the dramatis personae of *Ten Nights*. In the closing years of the nineteenth century, temperance lecturers frequently illustrated their sermons with colored magic lantern slides – glass slides painted with the scenes of the story that were projected upon a makeshift screen in a local opera house or town meeting hall. While lacking the emotional impact of the acted drama, magic lantern shows nevertheless effectively depicted the searing scenes of the story and, with "the artist's conception of the borers and the crawling things that devoured tissues and left lumps in a drunkard's stomach," vividly depicted in graphic enlargement the destruction of a town by intemperance.[58] One of the most famous sets of slides traveled the Chautauqua circuit and, according to accounts, convinced thousands of drunkards to embrace sobriety. By the early years of the twentieth century, however, *Ten Nights in a Bar-room*, that strange intermixture of Swedenborgian anti-individualism, Neal Dow Maine Law prohibition politics and melodramatic conventions, had begun to disappear from the public consciousness; but before it did, it is credited with being as influential at disseminating the temperance message as its famous predecessor, *The Drunkard*.

The second of Arthur's temperance narratives to be translated to the stage, *Three Years in a Man-Trap*, was considerably less successful both as a novel and as a stage play. The novel, in which "the author grapples with the monster intemperance, but in a new field, and with enemies more thoroughly disciplined and organized," was published by J. M. Stoddart in 1872 and was adapted by dramatist Charles H. Morton the following year.[59] Subsequently, it was mounted at Wood's Museum and was seen for only a week in August (1873), was revived briefly at Niblo's Garden in 1878, and thereafter was relegated to the road.

If *Ten Nights in a Bar-room* was a "phantasmagoria of shocking and sensational incidents," *Three Years in a Man-Trap* was even more so. In it, Arthur/Morton reemphasized Arthur's Swedenborgian belief that "men will drink liquor and if they take more than they ought, they have only themselves to blame" (stated by bar owner-to-be Tom Lloyd).[60] This said, the authors turned their attack on the demons of the piece: brewers, distillers and bar owners – the liquor industry itself, Arthur's "new field." No longer was the target the quaint, quiet country inn, but *Three Years in a Man-Trap* targeted the big-city saloon, which had proliferated after the Civil War despite local restrictions. Astonished and disgusted that his home city of Philadelphia contained between six to seven thousand saloons – a fact that is stressed in both the novel and the stage play – the then sixty-three-year-old author vowed to rectify the situation by focusing public attention upon "the deadly ulcer that is eating steadily down at the vitals of the people."[61] Despite the difference in focus, *Three Years in a Man-Trap* shared a number of characteristics with its more famous predecessor. The principal setting, like *Ten Nights in a Bar-room*, was the tavern itself and the claim to being the central character of the play was shared by the drunkard, Harry Glenn, and the tavern owner, Tom Lloyd, recapitulations of Joe Morgan and Simon Slade respectively.

While *Ten Nights in a Bar-room* evoked comparison with *Fifteen Years of a Drunkard's Life* because of the draconian punishments imposed upon the transgressor of the piece and upon anyone related to him, *Three Years in a Man-Trap* is even more deserving of the comparison. The first murder, that of bar owner John Glum, takes place before the end of the second scene, and thereafter both the guilty and the innocent perish with alarming regularity. Glum's murderer, an old drunkard named Perry Flint, dies in prison of the DT's; drunkard Harry Glenn's infant child dies in an apartment fire that results from his father's knocking over an oil lamp during a fit of delirium tremens; tavern owner Tom Lloyd's daughter, Maggie, consumed by guilt about her father's having amassed a fortune by destroying human lives, wanders into a blizzard, catches pneumonia and dies; Lloyd's son, although allowed to live, has his character "eroded" by his father's occupation and is destined to live out his life as a petty criminal; and finally Tom Lloyd, whose life has become meaningless after his daughter's death, dies in an especially agonizing bout of the DT's. Thus, despite a seemingly optimistic final scene in which Harry Glenn, who has signed the pledge, is reunited with his family and promoted to foreman at work, *Three Years in a Man-Trap* is arguably the darkest, most deterministic temperance drama ever written in America, surpassing even *Ten Nights in a Bar-room* in that regard.

Although Arthur/Pratt's little Mary is considered by many to have been the quintessential martyred child in temperance literature, arguably the most famous child-victim of the era was Little Katy, the hot corn girl, whose sad story was shown simultaneously in 1854 on the stages of the Bowery, Purdy's National Theatre and Barnum's Museum. The narrative of the pathetic twelve-year-old corn seller who was forced to return home without selling her corn and was beaten to death by her drunken mother who needed the proceeds of her daughter's enterprise to finance her drinking, gained fame first as a series of fictive editorials in the *New York Tribune* in 1853 and then as a novel the following year. Both depicted graphically the atrocious conditions on New York's streets and in its tenements; while at the same time, they focused attention upon the unseen victims of intemperance: children.

Figure 11. Little Katy, the Hot Corn Girl

The product (initially at least) of reporter Solon Robinson's pen and Horace Greeley's editorship, the exposé was a natural undertaking for both men. Greeley, for years, had been aligned with progressive causes and reformist activities, espousing at different times experimental utopianism, abolition, tariff protection for American business, women's rights, vegetarianism, political reform and temperance; while Robinson supported agricultural reform, temperance, protection of widows' rights, and improvements of living conditions of the poor. Robinson's admiration for his fellow reformer, Greeley, is evidenced by his dedication of the novel, which states: "To HORACE GREELEY, and his Co-laborers, Editors of the *New York Tribune*; The Friends of the Working Man; The Advocates of Lifting up poor-trodden-down Humanity; The Ardent Supporters of, and Earnest Advocates for the Maine Law…"[62] Together the two reformers co-produced "a temperance tale that [had] no equal," selling over 50,000 copies in the first six months following its publication.

Four months to the day after Robinson's exposé appeared in *The Tribune* (December 5, 1853), the first stage adaptation of his story opened at New York's National Theatre, already famous as the venue of *Uncle Tom's Cabin.*[63] Broadsides and programs for the Howard Company's production of *Hot Corn* advertised that it had been "dramatized expressly for the National Theatre by C. W. Taylor from Solon Robinson's popular story."[64] For the remainder of the 1853–54 season, on Monday, Tuesday, Thursday and Friday, the Howard company played *Hot Corn* in the afternoon and *Uncle Tom's Cabin* at night, requiring the child actress, Cordelia Howard, to perform two ascension scenes per day on the days *Hot Corn* played: one as Little Eva; the second as Little Katy. By the end of 1854, the young actress had played Little Katy more than fifty times and Little Eva more than double that number of performances.[65]

The day after Captain A. H. Purdy opened *Hot Corn* at the National, P. T. Barnum, reprising his appropriation of *Uncle Tom's Cabin* from Purdy, opened his own version of Robinson's tale. Although Barnum's cast was not the caliber of Purdy's, the American Museum production more than held its own at the box office and Barnum scored a minor coup in May 1854 by sponsoring the play as a benefit for C. W. "Drunkard" Clarke with Clarke as "the affluent, the degraded, the fallen" Eugene Sedley and the entire Howard Company, including Little Cordelia, in support.

By Spring 1854, *Hot Corn* had been mounted at Boston's National Theatre and had opened at a third New York theatre, the Bowery. Plunging into competition with the National and Barnum's Museum, the Bowery proudly

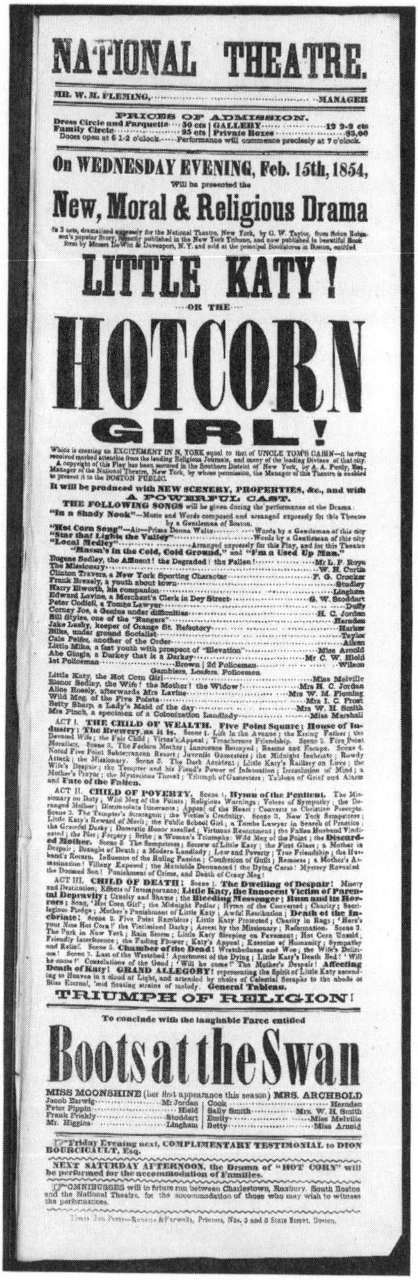
NATIONAL THEATRE.

MR. W. M. FLEMING, ... MANAGER

PRICES OF ADMISSION.

Dress Circle and Parquette ... 50 cts | GALLERY .... 12 1-2 cts
Family Circle .... 25 cts | Private Boxes $5,00
Doors open at 6 1-2 o'clock ...... Performance will commence precisely at 7 o'clock.

On WEDNESDAY EVENING, Feb. 15th, 1854,

Will be presented the

New, Moral & Religious Drama

In 3 acts, dramatized expressly for the National Theatre, New York, by C. W. Taylor, from Solon Robinson's popular Story, recently published in the New York Tribune, and now published in beautiful Book form by Messrs DeWitt & Davenport, N.Y. and sold at the principal Bookstores in Boston, entitled

LITTLE KATY!

OR THE

HOTCORN

GIRL!

Which is creating an EXCITEMENT IN N. YORK equal to that of UNCLE TOM'S CABIN—it having received marked attention from the leading Religious Journals, and many of the leading Divines of that city.
A copyright of this Play has been secured in the Southern District of New York, by A. A. Purdy, Esq., Manager of the National Theatre, New York, by whose permission, the Manager of this Theatre is enabled to present it to the BOSTON PUBLIC.

It will be produced with NEW SCENERY, PROPERTIES, &c., and with

A POWERFUL CAST.

THE FOLLOWING SONGS will be given during the performance of the Drama:
"In a Shady Nook"—Music and Words composed and arranged expressly for this Theatre by a Gentleman of Boston.
"Hot Corn Song"—Air—Prima Donna Waltz .... Words by a Gentleman of this city
"Star that Lights the Valley" .... Words by a Gentleman of this city
"Local Medley" .... Arranged expressly for this Play, and for this Theatre
"Massa's in the Cold, Cold Ground," and "I'm a Used Up Man."

Eugene Sedley, the Affluent! the Degraded! the Fallen! .... Mr L. P. Roys
The Missionary .... W. H. Curtis
Clinton Travers, a New York Sporting Character .... F. G. Crocker
Frank Brezely, a youth about town .... Studley
Harry Elworth, his companion .... Lingham
Edward Lavine, a Merchant's Clerk in Dey Street .... G. W. Stoddart
Peter Codicil, a Tombs Lawyer .... Duffy
Corney Joe, a Genius under difficulties .... H. C. Jordan
Bill Styles, one of the "Rangers" .... Herndon
Jake Lushy, keeper of Orange St. Refectory .... Harker
Bilks, under ground Socialist .... Taylor
Cale Pelfer, another of the Order .... Aiken
Little Mike, a fast youth with prospect of "Elevation" .... Miss Arnold
Abe Gingle, a Darkey that is a Darkey .... Mr C. W. Hield
1st Policeman .... Brown | 2d Policeman .... Wilson
Gamblers, Loafers, Policemen.
Little Katy, the Hot Corn Girl .... Miss Melville
Elenor Sedley, the Wife! the Mother! the Widow! .... Mrs H. C. Jordan
Alice Rosely, afterwards Mrs Lavine .... Mrs W. M. Fleming
Wild Meg, of the Five Points .... Mrs I. C. Frost
Betty Sharp, a Lady's Maid of the day .... Mrs W. H. Smith
Mrs Pinch, a specimen of a Colonization Landlady .... Miss Marshall

ACT I. THE CHILD OF WEALTH. Five Point Square; House of Industry; The Brewery, as it is. Scene 1. Life in the Avenue; the Erring Father; the Devoted Wife; the Fair Child; Virtue's Appeal; Treacherous Friendship. Scene 2. Five Point Moralists. Scene 3. The Forlorn Mother; Innocence Betrayed; Rescue and Escape. Scene 4. Noted Five Point Subterranean Resort; Juvenile Gamesters; the Midnight Inebriate; Rowdy Attack; the Missionary. Scene 5. The Dark Accident; Little Katy's Raillery on Love; the Wife's Despair; the Tempter and his Fiend's Power of Infatuation; Irresolution of Mind; a Mother's Prayer; the Mysterious Threat; Triumph of Gamesters; Tableau of Grief and Alarm and Fate of the Fallen.

ACT II. CHILD OF POVERTY. Scene 1. Hymn of the Penitent. The Missionary on Duty; Wild Meg of the Points; Religious Warnings; Voices of Sympathy; the Deranged Mother; Disconsolate Itinerants; Appeal of the Heart; Converts to Christian Precepts. Scene 2. The Tempter's Stratagem; the Victim's Credulity. Scene 3. New York Sempstress; Little Katy's Reward of Merit; the Public School Girl; a Tombs Lawyer in Search of Practice; the Grateful Darky; Domestic Honor assailed; Virtuous Resentment; the Fallen Husband Vindicated; the Plot; Forgery; Bribe; a Woman's Triumph: Wild Meg of the Point; the Discarded Mother. Scene 5. The Sempstress; Sorrow of Little Katy; the First Glass; a Mother in Despair; Draught of Death; a Modern Landlady; Law and Poverty; True Friendship; the Husband's Return. Influence of the Ruling Passion; Confession of Guilt; Remorse; a Mother's Assassination! Villany Exposed; the Matricide Denounced! the Dying Curse! Mystery Revealed the Doomed Son! Punishment of Crime, and Death of Crazy Meg!

ACT III. CHILD OF DEATH! Scene 1. The Dwelling of Despair! Misery and Destitution; Effects of Intemperance; Little Katy, the Innocent Victim of Parental Depravity; Cruelty and Shame; the Bleeding Messenger; Rum and its Horrors; Song, 'Hot Corn Girl'; the Midnight Pedlar; Hymn of the Converted; Charity; Sacrilegious Pledge; Mother's Punishment of Little Katy; Awful Retribution; Death of the Inebriate! Scene 2. Five Point Ramblers; Little Katy Protected; Charity in Rags; 'Here's your Nice Hot Corn!' the Victimized Darky; Arrest by the Missionary; Reformation. Scene 3. The Park in New York; Rain Storm; Little Katy Sleeping on Pavement; Hot Corn Unsold; Friendly Interference; the Fading Flower; Katy's Appeal; Exercise of Humanity; Sympathy and Relief. Scene 5. Chamber of the Dead! Wretchedness and Woe; the Wife's Delirium! Scene 7. Last of the Wretched! Apartment of the Dying; Little Katy's Death Bed! 'Will he come?' Consolations of the Good; 'Will he come?' The Mother's Despair! Affecting Death of Katy! GRAND ALLEGORY! representing the Spirit of Little Katy ascending to Heaven in a cloud of Light, and attended by choirs of Celestial Seraphs to the abode of Bliss Eternal, 'mid floating strains of melody. General Tableau.

TRIUMPH OF RELIGION!

To conclude with the laughable Farce entitled

Boots at the Swan

MISS MOONSHINE (her first appearance this season) MRS. ARCHBOLD

Jacob Earwig	Mr Jordan	Cook	Herndon
Peter Pippin	Hield	Sally Smith	Mrs. W. H. Smith
Frank Friskly	Stoddart	Emily	Miss Melville
Mr. Higgins	Lingham	Betty	Miss Arnold

☞ Friday Evening next, COMPLIMENTARY TESTIMONIAL to DION BOURCICAULT, Esq.

NEXT SATURDAY AFTERNOON, the Drama of "HOT CORN" will be performed for the accommodation of Families.

☞ OMNIBUSSES will in future run between Charlestown, Roxbury, South Boston and the National Theatre, for the accommodation of those who may wish to witness the performances.

Times Job Press—Roberts & Farwells, Printers, Nos. 3 and 5 State Street, Boston.

Figure 12. Broadside, Hot Corn

announced its debut of the "New Moral and Local drama of HOT CORN or Life Scenes in New York on the Five Points and in the Fifth Avenue, In four parts, 18 scenes & 8 tableaux, all from real life."[66] By the summer of the same year, with numerous productions mounted in America's major cities, with songs like "Little Katy, or Hot Corn" and "Katy's Cry 'Come Buy my Hot Corn'" sung by Wood's Minstrels and other minstrel troupes in halls throughout New York, and with endorsements by "leading Divines" published in religious journals, no one was surprised by claims such as, "*Little Katy, or the Hot Corn Girl* is creating an EXCITEMENT in New York equal to that of UNCLE TOM'S CABIN" that appeared in newspapers and advertisements.[67] Nor was it surprising that *Hot Corn* should thereafter become an arch rival of *Uncle Tom's Cabin* and tour the United States for decades.

In the history of temperance dramaturgy, however, *Hot Corn* is considerably more than yet another example of a martyred child drama and a popular success; it is one of a handful of plays on record that directly and publicly displayed the impact of intemperance upon the Irish-American community. Contrary to Know-Nothing and other nativist propaganda claiming that Irish-Americans demonstrated their inferiority to native-born Protestants by their indifference to alcoholism and their seeming willingness to have their families decimated by drink, *Hot Corn* showed thousands of theatre patrons that Irish-Americans not only suffered because of intemperance, but that they were acutely aware of the problem and believed that it was resolvable. This was *Hot Corn*'s "message," which was disseminated to Irish-Americans and non-Irish alike.

Irish immigrants had been initially attracted to the theatre by Mose the Bowery B'hoy, Frank Chanfrau's famous stage incarnation of an Irish-American fireman and neighborhood tough, in *A Glance at New York in 1848* and once they had discovered the theatre, they stayed for further Mose plays.[68] Set in the Bowery near the infamous Five Points, these plays introduced audiences for the first time to the pitiful living conditions and human misery in the slums and, in effect, primed working-class audiences for the hard-hitting *Hot Corn* to follow. When *Hot Corn* followed Mose in 1854, both Irish-Americans and native-born were shown graphically, not only the consequences of intemperance and poverty, but the consequences of Irish intemperance and poverty as well as Irish-Americans' resolve to eradicate, or at least to reduce, drunkenness.

Hot Corn was unique in a second regard: it featured a female (Katy's mother) as the principal drunkard and, in so doing, revealed to the American public a problem that plagued principally the Irish community in the United States. While in all other cultures it was mainly the men who drank, Irish-American women were as likely to drink to excess as the men. As Blocker and others have noted, "their poverty, the gender segregation of Irish immigrant communities, and the domestic violence and desertion that marked their marriages [led to a high incidence of intemperance and] made their drinking more an act of desperation than celebration."[69] Ostensibly ignored by other temperance writers (dramatists included) who presumably sought to preserve the moral superiority of the American woman, female drunkenness was instead foregrounded by Robinson and the playwrights who translated his narrative for the stage and the drunken woman thus entered the cast of characters in nineteenth-century temperance dramaturgy.

These observations notwithstanding, full assessment of this "temperance tale that has no equal" is not possible, for despite *Hot Corn's* being nearly as popular as *Uncle Tom's Cabin* and being played simultaneously on three New York stages, there are no extant copies of any of the scripts. In fact, in light of its absence from the records of major play publishers of the era, it is possible that it was never published.[70] Research is further complicated by significant differences between the three versions of the play. According to observers and existing documents, the Bowery production preserved the Irish-American flavor of Robinson's original narrative by retaining Irish names for the characters (e.g., Katy, Maggie and Jim Reagan, Maggie's father, who was a reformed drunk and a role model for Irish-American men). The remaining productions, however, anglicized the characters, thereby de-emphasizing the impact alcoholism had upon Irish-Americans. Despite these "shifts," however, since the central character remained identifiably Irish-American, the supporting cast contained Irish-Americans (Wild Meg and Bridget in the National Theatre production and Hank Harrington in the Barnum version), since the setting was a known Irish ghetto and, since the public was familiar with Robinson's original versions, audiences were able to readily the recognize the narrative's Irish roots.

While *The Drunkard*, *Ten Nights in a Bar-room* and *Hot Corn* were indisputably the most popular, influential and ideologically complex temperance dramas of the era, other temperance dramas "had their day" on New York's stages. *The Fatal Glass* by J. J. McClosky was successfully staged at the Brooklyn Park Theatre in 1872 and the Bowery two years later; Mrs. L. D. Shears saw her play, *The Wife's Appeal*, produced at the Academy of Music in 1878; H. J. Conway "appropriated" and adapted Dibdin Pitt's *The Last Nail*, which had been popular on the London stage in the 1830s, for Barnum in 1852; John Allen's *Fruits of the Wine Cup* was shown at the Bowery in 1858; and *The Drunkard's Warning* by C. W. Taylor was mounted at Barnum's American Museum (1856). The latter two in particular achieved a degree of success and occupy a significant (albeit secondary) position in the history of temperance dramaturgy even though they both advocated a single ideological position – total abstinence.

Arguably the most "conventional" temperance drama at mid-century, Taylor's *The Drunkard's Warning* traces the downward alcoholic spiral of a young businessman (Edward Mordaunt) and the impact his decline has upon his family and friends. At the opening curtain, Edward is already well on the road to drunkenness, his appearance is becoming sloppy and he is increasingly negligent of his work. As proof that "the ladder of crime is easily surmounted, when once the first step (1st drink) is attained," he takes up gambling and is soon in debt to a scoundrel and blackmailer. In despair at being exposed as a drunkard and gambler, Mordaunt turns increasingly to drink for solace.[71] Only when his wife, who, like all drunkards' wives, has been reduced to poverty and is at the point of death, does he repent. As was customary in "conventional" temperance dramas, Mordaunt was rewarded with his wife's recovery and a new-found social status, in this case as a temperance reformer. The only departures from standard expectations were the absence of a clearly identified villain who seduces and then encourages the drunkard, and the author's espousal of the somewhat extremist stance of the Waterdrinkers, a group of reformers who advocated plain water as a substitute for alcohol.

Less extreme than Taylor's play, Allen's *Fruits of the Wine Cup* is likewise defined by its clear identification with a specific temperance stance – in this case teetotalism through membership in the Washingtonians. Unlike other temperance dramas like *The Drunkard* that depicted an unnamed fictive organization resembling the Washingtonians, *Fruits of the Wine Cup* identified the society by name repeatedly throughout the play. Although the Washingtonians no longer existed by the play's debut, their ideology – its emphasis upon moral suasion and the spirit of assimilative reform – continued even during the Maine Law era.

Writing in the eighteenth century, Edmund Burke identified the appeal and the power of the aesthetic, claiming, "there is a boundary to men's passions when they act from feeling; none when they are under the influence of imagination."[72] Burke's observation was no more true than during the height of temperance activisim in the 1840s and 1850s, when Americans of all classes were bombarded with novels, serialized newspaper exposés and dramas staged in the country's best theatres. Each of these vehicles staked out a position on the issue of temperance and each appealed to the American imagination – an imagination that envisioned middle-class status, respectability and freedom from all constraints.

5

"In the halls": temperance entertainments following the Civil War

The great but neglected truth is that moral education, in spite of all the labours of direct instructors, is really acquired in hours of recreation.

W. Cooke Taylor, *Notes on a Tour of the Manufacturing Districts of Lancashire*

Temperance is the control of appetite by reason. Intemperance is the control of reason by appetite.

Dawson Burns, *Temperance History: A Consecutive Narrative of the Rise, Development and Extension of the Temperance Reform*

ECONOMICALLY, THE ERA FOLLOWING THE CIVIL WAR WAS ONE of unprecedented expansion in America, marked by the "economic individualism" of the Robber Barons and the epic scale of enterprises and revolutions in finance, manufacturing, transportation and communication.[1] During the 1870s and 1880s, the transformation from a simple agrarian country into a highly urbanized, industrialized one was nearly a fait accompli; the small shop became an anachronism; incorporation became commonplace; and, roughly 300 large corporations gained control of 40 percent of all manufacturing and directly or indirectly influenced 80 percent of America's commerce. During the same period, the railroads completed the links between America's small towns and major cities, creating the possibility of nationwide distribution of products and a national market for goods, either through catalogue sales or chains of stores like The Great American Tea Company, which, by 1870, maintained sixty-seven stores throughout the country selling everything from tea and coffee to fancy soaps to condensed milk. By the 1890s, the national scope of American industry, a relatively unstable economy and a veritable mania for mergers created an environment which encouraged the consolidation of control in the hands of relatively few men and culminated in a major realignment of the nation's economic power. In the waning years of the nineteenth century, centralization of organizational power became commonplace and conglomerates exerted their influence upon all aspects of American life from politics to family life and education to literature, the arts and the use of leisure time.

In the latter years of the nineteenth century, the theatre reflected similar organizational and financial trends as artists and entrepreneurs waged private wars for this most public of cultural institutions. The changes they wrought, in the process, markedly transformed the structure and functioning of the American stage. The theatre, by the beginning of the twentieth century, had become yet another American industry composed of a series of interlocking professions, each dependent upon the others, with its business operations centralized structurally and geographically. It had, in the course of the nineteenth century, become less democratic in both its administration and appeal, and had assumed the role of manufacturer of a product prepared and packaged for nationwide distribution. The long run had become its principal goal; the star system and the star vehicle had become the means to that end; the combination company had become recognized as the standard producing unit of the commercial theatre; the practices of theatre management and play production, once the domain of the actor/manager, had become discrete and separate endeavors; and the American theatre, although it began and ended in New York City, had taken to the road.[2]

During the latter half of the nineteenth century, it became practically axiomatic among the country's company managers and theatre owners that rural audiences were as interested in seeing "hit" plays as they were in seeing stars and that "exporting" shows from Broadway to America's hinterlands provided a viable economic alternative to remaining in New York. Thus, from the 1870s onward, "duplicate" companies composed of minor performers willing to work for "ten or fifteen a week and cakes" and billed as "straight from New York" criss-crossed the country, playing America's small towns for one or two nights and then moving on. As an example of this trend, in just one season (1882–83) *Hazel Kirke*, which had been on Broadway for 486 performances, was brought to the nation's heartland by no less than fourteen separate road companies playing just that one play.[3] During the waning years of the nineteenth century, it was generally accepted that the phrase, "Straight from a Year in New York," on the marquees of rural theatres was so intoxicating that managers were willing to suffer severe losses on Broadway just to reach the one-season mark.

Once a play had been deemed a hit in New York, the means of effecting its nationwide distribution was the theatrical circuit, a construct that had existed as a formal, organized practice since the close of the Civil War. Initially a local business, a circuit was a group of contiguous theatres on a logical transportation route for a traveling company, usually a railroad line, that banded together for mutual protection. Since, in the laissez-faire days before centralization, small theatre owners were the most vulnerable to performers' whims, a circuit significantly increased their bargaining power. As Alfred Bernheim states the case in *The Business of the Theatre*, before circuits, an attraction could skip an engagement with a single theatre with little fear of penalty; but, once circuits were established, it would hesitate to cancel, knowing that a number of theatres between major cities might boycott it.[4] The circuit offered an additional advantage in that it was considerably less expensive and far more convenient to book a series of theatres at once than it was to book each one separately, since just one man could handle the booking for many theatres.

Not coincidentally, the development of theatrical circuits paralleled that of the American railroad network, which, by the 1870s, had already transformed the country from a collection of isolated, independent villages into an interconnected national community. America's railroads, little more than a broken skein of just 9,000 miles of track in 1850, had mushroomed into a national rail network after the Civil War – from 35,000 miles of connected track in 1865 to 80,000 miles by 1880. By the beginning of their second decade of existence, therefore, traveling companies had access to hundreds of towns, both large and small, on rail lines from New York to San Francisco and from Minnesota to Texas.

Although independent circuits like Tom Davy's Louisiana Circuit and Henry C. Jarrett's New England Circuit had existed in the 1860s before the combination system, the circuit as a construct designed specifically to deal with traveling companies did not emerge until the seventies. The earliest circuits were true cooperatives composed of equal partners; but gradually, circuits underwent an organizational transformation, as one person with enough wealth or power to assume control and set policy for the entire circuit gained dominance. This "ownership" of the means of distribution was reflected in the designations of the various circuits – the Mishler Circuit in eastern Pennsylvania, Schwartz's Wisconsin Theatrical Circuit, Craig's Kansas–Missouri Circuit and Harry Greenwall's Lone Star Circuit.

While undeniably a period of major industrial and economic change and expansion, "the century after the Civil War," historian Daniel Boorstin writes, was also an age of "countless, little-noticed revolutions, which occurred not in the halls of legislatures or on battlefields or on the barricades but in homes and farms and factories and schools and stores, across the landscape and in the air – so little noticed because they came so swiftly, because they touched Americans everywhere and every day."[5] Had Boorstin scrutinized post-war developments in both temperance reform and the dramaturgy that supported and documented it, he would have found that similar small "revolutions" took place in those sectors as well – "small," not in their scope or impact, but because they initially occurred outside of the cities of the Northeast, beyond the public spotlight and hence unnoticed; revolutionary because they signaled significant social change.

Unlike other forms of theatre, temperance drama, both in its production and its reception, defied the national trend toward centralization. Although post-Civil War America was rapidly moving toward becoming a fully urbanized, industrialized and centralized society, small town life was still the norm for many, for as late as the 1870s, emotionally at least, the country was still composed of what Robert Wiebe has termed "island communities."[6] The production of temperance drama likewise defied national trends in temperance activism. While temperance reform was, for a short time in the 1870s, grass-roots in nature – organized into the small cells of the Women's Crusade that retained a distinctly local identity – by the end of the decade, it had become centralized in national organizations like the WCTU, and later, the Prohibition Party and the Anti-Saloon League. When temperance activities coalesced into more centralized institutions, however, the entertainments that supported the movements remained decentralized and the production of temperance drama, which was born and nurtured in the cities of the Northeast during the antebellum period, spent its adult life in the myriad island communities that dotted the landscape between and around America's major urban centers.

After their popularity in the cities of the Northeast waned in the late 1870s and early 1880s, *The Drunkard* and *Ten Nights in a Bar-room* joined other popular nineteenth-century stage favorites like *East Lynne*, *The Octoroon*, *Uncle Tom's Cabin*, *The Two Orphans*, *The Ticket of Leave Man*, *Rip Van Winkle* and *The Old Homestead* on the road to America's secondary cities and small towns. While *The Drunkard* quickly disappeared from the repertories of touring companies, *Ten Nights in a Bar-room*, along with *Uncle Tom's Cabin*, became the "meat and potatoes" of practically every one-night stand dramatic company. Commonly billed as a "Vivid Temperance Lesson," *Ten Nights* rivaled its abolitionist counterpart in popularity on the road and no theatrical season in America's heartland was complete without at least one production of it coming to the local town hall or opera house.

The touring versions of *Ten Nights in a Bar-room* were hardly the large, accomplished duplicate companies (like those of *Hazel Kirke*) that were formed in New York. Nor did they follow the larger, more prominent circuits. Instead, they were family touring troupes or "mom and pop" affairs that followed the country's small opera house circuits. The Thorne Comedy Company, for example, toured only in North Carolina, presenting a repertoire that included *Rip Van Winkle* and *Fanchon the Cricket* (in addition to *Ten Nights*) in front of scenery that the actors painted themselves; The Grace George Dramatic Company, featuring Luke Cosgrove as leading man, toured mining towns in the West; while The Switzer Comedy Company toured *Ten Nights*, along with a repertoire of ten other favorites, throughout the upper Midwest.[7] One of the largest, the Old Reliable Company that toured principally in the Southeast, employed a company of twenty-five and featured journeyman performers Helen d'Este and J. G. Stuttz.[8] Although there certainly were individual differences between these companies, they nevertheless shared some common characteristics. According to contemporary accounts, "the acting company of these small outfits was a strange assortment. The manager's wife insisted on being the leading lady; the character woman usually had a little girl that was billed as the 'Child Wonder' and as such was featured in all children's roles throughout the week, did specialties, and continually looked like Little Eva"; the leading lady was invariably too old for the roles she played and attempted to create the "illusion of the ingénue," intoning her lines in a "birdlike voice that carried to the far corners of the hall"; and, since the companies played largely the same repertoire, they respected each others' territory.[9] Nevertheless, despite their lack of sophistication, these companies brought a mainstream temperance classic to America's small towns.

Conceivably more important in the history of temperance dramaturgy than touring professional productions were the myriad presentations mounted by amateur stock companies in local opera houses, town halls, church basements, schools and temperance halls – the most common venues for non-professional temperance performances. While temperance advocates proved willing to stage their anti-drink dramas anywhere they could find adequate space, from roughly the mid-1840s onward the venue of choice was the center of local activism: the temperance hall. In the era before the erection of town halls and opera houses (the community gathering places of the last half of the nineteenth century), often the local temperance hall was the only facility in town large enough to accommodate popular assemblies.[10] Occasionally started by a local philanthropist interested in

Figure 13. Temperance Hall, Oak Park, Illinois

reform or by an ad hoc band of activists, most frequently the temperance hall was commissioned by formal organizations like the Salvation Army, the Sons of Temperance or the WCTU to serve as the local headquarters for their representatives. While the more generously endowed halls could be reserved exclusively for temperance activities sponsored by the organization that owned them, less wealthy halls were frequently rented to "temperance-friendly" political clubs, traveling stock companies, or lecturers.[11]

A common feature on both the urban and rural landscapes of the mid to late nineteenth century, the temperance hall assumed various forms, from small, one-story, single-room buildings; to rented rooms in commercial buildings in America's small towns; to large, multi-room structures in major cities furnished with meeting rooms, libraries and frequently a reasonably well-equipped auditorium or theatre. The first variation, whether located in Still Pond, Maryland; Oak Park, Illinois; Pine Grove, California; or anywhere in between, was a small, single-story frame building with one or two large rooms that could be converted for a variety of uses from lectures to dances to amateur theatricals. Many resembled small rural churches or one-room school houses. Often serving as meeting space for organizations other than the local temperance society, such structures were the first temperance halls erected and were ubiquitous from Maine to California.

An elaboration on this architectural scheme was built for $4,300 in Charlottesville, Virginia in 1855–56 to serve the needs and purposes of the Sons of Temperance. Convinced that lectures sponsored by the temperance society had "been effective in fixing and strengthening the convictions of... the community [and] that the evils of intemperance were corrected... through personal appeal... promulgated through their organization," the Board of Visitors of the University of Virginia authorized the erection of a sixty- by eighty-foot stone building on the grounds of the university.[12] The single floor was divided into two rooms that ran the eighty-foot length of the structure, with one of the larger rooms divided in two. The three rooms were used alternately as student reading rooms, for business meetings, for lectures, for club meetings, for musical presentations, for student meetings and as the headquarters and "rallying point" for temperance activists and for the local YMCA. The location of the hall on campus enabled both the Sons of Temperance and the Y to "come in contact with and get hold of the new students, to assist them in procuring rooms and room-mates and to guard them against dissipations and temptations as they enter[ed] upon university life."[13]

Big-city temperance halls, like the one at 403 Greenwich Street in New York or Dashaway Hall in San Francisco, were, for the most part, significantly larger and more sophisticated than their rural counterparts. Built on a strip of land "reclaimed from the city's notorious sand dunes," Dashaway Hall was a two-story, stone structure that contained private club rooms, a library, reading rooms "open to members at all hours, and a gallery that seated 1,000 people in front of a stage 50 feet wide."[14] A survey of the events scheduled at the hall, according to Jim Baumohl, who studied the Dashaway Association, a working men's temperance society that closely resembled the Washingtonians, provides a "telling glimpse of the alternative world the [Society] attempted to create."[15] On Sundays, the hall hosted a series of lecturers; business meetings were held on Tuesday evenings; on Wednesdays the hall hosted dances; Thursdays were devoted to experience speeches; and Friday nights were reserved for singing by the association's Glee Club and for the "Histrionic Society's" rehearsals of its next production. In all, the activities sponsored by the Dashaways in their hall afforded members the opportunities to meet members of both sexes and to socialize outside the "roiling world of the boarding house, street corner, or saloon."[16]

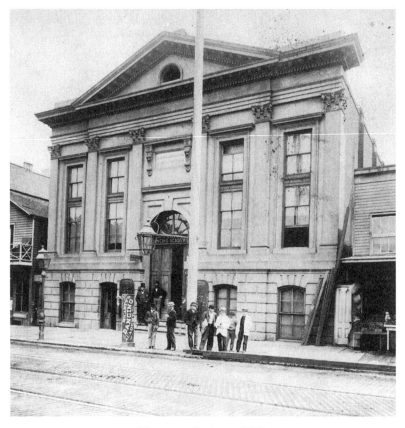

Figure 14. Dashaway Hall

One of the most elaborate temperance halls was planned by the Washingtonians in Baltimore. At the height of their popularity in 1842, the Washingtonians announced plans to raise $75,000 to pay for the erection of a two-story building that would house stores on the ground floor and a 2,500 seat hall on the upper floor. According to Leonard Blumberg and William Pittman, who describe the planned hall in their book *Beware the First Drink*, the Washingtonian Hall was to have been patterned after Exeter Hall in London, the Music Fund Hall in Philadelphia and Boston's Faneuil Hall; it would have sponsored a full range of Washingtonian activities; and would have been "a symbol of the general acceptance of temperance advocacy by the general community."[17]

Figure 15. Berlin Hotel and WCTU Hall

When local temperance activists were unable to build their own build-ing, they frequently rented quarters in existing commercial buildings. Many, like the WCTU Hall in Berlin, Illinois, resembled those mid-western opera houses that shared space with hardware or feed stores, with the main hall oc-cupying a back room or the upper floor(s) of a multi-story structure. Erected and opened as the Leonard Hotel, from the outset the Berlin WCTU Hall shared its space with shopkeepers. By the early 1890s, the hotel occupied the second floor and there was a grocery store housed in the building. Several years later, "there was a harness shop and the WCTU on the first and bot-tom floors" while the Borrowed Time Club maintained headquarters there as well.[18]

The temperance hall, as an institution, was hardly an American inven-tion; similar halls existed as early as 1830 in England, Scotland, Ireland and Canada as well. In Bradford, England, for example, the Bradford Long Pledge Association first rented space in an existing building and opened the Victorian Temperance Room. When they were evicted from those quarters, the Association erected its own building where, in addition to "standard" temperance activities, "concerts and other entertainments" were sponsored.[19] In Ireland, halls such as the Cork Temperance Institute provided a retreat where young men and boys "might pass their evenings and devote themselves to reading, study, and the intelligent interchange of ideas." The "spacious, handsome and well appointed" centre hall of the Institute was constructed specially to accommodate lectures and other edifying entertainments too large to stage in the reading rooms.[20] And, in Canada rural halls like the one in Durham, Ontario were erected to sponsor "Public, Private and Social Assemblies, Meetings and Entertainments...upon STRICTLY TEMPERANCE PRINCIPLES."[21] While information about the specific entertainments mounted in Canadian temperance halls is scant, there is a report that when the American actor E. A. Sothern attempted to rent the temperance hall in Halifax, Nova Scotia in the 1850s, his request was denied because "theatricals" were not permitted there; but just one decade later, the hall was being used for temperance productions.[22]

Regardless of their size or spatial characteristics, temperance halls served the same functions: they provided space for the "business" aspects of the organization; they afforded space for temperance-related meetings; and they presented or hosted a variety of entertainments, from dances to lectures to dramatic presentations to musical concerts for members. This latter function, entertainment, was arguably its most important, for it put temperance hall entertainments in step with then-current notions of the constructive use of leisure time, a set of trends labeled "rational recreation."

As outlined by Peter Bailey, British "rational recreation proceeded from a basic humanitarian sympathy with the plight of the urban masses [and middle-class efforts to ensure] a socially tractable working class in a fluid and anonymous urban society."[23] Disturbed by "traditional" working-class recreations like gambling, drinking, blood sports and other forms of "blasphemy that occurred in such settings as the pub, the fair and the street," nineteenth-century Christians sought first to eradicate these excesses; then, after failing to suppress the undesirable behaviors and to close the venues that sponsored and supported them, they chose instead to create a substitutive culture and alternative recreational setting that would rival the more objectionable facets of popular culture.[24] Consequently, by the late 1830s in Great Britain, there was a widespread effort to supplant the fair and the pub by sponsoring counter-attractions, "alternative recreations which stimulated and then restored the mind rather than merely debilitated the body."[25] The movement historians refer to as rational recreation thus was an attempt by the respectable classes to create "communities of enjoyment." These communities would be "conventicles of respectability" that would substitute for the "degrading" working-class recreation sites like the pub, gaming hall and the street, and would fill the need for regulated amusement.[26]

Rationality, as Hugh Cunningham has written, "implied both order and control."[27] However, making recreation rational meant significantly more than simply imposing middle-class values upon an unsuspecting working class – was far more complex than a simple, crude attempt at the social control of the intractable masses. Instead, it had roots in the "middle-class experience itself, in the problem felt by [the] growing . . . leisure class which had an excess of time on its hands and yet wished to avoid aristocratic dissipation."[28] Adopting Cooke Taylor's notion that "the great but neglected truth [was] that moral education, in spite of all the labours of direct instructors, [was] really acquired in hours of recreation," nineteenth-century reformers proposed that the constructive use of leisure-time was the "ideal" means to inculcate self-control, familialism and respectability – those values necessary for a successful life in an urban, commercialized society.[29] Spurred on by this new way of effecting their reforms, activists shaped their efforts toward the amelioration of social ills by stressing individual improvement and by providing new leisure activities and venues conducive to forming a "new type of personality" better equipped to resist the temptations prevalent in the urban environment. "The objective," as Gary Cross summarized it, "was not only to provide a new community-controlled leisure but to transform the individual – in a kind of semi-religious experience."[30]

The dual stress upon maintenance of order and individual improvement had great appeal to temperance reformers. The use of community-controlled leisure as a form of secular conversion was especially attractive to the Washingtonians, for shortly after the advent of rational recreation and temperance halls in England, American reformers emulated their British counterparts and the United States became a second center of rational recreation. Throughout the United States, temperance activists readily adopted and adapted controlled leisure to their specific uses and routinely offered a liberal selection of activities – lectures, balls, poetry readings, musical concerts and miscellaneous theatricals in the halls themselves and, beyond the confines of the hall, train excursions, parades and picnics – aimed at "the improvement of mental culture."[31]

Of these activities, it was musical concerts and theatricals that recurred with regularity, that were the most effective "engines of propaganda warfare" and that had the greatest impact upon large audiences. From the 1840s onward, singing added a major new attraction to the temperance movement whether presented as the principal entertainment of the evening or when interpolated into a melodrama such as *Ten Nights in A Bar-room* or *Hot Corn*. Next to melodramas, few temperance vehicles were more effective than the vast array of songs advising women to use their innate moral influence to save their families from the ravages of intemperance, admonishing them to "beware the man who drinks," or urging men to sign the pledge for the sake of their children. Bearing plaintive titles like "Dear Father, Drink No More," "Oh! Help Little Mary, the Drunkard's Poor Child" and "Father's a Drunkard and Mother is Dead," the power of these songs, like that of melodrama, "lay in their ability to combine the persuasive techniques of performance with the messages of temperance."[32]

Like melodramas, to which they were related thematically, musical texts tended to mirror the dominant temperance ideology of the era. Thus, at a time when moral suasion and assimilative reform were ascendant, songs like "He is Thy Brother Still," "Deal Gently with the Fallen," "Sympathy Rather than Scorn" and "Moral Suasion" (which began with the lines "Moral suasion for the man who drinks; Mental suasion for the man who thinks)" were popular, only to be supplanted in the public consciousness in the 1850s by tunes with titles like "The Prohibitory Song," "Hurrah for Prohibition" and "O Comrades in this Conflict of Right & Wrong, to the Battle of the Ballots."[33] When women dominated temperance activism through the WCTU, they penned temperance songs too numerous to mention; while anti-saloon agitation spawned a plethora of songs on the subject with titles like "The Saloon Must Go" and "A Saloonless Nation by 1920." With songs like "We'll Smash the Saloon When We're Men" even extremist vigilantism was musically represented.

While temperance plays and songs concentrated upon many of the same themes and expressed the same ideologies, temperance music possessed a number of advantages over drama. It could be rendered by a single performer; no specialized space was needed; relatively little rehearsal was required prior to performance; and the costs of production were low. Like playtexts, which were distributed by both commercial distributors like Thomas Lacy and Samuel French, Inc. and specialized publishers like The National Temperance Society and Publications House and A. D. Ames, Publisher, songs could be printed in bulk and sold to an eager public. Furthermore, compared to drama, music was a condensed form that, with its focus upon the results of drinking rather than the process of a drunkard's deterioration, was considerably more concentrated emotionally.

Many of the temperance songs of the era were written for women *by* women whose "narrative voices embodied the power that [their female] audience lacked."[34] Where drinking was concerned, the problem for men "was first of all self-control; for women the principal problem was controlling the behavior of men" whose intemperance affected every aspect of family life.[35] Given the reality that family welfare and happiness could be destroyed by a husband/father's drunkenness, it is understandable that much of the emotional power of temperance music should derive from its being written from the point of view of a woman or, almost as frequently, a child. Consistent with this orientation, many temperance songs were, to reiterate, admonitions to women to "Marry No Man if He Drinks," "Don't Marry a Drunkard to Reform Him," or to "Wait for a Temperance Man." Although not as numerous as admonitory music intended for mature women, musical pleas with titles like "Dear Father, Drink No More" and "Come Home Father" were written expressly for children who, like Little Effie Parkhurst, frequently performed them publicly "at the great temperance gatherings in New York and Boston."[36]

Conceivably, one of the most recurrent themes in temperance music was the cruelty imposed by drunkards upon innocent children. With titles like "The Drunkard's Child," "The Dying Girl's Appeal" and "Father's a Drunkard and Mother is Dead," temperance music mirrored the poignancy of the deaths of Little Mary in *Ten Nights in a Bar-room* and Little Katy in *Hot Corn*, both of whom were represented in song as well as in drama. Little Mary's plea was musically rendered in "Father, Dear Father, Come Home with Me Now," while Little Katy was musically immortalized in "Little Katy, or Hot Corn" and "Katy's Cry 'Come Buy My Hot Corn'." These and other "dying child" songs were among the most effective vehicles as temperance propaganda, largely because they were the least subtle and the most sentimental, as the following lyrics from "The Drunkard's Child" illustrate: "I wish my father'd come, mother; I do not fear him now; He'll never beat me more, mother, for I am dying now." The song ends with the narrator's voice intoning, "for there, past all pain and sorrow, the drunkard's child lay dead."[37]

Not all temperance songs, however, were aimed at women and children. Some, like temperance dramas of the era, displayed a distinct psychological dimension by exploiting men's guilt about abusing or neglecting their families, thereby representing drunkards' unconscious fears and hopes. In this regard, songs like "The Drunkard's Dream," "The Husband's Dream," "The Drunkard's Hell," "A Drunken Dream" or "A Drunkard's Confession" featured dreams of a wife's death or the death of a child and ended with the drinker's becoming a teetotaler and even praying for prohibition legislation.

By the middle of the nineteenth century, the writing and performing of temperance songs had attracted entertainment professionals and amateurs alike. Groups as renowned as Wood's Minstrels were regularly performing popular temperance tunes like "Katy's Cry 'Come Buy My Hot Corn'"; temperance singers like Ossian E. Dodge and Charley White (later a famous minstrel entertainer) were able to earn in excess of $10,000 per year playing teetotalers' halls; and books of music like *The Temperance Entertainer* and *The Variety Theatre Songster*, which contained "songs sung with great success in all the principal theatres of the United States" were sold at variety halls and news stands.[38]

For some in the entertainment world, the temperance cause shaped or helped shape their careers. The Hutchinson Family Singers, for example, "one of early nineteenth century America's best loved popular entertainment groups and one of its most effective protest voices," incorporated temperance into the lexicon of reforms they advocated on both national and international stages.[39] Although the group also sang about women's rights and trade unionism, their principal concerns were slavery and temperance. Their most famous song, in fact, which they and their numerous imitators popularized, was "King Alcohol," which targeted "'rum and gin and beer and wine and brandy of longwood hue and hock and port and flip and cherry... and champagne and perry' and the spirits of every hue found in the devil's toolkit."[40]

While not as widely recognized as the Hutchinson Family Singers outside of the Northeast, Mrs. E. A. Parkhurst had a long and illustrious career as a composer of every sort of song, from gospel music to "abolitionist and patriotic political songs" in support of the Union cause in the Civil War to Sunday School songs to temperance music, all rendered in the popular styles of the day and many published by Horace Waters, who also served as Stephen Collins Foster's publisher near the end of his career. Of these, however, she is best remembered for her temperance songs – songs like "Don't Marry a Man if He Drinks" and "Father's a Drunkard and Mother is Dead," arguably the most famous of her songs. Temperance, in fact, was so much a part of the Parkhurst family life that the song, "Sign the Pledge for Mother's Sake," with words by Mrs. M.A. Kidder and lyrics by Mrs. Parkhurst, was first sung on stage by Little Effie Parkhurst.[41]

While some songs, like those contained in *The Variety Theatre Songster*, were written for the theatre and were sung in New York's variety halls, the vast majority were written expressly for use by organizations like the children's Cold Water Army, the Daughters of Temperance and the 13th Ward Temperance Society. To support their efforts a veritable cottage industry composed of small, specialized publishers sprang up to turn out volumes like *Bugle Notes for the Temperance Army*, *A Boy's Temperance Book*, *Platform Pearls for Temperance Workers* and similar publications. These cheap volumes contained hundreds of exercises, recitations, poems and dialogues, in addition to temperance parlor songs. The temperance song, in fact, proved so successful that collections of teetotal melodies became the most profitable item for Washingtonian publishers until the decline of the society.

In their endeavors to write songs and/or verse that would advance their cause, temperance enthusiasts were not necessarily required to be accomplished tunesmiths. Adopting the common nineteenth-century practice of setting new lyrics to already popular tunes, temperance song writers "adapted" some of the best-known tunes of the day to reform purposes. Phineas Stowe appropriated the tune "Home, Sweet Home" into his song, "Compassion for the Drunkard"; the popular "Tramp, Tramp, Tramp" became "Prohibition's Might"; the Rev. John Pierpont, the alleged co-author of *The Drunkard*, used the tune of "America" for his "Fourth of July Ode"; and even "The Star-Spangled Banner" was co-opted and republished with the title "Flee as a Bird to Your Mountain." Not even literary giants like Shakespeare and Tennyson were exempt from such treatment. Tennyson's "Charge of the Light Brigade" was rewritten by Mary Wheeler into "The Charge of the Rum Brigade"; "The Seven Ages of Intemperance" began with the lines, "All the world's a barroom, / And all the men and women merely tipplers"; and a temperate Hamlet mused: "To drink or not to drink, THAT IS THE QUESTION."[42]

Songs were not the only temperance texts written by amateurs in post-Civil War America. While temperance dramas like *Three Years in a Mantrap*, *The Stolen Child* and *The Drunkard's Home* continued to be written and produced professionally in New York and other major cities as well as on the road, the post-Civil War period was marked by the "de-professionalization" of temperance dramaturgy; de-professionalization in the writing of the plays, their production and their distribution. Increasingly, from the 1860s onward, the principal production site for temperance plays shifted from the big city to America's small towns. A. D. Ames' two-act drama, *Wrecked*, first opened in February 1877 at the Opera House in Clyde, Ohio with Ames himself as the drunkard; Frank Lee Miles and H. W. Phillips' *The Wine-Cup; or the Tempter and the Tempted* was first performed in Danville,

Pennsylvania in 1878; *The Drunkard's Dream* by George Booth debuted in 1872 in Thompsonville, Connecticut; "W. Henri Wilkins' *Three Glasses a Day; or, The Broken Home* was performed at the Green Mountain Perkins Academy in South Woodstock, Vermont in 1871 and twice at the Union Dramatic Club of Felchville, Vermont in 1872; [and] T. Trask Woodward's *The Social Glass; or, Victims of the Bottle* was originally produced at the Masonic Temple in Louisville, Kentucky, followed by productions at the Register Hall in Effingham, Illinois, the Opera House in Seymour, Indiana, the Vermillion Opera House in Danville, Illinois and Parker's Opera House in Shelbyville, Illinois."[43]

To meet the needs of the myriad amateur theatrical producing groups that flourished in the late nineteenth century in small towns and cities, a new industry sprang into being to supply the temperance playtexts required by local companies.[44] Z. Pope Vose, editor of the Rockland, Maine *Courier-Gazette*, ran a small publishing house specializing in temperance dramas; the Happy Hours company of New York advertised "harmless home amusement for old and young" and distributed plays like John Delafield's *The Last Drop*; actor and playwright A. D. Ames distributed temperance plays through his small publishing house in Clyde, Ohio; and Thomas Stewart Denison sent out thousands of copies of his own plays, *Hard Cider: A Temperance Sketch*, *Only Cold Tea* and *The Sparkling Cup* from his Chicago publishing company.[45]

The play booklets, which cost between fifteen and twenty-five cents each, were ordered by mail and routinely included, not only the playtexts themselves, but directions for their staging and costuming. Typical of the aids provided amateur companies by publishers of cheap temperance dramas were the "inclusions" in the text of *Switched Off: A Temperance Farce in One Act*, written by Lizzie May Elwyn. Inside the front cover, just below the title and the notice that this script was No. 413 of the Ames Series of Standard and Minor Drama, the publisher printed the following: "WITH CAST OF CHARACTERS, ENTRANCES AND EXITS, RELATIVE POSITIONS OF THE PERFORMERS ON THE STAGE, DESCRIPTION OF COSTUMES AND THE WHOLE OF THE STAGE BUSINESS; CAREFULLY MARKED FROM THE MOST APPROVED ACTING COPY."[46] Some scripts, like William Comstock's *Rum: or, The First Glass*, arrived with complete descriptions of the scenery required, a props list and diagrams of the blocking, while many plays included scores for the music interpolated into the action.[47] For nominal fees, amateur companies could also purchase "handbooks on managing private theatricals (including directions on how to produce thunder, lightning, rain and moonlight)...instructional manuals on the Actor's Art for Beginners...burnt cork for the Ethiopian plays, whiskers and waxed and unwaxed moustaches, Yankee and Irish wigs and 'Chinaman' pigtails for the players and tableau and magnesium lights for the stage."[48]

The decline in the professionalization of temperance dramaturgy and production following the Civil War was predictable, for increasingly the writers, producers and publishers of these plays were active temperance reformers with little or no experience in the theatre. For example, the National Temperance Society and Publications House and the Woman's Temperance Publishing Association, neither a commercial publisher, printed and distributed a wide variety of literature from tracts to recitations to novels; while independent publishers like J. N. Stearns not only distributed a number of Nellie Bradley's temperance dramas but printed a temperance newsletter, *The Youth's Temperance Banner*, and sold Band of Hope supplies as well.[49] Likewise, in lieu of names like C. W. Taylor, H. J. Conway and T. S. Arthur on the title pages of temperance dramas, during the post-war period names like H. Elliot McBride, Ida M. Buxton, Lizzie May Elwyn and Nellie Bradley – names unknown outside of temperance circles – appeared. One of the inevitable by-products of the de-professionalization of temperance dramaturgy was that, while plays tended to be increasingly passionate about reform, they also tended to be more simplistic and crude than their predecessors.

Not surprisingly, during the 1870s and 1880s, a temperance cycle dominated by the WCTU, a growing number of plays were written by women. As Ruth Bordin has documented, by 1875 writing was one of the more popular vocations for WCTU members, with roughly 15 percent of the women listing "author" as their profession of choice and "women were writing approximately three-quarters of the temperance tracts and books published in the United States."[50] As a result, by the early 1880s the "typical" temperance dramatist was as likely to be female, amateur (or a newcomer to theatre) and, in David Reynolds' terms, a conventional reformer as they were to be male, professional and subversive in their reform. They, like their antebellum predecessors, were also likely to be involved in a variety of temperance-related activities. Thus, reformer/writers like Julia Colman and Nellie Bradley were activists first and disseminated their respective messages in more than one medium. As Ann Ferguson discovered, Colman, author of *No King in America*, was a writer of both temperance and hygiene leaflets, the chair of a committee on leaflets and the author of the

Sunday-School Temperance Catechism (National Temperance Publishing House, 1892), *Beauties of Temperance, Readings on Beer* and *Alcohol and Hygiene: A Lesson Book for Schools.*[51] These non-dramatic writings and activities led Ferguson to conclude that even when Colman wrote plays she wrote "with her role as reformer, rather than playwright, foremost in her mind."[52]

Nellie Bradley likewise was an active reformer as well as being a noted poet, lyricist and playwright. She was one of the original signers of the WCTU Incorporation Papers and in 1887 she showed her versatility as a reformer by carrying on a "most vigorous campaign against lewd pictures in cigar stores and barber shops" in Washington, D.C.[53] For years, during the late 1880s and early 1890s, she was Superintendent of the District of Columbia Chapter of the WCTU and an acknowledged leader in temperance reform in the Washington area, an endeavor she shared with her husband, Francis M. Bradley, who was Superintendent of Young People's Work of the Sons of Temperance and who ran the Sons of Temperance Insurance Company.

Bradley's "other life" was as a temperance artist – a writer of all forms of entertainment from poems like "Hold High the Torch" (in *The Youth's Companion*, nd) to parlor recitations like "Save the Boys" (in *Women in Sacred Song*, 1885). As a member of a standing committee within the WCTU dedicated to the utilization of music for reform purposes, Bradley pledged "to elevate the standard, and use her influence to have only such music rendered as shall tend to advance the cause for which we labor and make sacrifice."[54] Long before joining this committee, however, Bradley had distinguished herself musically, having written the lyrics for, "Father's a Drunkard and Mother is Dead," one of the most famous temperance songs ever written. With lyrics by Bradley and music by noted composer Mrs. E. A. Parkhurst, the song began with the then-famous lines:

> *"One dismal, stormy night in winter, a little girl, barefooted and miserably clad, leaned, shivering against a large tree near the President's House. 'Sissie,' said a passing stranger, 'why don't you go home?' She raised her pale face, and with tears dimming her sweet blue eyes, answered mournfully: 'I have no home, Father's a drunkard, and Mother is dead'."*[55]

As a playwright, Bradley was considerably more prolific than Colman. During a career that spanned two decades Bradley penned nine known temperance dramas: *The Young Teetotaler; or Saved at Last* (1867); *Marry No Man If He Drinks* (1868); *Reclaimed, or the Danger of Moderate Drinking* (1868); *The First Glass; or the Power of a Woman's Influence* (1868); *The Stumbling*

Block, or Why the Deacon Gave Up his Wine (1871); *Wine as a Medicine, or Abbie's Experience* (1873); *Having Fun* (1883); *The Bridal Wine Cup* (c. 1887); and *A Temperance Picnic with the Old Woman Who Lived in the Shoe* (1888). During roughly the same time period, she was also the author of recitations, dialogues and declamations designed to be delivered by women or children to women and children who were rapidly replacing the recent immigrant, the urban poor and the newly minted bourgeoisie as the "average" spectator.

One of the first endeavors of the WCTU after it gained ascendance was the institution of temperance-oriented activities for children. Emulating the British juvenile temperance movement of the 1830s, during the mid-1870s the WCTU organized Bands of Hope and other juvenile temperance clubs "because little formal entertainment was available for youngsters, and the excursions, lantern shows, and other club-sponsored outings filled this lack."[56] By 1878, the WCTU division dedicated to the promotion of children's activities was reporting to the national association at its annual convention and by the 1880s, marching and exhibitions mounted by the Loyal Temperance Legions and Bands of Hope were regular and popular features at WCTU conventions.[57]

Beginning in the 1870s, temperance authors were more than willing to write plays, skits and short musicals that not only were intended to be witnessed by children, but were designed specifically for child actors. Typical of these child-oriented dramas, Ida Buxton's *On to Victory*, written expressly for "the little ones," featured an Uncle Sam character who joined forces with Captain Prohibition and a chorus of boys and girls to "strike a blow at the sin" of intemperance.[58] This musical play, which took advantage of juvenile marching societies' training and afforded ample opportunity for choral singing, ended with performers representing Maine, Iowa, Kansas and Rhode Island – the four prohibition states – singing the song of victory. A second children's play, Effie Merriman's *The Drunkard's Family*, written without music and published in a volume of "Parlor Theatricals, Evening Entertainments and School Exhibitions," espoused the view that since moral suasion had proven ineffective, the only solution to national intemperance was prohibition and the elimination of the saloon. Described as a "realistic play for children," *The Drunkard's Family* was based upon the premise that in 1898 children were old enough to be told the truth about the politics of temperance.[59]

Conceivably, the most elaborate example of the children's play was Nellie Bradley's *A Temperance Picnic with the Old Woman Who Lived in a Shoe* published in 1888 by the National Temperance Society and

Publication House. Described as a pro-prohibition musical for children, *A Temperance Picnic with the Old Woman Who Lived in a Shoe* featured a narrative, two recitations, a colloquy and no less than seventeen songs (one sung by three characters labeled the Prohibition Trio) that advocated the vote as the remedy for intemperance and stressed the importance of exerting political pressure upon legislators.[60] The central character of Bradley's musical was Mother Merryheart, who, rather than lament the loss of her own son to drink, instead ministered to the happiness of others, mainly children of drunkards who had been abandoned. Her adopted brood at the beginning of the play included an Irish boy, a German boy, a Chinese boy and an African-American boy, all of whom Mother Merryheart took on a temperance picnic for their "entertainment and edification." After a series of pro-temperance songs, speeches and marches, the picnic ended with the hanging of *Al Kohol* and *Nick O'Teene* followed by more eating, singing and recitations.[61]

The increased presence of women in the ranks of temperance dramatists during the 1870s produced yet another significant change in the focus of the plays written. After a shift toward espousing prohibition as the means of eradicating intemperance following the Maine Laws and plays like *Ten Nights in a Bar-room*, during the WCTU era there was a partial return to a belief in the efficacy of moral suasion, or at least the moral authority of women. Written by both men and women, plays like *The First Glass; or the Power of a Woman's Influence* and *Marry No Man if He Drinks*, both by Nellie Bradley, and Edwin Tardy's *Saved* reasserted the proposition that women possessed the power to either exert enough influence upon their men to reform them or to refuse to enter a relationship with a drinker – even a moderate drinker – in the first place. Woman's choice was perhaps most clearly outlined in H. Elliot McBride's *Don't Marry a Drunkard to Reform Him* in which two women, each faced with the prospect of marrying moderate drinkers, elected different paths. Emily Bell chose to marry her beloved even though she knew that he drank, often to excess; while Pauline Knox steadfastly refused to marry the man she loved until he signed the pledge. Before the second act had ended, McBride had begun to focus upon the importance of woman's choice by graphically representing the responsibilities that accompany woman's power to choose a mate or a course of action and the consequences of abrogating those responsibilities. Pauline's marriage to a man willing to sign the pledge as a precondition of nuptials had thrived; while Emily's had quickly deteriorated into the standard nightmare of the drunkard's wife and children. These and other plays that dealt with moral suasion were dramatic reflections of Frances Willard's hope that women would become empowered to unite and "clasp hands in one common effort to protect their homes and loved ones from the ravages of drink" and that they would succeed in their efforts.[62]

Late nineteenth-century temperance dramas were hardly limited to women's and children's issues, however. In retrospect, post-Civil War dramaturgy, with its themes, settings and characters drawn from small-town America, was well suited to the entire demographic range of late nineteenth-century audiences that were increasingly rural. Operating from the premise that rural Americans would prefer plays that offered familiar, village settings and characters like themselves, late nineteenth-century playwrights accommodated their audiences' more agrarian tastes. Thus, unlike the protagonists in earlier plays like *The Drunkard* and *The Bottle*, who were likely to be city-dwellers (or at least city-educated), the central characters in post-Civil War temperance dramas were most frequently farmers or small-town businessmen; and, unlike Edward Middleton or Richard Thornley, who became drunkards and fell to their most degraded state in an urban setting, most post-war theatrical drunkards, while they may have met the same fate as their big-city counterparts, did so in their home environment, the rural village. Such a shift from urban settings, populations and problems was consistent with the dominant thinking of the era, for late in the nineteenth century, the rural once again became popular as a "source of authenticity, finding in the 'folk' the attitudes, beliefs, customs, and language to create a sense of national unity."[63]

This more rural perspective was also reflected in the theatrical representation of immigrants. While nativist attitudes certainly existed in the rural America of the 1870s and 1880s, they were rare in the dramatic representations of the era. Since most rural Americans had little first-hand knowledge of immigrants, were not in daily competition with them for jobs and daily necessities and were generally unaffected by urban ethnic tensions, they readily accepted the more benign stereotypes of "foreigners."[64] Most frequently, immigrants were utilized for comic relief, much as they were in George Baker's *Seeing the Elephant* and *A Drop Too Much* and J. McDermott's *The Wrong Bottle*, which lampoon Irish-Americans, and George S. Vautrot's *At Last*, which makes fun of Germans. On occasion, temperance playwrights even allowed immigrants to serve as reformers, as Lizzie May Elwyn did in *Switched Off*, which featured two Irish servants: one pro-drinking; the other aggressively pro-temperance.

One notable exception to the benign representation of ethnicity, however, was Julia Colman's *No King in America* (1888), a particularly vitriolic attack upon the Irish and the Germans that accused them of subverting American values through their drinking habits. More a sermon with characters than a play per se, *No King in America* opened with a scripture reading (the 10th Psalm), a prayer, and the singing of "My Country 'Tis of Thee." The "play" then proceeded to tell the Germans' own story of the origin of beer, "an invention of the devil." Narrated by two characters – Americus, a young man wrapped quite literally in the American flag, and Columbia, a young woman similarly costumed – the first part of *No King in America* indicted the Germans and their King Gambrinus (who sold his soul to Satan in exchange for the secret formula to make "peer") for introducing the "devil's brew" into the world and made an impassioned appeal for prohibition.[65] With similar polemics, in Part II, "The Whiskey King," Americus likewise denounced the Irish, branding them "as corrupt, criminals, drunks and Democrats" and compared whiskey to an invading army.[66] Addressing two Irish-Americans – Patrick and Michael – Americus asserted that "if a man is going to come here & help rule this country, he must learn how to rule himself first, & he can't do that when he is full of whiskey."[67] Colman's diatribe ended with Americus thanking Americans for waging war on "the delusions of German beer and the blarney of Hibernian whiskey" as well as the "duplicity and trickery of the American liquor industry in quest for the 'almighty dollar'."[68]

No King in America is unique among late nineteenth-century temperance entertainments for yet another reason. It is one of a handful of plays, all written after the Civil War, that were structured, not as narratives, but rather as debates. In the first part of her piece, Colman pitted Americus and Columbia, the representatives of temperance, against a character named Teuton who stated the case for the manufacture and consumption of German beer. This was immediately followed by a vigorous rebuttal delivered by Americus. Likewise, in Part II of Colman's piece, Americus rebutted the pro-whiskey arguments advanced by Patrick and Michael. While few other plays displayed this structure as overtly as did Colman's, Nellie Bradley's *Marry No Man If He Drinks* (1868), *Three Glasses a Day; or the Broken Home, Reclaimed; or the Danger of Moderate Drinking* (Henri Wilkins, 1878), *The Temperance Doctor* (Harry Seymour, c.1870) and *Which Will You Choose?* (Mary Dwinell Chellis, 1869) also centered around a debate between characters who represented opposing positions on drinking; and each first presented the case in favor of moderate drinking followed by an aggressive rebuttal. Most frequently the rebuttal was verbal, but on occasion it could be solely visual. *Marry No Man If He Drinks*, for example, began with a debate between Susie Gray, who defended her fiancé's moderate drinking, and her friend, Laura Bell, whom she ridiculed for being a temperance woman and for "trying to make out innocent things to be great sins."[69] When Susie's husband turned out to be a drunkard who abused his family, there was no need for a verbal rebuttal. The *mise-en-scène* representing the decimation of the drunkard's family more than sufficed to counter Susie's pro-drink arguments. In similar fashion, *The Last Drop* by John Delafield represented the pro-/anti-drink debate visually by contrasting two separate homes: the first of a teetotaler; the second of a drunkard.

On occasion, temperance playwrights utilized a dream sequence to present temperance arguments. Used in plays like George Booth's *The Drunkard's Dream* (1872), James J. McCloskey's *The Fatal Glass; or the Curse of Drink* (1872), James A. Herne's *Drifting Apart* (1888) and C. Z. Barnett's adaptation of *The Bottle* (1847), this dramatic device seemingly represented the drinker's reality, which ultimately ended with the decimation of a family and the drunkard's demise. Before the drunkard himself succumbed to drink, however, the horrific reality of his condition was revealed to be nothing more than a scenario played out in the mind of the sleeping protagonist. When employed, the dream sequence allowed the playwright to represent the inevitable consequences of intemperance in extreme terms while allowing the drinker to escape those consequences by altering his behavior and signing the pledge.

Intriguingly, while the temperance drama of the period was more simple structurally, more polemical and generally less sophisticated overall than pre-Civil War plays, it also exhibited a slight, barely perceptible shift toward a more modern stance on the addictive capacity of alcohol. Following the Civil War, playwrights increasingly adopted the position that intemperance was not

> merely the result of personal weakness. Rather, they demonstrate that liquor [was] a potentially irresistible force to which anyone can fall victim, no matter how strong his moral character or self-will may be.
>
> This message [was] at odds with the commonly held belief throughout most of the nineteenth century that drunkards were morally weak and that it was their own lack of character which was responsible for their alcoholism... [Dramatists] were, nonetheless, presenting a position about alcoholism not yet accepted in the United States. While it is difficult to assess the impact of these [dramas] on audience members' views of drunkards, it is significant that these ideas were suggested at all given the conventional contemporary view that alcoholism was the result of personal weakness.[70]

Figure 16. The Home of Sobriety and The Home of Drunkenness

While this shift hardly signaled an end to intemperance being the result of a moral failing (i.e., an internal character flaw), it did transfer some of the blame to external causes and shade the late nineteenth-century temperance drama toward alcohol's inherent qualities and capacity to enslave the drinker. This subtle shift to a loss of faith in the drinker's will to resist liquor's power to enslave constituted an intermediate step toward a modern concept of addiction — a concept the temperance drama was never to fully embrace.

Movement toward a more realistic realization of the addictive capacity of alcohol was accompanied by more pessimistic temperance dramas. Possibly influenced by a general loss of optimism following the Depression of 1873, an increasing number of late nineteenth-century temperance plays (albeit still a minority) became considerably "darker" and, like *The Bottle*, refused the drunkard redemption, condemning both him and his family to death. Emblematic of this trend, in F. L. Cutler's *Lost! Or, the Fruits of the Glass*, the drunkard's wife perishes and the drunkard himself commits suicide; H. Elliot McBride's *Under the Curse* ends with the drunkard's attacking his wife and daughter with a table leg. After realizing he has killed his wife and severely injured his daughter, the drunkard drinks himself to death; and T. Trask Woodward's protagonist-drunkard in *The Social Glass; or Victims of the Bottle*, who, in a fit of the DT's believes his wife to be a monster, kills her with a liquor bottle and then laces his drink with poison to kill himself. As indicated by Woodward's title, in his narrative it was the bottle, rather than the drinker's moral weakness, that victimized and destroyed husband and wife.

By the 1870s, the American temperance drama, spreading across America, had reached California. The play that heralded its arrival on the west coast was titled, simply, *Drink*. Adapted from Emile Zola's novel, *L'Assommoir* (1877), the story traces the downward spiral of Gervaise, a good-hearted Parisian washerwoman, who follows her lover (Lantier) from the country to the big city; is abandoned; marries a hardworking carpenter (Coupeau) who falls victim to drink and dies in a fit of the DT's; and, despite the efforts of the kind-hearted metal worker Gouget, ultimately succumbs to drink herself. In one of many stage versions, the play, in an adaptation by the budding impresario David Belasco, opened on July 15, 1879 at the Baldwin, one of San Francisco's premiere theatres. By Belasco's own admission, the cast was "practically an all star one" that featured James O'Neill as Coupeau, Rose Coghlan as Gervaise, Blanche Thorne as Clemence, James A. Herne as Bibi-La-Grillade (one of the comic characters) and Herne's wife, Katherine Corcoran as Coupeau's and Gervaise's daughter, Nana.[71]

Aided by excellent acting and direction, as well as a rousing fight between Gervaise and another washerwomen, Virginie, and a show-stopping depiction of the DT's by O'Neill, this "new drama of violent sensation" had a "respectable" run until July 30, 1879, when Coghlan left the Baldwin company for another engagement.

Belasco's adaptation at the Baldwin was actually the second version of Zola's story mounted in the United States. Several months earlier, on April 30, 1879, Augustin Daly had opened his own adaptation at New York's Olympic Theatre. Although "competently" acted and employing the latest stage equipment, Daly's *Drink* was a commercial failure, closed quietly after just three weeks and was withdrawn from the repertoire. While Daly's brother claimed that "the New York public was not to be attracted by such moral dramas," much of the blame was due, at least in part, to Daly's lack of dexterity in staging the drama.[72] As William Winter, measuring Daly's production against Belasco's pointed out, "a single comparative incident is significantly suggestive: in Daly's New York production the fall of Coupeau from a ladder was, palpably, made by substituting a dummy figure for the actor who played the part; in Belasco's San Francisco presentment, the fall of Coupeau was so skillfully managed that, on opening night, it was for several moments supposed by the audience that an actual accident had occurred."[73]

Drink was a "milestone in the line of Daly mistakes" for another reason; it embroiled him in a dispute over authorship rights with Olive Logan (Sykes) whom Daly employed as a "spotter" of promising European plays that might be translated for the American stage. Alerted by Logan to successful stage adaptations of Zola's novel in both Paris and in London, Daly sampled both and, despite his having "little faith in melodramas of low life," was convinced by the London production to stage the play in the United States.[74] Subsequently, Logan negotiated the rights for Daly, translated the play from its original French and adapted it for the stage. When the play opened at the Olympic, however, no mention of Logan's role was included in the playbill. Instead, the bill read, "Adapted and Arranged by Mr. Augustin Daly." Shortly thereafter Daly was granted a copyright in his name; Logan was forced to sue for even her finder's fee.[75]

Daly's and Belasco's adaptations were not the only American incarnations of Zola's story. At roughly the same time that they were mounting their productions, Dion Boucicault penned a third adaptation. Listed until recently as "lost," the typescript of the Boucicault version, like Daly's and Belasco's titled *Drink*, was discovered in Illinois with a trove of other nineteenth-century melodramas and is now housed in the Sherman

Collection at Southern Illinois University. To date, however, no evidence exists to prove it was ever staged.

While adaptations of Zola's story about the fall of Gervaise and Coupeau elicited mixed responses in America, they were highly successful in both Paris and London. The plays staged in both cities were free adaptations of Zola's work, which literary critics have described as "one of the masterpieces of the French novel, innovative in subject and technique, very controversial at the time of its publication (1877) . . . immensely influential throughout the world" and, considering its potential for projecting the pathos of its protagonists and the sensationalism of both the washroom fight and Coupeau's death, a logical choice for adaptation for the stage.[76]

The task of "translating" *L'Assommoir* to the Paris stage was assigned to Octave Gastineau and William Busnach, the latter responsible for adapting no less than six Zola novels for the theatre. In their efforts, Gastineau and Busnach had a secret collaborator: Zola himself, who was eager to prove that the naturalism he zealously espoused was the future of not only the modern novel, but the theatre as well. In fact, Zola was so driven to see *L'Assommoir* succeed on the stage that he wrote several newspaper reviews of the play himself – reviews that not only praised the play and its production, but afforded him the opportunity to deny any active participation in the adaptation. According to David Baguley, who has studied the adaptation process from the novel through the British adaptation, Zola himself "worked extensively on the plan and the drama and on the outline of each scene, leaving his collaborators to write the dialogue."[77] It was Zola, then, who shaped the central actions of the novel's plot into a series of *tableaux vivants* that constituted the framework of the stage plays.

The Busnach/Gastineau/Zola *L'Assommoir* opened at the Théâtre Ambigu on January 18, 1879 with Hélène Petit in the role of Gervaise and Gil Naza as Coupeau. Spurred by the controversy surrounding the novel and a veritable deluge of publicity for the play, all seats for the first night had been sold more than three weeks before the play opened. Before the production closed the following January, it had run for 250 performances, was equally successful in the provinces and in Belgium, and *L'Assommoir* was "revived in 1885, 1890, 1893, 1900, and almost annually after Zola's death in 1902 until 1933."[78]

From the outset, the play was as unpopular with the critics as it was popular with the average theatregoer. Francisque Sarcey, the crusty critic for *Le Temps*, for example, never tired of denigrating the play, publicly branding it as "repugnant" and considering it devoid of literary merit. Negative criticism, however, failed to dampen the "frenzy of admiration [the play] inspired in its audience" and did nothing to discourage British and American theatre managers from importing *L'Assommoir* for presentation to their audiences.[79]

Arguably, the most famous stage rendition of *L'Assommoir* was Charles Reade's adaptation, titled *Drink*, which opened on June 2, 1879 at the Princess' Theatre, Oxford Street, London and ran until February 14, 1880. Widely regarded as "Zola's nearest spiritual kin among English men of letters," known for his reformist novels like *It is Never too Late to Mend* (1856), and "a writer thoroughly in harmony with Victorian taste and pre-occupations, who saw life in melodramatic terms as a battleground for the struggle between the contending forces of good and evil," Reade was the logical choice to adapt Zola's story.[80] Consequently, when John Hollingshead, the manager of London's Gaiety Theatre saw the Busnach/Gastineau/Zola *L'Assommoir* in Paris, Reade was the first person he thought of as a potential English adapter.[81]

Aided by a tour de force performance by noted actor Charles Warner, who became acclaimed for his portrayal of Coupeau and for the intensity of his delirium tremens scene, Reade's *Drink* met with success, not only in London, but throughout Great Britain, in the United States and even as far afield as Australia.[82] In 1891, Reade's play was revived at the Drury Lane Theatre and most likely would have exceeded its initial London run had not Warner been injured in a stage accident. *Drink* was subsequently revived successfully at the Adelphi Theatre in 1899.

In one of its most interesting incarnations, *Drink* was featured as the centerpiece of a D. W. Griffith temperance film titled *The Drunkard's Reformation* (Biograph, 1909). In it, a father who is rapidly becoming a chronic drunkard, takes his young child to a performance of *Drink*, witnesses a narrative in which the drinker perishes and his family is decimated, is frightened by actions that parallel his own, anticipates his own fate should he continue drinking and consequently reforms, thereby saving both himself and his family from certain destruction. To theatre and film historian David Mayer, Griffith's movie was an act of homage, not only to an earlier temperance classic, but to Charles Warner, who had popularized Coupeau on three continents and who had committed suicide in a New York hotel shortly before filming started.[83] To document his contention, Mayer points to unmistakable similarities in costuming, makeup and mannerisms between Warner and Arthur Johnson, the male lead in the film – similarities possible only if Griffith had been exposed to one or more of the tours of *Drink*.[84]

To Mayer, Griffith's conceptual scheme for *A Drunkard's Reformation* has added significance for both theatre and film historians. Using *Drink* as the play-within-the movie to illustrate parallel actions was, to Mayer, a prime example of the inter-textual adaptation that was occurring at the turn of the century. "The development of *A Drunkard's Reformation* from specific theatrical sources," Mayer maintains, "points, not to separation of theatre and film, but to a continuing linkage or mutuality of subject-matter and performing styles between the two media and also, but perhaps harder to argue, to audiences still shared between theatre and film."[85] Conceivably, it was this shared audience and Griffith's confidence that it had a thorough knowledge of the methods for inculcating temperance ideology in the young that dictated his choice of characterization, *mise-en-scène* and acting style for *A Drunkard's Reformation*.

Throughout its illustrious history, *Drink* underwent countless transformations, from naturalistic novel to stage melodrama to classic temperance film. While moralists in both the United States and Great Britain almost immediately translated his novel "into a homily against alcohol, [with the book's becoming] a Bible to the temperance movement which, to advance its cause, thumped its covers unceasingly," Zola had wider and more ambitious goals than simply adding to temperance literature.[86] While he certainly hoped to expose the evils of cheap liquor and graphically represent the fate of drunkards, his central focus was the poverty, squalor, violence and sense of hopelessness of slum life. Through his writing, Zola planned to alert the "ruling classes" to the hideous living conditions of the urban proletariat and to encourage them to "mend matters by providing better housing for the labouring poor and better education for their children, and by legislating against excessively long hours of work for an inadequate wage. The evils he showed – promiscuity, delinquency, alcoholism – were, he insisted, the inevitable results of a bad environment, which only needed to be changed for the evils to disappear."[87]

Even though Zola maintained publicly that he had assiduously represented the truth about the working poor and had remained dispassionate in his treatment of his characters in his novel, when he came to adapt his work for the stage, he made significant compromises in order to meet pubic expectations. Possibly remembering the critics' mockery of his earlier play, *Le Bouton du Rose*, he "insisted on ... radical modifications of the novel in the direction of the popular melodrama" and it was Busnach, not the novelist, who remained faithful to the naturalism Zola purported to promote in the theatre and retained vestiges of the naturalistic elements Zola had employed in his original narrative.[88] In addition to suggesting the *tableaux vivants* that served to shape the action of *L'Assommoir*, Zola rewrote the character of Gervaise's adversary, Virginie, providing her with a revenge motive – a desire for retribution for being humiliated in the washroom scene – that transformed her into the villainess of the piece, the embodiment of evil who led her prey to their destruction through drink. Thus, when first Coupeau and then Gervaise are led to drink as the result of Virginie's machinations, they are the "victims of a character's malevolence rather than of their environment."[89] In additional concessions to popular expectations, Virginie was murdered by her jealous husband thereby satisfying audience expectations for poetic justice; while an unmistakable temperance theme was added to the original narrative by transforming Gouget into a temperance spokesman, a change that did not go unnoticed in England and the United States.

Reade's adaptation moved Zola's story further into the melodramatic mode. Whether it was Reade's natural "penchant for melodramatic plots, [his] inexhaustible taste for realistic detail, for 'human documents'," or his reformist tendencies that resulted in his "ventilating working-class concerns and providing middle-class solutions," his departures from the Busnach/Gastineau/Zola *L'Assommoir* were significant.[90] In a concession to Victorian sensibilities, Gervaise and Lantier were married; the character of Phoebe Sage, a sort of moral exemplar, was introduced into the plot to serve as friend, confidante and foil to Gervaise; Gouget's role as temperance activist was strengthened; liquor was identified as a contributory cause of Lantier's evil; a new scene, in which Gouget recognizes Gervaise as the woman he has loved from afar in the past, was incorporated into Reade's script; a second new scene informed the audience that Lantier is a bigamist; and, unlike the French version, Gouget was reintroduced in the scene where Gervaise turned to drink. Possibly the most significant change, however, was Reade's decision to allow Gervaise to live at the end of the play. Through the intervention of Phoebe, the agent of redemption, who exposes the treachery of Virginie and Lantier and arranges for Gouget to be present in Gerviase's time of need at the end of the play, Reade's *Drink* ended in a "triumph of retribution and salvation."[91] By this one change, Reade, in a sense, mixed the then-popular melodramatic mode with Zola's original naturalistic mode, thereby effecting a compromise between the earlier, more catastrophic British temperance dramas and the more optimistic American pattern. Like Douglas Jerrold and Cruickshank's many adaptors, Reade punished the drunkard, Coupeau, by having him suffer horrendously through a fit of the DT's before his death; yet, Gervaise, who had tasted the "fatal first glass" herself and also perished in Zola's original story, was spared and there are even indications that she may have found eventual happiness with her devoted admirer, the temperance activist Gouget. Perhaps, in Reade's *Drink* the balance between the demands of melodrama and determinism that had eluded earlier British temperance dramatists had finally been achieved.

A study of American adaptations add little to the history of the changes made in Zola's narrative from its inception through Griffith's film. Both Belasco's and Daly's version have been lost and Boucicault's is nearly identical to Reade's in *dramatis personae*, structure and wording. Other than documenting the fact that all versions retained the washroom and the DT's scenes (the most overtly dramatic actions of the play), written accounts concentrated upon highlights of production (e.g., the comparison of Coupeau's fall from the scaffold in Daly's staging to the same scene in Belasco's production), but offer no insight into the missing versions of one of the most important temperance texts of the nineteenth century.

Writing of mid to late nineteenth-century temperance efforts, historians are wont to stress that, "raging throughout most of the nineteenth century and...into the twentieth, America's own Hundred Years' War between traffickers in liquor and progressives heaven-bent on reform was more than a light skirmish or even a major campaign. It was a full-scale conflict in which opposing forces, locked in battle [from coast to coast], engaged in all the fearful engines of propaganda warfare – including music, drama and song – in a desperate struggle to win."[92]

By the final decades of the nineteenth century, the writing and staging of temperance dramas, like the reforms they supported, were truly nationwide endeavors, with productions in America's small towns and big cities witnessed by audiences that were inclusive and mixed in terms of age, sex, race, ethnicity, educational background and geographical distribution. Despite their admitted lack of sophistication and literary merit, post-Civil War temperance dramas nevertheless were ubiquitous, immensely popular and remained valuable weapons and integral elements in America's continued campaign to combat intemperance.

6

Epilogue: "theatrical 'dry rot'?"; or what price the Anti-Saloon League?

"Taste not, handle not, touch not," should be inscribed on every vessel that contains spirits in the house of man.

> Benjamin Rush, *An Inquiry into the Effects of Ardent Spirits on the Human Body and Mind*

The residual, by definition, has been effectively formed in the past, but is still active in the cultural process, not only and often not at all as an element of the past.

> Raymond Williams, *Marxism and Literature*

To those who lived through it, america's gilded age was a turbulent time, an inchoate era marked by a complex, often bewildering, transformation from a Victorian world to what we have come to regard as the modern one. To many, it was an exhilarating time characterized by the final pacification and "colonization" of the American West; by the consolidation of nineteenth-century industrialization in a flurry of mergers, incorporation and unionization; by the drive toward professionalization in the workplace; by unprecedented changes in gender roles, interclass relations, sexual norms, business practices, social mobility, education, family life, democratic politics and daily living; and by the realization that America was on the threshold of becoming not just a nation, but a great nation. To others, however, it was nothing less than "a period of trauma, of change so swift and thorough that many Americans seemed unable to fathom the extent of the upheaval."[1] As Alan Trachtenberg has characterized it, *fin-de-siècle* America was a veritable watershed of shifting practices and clashing perspectives – practices and perspectives that could not help but trigger radical cultural change.[2]

Such cultural change and the anxieties and dislocations they necessarily precipitated were perhaps no more severe than they were in the area of the nation's moral foundation, for, historians tell us, post-Victorian pluralism first challenged and then undermined the "Victorian worldview that valued hierarchy, order, and a single standard of culture, morality, and values."[3] The growing skepticism that inevitably resulted from this crisis in values amounted to nothing less than a loss of faith in traditional social, moral and religious norms. "While America would always experience religious revivals and public approval of the role of the church would continue, the theological core was gone and religiosity had replaced the complex ideas and strenuous practices of earlier generations. Religious energies were channeled into economic activity and then into political faith."[4]

Cultural historian Warren Susman has located in the late nineteenth-century "crisis in thought" the seeds of a profound social change, from what he terms the "culture of character" to a "culture of personality." Man in each era, he has theorized, adopts a particular manner of "presenting the self to society, offering a standard of conduct that assure[s] the interrelationship between the 'social' and the 'moral'."[5] Each then defines his own "modal type" which he feels is necessary for the preservation of morality and social order. From roughly 1800 on, the dominant modal type – "the *sine qua non* of all collective adjustment and social intercourse" – was the man of sound character, the man who was identified by such descriptors as "honor," "duty," "reputation," "integrity" and "manners." Beginning in the 1880s, however, words such as "glowing," "attractive" and "charming," each applied to a person's individual style, began to appear in routine discourse.[6] Such rhetoric, plus the increasing de-emphasis of moral issues and the growing fascination with personality, disseminated through advice manuals, popular literature, psychological writings and popular culture in general, were all symptomatic of the shift away from the importance of building sound character traits to developing those traits associated with a "winning personality." In the emerging mass culture of the late nineteenth century, in which making a good first impression was frequently more important than proving oneself a good friend for a lifetime or dealing honestly with others, more emphasis was placed upon perceptions of surface values than upon those substantive moral values by which people lived and conducted their personal relations with others earlier in the century.[7] Invariably, this radical shift from a culture of character to one of personality permeated all thought and activity of the era, reform efforts included.

In 1900, soon-to-be President Teddy Roosevelt recognized the impact of the incipient modernization and the radical reformulation of cultural values on those who sought redress for social evils when he identified two "gospels" of reform. The first gospel, Roosevelt said, dealt with morality; the second with efficiency.[8] All reform, Roosevelt maintained, mixed moralism with the search for the most efficient means of effecting solutions to social problems. Mirroring Roosevelt's analysis, changes in twentieth-century thinking resulted in the realization that perhaps the means of reform, rather than the results, deserved the focus. With the advent of the Anti-Saloon League in 1895, temperance activists fell into lockstep with the more method-oriented approach to reform, as "dry" ideology became skewed sharply in favor of efficiency. Although, after the decline in evangelical fervor and the disappearance of the charismatic (and frequently subversive) antebellum reformers, activists continued to give lip service to the nineteenth-century notion that temperance was in essence a moral imperative, the ASL adopted a pragmatic and workmanlike approach to the regulation of liquor. By doing this, it ostensibly shifted focus from the sinful nature of intemperance to reformers' interaction with the polity and the legal establishment.

With the loss of a clear moral imperative and the sense of urgency that had defined earlier activism and playwriting, dramaturgy at the turn of the century, like its host culture, displayed first ambivalence toward temperance and then even outright hostility. Some, like James A. Herne's *Drifting Apart* (1888) and Elliot McBride's *As by Fire* (1895) maintained at least a surface fidelity to established temperance imperatives; others, like Charles Hoyt's *A Temperance Town* (1892) and J. W. Todd's *Arthur Eustace; or, A Mother's Love* (1891) betrayed doubts about temperance philosophy and tactics, especially those of the ASL; while still others, like Edward Locke's *The Drunkard's Daughter* (c.1905) overtly attacked, lampooned and/or dismissed reform efforts and the attitudes and the activists who initiated them.

Clearly the most "traditional" of the five plays mentioned, *As by Fire* treats intemperance as a violation of hegemonic norms, with drunkenness still regarded as a moral failing, and employs a number of devices considered standard for a nineteenth-century temperance drama. The protagonist, William Gordon, is "enslaved" by liquor; his drinking is encouraged by the villain of the piece; he loses a family member (his son) to drink; and his physical, moral and mental condition deteriorates to such a degree that he has a fit of the DT's in the fourth act. By Act v, Gordon has reformed and delivers the obligatory temperance harangue: "Intemperance and retribution! As by fire I have been saved from the drunkard's doom, and I go forward now with a determination, while life lasts, to battle against the assaults of King Alcohol; to endeavor to help those who, like myself, have been on the brink of ruin – on the verge of destruction."[9] In all regards, *As by Fire* faithfully conformed to expectations for a nineteenth-century temperance melodrama, and, since it characterized intemperance as a moral failing, it continued nineteenth-century reform polemics and was consequently reminiscent of *The Drunkard* and other earlier temperance dramas.

In comparison, Herne's *Drifting Apart* exhibited signs of modernity, although it remained as moralistic as McBride's drama and it too continued to rely upon melodramatic conventions. Characters, for example, were inserted for comic relief; the drunkard was a backslider who abandoned his wife and child; they were forced to suffer in poverty; the drunkard returned too late to save his family from starving to death; and there was a residual sentimentalism that permeated the entire piece.

Nevertheless, had Herne ended *Drifting Apart* with the deaths of the wife and child and possibly had his protagonist perish as well, his drama, despite the preponderance of melodramatic elements, might have joined *Three Years in a Man-Trap, Lost! Or, the Fruits of the Glass* and *Under the Curse* as one of the most deterministic temperance dramas written to that date. However, instead of sentencing the drunkard and his family to death and ensuring a "realistic" conclusion, Herne opted to use just one more melodramatic device: a dream sequence. In it, at the juncture of the plot where the protagonist, Jack Hepburn, returned home to find his wife and daughter dead, he awoke to discover that the entire drunken odyssey had been a nightmare and that he still had the opportunity to avert domestic disaster and ensure a happy ending by abstaining from drink.[10] Reminiscent of the final tableau of *The Drunkard*, stage directions for Hepburn's reunion with his family, which takes place on Christmas Day, call for sleigh bells and the popular temperance song, "Turn Your Glasses Upside Down" to be heard in the background.

Despite its melodramatic elements and residual sentimentalism, however, *Drifting Apart* contained enough that was recognized as realistic at the time to qualify as one of a handful of "transitional" works – plays that straddled the divide between the still-popular melodrama and the then-emerging theatrical realism. Presaging his drama *Margaret Fleming*, generally acknowledged as a milestone in early American stage realism, Herne in *Drifting Apart* dispensed with the conventional melodramatic villain, avoided the hackneyed final act harangues of his predecessors, utilized colloquial speech rhythms, created characterizations deeper and more psychological than those in earlier dramas and provided detailed stage directions that created the environment and set the atmosphere for the play. His mixture of melodramatic devices and conventions with realistic ones resulted in a hybrid not unlike those being written by Ned Sheldon, William Vaughn Moody and other playwrights at the turn of the century – playwrights who, although attracted to the new realism, were nevertheless either unwilling or unable to break with older conventions. Conceivably, in retrospect, had Herne been able to script his play minus the melodramatic dream sequence (a device that guaranteed a happy ending, but destroyed a realistic outcome and violated the internal logic of the piece), *Drifting Apart* might today be regarded as a true harbinger of realism.[11] As written, however, *Drifting Apart* is a work clearly caught in the cusp between two different theatres and two different cultures.

This "flaw" (the dream sequence) notwithstanding and despite his continued use of melodramatic devices, *Drifting Apart* exhibited signs of Herne's growing attraction to realism – an attraction immediately recognized by such early advocates of the style as William Dean Howells and Hamlin Garland. After seeing the play in a "cheap, second-rate" theatre in Boston's South End in 1889, Garland wrote in *The Literary World*: "Knowing nothing of Mr. Herne or the play, I went with little curiosity and no special interest, intending to go out after a couple of acts. I stayed throughout the whole play, more stirred to thought as well as feeling than I have been for years. I said, 'Here is a play which, with all its faults, deals with the *essentials* of American domestic life'."[12] Later, writing in *The Arena*, he compared the play's fourth act to "one of Millet's paintings, with that mysterious quality of reserve – the quality of life again."[13]

Unfortunately, Garland's was the minority opinion, as most agreed with *New York Tribune* critic William Winter, who despised the "problematic, polemic, didactic...disquisition" of the play and set the stage for its financial doom.[14] After a disastrous opening at New York's People's Theatre on May 7, 1888, Herne was forced to take the production on the road, where he managed to keep it alive for a total of 250 performances. The critical and financial failure of the play, however, did little to diminish its place in American theatre history. Had the pro-temperance drama survived in the twentieth century and had Herne eliminated the happy ending, his simple, transitional drama might have served as the prototype for a more realistic temperance play. As it stands, simply because it is one of a handful of plays on the subject written by a major American dramatist, *Drifting Apart* remains an important work in the history of temperance dramaturgy.

Despite the efforts of Herne and his playwriting contemporaries, however, the waning years of the century were difficult and confusing ones for temperance dramatists. After 1900, although "temperance values permeated the novels, plays and films of the time...the nineteenth-century flood of [actual] temperance plays and novels ebbed" as the reform-minded turned their attention toward other vices and social problems and audiences found other topics to engross them.[15] Fortunately for temperance activists, as the fervor for temperance on stage declined, the anti-liquor attack was taken up by the early narrative film, with movies like *In the Grip of Alcohol* (1912) and *John Barleycorn*, a six-reel feature adapted from a Jack London novel by reformist filmmaker Lois Weber in 1914, representing the horrors of alcoholism as faithfully and effectively as did the legendary temperance dramas of the nineteenth century. Much to the dismay of the liquor industry, films like *Prohibition* (1915), arguably the classic of the genre and a movie publicly endorsed by the Anti-Saloon League as political propaganda, contained as many "scenes depicting the misery inflicted upon the innocent wife" as did *The Drunkard*.[16] Reformers' reactions in general to anti-liquor films were as favorable as activists' responses had been to their mid and late nineteenth-century stage ancestors.

Although such films were a distinct minority (albeit a vocal one), they and other reformist films like *The Hypocrites* (1915), *Shoes* (1916), *The People vs. John Doe* (1916) and *The Hand that Rocks the Cradle* (1917) that dealt with political corruption, poverty and the slums, the injustices of capital punishment and birth control respectively, were nevertheless reflective of the times in which they were produced. During this period, which we now call the "Age of Reform," the progressive spirit was manifested in a vast array of social "documents" created by reformers of all stripes. It pervaded popular magazines like *Everybody's*, *Collier's*, *Cosmopolitan*, *Hampton's*, *Pearson's* and most notably *McClure's*, which regularly printed exposés of everything from monopolies to child labor to unsanitary conditions in meat packing plants; reformist themes were subjects of novels; and book-length exposés were penned by such noted muckrakers as Upton Sinclair, Lincoln Steffens and Ida Tarbell. In such a socially aware, progressive climate it is hardly surprising that early silent filmmakers like George Nichols, Barry O'Neil, Oscar Apfel and Lois Weber would view their medium as a means of correcting social ills and would be attracted to many of the same subjects (white slavery, political corruption, exploitation of immigrants, alcoholism) that were the foci of the muckrakers. In the words of one advocate of reformist filmmaking, "motion pictures are going to save our civilization from the destruction which has successively overwhelmed every civilization of the past."[17] And, like their nineteenth-century reformist predecessors, early twentieth-century reformer/filmmakers deemed intemperance as among the most destructive vices plaguing modern society.

Before the heyday of the temperance film was unceremoniously cut short by the passage of the Eighteenth Amendment in 1919, the form even proved attractive to the father of the narrative film, D. W. Griffith. During his career at Biograph, Griffith directed thirteen temperance films; he once considered converting Herne's *Drifting Apart* to film (he made *Way Down East* instead); and his final movie, *The Struggle* (1931), dealt directly with Prohibition, still a controversial issue in the early thirties. Raised in an abstemious Methodist home and instilled with a fear of alcoholism at an early age, intemperance, according to Griffith's biographers, held a near-compulsive fascination for him.[18] Not coincidentally, at the core of one of his best-know temperance films, *A Drunkard's Reformation*, Griffith focused upon the very act of inculcating temperance values in the young, something that had an impact upon him when he was a child. Through the unique play-within-a-play device that framed the film, Griffith depicted a drunkard father teaching his child about the horrors of alcoholism by means of a staged temperance drama, a tactic generations of the temperate had been employing to instruct their children for years.[19]

Sadly, in the early 1920s, Griffith succumbed to the temptation he feared most and became the very drunkard he decried in *A Drunkard's Reformation* and other Biograph films. Given his new habit and a lifelong distrust of reformers of any stripe, it was perhaps unavoidable that at this time, Griffith would ally himself with the repeal movement; nor was it unexpected that he would attempt to use his art to advance the anti-prohibition cause. Unfortunately, *The Struggle*, the film he produced to attack prohibition and perhaps to justify his own habit, was both an artistic and commercial failure. According to Richard Schickel, one of Griffith's biographers, "this film, which seems to have started out to be an anti-prohibition tract... ended up looking like a [pro-]temperance drama" with more than one critic comparing it unfavorably to *Ten Nights in a Bar-room*.[20] On a strictly personal level, it betrayed a drunkard's internal battle with his Methodist conscience; in a artistic sense, it served as yet another indication that the moralism of melodrama no longer satisfied the American public; and, on a social level, it reflected the era's ambivalence about coercion in the name of temperance and questioned the legitimacy of moralistic pronouncements of any sort in the twentieth century.

Like Griffith's final film, many late nineteenth- and early twentieth-century temperance dramas contained similar mixed messages. This was due, in part, to the especially harsh coercive methods of the Anti-Saloon League which angered and alienated a number of people, reformers and non-reformers alike. By the 1890s, facing a proliferation of new saloons in America's major cities, the increase in alcoholism that resulted, and forced to admit the relative ineffectiveness of the assimilative attitudes of the WCTU and the political tactics of the Prohibition Party, a number of temperance activists, many with populist leanings, began to opt for a more aggressive approach to reform and intensified their efforts to effect legal restrictions upon the sale of liquor.

To temperance activists and "small-town native American Protestants" alike, the urban saloon was regarded as a source of corruption and cultural subversion and hence the logical target for reformers. As historians Joseph Gusfield, Herbert Gutman and Roy Rosenzweig point out in separate studies, beginning in the 1880s and continuing until the second decade of the twentieth century, millions of Italians, Slavs, Greeks and Russian Jews entered the United States, in the process introducing into American society work and drinking habits, values and behavioral codes not favored by the American middle class. And, rightly or wrongly, these "foreign" habits, values and behavioral codes became associated with the rise of the urban saloon.[21]

Populist in its origins, the Anti-Saloon League, the antidote to the threat of the saloon, was a single-interest pressure group and from its outset was narrow in its focus. Furthermore, built as it was upon a foundation of geographical and ethnic differences, it could not avoid polarizing Americans, both within and outside of temperance ranks. As Gusfield has assessed the effect of the League: "It maximized the cultural differences between pro- and anti-Temperance forces while minimizing the class differences. In this fashion it promoted an atmosphere in which the meaning of Prohibition as a symbol of Protestant, middle-class, rural supremacy was enhanced."[22]

Throughout the history of dramaturgy, playwriting tended to lag behind the emergence of a particular temperance stance or ideology, just as Pratt's *Ten Nights in a Bar-room* represented prohibitionist sentiments seven years after the adoption of the Maine Law.[23] Intriguingly, however, in the early 1890s, several years before the formal founding of the Anti-Saloon League in 1895, two plays – *A Temperance Town* (1892) and *Arthur Eustace; or A Mother's Love* (1891) – actually predicted negative reactions to the ASL brand of coercive reform and represented on page and stage the divisiveness of late nineteenth-century attempts at national prohibition. Both began with the stated premise that the presence of a saloon was tantamount to having a cancer on the body of the community; and both, in differing degrees, questioned whether the price of coercive reform was too high.

At the beginning of *Arthur Eustace*, the more doctrinaire of the two works, entrepreneur Robert Eustace has just leased a vacant piece of property to a man who plans to convert it into a saloon. Ideological positions are staked out and battle lines are drawn immediately upon his wife's entrance. She is a Temperance Woman in the mold of the WCTU and has just come from a meeting of her local society convened to prevent the opening of a saloon in their midst. On hearing of the female opposition to his ventures and the fact that morality threatens his well-being, Eustace reacts predictably, railing: "Has it come to such a point that a man must lose money for the sake of gratifying the whims of a pack of fanatical women who call themselves temperance women? Bah! they had better be at home attending to their household duties rather than gadding around on a wild goose chase. What has that self-styled temperance crowd ever accomplished, I would like to know?"[24] Eustace's defense – on its surface, a businessman's justification of investing in a saloon – in both tone and content is a thinly disguised mockery of the WCTU's ineffectiveness and a deprecation of any female intervention in social matters. By the last act of the play, however, even the ASL, a male-dominated organization and supposedly an effective check on the unlimited proliferation of saloons on the national landscape, has been questioned and portrayed as a divisive cultural force. In the end, ironically, it is the saloon keeper, Harry Gordon, who saves the drunkard and, while the businessman affiliated with the liquor interests is defeated, temperance activists have proven both ineffective and destructive of the fabric of the nuclear family. Although *Arthur Eustace* fell short of mounting a direct challenge to the ASL, it nevertheless raised doubts about its aims and tactics.

Charles Hoyt's *A Temperance Town* was an even more extreme, almost anti-temperance, play. Set in a town threatened by the opening of a saloon, like *Arthur Eustace*, Hoyt's drama trots out the usual arguments against the sale of liquor – families decimated, poverty, increased gambling, younger generations ruined by drink – but just at the point when Hoyt appeared poised to defend established temperance doctrine, he abruptly reversed his stance. Instead of society's heroic saviors and guardians of the public morality, Hoyt depicted his reformers as hypocrites, moralistic meddlers who would resort to unethical and even illegal means to remove "the blight" from their community; while the saloon keeper was portrayed as an honest victim of unscrupulous local officials and the drunkards were represented as being harmless. Because of its reversal of the roles (drunkard and bar keeper) defined earlier by T. S. Arthur and William Pratt in their temperance classic, some critics have interpreted Hoyt's play as a repudiation of Arthur/Pratt's staunch prohibitionist stance.

While there is no evidence that Hoyt's play was intended as a direct response to Arthur's *Ten Nights in a Bar-room*, the similarity in *dramatis personae*, the centrality of the saloon and the socially vulnerable position of the tavern keeper raise the question of whether Hoyt was coming to Simon Slade's defense, albeit many years after Slade was created and then destroyed. Lending weight to this speculation was Hoyt's treatment of his analog to Little Mary, Arthur's most sympathetic character. Rather than treat her with the sympathy due a drunkard's child, Hoyt instead lampoons her and ridicules her attempts to drag her father from the bar. When Hoyt's bar tender says to the girl (simply called "child" in *A Temperance Town*), "a saloon is no place [for] a little girl! Here's a nickel for you to buy some candy with," his tone is patronizing, dismissive.[25]

Starting, then, from the "official" ASL position that local political action supported by the local religious establishment was the way to destroy the liquor interests, *A Temperance Town* ended by illustrating the evils of local ordinances and demonstrating that late nineteenth-century reform was "superimposed" and hardly pluralistic.[26] It also demonstrated that while temperance remained an important social concern, the coercive tactics of the Anti-saloon League and the proposed constrictions of national prohibition alarmed many Americans who perceived the ASL platform as rigid and narrow and their tactics as repressive and threatening to personal liberty. Thus, just as previous temperance dramas had represented the tensions and reformist measures of earlier eras, turn-of-the-century works proved just as reflexive by revealing the fissures in the temperance community and the cultural shifts that caused them.

In the early years of the twentieth century, the thinly veiled anti-temperance stance that Griffith attempted in *The Struggle* was hardly an anomaly. If the nineteenth-century American stage readily embraced the issue of temperance, conveying a positive image of the reform and reformers, the twentieth-century theatre did not. Perhaps the most common departure from the traditional temperance drama was the depiction of reformers as hypocritical cranks and drunkards as harmless and comical. As mentioned, *A Temperance Town* was ambivalent, even contradictory, in terms of its stance on temperance reform and tactics. One of the means of subverting its initial pro-ASL position was the dramatic representation of the drunkards in the play as fun-loving and hardly the pariahs of earlier dramas. As the reformers in the play became increasingly rigid, humorless and mechanistic, the drunks, by contrast, came to be regarded as more human. At the conclusion of the play, it was the reformers, not the tavern keeper nor the liquor industry, who had violated both law and common ethics, and it was the drinkers who had the most tenable moral position and who ultimately represented American ideals.

During the twentieth century, the depiction of the drunkard as a "lovable old sot" – a depiction that perhaps crystallized in W. C. Fields' characterizations in the films *Poppy* and *The Fatal Glass of Beer* – became far more common than the drunkard-as-moral-leper of the nineteenth century. In Edward Locke's *The Drunkard's Daughter* (c.1905), the title of which creates the expectation of yet another neglected waif suffering because of her father's drinking, the drunkard is hardly a threat to his family, society, or even himself. His daughter, finding him drunk early in the play, rather than tugging on his shirt sleeve and imploring him to come home with her, instead smiles and refers to him as "dear old dad."[27] Later in the play, an entire comic scene revolves around two roguish Irish sots playfully hiding a bottle from a third drinker while affectionately calling each other "old soaks." Placed along side the scene from *Ten Nights in a Bar-room* (Act 1, Scene 2), in which the villainous drunkard (Harvey Green) preys upon an intoxicated victim (Willie Hammond), Locke's scene serves as a convenient benchmark against which we can measure just how far drama on the temperance theme had departed from its original message(s). Locke's drunks were hardly the predatory beasts (or their victims) of earlier dramas and drunkenness was reduced to a minor theme of *The Drunkard's Daughter*, which centered instead on the daughter's marital problems. In fact, when the drunkard disappeared after Act 1, his absence (and the absence of alcohol) was barely noticed.

Beginning early in the century and continuing until the 1990s, when the movement dubbed "political correctness" by its critics made the comic treatment of drunkenness intolerable to large segments of the American public, the lovable "old soak" representation was a common characterization of the drunkard in popular culture – a representation that virtually ignored the social damage done by nearly a century of intemperance and sidestepped moral judgments altogether. It was a characterization that, in addition to W. C. Fields' film drunkards, was one that Thornton Wilder used effectively in his 1957 one-act comedy, *The Drunken Sisters*, in which Apollo tricks the Fates into getting drunk and making fools of themselves; one that served William Saroyan well in his revisionist representation of the mythical Kit Carson as a "cadger of drinks" in *The Time of Your Life* (1939); and was the basis of comedian Foster Brooks' popular stage and television persona, "the lovable lush," in the 1970s and 1980s. But the play in which this depiction coalesced and crystallized was Mary Chase's gentle comedy, *Harvey* (1944). In it, inebriate Elwood Dowd routinely drinks too much, after which he sees a giant rabbit beside him. Rather than being regarded as a deviant from dominant norms, however, Dowd, in the opinion of theatre historian Gerald Larson, is the person "society finally accepts with all his imperfections. He is friendly, curious, talkative, polite, without the aggressive habits of modern man. He is not sullen, he is not prejudiced, he would rather follow than lead. He is the one person in *Harvey* who has adjusted and adapted himself to his environment. One might say that *he's* not crazy, but everyone else is."[28] Possessing these twentieth-century traits, Larson continues, makes Dowd the "very antithesis of the conscience-stricken ruined wreck found in earlier 'morality' plays about drinking."[29]

Social historians note that such contradictory, even oppositional, attitudes within one form of cultural expression (temperance dramaturgy in this case) might be explained by the theory that "popular text[s] and performance[s] are sites of multiple, sometimes conflicting meanings, and that apprehension of [even a single] text involves multiple appropriations of it by different groups of viewers or readers for different purposes."[30] Some in the historical community openly embrace and endorse an even more confrontational cultural theory, finding that "every expressive act is embedded in a network of material practices," and regard tension and conflict as essential cultural catalysts, postulating a dialectical process of change in which one set of beliefs actively supplants another.[31] In such a "charged" atmosphere, as burlesque scholar Robert Allen has noted, frequently "popular entertainment becomes an arena for 'acting out' cultural...contestations and is exemplary of the complexities and ambiguities of this process."[32] As a powerful medium for the dissemination of ideas and opinions, the stage therefore becomes contested terrain, the site of ideological struggles through which nativist and middle-class temperance interests alike express their hostility toward working-class, under-class and ethnic drinkers who, in their turn, use the same medium for their responses.

Viewed in this context, plays in which the drunkard is presented in a positive manner – even as an attractive, loveable character – can be interpreted as a logical and necessary resistance to the containment efforts of the middle-class, "dry" hegemony. Thus, as lower-class and ethnic drinkers found themselves under an escalating assault on all fronts (the theatre included) from temperance activists, they found refuge in the antics of

characters like Fields' Eustace McGargle or the playful boozers in Locke's
The Drunkard's Daughter – happy-go-lucky, fun-loving drunks like those
with whom they associated in their neighborhood bars and who circulated
the message that the drinker was not necessarily evil.

Such challenges, negotiations with, or resistance to the dominant temperance ideology were hardly twentieth-century phenomena, as evidenced
by the fact that even Barnum's museum, a temperance stronghold, could
be invaded by subversive acts like "I Likes a Drop of Good Beer" sung in
1859 by Harry Pearson in *Fortune's Frolic*. While the nineteenth-century
representation of the inebriate as a loveable, even admirable, character remained far less common than the drunkard as social pariah and destroyer of
families, it was nevertheless written into some of the century's most appealing and durable stage personae. In 1878, at the height of WCTU activity
and influence, playwright/actor Ned Harrigan introduced audiences to one
of his most endearing and enduring characters, Ole Lavender, "a rogue as
sweet as the fragrant herb from which he takes his name."[33] As described
by Harrigan biographer, Richard Moody,

> the seedy and loveable reprobate, Ole Lavender, copied after an eccentric
> who had achieved celebrity on [New York's] Corlear's Hook, was one
> of Harrigan's finest portraits. His counterpoint might be found among
> the soggy inhabitants of any waterfront saloon, but few devout drunks
> could match Lavender's astonishing resistance to inebriation and to the
> deprivations of poverty. His elegant circumlocutions emerged in greater
> profusion with each dash of lubrication, and his natural dignity was unim-
> paired by his damaged top hat, his ragged frock coat, and his fingerless
> gloves.[34]

Given to "loquacious arrogance" and overblown pronouncements like
"[let us] pause to refresh the inner man with the nutriment which is dispensed by the connoisseur who presides over this cafe" (uttered as he made
a grand entrance into the dining room of Delmonico's elegant restaurant),
Ole Lavender, Moody continues, might well have been one of W. C. Fields'
boozy impersonations and most certainly would have been admired by
Fields. With little difficulty, you can hear Fields utter one of Ole Lavender's
most famous lines, "I've been imposed upon by water."[35]

As popular as Harrigan's "old soak" might have been in the last decades
of the nineteenth century, he hardly matched the audience appeal of Joseph
Jefferson's impersonation of Washington Irving's drunkard-hero, Rip Van
Winkle. Irving's "Sketch Book," completed in 1819, was first adapted to the

OLD LAVENDER

Figure 17. Ned Harrigan as Ole Lavender

stage in 1828 by "an Albanian" and debuted at the South Pearl Street Theatre in Albany, New York. The following year, Charles B. Parsons introduced his own version in Cincinnati and in 1829, William Chapman appeared as Rip at Philadelphia's Walnut Street Theatre. Thereafter, such noted actors as James H. Hackett and Sol Smith assumed the role of the loveable drunk.[36]

Figure 18. Joseph Jefferson as Rip Van Winkle

Jefferson first appeared in the play in 1850 when he played opposite his half-brother Charles Burke's Rip in Burke's dramatization of the story. He moved into the title role in 1865 and immediately began "tinkering" with the script, an activity that continued for the remainder of his life. The most extensive revision of the text took place shortly after he "inherited" the role of Rip. While on tour in England in June 1865, Jefferson contracted playwright Dion Boucicault to rewrite the play. Boucicault's adaptation was premiered at London's Adelphi Theatre later in 1865, played for 170 nights there and became the version that Jefferson played for the remainder of his career.[37]

From its inception, the Boucicault/Jefferson *Rip Van Winkle* aroused controversy and the ire of temperance activists. Not only did Jefferson and Boucicault refuse to idealize the rural setting of the piece, creating an environment as teeming with vice and corruption as any big city, but their protagonist, like Irving's original representation, was a confirmed drunk and was proud of it. Unlike the drunkards Edward Middleton in *The Drunkard* and Joe Morgan in *Ten Nights in a Bar-room*, however, Rip is not a mean, abusive drunk who dominates family life; rather, as his wife Gretchen testifies, he comes home drunk and "helplessly good-humored" and is so affable when "in his cups" that the village innocents – dogs and small children – follow him about. As one critic observed, "Rip's domestic vice turns out to be a charming peccadillo."[38]

Reformers were equally disturbed by the representation of the "voice of temperance" in the play. Despite her complaints that Rip's drinking is the cause of her poverty, Gretchen is hardly the meek, helpless, long-suffering wife of temperance dramaturgy. Rather, she is, in fact, the dominant figure in the family and browbeats Rip to the extent that he is afraid of her. Thus, the reformer of the piece is characterized as a shrew, a characterization that would gain popularity late in the century and would culminate in the twentieth-century stereotype of the temperance activist as busybody.

Jefferson's impersonation of Rip was especially problematical for temperance advocates because the text was what David Reynolds and others would regard as an "open" text. The play was not without pro-temperance messages. Rip does swear off alcohol; it is drinking that gets him turned out of his home in Act II; it is drinking with Hendrick Hudson and his men that results in the twenty-year nap that renders Rip "a stranger in a strange land"; and by end of play, Rip has ostensibly sworn off drinking. Yet, a pro-temperance stance is undermined by occurrences and statements that seemingly carry a pro-alcohol message. Immediately after his initial pledge that he "don't touch another drop," Rip takes a drink that he justifies with the disclaimer, "Well, I won't count this one"; during the obligatory reunion scene after Rip is restored to his family, Gretchen gives Rip her permission to "get tight as often as you please"; and Rip's final gesture of the play is to propose his famous toast, "Here's to your good health and your family's, and may they live long and prosper!" The latter was especially disturbing to reformers for, as Tom Scanlan has observed, the toast is "an emblem of the ambiguous action of the play as a whole," for while the words are an affirmation of family renewal, the drinking is "a gesture of irresponsibility."[39] Given such mixed messages embedded in their text, it is little wonder that Jefferson and Boucicault constantly argued about the "disagreeable" aspects of Rip's character and that temperance reformers repeatedly tried to convince Jefferson to revise Rip's character to conform with temperance orthodoxy.

In light of current theory, however, such apparent subversions of the "drunkard as moral leper" stereotype and the theory of "progress through oppositional struggle" may not conflate as neatly into full-scale anti-temperance readings of these two texts as cultural historians might wish. After all, the loveable drunk was loveable despite his drinking, not because of it. Furthermore, there is no record that the production of these texts was intended in any way to be anti-temperance; no indication that their authors harbored anti-temperance sentiments. The lack of such evidence exposes the problems of a position based solely upon theories of oppositional struggle and the hazards of using politicized terms and phrases like "appropriation" and "negotiation" that imply some sort of directed, volitional action. Just as popular cultural forms should not be viewed as "entirely the 'social control' of the ruling class," they should not be construed as "the 'class expression' of the dominated."[40]

In fact, a non-ideological reading is equally plausible here, for there is a likelihood that *Ole Lavender* and *Rip* were, in fact, examples of what John Fiske labels "producerly texts." The producerly text, Fiske argues,

> exposes, however reluctantly, the vulnerabilities, limitations, and weaknesses of its preferred meanings; it contains, while attempting to repress them, voices that contradict the ones it prefers; it has loose ends that escape its control, its meanings exceed its own power to discipline them, its gaps are wide enough for whole new texts to be produced in them – it is in a very real sense, beyond its own control...The social experience that determines the relevances that connect the textual to the social is beyond textual control.[41]

Unlike Barthes' "readerly text," which, like the majority of temperance dramas written during the nineteenth century, invites the reader/viewer to passively accept its meanings, the producerly text is open, devoid of set meanings and any sense of right and wrong, de-politicized. A producerly text, since it escapes control and manipulation by its producer immediately upon its creation, is consequently useless as a political tool, as an ideological weapon. In the final analysis, then, the question of whether playtexts like *Ole Lavender* and *Rip Van Winkle* were ideological or producerly is irresolvable. In the absence of evidence of the authors' involvement in anti-temperance activity or anti-temperance writing and lacking evidence of anti-temperance motives in the productions of these plays, the degree to which *Ole Lavender* and *Rip* were politicized, either in production or in reception, is impossible to assess.

There is no such problem in "reading" twentieth-century attitudes toward temperance classics – attitudes that resulted in the saddest chapter in the history of temperance dramaturgy. Even before Prohibition had been repealed, enterprising showmen capitalizing upon the national repudiation of temperance reform and the reformist mindset, targeted two temperance stage classics, *The Drunkard* and *Ten Nights in a Bar-room*, for ridicule. After decades of being consigned to the road and nearly disappearing from the theatrical landscape, both *Ten Nights in a Bar-room* and *The Drunkard* were once again produced in the "big city." The former was revived twice in New York during the waning years of prohibition: the first, by Kathleen Kirkwood at the Triangle Theatre in Greenwich Village in 1927; the second by Billy Bryant's Showboat Troupe at Broadway's Golden Theatre in January of 1932.

While the first production was "played by a sincere, serious cast, the lines and situations…[were] played with as much seriousness as seen by the fathers and grandfathers in a multitude of past productions, [and there were] solemn nods of righteous heads as wayward Willie Hammond is led astray and when the tavern of demon rum crashes about Simon Slade and his son, Frank," the same could hardly be said of Bryant's rendition.[42] In a curtain speech before his troupe – veterans of more than thirty years of performing on the Ohio and Mississippi Rivers – launched themselves into Pratt's play, Billy Bryant himself cued the audience as to what they might expect from his company and their production. He openly bragged that they were diehard "hams" and "bad actors"; that when they played *Hamlet*, they did away with the King and Queen and "no one missed them"; said that he would not blame the audience for walking out of the show since his troupe was "getting away with murder" and cheating them out of the price of admission; and concluded his good-natured, home-spun, self-deprecatory address by inviting the audience onto the stage (and into the Sickle and Sheaf set) during intermission to partake of beer and pretzels.

Predictably, Bryant's *Ten Nights in a Bar-room* was replete with a villain "made up with a burlesque red nose and huge black moustache," a rousing DT's scene (with "extra-long" snakes), egregious overacting and shameless appeals to the audience to "hiss the villain." Not content, however, with relying upon what were becoming stock devices for burlesquing nineteenth-century melodramas, Bryant hedged his bets by interpolating a

Figure 19. Broadside, Billy Bryant's showboat troupe production of Ten Nights in a Bar-room

corn-fed comedienne executing a bustle dance; a yokel playing "the Stars and Stripes Forever on the harmonica"; a Swiss bell ringer; and countless songs, including the latest hit, "Yip I Addy I Ay."[43] Even the villain, Harvey Green, was allowed a chance to sing, delivering a rendition of "She's More to Be Pitied Than Censured" and several other incidental tunes while he simultaneously led the innocent to ruin and death.

Like burlesques of other nineteenth-century classics (e.g., *Uncle Tom's Cabin*, *Rip Van Winkle*, *East Lynne*, *Human Hearts*), Bryant's *Ten Nights in a Bar-room* was popular with "sophisticated" twentieth-century audiences who regarded earlier progressive notions as absurd and even found in the death of Little Mary an occasion for "raucous laughter." To others, however, the production was self-indulgent, self-important and as "subtle as a threshing machine." In the words of one critic, it was "one of those smart and self-conscious betrayals of an old relic through which . . . the players leer knowingly at the audience to make sure that every one sees how aware they are of the absurdities in their silly old lines."[44]

The Drunkard, the second antebellum temperance classic to be revived in the twentieth century, received much the same treatment. After a celebrated revival at the Boston Museum in 1884 that featured Sol Smith Russell and William Seymour, the play was consigned to road companies. One of the earliest touring companies was headed by Artemus Ward and featured an actual drunkard in the drunkard's role. By 1920, however, after struggling for decades in the hinterlands and almost ceasing to exist, *The Drunkard* had been dismissed as a ridiculous sermon. It was revived briefly in 1926 by the Berkeley (California) Playhouse and four years later at New York's MacDougal Street Playhouse, a production that the critics "did not take seriously."

The first intentional spoof of the play was mounted at the American Music Hall in New York in 1934 and introduced the formula that would be applied to the text for years to come: "Drink beer and hiss the villain." Like Bryant's lampoon of *Ten Nights in a Bar-room*, which had been staged several blocks south in 1932, the producers, the Fifty-fifth Street Group, not only allowed, but encouraged beer drinking, smoking, munching of pretzels and vocal interaction with performers; acting was exaggerated and overblown; and the action of the play was "liberally augmented" by song. The tone of the evening was perhaps best captured by John Mason Brown, who wrote: "Of course making fun of antique melodramas is no longer the new sport that it once was. But for those who like to hear the songs of a bygone age and enjoy the irony of drinking beer in comfort at the same time they are laughing at a ridiculous sermon on the subject of a drunkard's degradation and redemption, this production at the American Music Hall offers a pleasant evening."[45]

Perhaps unbeknownst to the Fifty-fifth Street Group and their audiences, the same formula had been in practice for more than a year in California. In 1932, a company of amateur actors staged *The Drunkard* in Carmel. After the production closed, Galt Bell, one of the original actors, decided that a more professional production might have commercial potential, formed a professional company later to be known as the Los Angeles Players and on July 6, 1933 opened a new version of the play at the Palace Hotel in San Francisco. The initial run was scheduled for one week; the production lasted eight months. Convinced of the economic viability of his show, Bell moved the production to Los Angeles where, unable to find a suitable theatre in the downtown area, he was forced to rent an abandoned movie studio miles from the center of activity. This he renamed the Theatre Mart.

Considering the poor location, it is likely that Bell's venture would have failed had not the movie community discovered and adopted *The Drunkard*. Shortly after Bell opened his production, a contest developed among actors to determine who could see the show the most times. As a result, audiences at the Theatre Mart routinely found themselves seated near Mary Pickford, Edward G. Robinson, Harold Lloyd, Irene Dunn, Al Jolson, Ginger Rogers, Bing Crosby, Bob Hope, Earl Carroll, Joan Crawford, Billie Burke or Jimmy Durante. Before the end of his first year of operation, Bell's theatre had become a well-known tourist attraction for those who wanted to see stars of the stage and screen while they enjoyed a show and refreshments.

As more performers gravitated to the Theatre Mart, Bell realized another, tangential benefit. Given their natural propensity to perform and the informal, interactive, improvisational atmosphere Bell created, before long some of Hollywood's most celebrated performers were appearing impromptu in the olios at intermission and at the end of the play. It is a matter of record, for example, that Will Rogers, Fred Stone, and Olsen and Johnson took their turns on Bell's stage and, while there is no record of his having performed in an olio, W. C. Fields, who claimed to have seen *The Drunkard* twenty-seven times, conceivably may have been cajoled into juggling or recreating one of his cinematic personae on one of these occasions.

Like his New York counterparts, Bell's formula for success included eating, beer drinking, smoking, hissing the villain and cheering the hero. The latter responses quickly became codified so that when Mary Wilson was being threatened by Cribbs, audiences shouted "shame! shame!" and when Cribbs first attempted to convince Middleton to take a drink, in unison they exhorted, "Don't take it, boy." However, unlike performers in other burlesques of nineteenth-century dramas, Bell and his actors avoided over-acting or exaggeration of any sort, electing instead to "play it straight." In doing so, they quickly discovered that audiences considered the play funnier than if they had overplayed it. The seriousness of the company's acting also revealed a second truth; it highlighted the degree of the changes in the reception of temperance imperatives that had transpired during the course of a century.

Commenting on the nature of social change, John Fiske writes: "Changes at the level of the system itself, in whatever domain – that of law, of politics, of industry, of the family – occur only after the system has been eroded and weakened by the tactics of everyday life."[46] To this list Fiske might have added popular entertainment, for in no other human endeavor are themes and forms supplanted by new themes and forms more quickly. In light of this observation, it is amazing that the temperance drama held the stage for as long as it did, considering that, from the end of the nineteenth century on, temperance reform was eyed with increasing suspicion – as a set of restrictions upon individual liberty – and realism in both writing and production was rapidly gaining popularity while simultaneously melodrama was starting to look transparent, unsophisticated and unnecessarily sentimental.

Just as Repeal was a nullification of federal efforts to establish an "official morality," subversive performances (burlesqued versions of temperance classics and dramas that represented the drunkard sympathetically), occurring as they did near the end of Prohibition, represented the nation's emerging public repudiation of coercive reform and temperance extremists. In a larger sense, these performances were an acknowledgement of major societal changes taking place during the Depression; changes that saw a resurgence of individual liberty and the introduction of ethnic and labor groups, previously marginalized, into positions of political influence. As Mark Edward Lender and James Kirby Martin summarize it: these changes "flowed from the same evolution of social values that had finally brought Repeal. If increasing tolerance for individual freedom during the 1920s was a measure of broadened acceptance of a dawning pluralist culture in the United States, the election of 1932 (and with it Repeal) was emblematic of a dramatic shift away from neo-republican reform goals."[47] Such cultural shifts demanded immediate and significant reformulation of ideological stances and tactics; yet, in the face of such changes, temperance activists refused to abandon their "all-or-nothing posture" and either overlooked or ignored what many considered a new reality.[48]

It was in representing this new reality – a reality signaled by the emergence of a new perception of the root causes of intemperance – that post-Prohibition playwrights failed. Inexplicably, even in the face of scientific findings that documented the addictive potential of alcohol, late nineteenth- and early twentieth-century temperance dramatists continued to depict drinking either as an individual moral failing or as a social problem (the result of the proliferation of the saloon and, by extension, the liquor industry). Their ignorance of or refusal to embrace a modern definition of addiction put them out of touch with the more progressive and informed members of the reform community.

Before the term was applied to a physiological reaction to a particular substance, addiction had been a legal term used to describe a "performative act of bondage" and its adoption by the scientific and medical communities actually predated organized temperance reform by more than a century.[49] Historian Carol Steinsapir points to seventeenth-century laws in the colonies that prohibited the sale of liquor to "habitual drunkards," and concludes that these laws illustrated colonists' "belief that habitual drunkards were not capable of drinking in moderation."[50] However, the concept of addiction was not codified until the late eighteenth century when Dr. Benjamin Rush first publicly declared chronic drunkenness a disease. In 1784, in his *Inquiry into the Effects of Ardent Spirits Upon the Human Body and Mind*, Rush published the first recognized theory of addiction, arguing that the consumption of distilled beverages had "deleterious physiological effects" and warning that over time even moderate drinking could "undermine a drinker's constitution."[51] Although hardly a sophisticated theory of addiction by twenty-first century standards, Rush's findings nevertheless reflected a basic belief that both acute and chronic alcoholism would somehow result from continued drinking. For generations of physicians to follow, Rush had not only identified the addictive agent, but he accurately outlined the progress of the disease from its inception to its inevitable conclusion. Interestingly, Rush hardly mentions intemperance as a moral failing, stressing instead the physiological causes and the damage caused by alcohol.

Throughout the nineteenth century, the addiction theories of Rush, the English doctor Thomas Trotter and others found support within the medical community and by the Civil War even a segment of the temperance reform movement(s) had become aware of the physiological dimension of intemperance; but it was not until the efforts of Dr. Joseph E. Turner in the 1860s and the American Association for the Cure of Inebriates in the 1870s that addiction theory "evolved into concepts roughly comparable to those that [became] widely accepted in the last half of the twentieth century."[52]

From the outset, addiction presented problems for temperance reformers regardless of whether their principal strategy was moral suasion and their goal was the reclamation of drunkards or was coercion aimed at destroying the liquor industry and thereby removing the temptation to drinkers. While activists of both camps tacitly accepted some notion or other of addiction, which they characterized in political terms (i.e., liquor's capacity to "enslave" a drinker), they nevertheless retained a belief in the volitional nature of the drinker's habit. Proponents of moral suasion found it necessary to de-emphasize or even deny the physiologically addictive qualities of alcohol, for their tactical approach to intemperance required the drunkard to sign the pledge (the instrument by which one rejected alcohol), to voluntarily and immediately swear off drink forever and, through the exercise of will power, to refrain from drinking. In similar manner, prohibitionists needed to believe that drunkards could readily live without drink once the taverns had been closed and the liquor supply cut off. Both approaches, relying as they did upon the drinker's being able to survive without alcohol (or, in the case of the suasionists, to even willfully reject it), neatly skirted the issue of addiction and sought instead to deny the impossibility of an individual's simply walking away from drink; in other words, denied the existence of what we today regard as alcoholism.

While some temperance activists, albeit a minority, acknowledged addiction and physiological reactions to alcohol as the reason for a drunkard's "enslavement," temperance dramatists aligned themselves almost uniformly with the majority opinion and chose to avoid the issue altogether, opting instead for both a moral cause and either a moral or legal cure for intemperance. To a degree, they were constrained by their choice of art form, for as already noted, the moral reform drama was essentially the nineteenth-century morality play and consequently "right thinking," not medical intervention, was the necessary route to salvation. Writing within these conventions, most dramatists maintained belief in the free will of the drinker, claiming that he could quit at any time. Others, a distinct minority (but seemingly more realistic), appeared to be embracing addiction theory by stressing the danger of the "fatal first glass."

From a current perspective, neither was correct. While the exercise of free will might "save" a drinker early in the progression from moderate drinker to full-blown alcoholic, it alone seldom saved drunkards late in the development of the habit. Those targeting the fatal first glass, while more aware of liquor's addictive properties, chose to portray it as a "poison" that acted immediately, failed to acknowledge the progressive nature of alcoholism and consequently missed the opportunity to represent intemperance as a disease. Written by reformers, not scientists, physicians or even the more scientific-minded temperance activists, such characterizations were likely inevitable, given that as moralists they were more interested in the effects, rather than the causes, of drunkenness. It is little wonder, then, that the "redeemer," in a temperance drama was simply a man of "high moral character," not the family doctor or a scientist. And, it is little wonder that the promise of the "darker" late nineteenth-century temperance plays, those that dealt with the enslavement of the drinker, was never fulfilled.

After the repeal of Prohibition, this "oversight" immediately put what remained of temperance dramaturgy out of step with temperance ideology and activism. The emergent reform organization, Alcoholics Anonymous, the self-help support group begun in 1935 by two alcoholics, Robert G. Wilson and Dr. Robert Smith, combined Christian values and a suasionist approach with the belief that intemperance was a disease. The first of AA's famous Twelve Steps toward temperance, in fact, urges alcoholics to admit that they are "powerless over alcohol" and that they have lost control over their daily lives – both admissions of the addictive power of liquor. Although the same admissions – that alcoholism was a disease and that simply walking away from alcohol was no solution – underlay O'Neill's representation of the drunkards in *The Iceman Cometh* (1946) and Lillian Hellman's drawing of the "boozy" Birdie in *The Little Foxes* (1939), neither work sought to eradicate intemperance and hence neither was regarded as a temperance play. Nor was a concept of addiction incorporated into post-Prohibition temperance plays like Marion Wefer's *A Net is Cast* (1938). Instead, the portrayal of the drunkard as addict was ceded to films like Billy Wilder's *The Lost Weekend* (1945), *I'll Cry Tomorrow* (1955) and *The Days of Wine and Roses* (1962), that represented, not only the horrors of intemperance – the impact upon the drinker and his/her family – but the drunkard's struggle to "kick the habit." All three films, while incorporating stock temperance drama devices like the impact of the first glass, rousing DT's scenes (*I'll Cry Tomorrow* and *The Lost Weekend*) and a child's questioning when the drunken parent will "be coming home" (*The Days of Wine and Roses*), demonstrated their modernity by embracing addiction as the reason that drinkers were incapable of shedding their habit and by stressing that the public admission of addiction and membership in AA were the means to sobriety. These were issues that live theatre, in the few post-Prohibition temperance dramas written, nevertheless chose to ignore. By the end of the 1930s, the staged drama, as an effective weapon in the temperance arsenal, was dead.

It has been said that a culture is "defined by its tensions, which provide both the necessary tensile strength to keep the culture stable and operative and the dynamic force that may ultimately bring about change or complete structural collapse."[53] For nearly a century, temperance reformers actively and publicly participated in the cultural dynamics of America, pitting moralistic zeal against what they considered the most destructive by-products of industrialism: the urban environment, the bachelor subculture that emerged during the era of separate spheres and a liquor industry that constantly gained political strength from the 1820s onward – all social forces that either tacitly or overtly supported drinking. Facing formidable adversaries, temperance activists from the beginning of the nineteenth century to the end adopted any weapons that might aid their efforts. During their times of crisis, American reformers relied increasingly upon the American "drama's faith in historical process, and particularly in the superiority of the American experiment . . . the social equivalent of [the] belief that providence would reward the virtuous individual" to vividly represent the destructive capacity of alcohol, to legitimate their cause and to eradicate the scourge of intemperance. In doing so, reformers disseminated their warnings to a segment of the American populace that did not read tracts or attend lectures, and hence gave voice to that segment of the American populace that David Grimsted has labeled the "historically voiceless."[54]

Notes

Introduction: a complex causality of neglect

The title of this chapter was originally the title of an article by Joyce Flynn published in *American Quarterly* in March 1989 and is used here with her permission.

1. Although historians routinely refer to nineteenth-century temperance reform as if it were a monolithic, unified and continuous movement, temperance agitation was, more precisely, a series of related, interlocking movements often with different motives and often radically different cultural missions.

2. Jed Dannenbaum, *Drink and Disorder: Temperance Reform in Cincinnati from the Washingtonian Revival to the WCTU* (Urbana: University of Illinois Press, 1984), pp. 32–42; Susan Davis, *Parades and Power: Street Theatre in Nineteenth-Century Philadelphia* (Berkeley: University of California Press, 1986), pp. 147–53; Joseph R. Gusfield, "Status Conflicts and the Changing Ideologies of the American Temperance Movement," *Society, Culture and Drinking Patterns*, ed. David J. Pittman and Charles R. Snyder (New York: John Wiley & Sons, Inc., 1962), pp. 115–16; Jack S. Blocker, *American Temperance Movements: Cycles of Reform* (Boston: Twayne Publishers, 1989), pp. xi–xvi; Paul Johnson, "Drinking, Temperance and the Construction of Identity in 19th Century America," *Social Science Information* 25 (1986): 521–30.

3. Ian R. Tyrrell, *Sobering Up: From Temperance to Prohibition in Ante-bellum America, 1800–1860* (Westport, CT: Greenwood Press, 1979), pp. 3, 4.

4. Gusfield, "Status Conflicts," p. 101; W. J. Rorabaugh, *The Alcoholic Republic: An American Tradition* (Oxford: Oxford University Press, 1979), pp. ix–xi.

5. Susan Harris Smith, *American Drama: The Bastard Art* (New York: Cambridge University Press, 1997); Susan Harris Smith, "Generic Hegemony: American Drama and the Canon," *American Quarterly* 41 (March 1989): 112–22. Volume 11 of the 5th edition of the *Norton Anthology* (1998) lists five plays (*Long Day's Journey into Night* by Eugene O'Neill, *Death of a Salesman* by Arthur Miller, Tennessee Williams' *A Streetcar Named Desire*, *Glengarry Glen Ross* by David Mamet and Amiri Baraka's *Dutchman*), seemingly a slight improvement over the first edition. However, when the amount of space devoted to drama is considered, 254 pages of a two-volume work of over 5000 pages, theatre's presence remains insignificant.

6. Smith, "Generic Hegemony," p. 114; Joyce Flynn, "A Complex Causality of Neglect," *American Quarterly* 41 (March 1989): 124–25.

7. Flynn, "A Complex Causality," p. 124; David Grimsted, "Melodrama as the Voice of the Historically Voiceless," *Anonymous Americans: Explorations in Nineteenth-Century Social History*, ed. Tamara K. Hareven (Englewood-Cliffs, NJ: Prentice-Hall, 1971), pp. 80–98.

8. Elaine Hadley, *Melodramatic Tactics: Theatricalized Dissent in the English Marketplace, 1800–1885* (Stanford, CA: Stanford University Press, 1995), p. 2.

9. Thomas Postlewait, "From Melodrama to Realism: The Suspect History of American Drama," *Melodrama: The Cultural Emergence of a Genre*, ed. Michael Hays and Anastasia Nikolopoulou (New York: St. Martin's Press, 1996), pp. 39–60.

10. *Ibid.*, p. 50.

11. *Ibid.*, pp. 42–44.

12. *Ibid.*, p. 54.

13. Arthur Schlesinger, *The American as Reformer* (New York: Athenaeum, 1968), p. XIII.

14. Postlewait, "From Melodrama to Realism," p. 54.

15. This paragraph is a distillation of Peter Brooks' description of melodrama in *The Melodramatic Imagination* (New York: Columbia University Press, 1985), pp. ix–35.

16. Jim Davis, "Melodrama, Community and Ideology: London's Minor Theatres in the Nineteenth Century," Paper, Melodrama Conference, Institute of Education, London, 1992; Michael Hays, "To Delight and Discipline: Melodrama as Cultural Mediator," Paper, Melodrama Conference, Institute of Education, London, 1992.

17. See Rosemarie K. Bank, *Theatre Culture in America, 1825–1860* (New York: Cambridge University Press, 1997); Jeffrey D. Mason, *Melodrama and the Myth of America* (Bloomington: Indiana University Press, 1993); Elaine Hadley, *Melodramatic Tactics*; Bruce A. McConachie, *Melodramatic Formations: American Theatre & Society, 1820–1870* (Iowa City: University of Iowa Press, 1992). See also Bruce A. McConachie, "'The Theatre of the Mob': Apocalyptic Melodrama and Preindustrial Riots in Antebellum New York," *Theatre for Working-Class Audiences in the United States, 1830–1980*, ed. Bruce A. McConachie and Daniel Friedman (Westport, CT; Greenwood Press, 1985), pp. 17–46; Bruce A. McConachie, "American Theatre in Context, From the Beginnings to 1870," *Cambridge History of American Theatre*, vol. 1, ed. Don B. Wilmeth and Christopher Bigsby (Cambridge: Cambridge University Press, 1998), pp. 111–81. The definition of "melodramatic mode" cited in the text appears on the rear dust cover of Hadley's book.

18. Marvin Carlson, "He Never Should Bow Down to a Domineering Frown: Class Tensions and Nautical Melodrama," *Melodrama: The Cultural Emergence of a Genre*, ed. Michael Hays and Anastasia Nikolopoulou (New York: St. Martin's Press, 1996), p. 168.

19. Michael Hays and Anastasia Nikolopoulou, "Introduction," *Melodrama: The Cultural Emergence of a Genre*, ed. Michael Hays and Anastasia Nikolopoulou (New York: St. Martin's Press, 1996), p. viii.

20. Postlewait, "From Melodrama to Realism," p. 54.

21. Gerald M. Berkowitz, *American Drama of the Twentieth Century* (London: Longman, 1992), pp. 1, 2.

22. Postlewait, "From Melodrama to Realism," pp. 54–55.

23. Leo Stein cited in David E. Shi, *Facing Facts: Realism in American Thought and Culture, 1850–1920* (New York: Oxford University Press, 1995), p. 5.

24. Postlewait, "From Melodrama to Realism," p. 40.

25. John Gassner, *Dramatic Soundings: Evaluations and Retractions Culled from 30 Years of Dramatic Criticism*, Introduction and posthumous editing by Glenn Loney (New York: Crown Publishers, 1968), pp. 242–43.

26. *Ibid.*, pp. 243.

27. Raymond Williams, *Keywords: A Vocabulary of Culture and Society* (New York: Oxford University Press, 1976), pp. 243–45.

28. Schlesinger, *American as Reformer*, p. 12.

29. Eric F. Goldman, *Rendezvous with Destiny: A History of Modern American Reform* (New York: Ivan R. Dee, 1952), p. 75.

30. Steven Mintz, *Moralists & Modernizers: America's Pre-Civil War Reformers* (Baltimore: Johns Hopkins University Press, 1995), p. 156.

31. Raymond Williams, *Marxism and Literature* (Oxford: Oxford University Press, 1977), pp. 121–27.

32. Robert Crunden, *A Brief History of American Culture* (London: North Castle Books, 1996, p. 130; Williams, *Keywords*, pp. 243–45.

33. Richard Hofstadter, *The Age of Reform* (New York: Vintage Books, 1955), p. 5.

34. Peter Davis outlines the local color or scenic realism of the nineteenth century as follows: "For nineteenth-century playwrights and producers, realism was not some profound socio-political philosophy, but a technical device (and occasionally a literary diversion), used with great discretion only as allowed by a moralistic middle-class audience hungry for melodrama on American themes" ("The Dual Nature of American Theatre in the Late Nineteenth Century: Ibsenism Versus Realism," *Studies in Popular Culture* 9[1986]: 21). While it is certainly true that moralism often took precedence over "objective truth," it is also undeniable that *fin-de-siècle* plays also were making significant strides toward what critics label environmental determinism and an approximation of Taine's milieu.

35. For existing studies in the literature (most in the form of journal articles) of temperance entertainments see: Michael Booth's rather brief 1964 article in *The Dalhousie Review* ("The Drunkard's Progress: Nineteenth-century Temperance Drama"); Judith McArthur's 1989 article in the *Journal of the Early Republic* ("Demon Rum on the Boards: Temperance Melodrama and the Tradition of Antebellum Reform") which concentrates upon the playtext as social document and never involves itself with issues of performance; Jeffrey Mason's 1990 article on temperance drama in *Pacific Coast Philology* ("Poison it with Rum," his subsequent chapter on temperance and *The Drunkard* in his book *Melodrama and the Myth of America*, which deals predominantly with only one script; my articles in *The Journal of American Theatre and Drama* and *Performing Arts Resources* ("He Drank From the Poisoned Cup: Theatre, Culture and Temperance in Antebellum America," 1992; "Victims of the Bottle from Printed Page to Gilded Stage," 1991); a doctoral dissertation, "Beyond The Drunkard: American Temperance Drama Reexamined" by Ann Louise Ferguson (Indiana University, 1991); and a portion of a second dissertation, "'I'll Never Touch Another Drop": Images of Alcoholism and Temperance in

American Popular Culture, 1874-1920" by Joan L. Silverman (New York University, 1979).

36. Mason, *Melodrama and the Myth of America*, p. 61. It is important to note here that the majority of the records cited by Mason as proof of temperance societies' rejection of dramatic means to disseminate their message were written prior to 1845, before the full impact of Washingtonian reform was felt.

37. Mason, "Poison it with Rum," p. 97. Some scholars, Mason included, imply that, since temperance reform before 1845 had effected a reduction of per capita consumption of alcohol from a high of more than seven gallons in 1830 to less than two gallons in 1845, intemperance had ostensibly been eradicated. With the battle already won, Mason contends, temperance dramas, emerging as they did after 1844, would have had little impact upon an already teetotaling public. While Mason is correct in his assertions regarding the efficacy of the first cycle of temperance reform, which was accomplished largely by religious and/or spiritually motivated groups, he overlooks several crucial factors: (1) that temperance dramas sprang up at a time when temperance reform was moving out of the middle classes and into more democratic and inclusive movements, characteristics which practically defined the second cycle of temperance reform according to Jack Blocker; (2) American melodrama as the vehicle for narrating and conveying moral lessons was entering what was arguably its most formative and vital phase; (3) and lastly, that the target audience for domestic melodrama – a mixture of middle-class and working-class males – was nearly identical to that of the Washingtonians and the democratic fraternal societies that succeeded them. Rather than appearing *after* intemperance had been eradicated and when they might simply have affirmed "a vision that had already come true," the temperance melodramas of the 1840s and 1850s were poised to convey temperance ideology and solutions to newly arrived immigrants from Ireland, Germany and America's heartland, in emotional terms which they readily comprehended and at a time when the American theatre was expanding to accommodate larger audiences.

38. See Blocker, *American Temperance Movements*, for a description of the various cycles of reform in American temperance activism.

39. David S. Reynolds, *Beneath the American Renaissance: The Subversive Imagination in the Age of Emerson and Melville* (Cambridge, MA: Harvard University Press, 1988), p. 59. Reynolds credits historians Bruce Laurie and Sean Wilenz with dividing reformist attitudes and approaches into two separate groups – the rationalists and the evangelicals – who frequently manifested the same or similar objectives, but who disagreed, often violently, over ideology and tactics. (See *ibid.*, pp. 56–57.) Reynolds, in turn, divides reformers first into the Conventional and the Subversive and later, in *The Serpent in the Cup: Temperance in American Literature* (David Reynolds and Debra J. Rosenthal, eds. Amherst: University of Massachusetts Press, 1997) into the Conventional, the Dark Reformer, the Ironic and the Transcendental. For purposes of this study, Reynolds' original categories will suffice.

40. Reynolds, *Beneath the American Renaissance*, p. 55; Reynolds and Rosenthal, *Serpent in the Cup*, p. 23.

41. Russell Nye, *The Unembarrassed Muse* (New York; The Dial Press, 1970), p. 153.

42. *Spirit of the Times*, July 13, 1850; clipping, *The Drunkard's Daughter*, Billy Rose Theatre Collection, New York Library for the Performing Arts, Lincoln Center; Program,

Ten Nights in a Bar-room, Theatre Royal, Spring Garden, June 9, 1866, Harvard Theatre Collection; Reynolds and Rosenthal, *Serpent in the Cup*, p. 3.

43. Claire McGlinchee, *The First Decade of the Boston Museum* (Boston: Bruce Humphries, Inc., *c.* 1940), pp. 24–25; clipping, *The First & Last Pledge* and *One Cup More, or the Doom of the Drunkard*, Harvard Theatre Collection.

44. Van Wyck Brooks, "On Creating a Usable Past," cited in Russell J. Reising, *The Unusable Past* (New York: Metheun, 1986), p. 12.

45. The total influence of temperance dramas written during the 1840s and 1850s and produced professionally includes the countless touring productions of these plays that visited America's rural areas from the end of the Civil War to the early years of the twentieth century.

46. Those readers desiring a more detailed study of individual plays and/or an analysis of various structures, themes and characters employed by temperance playwrights should consult two dissertations: Ferguson, "Beyond *The Drunkard*, and Silverman, "'I'll Never Touch Another Drop."

47. Stuart Hall, "Deconstructing the Popular," *People's History And Socialist History*, ed. Raphael Samuel (London: Routledge, 1981), pp. 227–28.

Chapter 1: "He drank from the poisoned cup": temperance reform in nineteenth-century America

1. Abraham Lincoln, Temperance Address, Springfield, Illinois, February 22, 1842; Lee Benson, *The Concept of Jacksonian Democracy* (Princeton: Princeton University Press, 1961), p. 199; Rev. David Pickering, Pamphlet, *Effects of Intemperance: A Discourse*, 1827.

2. Bayard Rust Hall, *Something for Every Body: Gleaned in the Old Purchase, from Fields Often Reaped* (New York: D. Appleton, 1846), p. 126.

3. William Cobbett cited in Ronald G. Walters, *American Reformers: 1815–1860* (New York: Hill and Wang, 1978), p. 124.

4. Rorabaugh, *Alcoholic Republic*, p. 25; Diana Ross McCain, "The Temperance Movement," *Early American Life* (February 1993): 16; Tyrrell, *Sobering Up*, p. 7; Mark Edward Lender and James Kirby Martin, *Drinking in America* (New York: Free Press, 1987), pp. 9–10.

5. Lyman Beecher cited in Tyrrell, *Sobering Up*, p. 17; Lender and Martin, *Drinking in America*, p. 12.

6. Increase Mather, *Wo to Drunkards* (Cambridge, MA, np, 1673), p. 4; in 1708, Cotton Mather repeated his father's opinion, although he was considerably more disturbed by the increase in drunkenness around him (Rorabaugh, *Alcoholic Republic*, p. 30).

7. Joseph R. Gusfield, "Temperance, Status Control, and Mobility, 1826–1860," *Antebellum Reform*, ed. David Brion Davis (New York: Harper & Row, 1967), p. 123.

8. Lender and Martin, *Drinking in America*, pp. 9–11.

9. Thomas R. Pegram, *Battling Demon Rum: The Struggle for a Dry America: 1800–1933* (Chicago: Ivan R. Dee, 1998), pp. 8–9.

10. Tyrrell, *Sobering Up*, p. 18.

11. *Ibid.*, p. 21.

12. Lender and Martin, *Drinking in America*, pp. 13–15; McCain, "Temperance Movement," p. 16.

13. *Ibid.*, pp. 16–17.

14. David W. Conroy, *In Public Houses: Drink and the Revolution of Authority in Colonial Massachusetts* (Chapel Hill: University of North Carolina Press, 1995), p. 4.

15. *Ibid.*, p. 2.

16. Rorabaugh, *Alcoholic Republic*, p. 27.

17. Gusfield, "Status Conflicts," p. 104.

18. Gusfield, "Temperance, Status Control, and Mobility," pp. 121–22.

19. Rorabaugh, *Alcoholic Republic*, p. 27.

20. Peter Bailey, *Leisure and Class in Victorian England: Rational Recreation and the Contest for Control, 1830–1885* (London: Routledge & Kegan Paul, 1978), pp. 39–40; Rorabaugh, *Alcoholic Republic*, pp. 25–57; Joseph R. Gusfield, *Symbolic Crusade: Status Politics and the American Temperance Movement* (Urbana: University of Illinois Press, 1986), pp. 13–35.

21. Tyrrell, *Sobering Up*, p. 24.

22. Gusfield, "Temperance, Status Control, and Mobility," pp. 122–23.

23. For an examination of incest as a result of intemperance see Karen Sanchez-Eppler, "Temperance in the Bed of a Child: Incest and Social Order in Nineteenth-century America," *American Quarterly* 47 (March 1995): 1–33.

24. Blocker, *American Temperance Movements*, p. 10.

25. Warren in Tyrrell, *Sobering Up*, p. 41.

26. Benjamin Rush, *An Inquiry into the Effects of Ardent Spirits Upon the Human Body and Mind* (Exeter, NH: Printed for Josiah Richardson, 1819).

27. Walters, *American Reformers*, p. 125; Blocker, *American Temperance Movements*, p. 7.

28. Blocker, *American Temperance Movements*, p. 6; Rush, *An Inquiry*, p. 11. Rush estimated that over 4,000 lives were sacrificed to distilled beverages each year.

29. Tyrrell, *Sobering Up*, pp. 59–61; Rorabaugh, *Alcoholic Republic*, pp. 181–83; McCain, "Temperance Movement," p. 17.

30. Tyrrell, *Sobering Up*, p. 61.

31. The ATS, as a voluntary reform society, was anticipated by general reform societies like the Bethany Tract Society in Kentucky and the Connecticut Society for the Reformation of Morals and local temperance societies like the Massachusetts Society for the Suppression of Intemperance (MSSI).

32. Beecher in Pegram, *Battling Demon Rum*, p. 20.

33. Blocker, *American Temperance Movements*, pp. 12–13.

34. Justin Edwards in Pegram, *Battling Demon Rum*, p. 21.

35. For over a century, temperance reformers were portrayed, in Blocker's words, as "fearful conservatives disoriented by the rapid pace of social change in nineteenth-century America." More recently, however, through the vigorous rebuttals of Blocker, Tyrrell, Gusfield and others, a different perception has been created. As these historians emphasize, temperance reform from its inception attracted ambitious, progressive, upwardly mobile men and women who maintained a stake in America's future, welcomed cultural change and were likely to be actively involved in other reform movements (abolitionism, women's rights, prison reform, improved treatment of the insane). See Ian R. Tyrrell, "Temperance and Economic Change in the Antebellum

North," *Alcohol, Reform and Society: The Liquor Issue in Social Context*, ed. Jack S. Blocker (Westport, CT: Greenwood Press, 1979), pp. 45–63.

36. The phrase, "great unmasking," appears in Sean Wilentz, *Chants Democratic: New York City and the Rise of the American Working Class, 1788–1850* (New York: Oxford University Press, 1984), p. 146.

37. Blocker, *American Temperance Movements*, p. xv.

38. Johnson, "Drinking, Temperance and the Construction of Identity," p. 522.

39. Gusfield, *Symbolic Crusade*, p. 3.

40. Gusfield, "Temperance, Status Control, and Mobility," p. 129.

41. *Ibid.*, pp. 131–32.

42. Christine Stansell, *City of Women: Sex and Class in New York, 1789–1860* (Urbana: University of Illinois Press, 1987), p. 66.

43. The founders and original members of the Baltimore Washingtonians included: William K. Mitchell (merchant tailor); Archibald Campbell (silver plater); John H. Hoss (carpenter); James McCurley (coach maker); George Steers (wheelwright); and David Anderson (blacksmith). See Leonard U. Blumberg, with William L. Pittman, *Beware the First Drink: The Washington Temperance Movement and Alcoholics Anonymous* (Seattle: Glen Abbey Books, 1991), pp. 58–59.

44. Blocker, *American Temperance Movements*, pp. 39–44.

45. Unfortunately, the focus upon reforming drunkards alienated many of the so-called respectable temperance reformers at the same time it encouraged artisans to sign the pledge, thus exacerbating classism associated with temperance reform.

46. Tyrrell, *Sobering Up*, p. 163.

47. T. S. Arthur, *Temperance Tales, or Six Nights with the Washingtonians* (Philadelphia: Leary & Getz, 1848), p. 49.

48. The Washingtonian experience speech was designated a "charismatic situation" by Leonard Blumberg, *Beware the First Drink*, p. 89.

49. Ian R. Tyrrell, "Women and Temperance in Antebellum America," *Civil War History* 28 (June 1982): 131; Blocker, *American Temperance Movements*, pp. 18–20.

50. Jed Dannenbaum, "The Origins of Temperance Activism and Militancy Among American Women," *Journal of Social History* 15 (Winter 1981): 236–37.

51. Edwin Tardy, *Saved; or a Woman's Influence* (Clyde, OH: A. D. Ames, nd), p. 3.

52. Ruth M. Alexander, "'We Are Engaged as a Band of Sisters': Class and Domesticity in the Washington Temperance Movement, 1840–1850," *Journal of American History* 75 (October 1988): 770.

53. Dannenbaum, "The Origins of Temperance Activism," p. 236.

54. Ruth Bordin, *Woman and Temperance: The Quest for Power and Liberty, 1873–1900* (New Brunswick, NJ: Rutgers University Press, 1990), pp. xxiv–xxvi.

55. Tyrrell, "Women and Temperance," p. 138.

56. Donald Yacovone, "The Transformation of the Black Temperance Movement, 1827–1854: An Interpretation," *Journal of the Early Republic* 8 (Fall 1988): 283.

57. *Ibid.*, p. 286.

58. Italics mine. Frederick Douglass cited in *ibid.*, pp. 290–91.

59. Lender and Martin, *Drinking in America*, pp. 80–81; Mark Edward Lender, *Dictionary of American Temperance Biography* (Westport, CT: Greenwood Press, 1984), pp. 331–33.

60. Lender and Martin, *Drinking in America*, p. 113.

61. Maureen Dezell, *Irish America: Coming into Clover* (New York: Doubleday, 2001), p. 18.
62. *Ibid.*, pp. 117–18. In the dissemination and perpetuation of the drunken Paddy myth, the American stage played a significant role. On stage, as Maureen Dezell, points out, the Irishman was "Sambo with a shillelagh."
63. Rorabaugh, *Alcoholic Republic*, p. 214; Tyrrell, *Sobering Up*, pp. 5, 321.
64. See Stanley K. Schultz, "Temperance Reform in the Antebellum South: Social Control and Urban Order," *South Atlantic Quarterly* 83 (Summer 1984): 323–39; Douglas W. Carlson, "'Drinks He to his Own Undoing': Temperance Ideology in the Deep South," *Journal of the Early Republic* 18 (Winter 1998): 659–91; Blocker, *American Temperance Movements*, pp. 26–27.
65. Blocker, *American Temperance Movements*, p. 26.
66. Schultz, "'Drinks He to his Own Undoing,'" p. 333.
67. Blocker, *American Temperance Movements*, p. 48.
68. Pegram, *Battling Demon Rum*, p. 40.
69. Gary Cross, *A Social History of Leisure Since 1600* (State College, PA: Venture Publishing, Inc., 1990), p. 92.
70. Stansell, *City of Women*, p. 67; Cross, *Social History of Leisure*, p. 92.
71. George Ewing, *The Well-Tempered Lyre* (Dallas: Louisiana State University Press, 1977), p. 133.
72. Bailey, *Leisure and Class*, p. 60.
73. Tyler Anbinder, *Five Points: The 19th-Century New York City Neighborhood that Invented Tap Dance, Stole Elections, and Became the World's Most Notorious Slum* (New York: The Free Press, 2001), p. 232
74. Dannenbaum, "Temperance Activism and Militancy," p. 240.
75. *Ibid.*, pp. 242–44.
76. Jack S. Blocker, Jr., "Separate Paths: Suffragists and the Women's Temperance Crusade," *Signs* 10 (Spring 1985): 462.
77. Dannenbaum, "Temperance Activism and Militancy," p. 246.
78. Pegram, *Battling Demon Rum*, p. 66.
79. Bordin, *Woman and Temperance*, p. xiv.
80. *Ibid.*, p. xxiv.
81. For an assessment of the methods and impact of the Anti-Saloon League of America see: Richard Hamm, *Shaping the 18th Amendment: Temperance Reform, Legal Culture, and the Polity, 1880–1920* (Chapel Hill: University of North Carolina Press, 1995); Edward Behr, *Prohibition: Thirteen Years that Changed America* (New York: Arcade, 1996); and Pegram, *Battling Demon Rum*, pp. 85–135.
82. Pegram, *Battling Demon Rum*, p. 85.
83. Richard Hofstadter cited in *ibid.*, p. 167.
84. *Ibid.*, p. 85.

Chapter 2: "Nine-tenths of all kindness": literature, the theatre and the spirit of reform

1. Schlesinger, *American as Reformer*, p. 51.
2. Stephen Railton, *Authorship and Audience: Literary Performance in the American Renaissance* (Princeton: Princeton University Press, 1991), p. 4.

3. Henry Steele Commager, *The Era of Reform, 1830–1860* (Princeton: D. Van Nostrand Company, 1960), pp. 8–9.

4. *Ibid.*, p. 9.

5. Mintz, *Moralists & Modernizers*, p. xiii.

6. *Ibid.*, p. xiv.

7. *Ibid.*, pp. xiv–xvi; Walters, *American Reformers*, pp. 15–18.

8. Mintz, *Moralists & Modernizers*, pp. xiii–xvii; Paul Boyer, *Urban Masses and Moral Order in America, 1820–1920* (Cambridge, MA: Harvard University Press, 1978), pp. vii–3; Warren I. Susman, *Culture as History: The Transformation of American Society in the Twentieth Century* (New York: Pantheon Books, 1984), pp. 245–47.

9. Boyer, *Urban Masses*, p. viii.

10. Williams, *Keywords*, pp. 244.

11. Emerson cited in Schlesinger, *American as Reformer*, p. x.

12. Gunther Barth, *City People: The Rise of Modern City Culture in Nineteenth-Century America* (New York: Oxford University Press, 1980), p. 22.

13. While violence in the form of duels, gouging matches and lynchings was certainly pervasive in the hinterlands during the nineteenth century, as Herbert Asbury points out, it lacked the scale and the "specularity" of dozens of armed thugs waging war on Broadway in the mid-day sun. (See Herbert Asbury, *The Gangs of New York: An Informal History of the Underworld* [New York: Paragon House, 1990].)

14. Timothy J. Gilfoyle, *City of Eros: New York City, Prostitution and the Commercialization of Sex, 1790–1920* (New York: Norton, 1992), pp. 18, 29. See also Claudia Johnson, "That Guilty Third Tier: Prostitution in Nineteenth Century Theaters," *American Quarterly* 27 (December 1975): 575–84, and Rosemarie K. Bank, "Hustlers in the House: The Bowery Theatre as a Mode of Historical Information," *The American Stage*, ed. Ron Engle and Tice L. Miller (Cambridge: Cambridge University Press, 1993), pp. 47–64.

15. Mintz, *Moralists & Modernizers*, p.4; Hone in Boyer, *Urban Masses*, pp. 70, 76.

16. Walt Whitman, *New York Dissected* (New York: Rufus Rockwell Wilson, Inc., 1936), p. 140.

17. Mitford M. Mathews, ed., *A Dictionary of Americanisms* (Chicago: University of Chicago Press, 1956) defines a pocketbook dropper as a thief who drops a wallet containing counterfeit money with the intention of finding someone gullible enough to exchange the counterfeit for real money (p. 1269). The pocketbook drop was a popular swindle in antebellum America.

18. Hofstadter, *The Age of Reform*, p 24.

19. *Ibid.*, pp. 7, 23; Paul Johnstone, "Old Ideas Versus New Ideas in Farm Life," cited in *ibid.*, pp. 26, 39.

20. *Ibid.*, pp. 7, 23–24.

21. Susman, *Culture as History*, p. 245; Max Weber cited in *ibid.*, p. 246; Hofstadter, *Age of Reform*, pp. 38–46; Clifford Geertz, *The Interpretation of Cultures* (New York: Basic Books, 1973), p. 3.

22. See Rosemarie K. Bank, *Theatre Culture in America*, pp. 42–59.

23. Boyer, *Urban Masses*, pp. 70–74; Reynolds, *Beneath the American Renaissance*, pp. 59–82.

24. Reynolds, *Beneath the American Renaissance*, p. 7; Michael Denning, *Mechanic's Accents: Dime Novels and Working-Class Culture in America* (London: Verso, 1987), p. 87.

25. Reynolds, *Beneath the American Renaissance*, pp. 55, 59. According to Reynolds, subversive reformers were largely responsible for transforming a culture of morality into a culture of ambiguity.

26. Carroll Smith-Rosenberg, "Misprisoning Pamela: Representations of Gender and Class in Nineteenth-century America," *Michigan Quarterly Review* 26 (Winter 1987): 14.

27. *Ibid.*, p. 14.

28. Invariably it was a youth (either male or female) who was imperiled and threatened with moral ruin. "To early-nineteenth-century Americans, a person's moral character was not innate; it was something that had to be nurtured and shaped . . . Americans [harbored] the notion that human nature was capable of being molded like fresh clay" (Mintz, *Moralists & Modernizers*, pp. 13–14). Thus, a youth, whose moral character had not yet had the chance to mature, was in the most danger when exposed to the vices omnipresent in the modern city.

29. Walter J. Meserve, *An Outline History of American Drama* (New York: Feedback Theatre Books, 1994), 99–100; Gary Richardson, "Plays and Playwrights: 1800–1865," *Cambridge History of the American Theatre*, vol. 1, eds. Don B. Wilmeth and Christopher Bigsby (Cambridge: Cambridge University Press, 1998), pp. 289–93; and Peter Buckley, "Paratheatricals and Popular Stage Entertainments," *Cambridge History of the American Theatre*, vol. 1, eds. Don B. Wilmeth and Christopher Bigsby (Cambridge: Cambridge University Press, 1998), p. 466.

30. Although H. J. Conway, C. W. Taylor and Charles Townsend also adapted Stowe's novel for the stage, none of their versions can be classed as a moral reform melodrama.

31. Reynolds, *Beneath the American Renaissance*, pp. 76–77.

32. George C. D. Odell, *Annals of the New York Stage* (New York: Columbia University Press, 1927–41), vol. IV, pp. 600, 602, 678–79, 696; vol. V, pp. 322–23; Davis, *Parades and Power*, pp. 47–53; Nye, *Unembarrassed Muse*, pp. 153–54; Martin Meisel, *Realizations: Narrative, Pictorial, and Theatrical Arts in Nineteenth-century England* (Princeton: Princeton University Press, 1983), pp. 124–41; William M. Clark, "Ten Nights in a Bar-room," *American Heritage* 15 (June 1964): 14–7.

33. Reynolds and Rosenthal, *Serpent in the Cup*, p. 4.

34. Daniel C. Gerould, *American Melodrama* (New York: Performing Arts Journal Publications, 1983), p. 8; David Grimsted, *Melodrama Unveiled: American Theatre & Culture, 1800–1850* (Berkeley: University of California Press, 1968), p. 219; Hays and Nikolopoulou, "Introduction," *Melodrama*, p. viii.

35. John Marsh, *Journal of the American Temperance Union* (September 1842): 138.

36. McConachie, *Melodramatic Formations*, pp. 189–90.

37. *Ibid.*, p. 190.

38. Although ample evidence exists to indicate that women as well as men were intemperate, temperance propaganda routinely assigned the role of drunkard to the male and portrayed alcoholism in terms of a power struggle between the sexes.

39. Solon Robinson, *Hot Corn: Life Scenes in New York Illustrated* (New York: De Witt and Davenport, 1854), p. 113.

40. Rorabaugh, *Alcoholic Republic*, pp. 169–70.

41. Meade Minnigerode, *The Fabulous Forties, 1840–1850* (New York: G. P. Putnam's Sons, 1924), p. 113.

42. Wilentz, *Chants Democratic*, p. 309.

43. Mason, "Poison it with Rum," p. 98.

44. While it is customary to credit nineteenth-century women with possessing superior moral strength and suasionist powers, in actual fact, women were more often than not ineffective in limiting their husbands' drinking.

45. McConachie, *Melodramatic Formations*, p. 42.

46. Johnson, "Drinking, Temperance and the Construction of Identity," p. 524.

47. Rosemarie K. Bank, "Melodrama as a Social Document: Social Factors in the American Frontier Play," *Theatre Studies* 22 (1975–76): 42–49; Grimsted, *Melodrama Unveiled*, pp. 222–26; Gerould, *American Melodrama*, p. 9; McArthur, "Demon Rum on the Boards," pp. 517–40.

48. Blocker, *American Temperance Movements*, p. 10.

49. William W. Pratt, *Ten Nights in a Bar-Room* (New York: Samuel French, *c.* 1858), p. 13.

50. All of the citations in this paragraph are from Karen Halttunen, *Confidence Men and Painted Women: A Study of Middle-class Culture in America, 1830–1870* (New Haven: Yale University Press, 1982), pp. 9–10.

51. McArthur, "Demon Rum on the Boards," p. 535.

52. Charles H. Morton, *Three Years in a Man-trap* (Camden, NJ: New Republic Press, 1873), p. 14.

53. Thomas Morton, *Another Glass* (London: John Duncombe, *c.* 1848), p. 5; C. W. Taylor, *The Drunkard's Warning* (London: John Dicks, 1856), p. 9.

54. W. H. Smith, and "A Gentleman," *The Drunkard, or the Fallen Saved*, *Dramas from the American Theatre, 1762–1909*, ed. Richard Moody (Boston: Houghton Mifflin Company, 1969), p. 283.

55. Grimsted, *Melodrama Unveiled*, p. 181.

56. Nellie Bradley, *Marry No Man if He Drinks* (New York: J. N. Stearns, 1868), pp. 5–6.

57. Richard Hofstadter, *The Paranoid Style in American Politics and Other Essays* (Cambridge, MA: Harvard University Press, 1952), pp. 29–32; Bruce A. McConachie, "'The Theatre of the Mob': Apocalyptic Melodrama and Preindustrial Riots in Antebellum New York," in McConachie and Friedman, *Theatre for Working-Class Audiences*, p. 26.

58. For a detailed treatment of themes expressed in temperance dramas, see Ferguson, "Beyond *The Drunkard*," chapter 3.

59. Jon M. Kingsdale, "The 'Poor Man's Club': Social Functions of the Urban Working-Class Saloon," *American Quarterly* 25 (October 1973): 476.

60. John H. Allen, *The Fruits of the Wine Cup* (New York: Dick & Fitzgerald, *c.* 1858), p. 6.

Chapter 3: "Every odium within one word": early American temperance drama and British prototypes

1. Walter J. Meserve, *Heralds of Promise: The Drama of the American People in the Age of Jackson, 1829–1849* (Westport, CT: Greenwood Press, 1986), p. 151.

2. McConachie, *Melodramatic Formations*, p. 164.

3. Odell, *Annals*, vol. IV, p. 489. See also Victor Emeljanow, *Victorian Popular Dramatists* (Boston: Twayne Publishers, 1987), p. 28; Louis James, "'The Bottle with No Label': The Curious Case of British Temperance Melodrama," Paper, Melodrama Conference, Institute of Education, London, 1992, p. 3.

4. Douglas Jerrold, *Fifteen Years of a Drunkard's Life* (New York: Samuel French, Inc., nd), p. 9.

5. In the first scene, the following exchange between Franklin, the temperance spokesman, and Vernon's servant, Dognose, takes place:

> FRANKLIN: Some desperate efforts must yet be made to save [Vernon].
> DOGNOSE: I know but one sir – destroy all the vineyards – demolish all the distillers, and cry down the trade of brewer as wicked and unlawful. (p. 3)

Dognose's retort seems to pose the thesis that, since drunkards were incapable of resisting alcohol, direct, even legal intervention (i.e., prohibition) was required. In 1828, such a notion would have been radical, not only in society at large, but in temperance circles as well. Yet, Franklin's use of the word, "desperate," just one line before, indicates that Jerrold regarded these measures as extreme.

6. Michael Booth *et al.*, *The Revels History of Drama in English* (London: Methuen & Co. Ltd., 1975), vol. IV, p. 219. The authors, in what is perhaps an act of charity, excuse Pratt's "borrowing," theorizing that he was a "man who had seen or perhaps acted in the earlier play and could not forget it." Nevertheless, they continue to point out that many "quotations are . . . exact, and the two plays [were] . . . similar in other small points" (p. 219).

7. Ernest Reynolds, *Early Victorian Drama (1830–1870)* (Cambridge: W. Heffer & Sons, Limited, 1936), p. 12.

8. Raymond Williams, *Culture and Society: 1780–1950* (New York: Columbia University Press, 1983), p. 130.

9. Lilian Shiman, *Crusade Against Drink in Victorian England* (London: Macmillan, 1988), pp. 1–9; Brian Harrison, *Drink and the Victorians: The Temperance Question in England 1815–1872* (Pittsburgh: University of Pittsburgh Press, 1971), p. 47; Henry Carter, *The English Temperance Movement: A Study in Objectives* (London: The Epworth Press, 1933), pp. 15–26; Brian Harrison, "Drunkards and Reformers: Early Victorian Temperance Tracts," *History Today* 13 (March 1963): 178–85; Dawson Burns, *Temperance History: A Consecutive Narrative of the Rise, Development and Extension of the Temperance Reform*, 2 vols. (London: National Temperance Publication Depot, 1889), vol. I, pp. 24–88; Norman Longmate, *The Waterdrinkers: A History of Temperance* (London: Hamish Hamilton, 1968). For a detailed analysis of the evolution and cultural role of the pub, see Harrison's chapter on pubs in *The Victorian City: Images and Realities*, vol. I, ed. H. J. Dyos and Michael Wolff (London: Routledge & Kegan Paul, 1973), pp. 161–90.

10. Harrison, *Drink and the Victorians*, pp. 67–68.

11. Temperance reform was spread in much the same manner to Scotland, to both upper and lower regions of Canada, to Nova Scotia and New Brunswick, as well as to the West Indies.

12. E. P. Thompson, *The Making of the English Working Class* (New York: Vintage, 1966), pp. 401, 412. See also David Hempton, *Methodism and Politics in British Society 1750–1850* (London: Huchinson, 1984).

13. Thompson, *English Working Class*, p. 57–58. Ironically, Methodism may have played a role in creating the ambivalence found in much English and American temperance writing, the drama included. As Thompson points out: "The Methodist Satan is a disembodied force located somewhere in the psyche ... with the result that so long as [he] remained undefined and of no fixed class abode, Methodism condemned working people to a kind of moral civil war – between the chapel and the pub, the wicked and redeemed" (pp. 40, 46). A similar inability to locate moral fault – either in the drunkard or in some outside, free-floating evil – permeates temperance tracts, novels and dramas written before 1850 and remains one of the legacies of the early temperance years.

14. Patrick Colquhoun, *Treatise on the Police of the Metropolis* (1797), and *Observations and Facts Relative to Public Houses* (1796), and *Treatise on Indulgence* (1806) cited in Thompson, *English Working Class*, pp. 56–57.

15. Harrison, *Drink and the Victorians*, p. 23.

16. *The Temperance Advocate*, May 3, 1862. According to temperance legend, the term "teetotal" entered the vocabulary when, during a temperance meeting in the Cockpit in 1833, former drunkard Richard "Dicky" Turner stood to take the pledge and stuttered: "I'll have nowt to do wi' this moderation, botheration pledge; I'll be reet down and out tee-tee-total for ever and ever"; whereupon Joseph Livesey shouted "that shall be the name" and declared "teetotalism" to be synonymous with temperance (Longmate, *The Waterdrinkers*, 46).

17. Victor Emeljanow, *Victorian Popular Dramatists*, p. 22.

18. James, "The Bottle with No Label," p. 3. By 1840, Jerrold, unable to earn a living in the theatre and discouraged by the desperate economic position of the house playwright, turned full-time to journalism, editing a series of journals including *Douglas Jerrold's Shilling Magazine*, *Lloyd's Weekly Magazine*, *Douglas Jerrold's Weekly Magazine*, and the legendary *Punch*.

19. Raymond Williams, *Problems in Materialism and Culture* (London: Verso, 1980), pp. 134–35. According to his biographers, most notably Richard Kelley, Jerrold shared many ideas about social injustice, hypocrisy and self-aggrandizement with his friends Dickens and Thackeray, who wrote for Jerrold's journals. Some of Thackeray's most incendiary articles were published in *Punch*, which, according to Kelley, was so politically outspoken that it was banned in France and nearly barred from sale in the United States because of its vigorous attacks upon slavery. Throughout his publishing career, Jerrold continued to piously espouse liberal causes and to champion the "humbler classes," dedicating his *Illustrated Magazine* to "the masses," appealing to the "social and economic underdog" in *The Shilling Magazine*, supporting Lord John Russell and the Whigs because of their promise to "help the poor and oppressed of England," and keeping prices of his publications low so that the working man could afford them. To the end of his life, Jerrold's beliefs were those of a radical democrat. (Richard Kelley, ed., *Douglas Jerrold: The Best of Mr. Punch* (Knoxville: University of Tennessee Press, 1970), pp. 5–13.)

20. Review, *Figaro in London*, cited in Williams, *Problems in Materialism and Culture*, pp. 135–36.

21. Jim Davis, "Melodrama, Community and Ideology," p. 1; Michael Hays, "To Delight and Discipline," p. 6.

22. Hadley, *Melodramatic Tactics*, p. 3. Hadley also points out that during the early years of the nineteenth century, the term "drama" in England became virtually synonymous with melodrama.

23. Robin Estill, "The Factory Lad: Melodrama as Propaganda," *Theatre Quarterly* 1 (October-December 1971): 22. In this play, the protagonist commits the radical, even revolutionary, acts of smashing machines in the factory where he works and setting fire to the building.

24. Michael R. Booth, *English Plays of the Nineteenth Century*, 2 vols. (Oxford: Clarendon Press, 1969), vol. 1, p. 6.

25. Booth *et al.*, *The Revels History*, p. 33; Davis, "Melodrama, Community and Ideology, pp. 1–4; Hays, "To Delight and Discipline," pp. 3, 5, 8.

26. Jim Davis and Victor Emeljanow, "New Views of Cheap Theatres: Reconstructing the Nineteenth-Century Theatre Audience," *Theatre Survey* 39 (November 1998): 55; H. Barton Baker, *The History of the London Stage and its Famous Players (1576–1903)* (London: George Routledge and Sons, Limited, 1904), p. 419.

27. William Hazlitt, "The Minor Theatres," *London Magazine* (March 1820); Baker, *London Stage*, p. 399; Henry Mayhew, "The Vic Gallery," *Theatre Quarterly* 1 (October-December 1971): 11–12; Charles Mathews cited in Baker, *London Stage*, p. 399.

28. Davis, "Melodrama, Community and Ideology," p. 23.

29. Simon Shepard and Peter Womack, *English Drama: A Cultural History* (Oxford: Blackwell, 1996), p. 205.

30. Williams, *Problems in Materialism and Culture*, p. 137.

31. James, "The Bottle with No Label," pp. 5–7.

32. Walter Jerrold, *Douglas Jerrold: Dramatist and Wit*, 2 vols. (London: Hodder & Stoughton, 1914), vol. 1, p. 214.

33. James, "The Bottle with No Label," p. 7.

34. *Ibid.*, p. 2.

35. *Douglas Jerrold's Weekly Paper*, September 11, 1847, p. 141.

36. Blanchard Jerrold, *The Life of George Cruikshank* (Chincheley, England: Paul P. B. Minet, 1971), p. 254. "Signing the pledge," is used figuratively here to denote Cruikshank's publicly espousing the teetotal philosophy, for the artist himself denied having ever signed the pledge, claiming there was no need to do so since he had committed himself to total abstinence.

37. *Illustrated London News*, May 20, 1854, p. 465.

38. Jonathan Mayne, ed., "Some Foreign Caricaturists," *The Painter of Modern Life and Other Essays* (London: Phaidon, *c.* 1964), p. 189.

39. Michael Wynn Jones, *George Cruikshank: His Life and London* (London: Macmillan, 1978), p. 80.

40. Henry Fielding cited in M. Dorothy George, *Hogarth to Cruikshank: Social Change in Graphic Satire* (London: Allen Lane, The Penguin Press, 1967), p. 21.

41. For a prime example of Hogarth's use of telling detail in a single illustration see Plate III of *A Harlot's Progress, Her Apprehension by a Magistrate*. "On the wall her witch-masquerade costume with its birch broom suggests [the harlot] has sunk to ministering to perversions. The medicine shows that she is already tainted. She plays with a stolen watch as the cat plays at her feet ... The knot in the bed curtain is twisted into a monstrous face, her nightmare" (Jack Lindsay, *Hogarth: His Art and His World* (London: Hart-Davis, MacGibbon, 1977), p. 60).

42. Hogarth cited in George, *Hogarth to Cruikshank*, p. 21.

43. Meisel, *Realizations*, pp. 148–49. Meisel's study of the relationship between theatre and serial illustrations in the eighteenth and nineteenth centuries is clearly the most incisive and comprehensive, offering special insights into Hogarth's socially progressive graphic plates and both *The Bottle* and *The Drunkard's Children*.

44. Broadsides for *The Bottle*, the Theatre Collection, University of Bristol; Meisel, *Realizations*, pp. 125ff. The play at the Royal Pavilion was titled *The Bottle*; at the Standard it was *Our Bottle; Or, A Drunkard's Progress*; Pitt's drama was *The Bottle Bane; or, A Drunkard's Life*; while Barnett's version was titled *The Bottle and the Glass; or, The Drunkard's Progress, A Drama of Everyday Life*.

45. Broadsides for *The Bottle* at The City Theatre and the Victoria Theatre, Theatre Collection, University of Bristol.

46. Jerrold, *Cruikshank*, p. 250.

47. *Ibid.*; Meisel, *Realizations*, p. 130; Jones, *Cruikshank*, p. 86.

48. Jerrold, *Cruikshank*, p. 251.

49. Meisel, *Realizations*, p. 3.

50. Shepard and Womack, *English Drama*, p. 203.

51. Meisel, *Realizations*, p. 130.

52. *Ibid.*, p. 125.

53. *Ibid.*, p. 131.

54. *Ibid.*, p. 124.

55. James, "The Bottle with No Label," p. 9.

56. Davis, "Melodrama, Community and Ideology," p. 2.

57. Meisel, *Realizations*, pp. 132–33; James, "The Bottle with No Label," pp. 11–12.

58. *The Era*, July 2, 1848.

59. George Cruikshank, *The Drunkard's Children*, Plate 1, 1848.

60. Meisel, *Realizations*, p. 133.

61. *Ibid.*, p. 138; in Johnstone's play, the daughter, Mary Reckless, is spared from drowning. She jumps from the bridge, but is saved by Martin Merit, her intended.

62. Meisel, *Realizations*, pp. 138–39.

63. Charles Dickens, *The Examiner*, July 9, 1848, p. 436.

64. Charles Dickens cited in Jones, *Cruikshank*, p. 87.

65. When it was first published in England in 1852, *The Drunkard* was advertised as "A Domestic Drama of American Life adapted to the British stage by Thomas Haile Lacy." Inexplicably, though, there is no record of a license issued by the Lord Chamberlain's office until 1890.

66. Shiman, *Crusade Against Drink*, p. 145. In the novel, all three of the drunkard sons died early. Moulds, possibly influenced by the more redemptive melodramas, allowed

one of the dissolute sons to survive. A fourth drunkard, a nobleman who marries the industrialist's daughter, reforms only after he is shot in a duel into which he is drawn while drunk.

67. James, "The Bottle with No Label," p. 2; Meisel, *Realizations*, p. 131.
68. Hilary Evans and Mary Evans, *The Man Who Drew The Drunkard's Daughter: The Life and Art of George Cruikshank, 1792–1878* (London: Frederick Muller Limited, 1978), p. 11; *The Era*, July 23, 1848; Odell, *Annals*, vol. VI, p. 376.
69. Meisel, *Realizations*, p. 4.

Chapter 4: Reform comes to Broadway: temperance on America's mainstream stages

1. *Herald*, October 8, 1850; *Tribune*, October 8, 1850; *Spirit of the Times*, October 12, 1850.
2. Odell, *Annals*, vol. IV, p. 696.
3. *Ibid.*, vol. IV, pp. 600–01, 678–79, 696; vol. V, pp. 232–33.
4. Andrea Stulman Dennett, *Weird and Wonderful: The Dime Museum in America* (New York: New York University Press, 1997), p. 6. See also Bruce A. McConachie, "Museum Theatre and the Problem of Respectability for Mid-Century Urban Americans," *The American Stage*, ed. Ron Engle and Tice L. Miller (Cambridge: Cambridge University Press, 1993): 65–80.
5. Dennett, *Weird and Wonderful*, p. 6; McGlinchee, *The First Decade*; clipping, Harvard Theatre Collection.
6. Dennett, *Weird and Wonderful*, p. 27.
7. Compilation from obituaries, Harvard Theatre Collection.
8. *Ibid.*
9. Clipping, Harvard Theatre Collection.
10. Walter J. Meserve, *When Conscience Trod the Stage* (New York: Feedback Theatre Books, 1998), p. 50. Sadly and inexplicably, obituaries in major papers failed to mention Smith's role in creating and popularizing *The Drunkard*.
11. Clipping from *Boston Transcript*, Harvard Theatre Collection.
12. McGlinchee, *The First Decade*, p. 24.
13. Grimsted, *Melodrama Unveiled*, p. 229; Henry Steel Commager, *Theodore Parker* (Boston: Beacon Press, 1947), p. 87.
14. Clipping, Andover-Harvard Divinity School Library.
15. *Proceedings of a Meeting of Friends of Rev. John Pierpont and His Reply to the Charges of the Committee of Hollis Street Society* (Boston: S. N. Dickenson, 1839).
16. Abe C. Ravitz, "John Pierpont: Portrait of a Nineteenth Century Reformer," PhD dissertation, New York University, 1955, p. 214.
17. Bluford Adams, *E Pluribus Barnum: The Great Showman and US Popular Culture* (Minneapolis: University of Minnesota Press, 1997), p. 76.
18. Dennett, *Weird and Wonderful*, pp. 24–25.
19. *Ibid.*, p. 34. For a complete description of the adornments of the Moral Lecture Room, see *ibid.*, chapter 2.
20. In his autobiography, *Struggles and Triumphs; or Forty Years Recollections* (Buffalo, NY: The Courier Company, 1882), Barnum mentions his drinking problem only

once when he admits downing a full bottle of champagne at one sitting (p. 93). See also Bluford Adams, *E Pluribus Barnum*; Philip B. Kunhardt, Jr., Philip B. Kunhardt III and Peter W. Kunhardt, *P. T. Barnum: America's Greatest Showman* (New York: Knopf, 1995); Neil Harris, *Humbug: The Art of P. T. Barnum* (University of Chicago Press, 1973).

21. Dennett, *Weird and Wonderful*, p. 55.

22. Adams, *E Pluribus Barnum*, p. 121.

23. Howard Becker, *Outsiders: Studies in the Sociology of Deviance* (New York: Free Press, 1966), p. 148. Christine Stansell calls this phenomenon "benevolent entrepreneurialism" (*City of Women*, p. 67).

24. Lewis A. Erenberg, *Steppin' Out: New York Nightlife and the Transformation of American Culture, 1890–1930* (Westport, CT: Greenwood Press, 1981), pp. 68–69.

25. Smith, *The Drunkard*, p. 282.

26. *Ibid.*, p. 293.

27. Broadside for the Boston Museum, February 26, 1844, Harvard Theatre Collection; *The Drunkard*, p. 300.

28. Smith, *The Drunkard*, p. 307.

29. Mason, *Melodrama*, pp. 77, 207.

30. In his preface to *The Drunkard* in *Early American Drama* (Penguin 1997), Jeffrey Richards objects to Mason's theory, claiming that the play derives from the theatre, not the pulpit; but Walter Meserve aligns himself with Mason, noting: "Crusades by definition have a theatrical quality, and the pictures, pamphlets and platform lecturers who supported the temperance crusade tended to be spectacular, wisely in step with the melodramatic tendencies of the age and the form of entertainment the people enjoyed. Playwrights had only to transform narrative into dialogue and story into dramatic plot" (Meserve, *Heralds of Promise*, pp. 151–52). In this way, imperatives which had their origins in America's churches early in the nineteenth century found their way to its stages by mid-century.

31. Terry Eagleton, *The Ideology of the Aesthetic* (London: Blackwell, 1990), p. 28.

32. Smith, *The Drunkard*, p. 283.

33. Smith-Rosenberg, "Misprisoning Pamela," p. 20.

34. Dannenbaum, "The Origins of Temperance Activism," p. 236.

35. Adams, *E Pluribus Barnum*, p. 124.

36. Blocker cites 1851 as the first institutional no-license laws (in Ohio) and notes that there was a negligible difference between active participation in religion between the Washingtonians and no-license advocates (*American Temperance Movements*, pp. 48–53).

37. Stuart Blumin, *The Emergence of the Middle Class: Social Experience in the American City, 1760–1900* (New York: Cambridge University Press, 1989), p. 203.

38. *Ibid.*, p. 204.

39. *The Spirit of the Times*, July 13, 1850.

40. Clipping, Harvard Theatre Collection.

41. Program, Radcliff Theatre Production, nd, Harvard Theatre Collection.

42. Donald A. Koch, "Introduction," *Ten Nights in a Bar-Room, and What I saw There* (Cambridge, MA: Harvard University Press, 1964), p. vii; Mathews, ed., *Dictionary of Americanisms*, p. 377.

43. Gusfield, *Symbolic Crusade*, pp. 6–7.

44. *Ibid.*, pp. 6–7.
45. Blocker, *American Temperance Movements*, p. xv.
46. Francis Lauricella, Jr., "The Devil in Drink: Swedenborgianism in T. S. Arthur's *Ten Nights in a Bar-room*," *Perspectives in American History* 12 (1979): 359.
47. *Ibid.*, p. 354.
48. *Ibid.*, pp. 354–55.
49. Mary Noel, *Villains Galore: The Heyday of the Popular Story Weekly* (New York: The Macmillan Company, 1954), p. 249.
50. Lauricella, "Devil in Drink," pp. 366, 379.
51. McArthur, "Demon Rum," pp. 523–24. See also Pratt, *Ten Nights in a Bar-Room*; T. S. Arthur, *Ten Nights in a Bar-Room and What I Saw There* (Bedford, MA: Applewood Books, nd.).
52. Koch, "Introduction," *Ten Nights*, p. lxv.
53. *Ibid.*, p. lxiv.
54. Pratt, *Ten Nights*, p. 44.
55. Lauricella, "Devil in Drink," p. 382.
56. Mason, "Poison it with Rum," p. 99.
57. Lauricella, "Devil in Drink," pp. 371–72.
58. Clark, "Ten Nights," p. 15.
59. While Morton was undisputedly the playwright, the copyright was recorded in Arthur's name.
60. Morton, *Man-trap*, p. 6.
61. Arthur, *Man-trap*, p. 3.
62. Robinson, *Hot Corn*, iii.
63. McArthur, "Demon Rum," pp. 522–23.
64. Playbill, *Hot Corn* at Boston's National Theatre, Harvard Theatre Collection.
65. McArthur, "Demon Rum," p. 522.
66. Clipping, Billy Rose Theatre Collection, New York Library for the Performing Arts, Lincoln Center.
67. Playbill, Harvard Theatre Collection.
68. Contemporary accounts of *A Glance at New York* report that Mose was seen both on the stage and, in significant numbers, in the auditorium. This observation is supported by David L. Rinear, who notes that "Chanfrau's Mose involved the tri-partite phenomenon of an actual bowery b'hoy playing a fictitious bowery b'hoy to audiences composed largely of bowery b'hoys ("F. S. Chanfrau's Mose: The Rise and Fall of an Urban Folk-Hero," *Theatre Journal* 33 [May 1981]: 212).
69. Blocker, *American Temperance Movements*, p. 37.
70. An extensive three-year search of the major repositories in the United States, Great Britain and Canada failed to unearth an extant copy of *Hot Corn*. Likewise, a survey of playtexts published by Samuel French, Inc., Walter H. Baker & Co., Dick & Fitzgerald and Thomas Lacy, failed to yield a script. Given the extent of this search and the failure of previous scholars to find an extant script or even a record of publication, it is possible that none of the various versions of *Hot Corn* were ever published.
71. Taylor, *Drunkard's Warning*, p. 5.
72. Edmund Burke, *The Works of Edmund Burke*, vol. iv, ed., George Nichols (Boston: Little, Brown, and Company, 1866), pp. 192.

Chapter 5: "In the halls": temperance entertainments following the Civil War

1. Alan Trachtenberg, *The Incorporation of America: Culture & Society in the Gilded Age* (New York: Hill and Wang, 1982), pp. 3–6.
2. John W. Frick, "A Changing Theatre: New York and Beyond, 1870–1945," *The Cambridge History of American Theatre*, vol. II, ed. Don B. Wilmeth and Christopher Bigsby (Cambridge: Cambridge University Press, 1999), pp. 196–99.
3. Jack Poggi, *Theater in America: The Impact of Economic Forces, 1870–1967* (Ithaca, NY: Cornell University Press, 1966), p. 6.
4. Alfred Bernheim, *The Business of the Theatre* (New York: Actors' Equity Association, 1932), pp. 34–40.
5. Daniel Boorstin. *The Americans: The Democratic Experience* (New York: Random House, 1973). p. x.
6. For a complete description of "island communities" see Robert Wiebe, *The Search for Order, 1877–1920* (New York: Hill and Wang, 1967), chapter 3.
7. Harlow R. Hoyt, *Town Hall Tonight: Intimate Memories of the Grassroot Days of the American Theatre* (Englewood Cliffs, NJ: Prentice-Hall, Inc., 1955), p.76; William Lawrence Slout, *Theatre in a Tent: The Development of a Provincial Entertainment* (Bowling Green, OH: Bowling Green University Popular Press, 1972), pp. 17, 21.
8. Slout, *Theatre in a Tent*, p. 17.
9. *Ibid.*, pp. 21–22.
10. Peter Bailey, *Leisure and Class*, p. 47.
11. Jon Miller, posting to Alcohol and Temperance History Group listserv, November 14, 1999.
12. F. P. Dunnington, "Matters concerning the University Temperance Hall," Manuscript, University of Virginia Special Collections, 1895, p. 3.
13. *Ibid.*, p. 4.
14. Jim Baumohl, "On Asylums, Homes, and Moral Treatment: The Case of the San Francisco Home for the Care of the Inebriate, 1859–1870," *Contemporary Drug Problems* (Fall 1986): 406; Jim Baumohl, "Dashaways and Doctors: The Treatment of Habitual Drunkards in San Francisco from the Gold Rush to Prohibition," dissertation, University of California, Berkeley, 1966, p. 106.
15. Baumohl, "On Asylums," p. 406.
16. *Ibid.*, p. 407; Baumohl, "Dashaways and Doctors," pp. 106–07.
17. Blumberg, with Pitman, *Beware the First Drink*, pp. 65–66; *Baltimore American*, February 10, 1841; *Baltimore American*, July 30, 1841.
18. Clippings, Historical Society of Oak Park and River Forest.
19. Shiman, *Crusade Against Drink*, pp. 33–35, 111–12, 159–63.
20. Justin McCarthy, *An Irishman's Story* (New York: Grosset & Dunlap, Publishers, 1904), pp. 33–34.
21. Janet Noel, *Canada Dry: Temperance Crusades Before Confederation* (University of Toronto Press, 1994), p. 121.
22. Correspondence with Patrick O'Neill, November 2, 2001.
23. Bailey, *Leisure and Class*, pp. 35, 37.
24. Harrison, *Drink and the Victorians*, p. 95.
25. Bailey, *Leisure and Class*, pp. 36, 46.

26. Cross, *Social History of Leisure*, pp. 95, 20, 36.
27. Hugh Cunningham, *Leisure in the Industrial Revolution* (London: Croom Helm, 1980), p. 90.
28. *Ibid.*, p. 90.
29. Cooke Taylor cited in Cross, *Social History of Leisure*, p. 87.
30. Cross, *Social History of Leisure*, p. 95.
31. Cunningham, *Leisure in the Industrial Revolution*, p. 101.
32. Barbara Cohen-Stratyner, "Platform Pearls; or 19th Century American Performance Texts," *Performing Arts Resources* 16 (October 1991): 70.
33. Ewing, *Well-Tempered Lyre*, pp. 136, 154–55.
34. Cohen-Stratyner, "Platform Pearls," p. 70.
35. Blocker, *American Temperance Movements*, p. 20.
36. Cohen-Stratyner, "Platform Pearls," p. 70.
37. "The Drunkard's Child" in *The Variety Theatre Songster* (New York: Popular Publishing Co., nd).
38. Cohen-Stratyner, "Platform Pearls," pp 69–77; Wilentz, *Chants Democratic*, pp. 308–11.
39. Jean Stonehouse, "We Have Come From the Mountains," *New England Journal of History* 51 (1994): 60.
40. *Ibid.*, p. 64.
41. So attractive was temperance as a subject for song that it even attracted "America's troubadour," Stephen Collins Foster, who wrote "Comrades, Fill no Glass for Me" and collaborated on "Mr. and Mrs. Brown," a popular temperance tune of the 1860s. Sadly, even though he wrote on the temperance theme, Foster was a known drunkard at the time of his death (Ewing, *Well-Tempered Lyre*, p. 146).
42. *Ibid.*, pp. 193–94.
43. Ferguson, "Beyond *The Drunkard*," pp. 56, 68, 98, 257–58.
44. Silverman, "'I'll Never Touch Another Drop'," p 40.
45. *Ibid.*, pp. 40–41.
46. Lizzie May Elwyn, *Switched Off. A Temperance Farce* (Clyde, OH: A. D. Ames, 1899), Frontpiece.
47. William Comstock, *Rum; or, the First Glass. A Drama in Three Acts* (New York: Dewitt, 1875), p. 2.
48. Silverman, "'I'll Never Touch Another Drop'," p. 41.
49. Ferguson, "Beyond *The Drunkard*," pp. 263–64.
50. Bordin, *Woman and Temperance*, pp. 48, 167.
51. Ferguson, "Beyond *The Drunkard*," p. 263.
52. *Ibid.*, p. 263.
53. "Suppression of Impure Literature," *Minutes of the National W.C.T.U.*, 1887, p. lix.
54. "The Chief Aim [of Music]," *Minutes of the National W.C.T.U.*, 1886, p. xvii.
55. Mrs. Nellie M. Bradley and Mrs. E. A. Parkhurst, "Father's a Drunkard and Mother is Dead," *Woman in Sacred Song*, ed. Eva Munsou Smith (Boston: D. Lothrop & Company, 1885), pp. 600–02.
56. Bordin, *Woman and Temperance*, p. 101.
57. *Ibid.*, p. 101.

58. Ferguson, "Beyond *The Drunkard*," pp. 93, 148–50; Ida M. Buxton, *On to Victory* (Clyde, OH: A. D. Ames, 1887).

59. Silverman, "'I'll Never Touch Another Drop'," pp. 51–52; Effie W. Merriman, *The Drunkard's Family* (Chicago: Dramatic Publishing Company, 1898).

60. Ferguson, "Beyond *The Drunkard*," pp. 92, 147; Nellie Bradley, *A Temperance Picnic with the Old Woman Who Lived in the Shoe* (New York: The National Temperance Society and Publication House, 1888).

61. Bradley, *A Temperance Picnic*.

62. Frances Willard in Bordin, *Woman and Temperance*, p. 9.

63. S. E. Wilmer cited in Jessica Hester, "What's a Poor Girl to Do? Poverty, Whiteness, and Femininity on the Carolina Playmaker's Stage," Theatre Symposium, April 2002.

64. Silverman, "'I'll Never Touch Another Drop'," p. 43.

65. Julia Colman, *No King in America* (New York: The National Temperance Society and Publication House, 1888), pp. 7, 8.

66. Silverman, "'I'll Never Touch Another Drop'," p. 43.

67. Colman, *No King in America*, p. 18.

68. Colman, *ibid.*, p. 23.

69. Bradley, *Marry No Man If He Drinks*, p. 6.

70. Ferguson, "Beyond *The Drunkard*," p. 26.

71. William Winter, *The Life of David Belasco*. vol. 1 (New York: Moffat, Yard and Company, 1918), pp. 185–88.

72. Joseph Francis Daly, *The Life of Augustin Daly* (New York: The Macmillan Company, 1917), p. 309.

73. Winter, *The Life of David Belasco*, p. 187.

74. Joseph Daly cited in Louise Cheryl Mason, "The Fight to be an American Woman and a Playwright: A Critical History from 1773 to the Present," Dissertation, University of California – Berkeley, 1983, p. 122. According to Joseph Daly, his brother felt that

> *L'assommoir* [was] a disgusting piece: One prolonged sigh from first to last over the miseries of the poor; with a dialogue culled from the lowest slang, and tritest claptrap. It gave me no points that I could use; & the only novelty was in the *lavoir* scene where two wash-women (the heroine & her rival) throw pails full of warm water (actually) over each other & stand dripping before the audience. (Mason, "The Fight to be an American Woman," p. 122)

He, nevertheless, elected to produce it in America.

75. *Ibid.*, p. 123.

76. David Baguley, "Introduction," *Naturalist Documents/Documents Naturalistes* (London, Canada: Mestengo Press, 1991), p. 6.

77. *Ibid.*, p. 9.

78. *Ibid.*, p. 12.

79. *Ibid.*, p. 12.

80. *Ibid.*, pp. 13–14.

81. There is no explanation in the literature as to why *Drink* was first produced at the Princess' Theatre and not the Gaiety.

82. Baguley, "Introduction," pp. 22–23.

83. See David Mayer, "The Death of a Stage Actor: The Genesis of a Film," *Film History* 11 (1999): 342–52.

84. It is possible that Griffith saw Daly's adaptation of *Drink*, but considering that it was relatively short-lived and that the Reade/Warner production toured several times in the United States, it is more likely that he saw the British version.

85. Mayer, "Death of a Stage Actor," p. 344.

86. Graham King, *Garden of Zola* (London: Barrie & Jenkins Ltd., 1978), p. 119.

87. F. W. J. Hemmings, *The Life and Times of Emile Zola* (New York: Charles Scribner's Sons, 1977), p. 85.

88. Baguley, "Introduction," p. 9.

89. *Ibid.*, p. 10.

90. *Ibid.*, pp. 13, 15.

91. *Ibid.*, p. 21.

92. Grovsner Fattic, "A Few Sterling Pieces: Nineteenth Century Adventist Temperance Songs," *Adventist Heritage* 2 (1975): 35.

Chapter 6: Epilogue: "theatrical 'dry rot'?"; or what price the Anti-Saloon League?

1. Trachtenberg, *The Incorporation of America*, p. 5.

2. *Ibid.*

3. Lynn Dumenil, *Modern Temper: American Culture and Society in the 1920s* (New York: Hill and Wang, 1995), p. 6.

4. Crunden, *A Brief History of American Culture*, p. 129.

5. Susman, *Culture as History*, p. 273.

6. A. A. Roback cited in *ibid.*, p. 273. For full treatment of personality and the making of twentieth-century culture see *ibid.*, chapter 14.

7. *Ibid.*, p. 273.

8. Richard F. Hamm, *Shaping the 18th Amendment*, p. 4.

9. H. Elliot McBride, *As by Fire: A Temperance Drama in Five Acts* (Philadelphia: Penn Pub. Co., c. 1895).

10. While the dream sequence in *Drifting Apart* was one of the earliest examples of the device in American theatre history, it was not without precedent in the history of temperance dramaturgy. C.Z. Barnett had employed it more than forty years before in his version of *The Bottle*. It is unlikely, however, that Herne had seen or read Barnett's play as it was one of the more obscure adaptations of Cruikshank's serial graphic illustrations.

11. According to his wife, Herne's principal weakness was his love of past theatrical traditions and his affinity for theatrical effects.

12. Hamlin Garland, cited in John Perry, *James A. Herne: The American Ibsen* (Chicago: Nelson-Hall, 1978), p. 84.

13. *Ibid.*, p. 86.

14. Herbert J. Edwards and Julie A. Herne, *James A. Herne: The Rise of Realism in the American Drama* (Orono: University of Maine Press, 1964), p. 41.

15. Blocker, *American Temperance Movements*, p. 111.

16. Kevin Brownlow, *Behind the Mask of Innocence* (Berkeley: University of California Press, 1990.), p. 127.

17. Mary Grey Peck in *ibid.*, p. 111.

18. Richard Schickel, *D. W. Griffith: An American Life* (New York: Simon and Schuster, 1984), pp. 182, 560–70, 572; Robert M. Henderson, *D. W. Griffith: His Life and Work* (New York: Oxford University Press, 1972), pp. 275–79. Joan L. Silverman believes that even *The Birth of A Nation* was prohibition propaganda that preached that unless liquor was banned, the country would be overrun by drunken African-Americans. In addition to the South Carolina legislature scene which depicted African-American representatives openly drinking while allegedly conducting state business, Griffith shows the mulatto villain Silas Lynch swigging from a champagne bottle; the "renegade" Gus hides in White-arm Joe's gin mill (an African-American bar) after killing Flora Cameron, the Little Colonel's sister; and the "good" African-Americans are portrayed as always sober. Silverman also points to the fact that in *The Clansman*, the novel from which the film was adapted, the author almost never used the word "Negro" without prefacing it with the adjective "drunken." See Joan Silverman, "*The Birth of a Nation*: Prohibition Propaganda," *Southern Quarterly* 19 (1981): 23–30.

19. A. Nicholas Vardac, *Stage to Screen: Theatrical Method from Garrick to Griffith* (New York: Da Capo Press., 1949), p. 202; Richard J. Meyer, "The Films of David Wark Griffith: The Development of Themes and Techniques in Forty-two of his Films," *Focus on D. W. Griffith*, ed. Harry M. Geduld (Englewood Cliffs, NJ: Prentice-Hall, Inc., 1971), p. 110.

20. Schickel, *Griffith: An American Life*, p. 560.

21. Gusfield, *Symbolic Crusade*, p. 99; Herbert Gutman and Roy Rosenzweig cited in Pegram, *Battling Demon Rum*, p. 88.

22. Gusfield, *Symbolic Crusade*, p. 99.

23. For an explanation of "cultural lag" in the nineteenth-century melodrama see Bank, "Melodrama as a Social Document," pp. 42–9.

24. Todd, *Arthur Eustace*, p. 4.

25. Charles H. Hoyt, *A Temperance Town, Dramas from the American Theatre, 1762–1909*, ed. Richard Moody (Boston: Houghton Mifflin Company, 1969), p. 645.

26. In a preface to *A Temperance Town*, Hoyt stated that his play was "intended to be a more or less truthful presentation of certain phases and incidents of life, relating to the sale and use of liquor, in a small village in a prohibition state. The author has endeavored to give all sides a fair show. But he is quite willing to be classed as protesting against the prohibitory laws of Vermont, where a man named Kibling is now serving a sentence of something like sixty years for selling about seven hundred glasses of liquor (less than most of our respectable city hotels sell in a day)." "Five Plays by Charles H. Hoyt," *America's Lost Plays*, ed. Douglas L. Hunt (Bloomington: Indiana University Press, 1940), p. 149.

27. Edward Locke, *The Drunkard's Daughter* (np: *c.* 1905), p. 11.

28. Gerald Larson, "From *Ten Nights* to *Harvey*. Drinking on the American Stage," *Western Humanities Review* 10 (1956): 390.

29. *Ibid.*

30. Robert C. Allen, *Horrible Prettiness: Burlesque and American Culture* (Chapel Hill: University of North Carolina Press, 1991), p. 28.

31. H. Aram Vesser, *The New Historicism* (New York: Routledge, 1989), p. xi.

32. Allen, *Horrible Prettiness*, p. 27.

33. Richard Moody, *Ned Harrigan: From Corlear's Hook to Herald Square* (Chicago: Nelson-Hall, 1980), p. 79.

34. *Ibid.*, pp. 78–79; E. J. Kahn, *The Merry Partners: The Age and Stage of Harrigan & Hart* (New York: Random House, 1955), pp. 267–69.

35. Kahn, *The Merry Partners*, p. 268.

36. This brief history is excerpted from Montrose Moses' introduction to the play in Moses, ed., *Representative Plays by American Dramatists* (New York: Benjamin Blom, Inc., 1964).

37. Stephen Johnson, "Evaluating Early Film as a Document of Theatre History: The 1896 Footage of Joseph Jefferson's *Rip Van Winkle*," *Nineteenth Century Theatre* 20 (Winter 1992): 101–22; Stephen Johnson, "Joseph Jefferson's *Rip Van Winkle*," *The Drama Review* 26 (Spring 1982): 3–20.

38. Tom Scanlan. "The Domestication of Rip Van Winkle: Joe Jefferson's Play as Prologue to Modern American Drama," *The Virginia Quarterly Review* 50 (1974): 56.

39. *Ibid.*, pp. 55–56.

40. Eric Lott, "The Seeming Counterfeit: Racial Politics and Blackface Minstrelsy," unpublished paper, p. 5; Gareth Stedman Jones, "Class Expression Versus Social Control? A Critique of Recent Trends in the Social History of 'Leisure'," in Gareth Stedman Jones, *Languages of Class: Studies in English Working Class History, 1832–1982* (New York: Cambridge University Press, 1983), pp. 76–89.

41. John Fiske, *Understanding Popular Culture* (London: Routledge, 1989), p. 104.

42. *The Herald Tribune*, March 29, 1928.

43. Clipping, "Ten Nights in a Bar-room," Harvard Theatre Collection.

44. Clipping, "Ten Nights in a Bar-room," Theatre Collection, Museum of the City of New York.

45. Clipping, "The Drunkard," Theatre Collection, Museum of the City of New York.

46. Fiske, *Understanding Popular Culture*, p. 20.

47. Lender and Martin, *Drinking in America*, p. 172.

48. *Ibid.*, p. 167.

49. Michael Warner, "Whitman Drunk," *Breaking Bounds: Whitman and American Cultural Studies*, ed. Betsy Erkkila and Jay Grossman. New York: Oxford University Press, 1996, p. 32.

50. Carol Steinsapir in Blocker, *American Temperance Movements*, p. 7; Warner, "Whitman Drunk," p. 32.

51. Blocker, *American Temperance Movements*, p. 7.

52. Lender and Martin, *Drinking in America*, p. 120.

53. Susman, *Culture as History*, p. 288.

54. Grimsted, "Historically Voiceless"; Grimsted, *Melodrama Unveiled*, p. 224.

Appendix: nineteenth-century temperance plays

Adkisson, Noble. *Ruined by Drink . . . in four acts.* New York: Samuel French, Inc., 1889.
   The Wages of Sin. A Temperance Drama in Three Acts. Sulpher Springs, Texas: N. Adkisson, 1888.
Allen, John Henry. *The Fruits of the Wine Cup.* New York: Dick & Fitzgerald, c. 1858.
Ames, A. D. *Wrecked.* Clyde, Ohio: A. D. Ames, c. 1877.
Anon. *Another Glass; or The Horrors of Intemperance,* n.p., 1845.
Anon. *The Drunkard's Home.* np., c. 1847.
Anon. *The Power of the Pledge, a Sequel to The Bottle.* New York: Oliver & Brother, 1848.
Anon. *Signing the Pledge.* Philadelphia: P. Garrett, 1887.
Anon. *Stanhope; or, by Hook or by Crook.* Ypsilanti, MI: The Band of Hope, 1882.
Anon. *The Wine Cup; or, Saved at Last.* New York: Happy Hours Company, 1876.
Arnold, Laura C. *Sauce for the Goose.* Columbus, IN: Democrat Office, 1880.
Arthur, T. S. *Ten Nights in a Bar-Room and What I Saw There.* Bedford, MA: Applewood Books, nd.
   Three Years in a Man-trap. Philadelphia: Hubbard Brothers, 1888.
Babcock, Charles W. *Adrift. A Temperance Drama in Three Acts . . . to which is added, a description of costumes, characters, entrances and exits; with the stage business carefully marked.* Clyde, OH: A. D. Ames, 1880.
Baker, George Melville. *A Drop Too Much.* Boston: Lee & Shepard, 1866.
   The Flowing Bowl. Boston: W. H. Baker Co., 1885.
   Handy Dramas for Amateur Actors. New Pieces for Home, School and Public Entertainment. [Includes The Flower of the Family, A Mysterious Disappearance, The Little Brown Jug], np., nd.
   The Last Loaf. Boston: W. H. Baker Co., 1898.
   The Little Brown Jug. Boston: W. H. Baker Co., 1876.
   A Little More Cider. Boston: Lee & Shepard, 1870.
   The Man with the Demijohn. Boston: W. H. Baker Co., 1876.
   Past Redemption. Boston: Lee & Shepard, 1875.
   Seeing the Elephant. Boston: Lee & Shepard, 1874.
   The Temperance Drama: A Series of Dramas, Comedies and Farces for Temperance Exhibitions and Home and School Entertainment. Boston: Lee & Shepard, Publishers, 1874.

The Tempter; or, The Sailor's Return. Boston: W. H. Baker Co., 1894.

We're All Teetotalers. Boston: W. H. Baker Co., 1866.

Barnett, C. Z. *The Bottle*. np. Produced 1847.

Booth, George H. *The Drunkard's Dream*. Springfield, MA: Clark W. Bryan & Co., 1872.

Boucicault, Dion. *Drink*. Typescript, Sherman Collection, Southern Illinois University, c. 1874.

Bradley, Nellie. *The Bridal Wine Cup* in *Dramatic Leaflets: Comprising Original and Selected Plays for Amateur Clubs, Parlor Theatricals, Temperance Societies, Church Entertainments, Exhibitions, Sociables, Etc*. Philadelphia: P. Garrett & Co., c. 1887.

The First Glass; or the Power of a Woman's Influence. New York: J. N. Stearns, 1868.

Having Fun. New York: The National Temperance Society and Publication House, 1883.

Marry No Man If He Drinks. New York: J. N. Stearns, 1868.

Reclaimed, or the Danger of Moderate Drinking. Rockland, ME: Z. Pope Vose, 1868.

The Stumbling Block, or Why the Deacon Gave Up his Wine. Rockland, ME: Z. Pope Vose, 1871.

A Temperance Picnic with the Old Woman Who Lived in the Shoe. New York: The National Temperance Society and Publication House, 1888.

Wine as a Medicine, or Abbie's Experience. Rockland, ME: Z. Pope Vose, 1873.

The Young Teetotaler or Saved at Last. Rockland, ME: Z. Pope Vose, c. 1867.

Brown, Charles P. and G. Tompkins. *A Glass of Wine. An Emotional Temperance Drama in Five Acts*. Brooklyn, NY: Brown & Tompkins, 1877.

Burleigh, George S. *The Conqueror Conquered* in *Dramatic Leaflets*. Philadelphia: P. Garrett, c. 1887.

The Evening Party in *The Temperance School Dialogues. A Collection of Dramatic and Effective Dialogues Calculated to Show the Evils of Intemperance; Designed for the Use of Temperance Societies, District Lodges, and all Interested in Temperance*. New York, H. J. Wehman, 1892.

Eyes and No Eyes in *The Temperance School Dialogues*. New York, H. J. Wehman, 1892.

First and Last in *The Temperance School Dialogues*. New York, H. J. Wehman, 1892.

Buxton, Ida M. *On to Victory*. Clyde, OH: A. D. Ames, 1887.

Our Awful Aunt. Clyde, OH: A. D. Ames, 1885.

Carswell, Edward. *Mind Your Business*. New York: The National Temperance Society and Publication House, 1884.

Chellis, Mary Dwinell. *Which Will You Choose?* Rockland, ME: Z. Pope Vose, 1869.

Colman, Julia. *No King in America*. New York: The National Temperance Society and Publication House, 1888.

Comstock, William. *Rum; or, the First Glass. A Drama in Three Acts*. New York: Dewitt, 1875.

Conway, H. J. *Hot Corn*. np. Produced 1854.

Cook, S. N. *Broken Promises ... in Five Acts*. New York: Happy Hours Company, 1879.

A Cure for a Bad Appetite in *The Temperance School Dialogues*. New York, H. J. Wehman, 1892.

Out in the Streets. New York: Dick & Fitzgerald, nd.

Courtney J. *Life: Founded on The Drunkard's Children*. np. Produced 1848.

Cowper, Will C. *Redemption*. np., 1898.

Cutler, F. L. *Lost! Or, the Fruits of the Glass*. Clyde, OH: A. D. Ames, 1882.

Daly, Augustin. *Drink*. np. produced 1879.

Delafield, John H. *The Last Drop*. New York: Happy Hours Company, 1876.

Denison, Thomas Stewart. *Hard Cider: A Temperance Sketch*. Chicago: T. S. Denison, c. 1880.

    Only Cold Tea. Chicago: T. S. Denison, c. 1895.

    The Sparkling Cup. Chicago: T. S. Denison, 1877.

Denton, Clara Janetta Fort. *The Drunkard's Home*, np., nd.

Dunn, E. C. *Lost*. Rockford, IL: Register Co., 1877.

    A Temperance Drama in Five Acts. Rockford, IL: E. C. Dunn, 1877.

Durivage, John E. *Hot Corn; Life Scenes of New York*, np., 1854.

Elwyn, Lizzie May. *Dot, the Miner's Daughter, Or One Glass of Wine*. Clyde, OH: A. D. Ames, 1899.

    Switched Off. A Temperance Farce. Clyde, OH: A. D. Ames, 1899.

English, Thomas Dunn. *The Doom of the Drinker*, np., 1844.

Fowle, William Bentley. *The Tear*. Boston: Morris Cotton, 1857.

Gilbert, Clayton H. *A Glass of Double X* in *The Temperance School Dialogues*. New York, H. J. Wehman, 1892.

    Rescued; an Original Temperance Drama. Clyde, OH: A. D. Ames, 1874.

Greenley, Jay. *The Three Drunkards*. New Albany, IN: np., 1858.

Heege, Phillip A. *One Month Married; or, Does He Drink?*, np., nd.

Herne, James A. *Drifting Apart* in *The Early Plays of James A. Herne*. Princeton, NJ: Princeton University Press, 1940.

Hill, F. S. *The Six Degrees of Crime; or Wine, Women, Gambling, Theft, Murder and the Scaffold*. Boston: Wm. V. Spencer, 1856.

Hotchkiss, Zort P. *The Good Templars' Drama of Saved, written expressly for the I[nternational] O[rganization] of G[ood] T[emplars]... and presented in "faith, hope and charity."* Richmond, IN: Telegraph Steam Printing Co., 1874.

Howe, William Oscar. *The Drunkard's Dream; or, The Spirit of 1876. A Moral Domestic Drama in Five Acts and Six Tableaux*. Fitchberg, MA: Sentinel Printing Co., 1876.

Hoyt, Charles H. *A Temperance Town. Dramas from the American Theatre, 1762–1909*, ed. Richard Moody. Boston: Houghton Mifflin Company, 1969.

Jerrold, Douglas. *The Devil's Ducat, or the Gift of Mammon*. London: John Cumberland, 1830.

    Fifteen Years of a Drunkard's Life. New York: Samuel French, Inc., nd.

    The Rent Day. New York and London: Samuel French, Inc. c. 1832.

Johnston, Robert. *Rum; or The Crusade of Temperance... in Four Acts*. Philadelphia: R. Johnston, 1874.

Johnstone, J. B. *The Drunkard's Children*. London: Samuel French, Inc., 1848.

Jones, William A. *The Drunkard's Home, his Cruelty, his Eccentricities, his Reflection, his Remorse, and Reformation*. Self-printed, 1895.

Kidder, John. *The Drama of the Earth*. New York: Adolphus Ranney, 1857.

Landis, Simon M. *Dick Shaw, the Fiend.* Detroit: Edna Powell Landis, 1888.

Latour, H. J. *True Wealth; a Temperance Drama in Four Scenes.* New York: The National Temperance Society and Publication House, 1889.

Linn, J. Henry. *The Fatal Step; or, Whiskey Unmasked.* Montezuma, IN: J. H. Linn, 1879.

McBride, H. Elliot. *As by Fire: A Temperance Drama in Five Acts.* Philadelphia: Penn Pub. Co., *c.* 1895.

Before the Execution. Chicago: Hennebery Co., nd.

A Bitter Dose. New York: The National Temperance Society and Publication House, 1879.

A Boy's Rehearsal. New York: The National Temperance Society and Publication House, 1879.

The Closing of the Eagle. New York: Dick & Fitzgerald, 1877.

Don't Marry a Drunkard to Reform Him. New York: Dick & Fitzgerald, *c.* 1877.

Maud's Command; or, Yielding to Temptation, a Temperance Play in Two Acts. New York: Dick & Fitzgerald, *c.* 1877.

On the Brink; or, the Reclaimed Husband. A Temperance Drama in Two Acts. Chicago: T. S. Denison, 1878.

Out of the Depths. A Temperance Drama in Three Acts. New York: Dick & Fitzgerald, *c.* 1877.

The Poisoned Darkys. New York: Wehman Bros., 1877.

Ralph Coleman's Reformation. New York: Roorbach, 188?.

Reclaimed; or Sunshine Comes at Last. Philadelphia: P. Garrett, 1891.

The Stolen Child; or, A New Hampshire Man in Boston. New York: Dick & Fitzgerald, 1882.

A Talk on Temperance. New York: The National Temperance Society and Publication House, *c.* 1879.

Temperance Dialogues Designed for the Use of Schools, Temperance Societies, Bands of Hope, Divisions, Lodges, and Literary Circles. New York: Dick & Fitzgerald, *c.* 1877.

Those Thompsons. New York: Dick & Fitzgerald, 1883.

Two Drams of Brandy; A Temperance Play. New York: O. A. Roorbach, 1881.

Under the Curse; A Temperance Drama. New York: O. A. Roorbach, 1881.

Well Fixed for a Rainy Day. New York: Wehman Bros., *c.* 1882.

McCloskey, James Joseph. *Across the Continent; or, Scenes From New York Life and the Pacific Railroad. Dramas from the American Theatre, 1762–1909,* ed. Richard Moody, Boston: Houghton Mifflin Company, 1969.

The Fatal Glass; or, the Curse of Drink. Brooklyn, NY: J. J. McClosky, 1872.

McConaughty, J. E. *The Drunkard's Daughter. A Collection of Temperance Dialogues for Divisions of Sons, Good Templar Lodges and Other Temperance Societies,* ed. S. Hammond, np., 1869.

McDermott, J. *The Wrong Bottle.* New York: Dick & Fitzgerald 1895.

McDermott, J. and Trumble, J. *A Game of Billiards.* New York: Happy Hours Company, *c.* 1875.

McFall, G. B. *Among the Moonshiners; or, A Drunkard's Legacy.* Clyde, OH: A. D. Ames, 1897.

Meriwether, Elizabeth Avery. *The Devil's Dance*. St. Louis: Hailman Bros., *c.* 1886.

Merriman, Effie W. *The Drunkard's Family*. Chicago: Dramatic Publishing Company, 1898.

Miles, Frank Lee and H. W. Phillips. *The Wine-cup; or The Tempter and the Tempted*. np., 1880. (First produced Danville, PA.)

Mitchell, Thomas. *The Household Tragedy*. Albany, NY: Weed, Parsons & Co., 1870.

Morton, Charles H. *Three Years in a Man-trap*. Camden, NJ: New Republic Press, 1873.

Morton, Thomas. *The Two Mechanics, or Another Glass*. Boston: W. H. Baker Co., nd.

Moulds, Arthur. *Danesbury House: A Temperance Entertainment*. Leicester: E. T. Lawrence, 1862.

The Village Bane. Leicester: E. T. Lawrence, 186?.

Murray, E. *Licenced Snakes*. Philadelphia: P. Garrett, 1887.

Murray, Ellen. *Cain, Ancient and Modern*. Philadelphia: P. Garrett, 1887.

Optic, Oliver. *The Demons of the Glass*. Philadelphia: P. Garrett, 1887.

Peake, Richard Brinsley. *The Bottle Imp*. Philadelphia: Frederick Turner, 1847.

Penney, Lizzie. *How to Fight the Drink; or, the Saloon Must Go!* New York: The National Temperance Society and Publication House, 1894.

Pitt, George Dibdin. *Basil and Barbara: The Children of the Bottle, or The Curse Entailed*. np. Produced 1848.

The Bottle Bane. np. Produced 1847.

The Drunkard's Doom; or, The Last Nail. London: John Dicks, *c.* 1832.

Pratt, William W. *Ten Nights in a Bar-room*. New York: Samuel French, Inc., *c.* 1858.

Reade, Charles. *Drink*. 1879. Reprinted in *Naturalist Documents/Documents Naturalistes*, ed. David Baguley. London, Canada: Mestengo Press, 1991.

Taylor, C. W. *Little Katy, or the Hot Corn Girl*. np. Produced 1854.

Seymour, Harry. *Aunt Dinah's Pledge*. New York: Wehman Bros., *c.* 1850.

The Temperance Doctor. A Moral Drama in Two Acts . . . Dramatized from the Story of The Temperance Doctor. New York: Samuel French, Inc., 187–.

Shears, Mrs. L. D. *The Wife's Appeal*. New York: np., 1878.

Sheridan, Eugene. *Wrecked and Saved*, np., 1887.

Smith, W. H., and "A Gentleman." *The Drunkard, or the Fallen Saved. Dramas from the American Theatre, 1762–1909*, ed. Richard Moody. Boston: Houghton Mifflin Company, 1969.

Tardy, Edwin. *Saved; or a Woman's Influence*. Clyde, OH: A. D. Ames, nd.

Taylor, Charles W. *The Drunkard's Warning*. London: John Dicks, 1856.

Taylor, T. P. *The Bottle; or, Cause and Effect*. London: Thomas Lacy, 1847.

The Drunkard's Children, or A Sequel to the Bottle. np. Produced 1848.

Thayer, Julia. *Fighting the Rum-fiend*. Philadelphia: P. Garrett, 1887.

Thayer, Mrs. J. *The Drunkard's Daughter*. Boston: William S. Damrell, 1842.

Todd, J. W. J. *Arthur Eustace; or, A Mother's Love*. Clyde, OH: A. D. Ames, 1891.

Vautrot, George S. *At Last; A Temperance Drama*. Clyde, OH: A. D. Ames, 1879.

Vickers, George M. *Two Lives* in *Dramatic Leaflets*. Philadelphia: P. Garrett, *c.* 1887.

Whalen, E. C. *Under the Spell; A Temperance Drama in Four Acts*. Chicago: T. S. Denison, 1890.

White, John Blake. *The Forgers*. c. 1829. Reprinted in *Southern Literary Journal* 1 (1968): 2–6.

Wilkins, W. Henri. *Three Glasses a Day; or, The Broken Home*. Clyde, OH: A. D. Ames, 1878.

The Turn of the Tide, or Wrecked in Port. Clyde, OH: A. D. Ames, 1880.

Woodward, T. Trask. *The Social Glass; or, Victims of the Bottle*. New York: Samuel French, Inc., 1887.

Bibliography

Books

Adams, Bluford. *E Pluribus Barnum: The Great Showman and US Popular Culture*. Minneapolis: University of Minnesota Press, 1997.

Allen, Robert C. *Horrible Prettiness: Burlesque and American Culture*. Chapel Hill: University of North Carolina Press, 1991.

Anbinder, Tyler. *Five Points: The 19th-Century New York City Neighborhood that Invented Tap Dance, Stole Elections, and Became the World's Most Notorious Slum*. New York: The Free Press, 2001.

Anonymous. *Select Temperance Tracts*. New York: American Tract Society, 1860.

Arthur, T. S. *Temperance Tales, or Six Nights with the Washingtonians*. Philadelphia: Leary & Getz, 1848.

Asbury, Herbert. *The Gangs of New York: An Informal History of the Underworld*. New York: Paragon House, 1990.

Bailey, Peter. *Leisure and Class in Victorian England: Rational Recreation and the Contest for Control, 1830–1885*. London: Routledge & Kegan Paul, 1978.

Popular Culture and Performance in the Victorian City. Cambridge: Cambridge University Press, 1998.

Baker, Benjamin. *A Glance at New York*. In *On Stage America*, ed. Walter J. Meserve. New York: Feedback Theatre Books, 1996.

Baker, H. Barton. *The History of the London Stage and its Famous Players (1576–1903)*. London: George Routledge and Sons, Limited, 1904.

Bank, Rosemarie K. *Theatre Culture in America, 1825–1860*. New York: Cambridge University Press, 1997.

Barnum, P. T. *Struggles and Triumphs; or Forty Years' Recollections*. Buffalo, NY: The Courier Company, 1882.

Barth, Gunther. *City People: The Rise of Modern City Culture in Nineteenth-Century America*. New York: Oxford University Press, 1980.

Baym, Nina, ed. *The Norton Anthology of American Literature*. New York: Norton, 1994.

Becker, Howard. *Outsiders: Studies in the Sociology of Deviance*. New York: The Free Press, 1966.

Beecher, Layman. *Six Sermons on the Nature, Occasions, Signs, Evils, and Remedy of Intemperance*. Boston: T. R. Marvin, 1828.

Benson, Lee. *The Concept of Jacksonian Democracy*. Princeton: Princeton University Press, 1961.

Berkowitz, Gerald M. *American Drama of the Twentieth Century*. London: Longman, 1992.

Blocker, Jack S., ed. *Alcohol, Reform and Society: The Liquor Issue in Social Context*. Westport, CT: Greenwood Press, 1979.

Blocker, Jack S. *American Temperance Movements: Cycles of Reform*. Boston: Twayne Publishers, 1989.

"Give to the Winds they Fears": The Women's Temperance Crusade, 1873–1874. Westport, CT: Greenwood Press, 1985.

Retreat From Reform: The Prohibition Movement in the United States, 1890–1913. Westport, CT: Greenwood Press, 1976.

Blumberg, Leonard U., with William L. Pittman. *Beware the First Drink: The Washington Temperance Movement and Alcoholics Anonymous*. Seattle: Glen Abbey Books, 1991.

Blumin, Stuart. *The Emergence of the Middle Class: Social Experience in the American City, 1760–1900*. New York: Cambridge University Press, 1989.

Boorstin, Daniel. *The Americans: The Democratic Experience*. New York: Random House, 1973.

Booth, Michael R. *English Melodrama*. London: Herbert Jenkins, 1965.

English Plays of the Nineteenth Century. 2 vols. Oxford: Clarendon Press, 1969.

Booth, Michael R., ed. *Hiss the Villain*. London: Eyre & Spottiswoode, 1964.

Booth, Michael R. *Theatre in the Victorian Age*. Cambridge: Cambridge University Press, 1991.

Booth, Michael R. *et al*. *The Revels History of Drama in English*, vol. IV (1750–1880). London: Methuen & Co. Ltd., 1975.

Bordin, Ruth. *Woman and Temperance: The Quest for Power and Liberty, 1873–1900*. New Brunswick, NJ: Rutgers University Press, 1990.

Boyer, Paul. *Urban Masses and Moral Order in America, 1820–1920*. Cambridge, MA: Harvard University Press, 1978.

Bradby, David, Louis James and Bernard Sharratt, eds. *Performance and Politics in Popular Drama*. Cambridge: Cambridge University Press, 1980.

Brooks, Peter. *The Melodramatic Imagination*. New York: Columbia University Press, 1985.

Brown, Eluned, ed. *The London Theatre, 1811–1866. Selections from the Diary of Henry Crabb Robinson*. London: Society for Theatre Research, 1966.

Brown, Herbert Ross. *The Sentimental Novel in America, 1790–1860*. Durham: np., 1940.

Brownlow, Kevin. *Behind the Mask of Innocence*. Berkeley: University of California Press, 1990.

Buntline, Ned. *The Mysteries and Miseries of New York: A Story of Real Life*. New York: Edward Z. C. Judson, 1848.

Burns, Dawson. *Temperance History: A Consecutive Narrative of the Rise, Development and Extension of the Temperance Reform*. 2 vols. London: National Temperance Publication Depot, 1889.

Carson, William G.B. *The Theatre on the Frontier*. Chicago: University of Illinois Press, 1932.

Carter, Henry. *The English Temperance Movement: A Study in Objectives*. London: The Epworth Press, 1933.

Clark, Norman H. *Deliver Us from Evil: An Interpretation of American Prohibition*. New York: W. W. Norton & Company, 1976.

Click, Patricia C. *The Spirit of the Times: Amusements in Nineteenth-Century Baltimore, Norfolk & Richmond*. Charlottesville: University Press of Virginia, 1989.

Commager, Henry Steele. *The Era of Reform, 1830–1860*. Princeton: D. Van Nostrand Company, 1960.

Conroy, David W. *In Public houses: Drink and the Revolution of Authority in Colonial Massachusetts*. Chapel Hill: University of North Carolina Press, 1995.

Cross, Gary. *A Social History of Leisure Since 1600*. State College, PA: Venture Publishing, Inc., 1990.

Crunden, Robert. *A Brief History of American Culture*. London: North Castle Books, 1996.

Cunningham, Hugh. *Leisure in the Industrial Revolution*. London: Croom Helm, 1980.

Dannenbaum, Jed. *Drink and Disorder: Temperance Reform in Cincinnati from the Washingtonian Revival to the WCTU*. Urbana: University of Illinois Press, 1984.

Darnovsky, Marcy, Barbara Epstein and Richard Flacks, eds. *Cultural Politics and Social Movements*. Philadelphia: Temple University Press, 1995.

Davis, David Brion, ed. *Antebellum Reform*. New York: Harper & Row, 1967.

Davis, Susan. *Parades and Power: Street Theatre in Nineteenth-Century Philadelphia*. Berkeley: University of California Press, 1986.

Dennett, Andrea Stulman. *Weird and Wonderful: The Dime Museum in America*. New York: New York University Press, 1997.

Denning, Michael. *Mechanic's Accents: Dime Novels and Working-Class Culture in America*. London: Verso, 1987.

de Walden, Thomas. *The Upper Ten and Lower Twenty*. Handwritten Manuscript, Harvard Theatre Collection.

Dezell, Maureen. *Irish America: Coming into Clover*. New York: Doubleday, 2001.

Dumenil, Lynn. *Modern Temper: American Culture and Society in the 1920s*. New York: Hill and Wang, 1995.

Eagleton, Terry. *The Idea of Culture*. London: Blackwell, 2000.

The Ideology of the Aesthetic. London: Blackwell, 1990.

Edwards, Herbert J. and Julie A. Herne. *James A. Herne: The Rise of Realism in the American Drama*. Orono: University of Maine Press, 1964.

Erenberg, Lewis A. *Steppin' Out: New York Nightlife and the Transformation of American Culture, 1890–1930*. Westport, CT: Greenwood Press, 1981.

Emeljanow, Victor. *Victorian Popular Dramatists*. Boston: Twayne Publishers, 1987.

Epstein, Barbara Leslie. *The Politics of Domesticity: Women, Evangelism and Temperance in Nineteenth-Century America*. Middletown, CT: Wesleyan University Press, 1981.

Evans, Hilary and Mary Evans. *The Man Who Drew The Drunkard's Daughter: The Life and Art of George Cruikshank, 1792–1878*. London: Frederick Muller Limited, 1978.

Ewing, George. *The Well-Tempered Lyre*. Dallas: Louisiana State University Press, 1977.

Felheim, Marvin. *The Theater of Augustin Daly*. Cambridge, MA: Harvard University Press, 1956.

Fiske, John. *Reading Popular Culture*. London: Routledge, 1989.

Understanding Popular Culture. London: Routledge, 1989.

Gassner, John. *Dramatic Soundings: Evaluations and Retractions Culled from 30 Years of Dramatic Criticism.* Introd. and posthumous editing by Glenn Loney. New York, Crown Publishers, 1968.

Geertz, Clifford. *The Interpretation of Cultures.* New York: Basic Books, 1973.

George, M. Dorothy. *Hogarth to Cruikshank: Social Change in Graphic Satire.* London: Allen Lane, The Penguin Press, 1967.

Gerould, Daniel C. *American Melodrama.* New York: Performing Arts Journal Publications, 1983.

Gilfoyle, Timothy J. *City of Eros: New York City, Prostitution and the Commercialization of Sex, 1790–1920.* New York: Norton, 1992.

Grimsted, David. *Melodrama Unveiled: American Theatre & Culture, 1800–1850.* Berkeley: University of California Press, 1968.

Gusfield, Joseph R. *Symbolic Crusade: Status Politics and the American Temperance Movement.* Urbana: University of Illinois Press, 1986.

Hadley, Elaine. *Melodramatic Tactics: Theatricalized Dissent in the English Marketplace, 1800–1885.* Stanford, CA: Stanford University Press, 1995.

Halttunen, Karen. *Confidence Men and Painted Women: A Study of Middle-class Culture in America, 1830–1870.* New Haven: Yale University Press, 1982.

Halttunen, Karen, and Lewis Perry, eds. *Moral Problems in American Life: New Perspectives on Cultural History.* Ithaca: Cornell University Press, 1998.

Hamm, Richard F. *Shaping the 18th Amendment: Temperance Reform, Legal Culture, and the Polity, 1800–1920.* Chapel Hill: University of North Carolina Press, 1995.

Hampel, Robert L. *Temperance and Prohibition in Massachusetts, 1813–1852.* Ann Arbor: UMI Research Press, 1982.

Harrison, Brian. *Drink and the Victorians: The Temperance Question in England 1815–1872.* Pittsburgh: University of Pittsburgh Press, 1971.

Hays, Michael and Anastasia Nikolopoulou, eds. *Melodrama: The Cultural Emergence of a Genre.* New York: St. Martin's Press, 1996.

Hemmings, F. W. J. *The Life and Times of Emile Zola.* New York: Charles Scribner's Sons, 1977.

Hempton, David. *Methodism and Politics in British Society 1750–1850.* London: Huchinson, 1984.

Henderson, Robert M. *D. W. Griffith: His Life and Work.* New York: Oxford University Press, 1972.

Hodge, Francis. *Yankee Theatre; The Image of America on the Stage, 1825–1850.* Austin: University of Texas Press, 1964.

Hofstadter, Richard. *The Age of Reform: From Bryan to F.D.R.* New York: Vintage Books, 1955.

Anti-intellectualism in American Life. New York: Vintage Books, 1962.

The Paranoid Style in American Politics and Other Essays. Cambridge, MA: Harvard University Press, 1952.

Hoyt, Harlow R. *Town Hall Tonight: Intimate Memories of the Grassroot Days of the American Theatre.* Englewood Cliffs, NJ: Prentice-Hall, Inc., 1955.

Hughes, Glenn. *A History of the American Theatre, 1700–1950.* London: Samuel French, 1951.

Ireland, Joseph N. *Records of the New York Stage from 1750 to 1860.* 2 vols. New York: Benjamin Blom, 1966.

Jerrold, Blanchard. *The Life of George Cruikshank*. Chincheley, England: Paul P. B. Minet, 1971.

Jerrold, Walter. *Douglas Jerrold: Dramatist and Wit*. 2 vols. London: Hodder & Stoughton, 1914.

Jones, Gareth Stedman. *Languages of Class: Studies in English Working Class History, 1832–1982*. New York: Cambridge University Press, 1983.

Jones, Henry Arthur, and Henry Herman. *The Silver King*, New York: Samuel French, 1907.

Jones, Michael Wynn. *George Cruikshank: His Life and London*. London: Macmillan, 1978.

Kahn, E. J. *The Merry Partners: The Age and Stage of Harrigan & Hart*. New York: Random House, 1955.

Kelley, Richard, ed. *The Best of Mr. Punch; The Humorous Writings of Douglas Jerrold*. Knoxville: University of Tennessee Press, 1970.

Kenny, Kevin. *The American Irish: A History*. London: Longman, 2000.

King, Graham. *Garden of Zola*. London: Barrie & Jenkins Ltd., 1978.

Kunhardt, Philip B. Jr., Philip B. Kunhardt III, and Peter W. Kunhardt. *P. T. Barnum: America's Greatest Showman*. New York: Knopf, 1995.

Laurie, Bruce. *Working People of Philadelphia, 1800–1850*. Philadelphia: Temple University Press, 1980.

Lender, Mark Edward. *Dictionary of American Temperance Biography*. Westport, CT: Greenwood Press, 1984.

Lender, Mark Edward and James Kirby Martin. *Drinking in America*. New York: Free Press, 1987.

Longmate, Norman. *The Waterdrinkers: A History of Temperance*. London: Hamish Hamilton, 1968.

Lott, Eric. *Love and Theft: Blackface Minstrelsy and the American Working Class*. New York: Oxford University Press, 1993.

Mason, Jeffrey D. *Melodrama and the Myth of America*. Bloomington: Indiana University Press, 1993.

Mathews, Mitford M., ed. *A Dictionary of Americanisms*. Chicago: University of Chicago Press, 1956.

Mayne, Jonathan, ed. *The Painter of Modern Life and Other Essays*. London: Phaidon, c. 1964.

McCarthy, Justin. *An Irishman's Story*. New York: Grosset & Dunlap, Publishers, 1904.

McConachie, Bruce A. *Melodramatic Formations: American Theatre & Society, 1820–1870*. Iowa City: University of Iowa Press, 1992.

McConachie, Bruce A. and Friedman, Daniel. *Theatre for Working-Class Audiences in the United States, 1830–1980*. Westport, CT: Greenwood Press, 1985.

McGlinchee, Claire. *The First Decade of the Boston Museum*. Boston: Bruce Humphries, Inc, c. 1940.

Meisel, Martin. *Realizations: Narrative, Pictorial, and Theatrical Arts in Nineteenth-century England*. Princeton: Princeton University Press, 1983.

Meserve, Walter J. *Heralds of Promise: The Drama of the American People in the Age of Jackson, 1829–1849*. Westport, CT: Greenwood Press, 1986.

An Outline History of American Drama. New York: Feedback Theatre Books, 1994.

When Conscience Trod the Stage. New York: Feedback Theatre Books, 1998.

Minnigerode, Meade. *The Fabulous Forties, 1840–1850.* New York: G. P. Putnam's Sons, 1924.

Mintz, Steven. *Moralists & Modernizers: America's Pre-Civil War Reformers.* Baltimore: Johns Hopkins University Press, 1995.

Moody, Richard, ed. *Dramas from the American Theatre, 1792–1909.* New York: Houghton Mifflin Company, 1966.

Moody, Richard. *Ned Harrigan: From Corlear's Hook to Herald Square.* Chicago: Nelson-Hall, 1980.

Morrow, Abbie Clemens. *Best Thoughts and Discourses of D. L. Moody.* New York: N. Tibbals & Sons, 1878.

Moses, Montrose J. *The American Dramatist.* Boston: Little, Brown, and Company, 1925.

Moses, Montrose J., ed. *Representative Plays by American Dramatists.* New York: Benjamin Blom, Inc., 1964.

Murphy, Brenda. *American Realism and American Drama, 1880–1940.* Cambridge: Cambridge University Press, 1987.

Nicoll, Allardyce. *A History of English Drama, 1669–1900.* Cambridge: Cambridge University Press, 1963.

Noel, Janet. *Canada Dry: Temperance Crusades Before Confederation.* Toronto: University of Toronto Press, 1994.

Noel, Mary. *Villains Galore: The Heyday of the Popular Story Weekly.* New York: The Macmillan Company, 1954.

Nye, Russell. *The Unembarrassed Muse.* New York: The Dial Press, 1970.

Odegard, Peter H. *Pressure Politics: The Story of the Anti-Saloon League.* New York: Columbia University Press, 1928.

Odell, George C. D. *Annals of the New York Stage.* 15 vols. New York: Columbia University Press, 1927–41.

Payne, Jayne Chancellor. *Diary of Jayne Chancellor Payne.* Np., nd.

Pegram, Thomas R. *Battling Demon Rum: The Struggle for a Dry America: 1800–1933.* Chicago: Ivan R. Dee, 1998.

Perry, John. *James A. Herne: The American Ibsen.* Chicago: Nelson-Hall, 1978.

Pittman, David J. and Charles R. Snyder, eds. *Society, Culture and Drinking Patterns.* New York: John Wiley & Sons, Inc., 1962.

Poggi, Jack. *Theater in America: The Impact of Economic Forces, 1870–1967.* Ithaca, NY: Cornell University Press, 1966.

Rahill, Frank. *The World of Melodrama.* University Park: Pennsylvania State University Press, 1967.

Railton, Stephen. *Authorship and Audience: Literary Performance in the American Renaissance.* Princeton: Princeton University Press, 1991.

Reising, Russell J. *The Unusable Past: Theory and the Study of American Literature.* New York: Methuen, 1986.

Reynolds, David S. *Beneath the American Renaissance: The Subversive Imagination in the Age of Emerson and Melville.* Cambridge: Harvard University Press, 1988.

Reynolds, David S., and Debra J. Rosenthal, eds. *The Serpent in the Cup: Temperance in American Literature*. Amherst: University of Massachusetts Press, 1997.

Reynolds, Ernest. *Early Victorian Drama (1830–1870)*. Cambridge: W. Heffer & Sons, Limited, 1936.

Rice, Charles. *The London Theatre in the Eighteen-thirties*. London: Society for Theatre Research, 1950.

Robinson, Solon. *Hot Corn: Life Scenes in New York Illustrated*. New York: De Witt and Davenport, 1854.

Rorabaugh, W. J. *The Alcoholic Republic: An American Tradition*. Oxford: Oxford University Press, 1979.

Rowell, George. *Nineteenth Century Plays*. Oxford: Oxford University Press, 1977.

The Old Vic Theatre: A History. Cambridge: Cambridge University Press, 1993.

The Victorian Theatre, 1792–1914. Cambridge: Cambridge University Press, 1978.

Rumbarger, John J. *Profits, Power and Prohibition: Alcohol Reform and the Industrializing of America, 1800–1930*. State University Press of New York, 1989.

Rush, Benjamin. *An Inquiry into the Effects of Ardent Spirits on the Human Body and Mind*. Exeter, NH: Printed for Josiah Richardson, 1819.

Ryan, Mary. *Civic Wars: Democracy and Public Life in the American City During the Nineteenth Century*. Berkeley: University of California Press, 1997.

Sargent, Lucius Manlius. *The Temperance Tales*. Boston: American Tract Society, 1863.

Saxon, A. H. *P. T. Barnum: The Legend and the Man*. New York: Columbia University Press, 1989.

Schickel, Richard. *D. W. Griffith: An American Life*. New York: Simon and Schuster, 1984.

Schlesinger, Arthur M. *The American as Reformer*. Cambridge, MA: Harvard University Press, 1950.

Scott, John Paul and Sarah F. Scott. *Social Control and Social Change*. Chicago: University of Chicago Press, 1971.

Siegel, Adrienne. *The Image of the American City in Popular Literature, 1820–1870*. Port Washington, NY: Kennikat Press, 1981.

Shepard, Simon and Peter Womack. *English Drama: A Cultural History*. Oxford: Blackwell, 1996.

Shi, David E. *Facing Facts: Realism in American Thought and Culture, 1850–1920*. New York: Oxford University Press, 1995.

Shiman, Lilian Lewis. *Crusade Against Drink in Victorian England*. London: Macmillan, 1988.

Slout, William Lawrence. *Theatre in a Tent: The Development of a Provincial Entertainment*. Bowling Green, OH: Bowling Green University Popular Press, 1972.

Smith, Susan Harris. *American Drama: The Bastard Art*. Cambridge: Cambridge University Press, 1997.

Smith, Timothy. *Revivalism and Social Reform in Mid-Nineteenth Century America*. Baltimore: Johns Hopkins University Press, 1980.

Smith-Rosenberg, Carroll. *Disorderly Conduct: Visions of Gender in Victorian America*. New York: Oxford University Press, 1985.

Stansell, Christine. *City of Women: Sex and Class in New York 1789–1860*. Urbana: University of Illinois Press, 1987.

Susman, Warren I. *Culture as History: The Transformation of American Society in the Twentieth Century*. New York: Pantheon Books, 1984.

Taylor, W. Cooke. *Notes on a Tour of the Manufacturing Districts of Lancashire*. New York: A. M. Kelley, 1968.

Thompson, Denman. *The Old Homestead*, in Walter J. Meserve, *On Stage America!* New York: Feedback Theatre Books, 1996.

Thompson, E. P. *The Making of the English Working Class*. New York: Vintage, 1966.

Tick, Judith. *American Women Composers Before 1870*. Ann Arbor: UMI Research Press, 1983.

Trachtenberg, Alan. *The Incorporation of America: Culture & Society in the Gilded Age*. New York: Hill and Wang, 1982.

Twain, Mark. *Contributions to the Galaxy, 1835–1871*. Ed. Bruce McElderry, Jr. Gainseville, FL: Scholars' Facsimiles & Reprints, 1961.

Tyrrell, Ian R. *Sobering Up: From Temperance to Prohibition in Ante-bellum America, 1800–1860*. Westport, CT: Greenwood Press, 1979.

Vardac, Nicholas. *Stage to Screen: Theatrical Method from Garrick to Griffith*. New York: Da Capo Press, 1949.

Vesser, H. Aram. *The New Historicism*. New York: Routledge, 1989.

Walker, Robert H. *Reform in America: The Continuing Frontier*. Lexington: University Press of Kentucky, 1985.

Walters, Ronald G. *American Reformers, 1815–1860*. New York: Hill and Wang, 1978.

Welter, Rush. *The Mind of America, 1820–1860*. New York: Columbia University Press, 1975.

Whitman, Walt. *New York Dissected*. New York: Rufus Rockwell Wilson, Inc., 1936.

Wiebe, Robert H. *The Search for Order, 1877–1920*. New York: Hill and Wang, 1967.

Wilentz, Sean. *Chants Democratic: New York City and the Rise of the American Working Class, 1788–1850*. New York: Oxford University Press, 1984.

Williams, Raymond. *Culture and Society: 1780–1950*. New York: Columbia University Press, 1983.

Drama From Ibsen to Brecht. London: Hogarth Press, 1987.

Keywords: A Vocabulary of Culture and Society. New York: Oxford University Press, 1976.

Marxism and Literature. Oxford: Oxford University Press, 1977.

Problems in Materialism and Culture. London: Verso, 1980.

Winter, William. *The Life of David Belasco*. vol. 1. New York: Moffat, Yard and Company, 1918.

Woolley, John G. and William E. Johnson. *Temperance Progress in the Century*. London: The Linscott Publishing Company, 1903.

Articles

Alexander, Ruth M. " 'We Are Engaged as a Band of Sisters': Class and Domesticity in the Washington Temperance Movement, 1840–1850." *Journal of American History* 75 (October 1988): 763–85.

Armao, Agnes Orsati. "Devout Legalists: Protestant Reliance on Law in Early Nineteenth-century America." *American Studies* 26 (Fall 1985): 61–73.

Baguley, David, "Introduction." *Naturalist Documents/Documents Naturalistes*. London, Canada: Mestengo Press, 1991.

Bank, Rosemarie K. "Hustlers in the House: The Bowery Theatre as a Mode of Historical Information." *The American Stage*, ed. Ron Engle and Tice L. Miller. Cambridge: Cambridge University Press, 1993, pp. 47–64.

"Melodrama as a Social Document: Social Factors in the American Frontier Play." *Theatre Studies* 22 (1975–76): 42–49.

Barker, Clive. "The Chartists, Theatre, Reform and Research." *Theatre Quarterly* 1 (October-December 1971): 3–10.

Baumohl. Jim. "On Asylums, Homes, and Moral Treatment: The Case of the San Francisco Home for the Care of the Inebriate, 1859–1870." *Contemporary Drug Problems* (Fall 1986): 395–445.

Blocker, Jack S. Jr., "Separate Paths: Suffragists and the Women's Temperance Crusade." *Signs* 10 (Spring 1985): 460–76.

Booth, Michael R. "The Drunkard's Progress: Nineteenth-century Temperance Drama." *Dalhousie Review* 44 (1964–65): 205–12.

"The Metropolis on Stage." *The Victorian City: Images and Realities*, vol. 1, ed. H. J. Dyos and Michael Wolff. London: Routledge & Kegan Paul, 1973, pp. 211–24.

Buckley, Peter. "Paratheatricals and Popular Stage Entertainments." *Cambridge History of the American Theatre*, vol. 1, ed. Don B. Wilmeth and Christopher Bigsby. Cambridge: Cambridge University Press, 1998, pp. 424–82.

Carlson, Douglas W. "'Drinks He to his Own Undoing': Temperance Ideology in the Deep South." *Journal of the Early Republic* 18 (Winter 1998): 659–91.

Child, Harold. "Nineteenth-century Drama." *The Cambridge History of English Literature*, vol. XIII, ed. A. W. Ward and A. R. Waller. Cambridge: Cambridge University Press, 1916, pp. 255–74.

Clark, William M. "Ten Nights in a Bar-room." *American Heritage* 15 (June 1964): 14–17.

Cohen-Stratyner, Barbara. "Platform Pearls; or 19th Century American Performance Texts." *Performing Arts Resources* 16 (October 1991): 69–77.

Dannenbaum, Jed. "The Origins of Temperance Activism and Militancy Among American Women." *Journal of Social History* 15 (Winter 1981): 235–52.

Davis, Jim, and Victor Emeljanow. "New Views of Cheap Theatres: Reconstructing the Nineteenth-Century Theatre Audience." *Theatre Survey* 39 (November 1998): 53–72.

Davis, Peter. "The Dual Nature of American Theatre in the Late Nineteenth Century: Ibsenism Versus Realism." *Studies in Popular Culture* 9 (1986): 14–23.

Davis, Susan. "'Making the Night Hideous': Christmas Revelry and Public Order in Nineteenth-Century Philadelphia." *American Quarterly* 34 (Summer 1982): 185–99.

Day, Robert, "Carry from Kansas Became a Nation All Unto Herself." *Smithsonian* 20 (April 1989): 147–64.

Dickens, Charles. "On the People's Theatres." *Theatre Quarterly* 1 (October-December 1971): 12–14.

"Douglas Jerrold." *The Dictionary of National Biography*, vol. X, ed. Sir Leslie Stephen and Sir Sidney Lee. Oxford: Oxford University Press, 1973.

Emerson, Ralph Waldo. "Man the Reformer." *The Prose Works of Ralph Waldo Emerson.* Boston: J. R. Osgood and Co., 1872.

Estill, Robin. "The Factory Lad: Melodrama as Propaganda." *Theatre Quarterly* 1 (October-December 1971): 22–26.

Fattic, Grovsner. "A Few Sterling Pieces: Nineteenth Century Adventist Temperance Songs." *Adventist Heritage* 2 (1975): 35–41, 68.

Flynn, Joyce. "A Complex Causality of Neglect." *American Quarterly* 41 (March 1989): 123–27.

Frick, John W. "A Changing Theatre: New York and Beyond, 1870–1945." *The Cambridge History of American Theatre*, vol. 11, ed. Don B. Wilmeth and Christopher Bigsby. Cambridge: Cambridge University Press, 1999, pp. 196–232.

"He Drank From the Poisoned Cup: Theatre, Culture and Temperance in Antebellum America." *Journal of American Drama and Theatre* 4 (Spring 1992): 21–41.

"'Nine-tenths of All Kindness...': The Nineteenth-century American Theatre and the Spirit of Reform." *New England Theatre Journal* 10 (1999): 47–62.

"Victims of the Bottle From Printed Page to Gilded Stage: T. P. Taylor's Dramatization of George Cruikshank's Serial Illustrations, *The Bottle*." *Performing Arts Resources* 16 (October 1991): 1–7.

Gabaccia, D. "Cheap Amusements – Working Women and Leisure in Turn of the Century New York," *Journal of American Ethnic History* 8 (1989): 127–33.

Gienapp, William. "The Antebellum Era." *Encyclopedia of American Social History*, vol. 1, ed. Mary Kupiec Cayton, Elliot J. Gorn and Peter W. Williams. New York: Charles Scribner's Sons, 1993, pp. 107–29.

Gorn, Elliot J. " 'Good-bye Boys, I Die a True American': Homicide, Nativism, and Working-Class Culture in Antebellum New York." *Journal of American History* 74 (September 1987): 388–410.

Grant, James. "Eye-witness at the Penny Gaffs." *Theatre Quarterly* 1 (October-December 1971): 15–18.

Grimsted, David. "Melodrama as the Voice of the Historically Voiceless." *Anonymous Americans: Explorations in Nineteenth-Century Social History*, ed. Tamara K. Hareven. Englewood Cliffs, NJ: Prentice-Hall, 1971, pp. 80–98.

Grose, Janet L. "G. W. M. Reynolds's 'The Rattlesnake's History': Social Reform Through Sensationalized Realism." *Studies in the Literary Imagination* 29 (Spring 1996): 35–42.

Guinn, John F. "Father Mathew's Disciples: American Catholic Support for Temperance, 1840–1920." *Church History* 65 (December 1996): 624–40.

Gusfield, Joseph R. "Social Structure and Moral Reform: A Study of the Woman's Christian Temperance Union." *American Journal of Sociology* 61 (November 1955): 221–32.

"Status Conflicts and the Changing Ideologies of the American Temperance Movement." *Society, Culture and Drinking Patterns*, ed. David J. Pittman, and Charles R Snyder. New York: John Wiley & Sons, Inc., 1962, pp. 101–120.

"Temperance, Status Control, and Mobility, 1826–1860." *Antebellum Reform*, ed. David Brion Davis. New York: Harper & Row, 1967, pp. 120–39.

Hall, Stuart. "Deconstructing the Popular." *People's History And Socialist History*, ed. Raphael Samuel. London: Routledge, 1981, pp. 227–40.

Hampel, Robert L. "The Contexts of Antebellum Reform." *American Quarterly* 33 (1981): 93–101.

Harrison, Brian. "Drunkards and Reformers: Early Victorian Temperance Tracts." *History Today* 13 (March 1963): 178–85.

"Pubs." *The Victorian City: Images and Realities*, vol. 1, ed. H. J. Dyos and Michael Wolff. London: Routledge & Kegan Paul, 1973, pp. 161–90.

"A World of Which We Had No Conception. Liberalism and the English Temperance Press: 1830–1872." *Victorian Studies* 13 (December 1969): 125–58.

Hazlitt, William. "The Minor Theatres." *London Magazine* (March 1820).

Johnson, Claudia. "That Guilty Third Tier: Prostitution in Nineteenth Century Theaters." *American Quarterly* 27 (December 1975): 575–84.

Johnson, Paul. "Drinking, Temperance and the Construction of Identity in 19th Century America." *Social Science Information* 25 (1986): 521–30.

Johnson, Stephen. "Evaluating Early Film as a Document of Theatre History: The 1896 Footage of Joseph Jefferson's *Rip Van Winkle*." *Nineteenth Century Theatre* 20 (Winter 1992): 101–22.

"Joseph Jefferson's *Rip Van Winkle*." *The Drama Review* 26 (Spring 1982): 3–20.

Kerr, Austin. "Organizing for Reform: The Anti-Saloon League and Innovation in Politics." *American Quarterly* 32 (1980): 37–53.

Kingsdale, Jon M. "The 'Poor Man's Club': Social Functions of the Urban Working-Class Saloon." *American Quarterly* 25 (October 1973): 472–89.

Koch, Donald A. "Introduction." *Ten Nights in a Bar-Room, and What I Saw There*. Cambridge, MA: Harvard University Press, 1964. vi–lxxxiii.

Larson, Gerald. "From *Ten Nights* to *Harvey*. Drinking on the American Stage." *Western Humanities Review* 10 (1956): 388–90.

Lauricella, Francis Jr. "The Devil in Drink: Swedenborgianism in T. S. Arthur's *Ten Nights in a Bar-room*." *Perspectives in American History* 12 (1979): 353–85.

Leach, Eugene E. "Social Reform Movements." *Encyclopedia of American Social History*, vol. III, ed. Mary Kupiec Cayton, Elliot J. Gorn and Peter W. Williams. New York: Charles Scribner's Sons, 1993, pp. 2001–30.

Lender, Mark Edward and Karen R. Karnchanapee. "'Temperance Tales': Antiliquor Fiction and American Attitudes Toward Alcoholics In the Late 19th and Early 20th Centuries." *Journal of Studies On Alcohol* 38 (1977): 1347–70.

McArthur, Judith N. "Demon Rum on the Boards: Temperance Melodrama and the Tradition of Antebellum Reform." *Journal of the Early Republic* 9 (Winter 1989): 517–40.

McCain, Diana Ross. "The Temperance Movement." *Early American Life* (February 1993): 16–19.

McConachie, Bruce. "Museum Theatre and the Problem of Respectability for Mid-Century Urban Americans." *The American Stage*, ed. Ron Engle and Tice L. Miller. Cambridge: Cambridge University Press, 1993, pp. 65–80.

Mason, Jeffrey D. "Poison it with Rum; or, Validation and Delusion: Antebellum Temperance Drama as Cultural Method." *Pacific Coast Philology* 25 (1990): 96–104.

Maxwell, Milton A. "The Washingtonian Movement." *Quarterly Journal of Studies on Alcohol* 11 (September 1950): 410–51.

Mayer, David. "The Death of a Stage Actor: The Genesis of a Film." *Film History* 11 (1999): 342–52.

Mayhew, Henry. "The Vic Gallery." *Theatre Quarterly* 1 (October–December 1971): 11–12.

Meyer, Richard J. "The Films of David Wark Griffith: The Development of Themes and Techniques in Forty-two of his Films." *Focus on D. W. Griffith*, ed. Harry M. Geduld. Englewood Cliffs, NJ: Prentice-Hall, Inc., 1971, pp. 109–28.

Monkkonen, Eric. "Urbanization." *Encyclopedia of American Social History*, vol. 1, ed. Mary Kupiec Cayton, Elliot J. Gorn and Peter W. Williams. New York: Charles Scribner's Sons, 1993, pp. 571–73.

Morantz, Regina Markell. "Making Women Modern: Middle Class Women and Health Reform in 19th Century America." *Journal of Social History* 10 (June 1977): 490–507.

Parker, Alison M. "'Hearts Uplifted and Minds Refreshed': The Woman's Christian Temperance Union and the Production of Pure Culture in the United States, 1880–1930." *Journal of Women's History* 11 (Summer 1999): 135–58.

Postlewait, Thomas. "From Melodrama to Realism: The Suspect History of American Drama." *Melodrama: The Cultural Emergence of a Genre*, ed. Michael Hays, and Anastasia Nikolopoulou. New York: St. Martin's Press, 1996, pp. 39–60.

Reckner, Paul E. and Stephen A. Brighton. "'Free From All Vicious Habits': Archeological Perspectives on Class Conflict and the Rhetoric of Temperance." *Historical Archeology* 33 (1999): 63–86.

Richardson, Gary. "Plays and Playwrights: 1800–1865." *Cambridge History of the American Theatre*, vol. 1, ed. Don B. Wilmeth and Christopher Bigsby. Cambridge: Cambridge University Press, 1998, pp. 250–302.

Rohrer, James R, "The Origins of the Temperance Movement: A Re-interpretation." *Journal of American Studies* 24 (August 1990): 228–35.

Rorabaugh, William J. "Rising Democratic Spirits: Immigrants, Temperance, and Tammany Hall." *Civil War History* 22 (1976): 131–57.

Sanchez-Eppler, Karen, "Temperance in the Bed of a Child: Incest and Social Order in Nineteenth-century America." *American Quarterly* 47 (March 1995): 1–33.

Scanlan, Tom. "The Domestication of Rip Van Winkle: Joe Jefferson's Play as Prologue to Modern American Drama." *The Virginia Quarterly Review* 50 (1974): 51–62.

Schultz, Stanley K. "Temperance Reform in the Antebellum South: Social Control and Urban Order." *South Atlantic Quarterly* 83 (Summer 1984): 323–39.

Silverman, Joan. "*The Birth of a Nation*: Prohibition Propaganda." *Southern Quarterly* 19 (1981): 23–30.

Smith, Susan Harris. "Generic Hegemony: American Drama and the Canon." *American Quarterly* 41 (March 1989): 112–22.

Smith-Rosenberg, Carroll. "Misprisoning Pamela: Representations of Gender and Class in Nineteenth-century America." *Michigan Quarterly Review* 26 (Winter 1987): 9–28.

Stonehouse, Jean. "We Have Come From the Mountains." *New England Journal of History* 51 (1994): 60–67.

Susman, Warren I. "Persistence of Reform." *Journal of Human Relations* 15 (1967): 94–108.

Trachtenberg, Alan. "Whitman's Lesson of the City." *Breaking Bounds: Whitman and American Cultural Studies*, ed. Betsy Erkkila and Jay Grossman. New York: Oxford University Press, 1996, pp. 163–173.

Tyrrell, Ian R. "Women and Temperance in Antebellum America." *Civil War History* 28 (June 1982): 128–52.

Warner, Michael. "Whitman Drunk." *Breaking Bounds: Whitman and American Cultural Studies*, ed. Betsy Erkkila and Jay Grossman. New York: Oxford University Press, 1996, pp. 30–43.

Yacovone, Donald, "The Transformation of the Black Temperance Movement, 1827–1854: An Interpretation." *Journal of the Early Republic* 8 (Fall 1988): 281–97.

Yeo, Eileen and Stephen Yeo. "Ways of Seeing: Control and Leisure Versus Class and Struggle." *Popular Culture and Class Conflict, 1590–1914*. Atlantic Highlands, NJ, 1981, pp. 128–56.

Dissertations; conference papers; unpublished materials

Baumohl, Jim. "Dashaways and Doctors: The Treatment of Habitual Drunkards in San Francisco from the Gold Rush to Prohibition." Dissertation. University of California, Berkeley, 1966.

Davis, Jim. "Melodrama, Community and Ideology: London's Minor Theatres in the Nineteenth Century." Paper, Melodrama Conference, Institute of Education, London, 1992.

Dunnington, F. P. "Matters Concerning the University Temperance Hall." Manuscript, University of Virginia Special Collections, 1895.

Ferguson, Ann Louise. "Beyond *The Drunkard*: American Temperance Drama Reexamined." Dissertation. Indiana University, 1991.

Hays, Michael. "To Delight and Discipline: Melodrama as Cultural Mediator." Paper, Melodrama Conference, Institute of Education, London, 1992.

Hester, Jessica. "What's a Poor Girl to Do?: Poverty, Whiteness, and Femininity on the Carolina Playmaker's Stage." Theatre Symposium, April 2002.

James, Louis. "'The Bottle with No Label': The Curious Case of British Temperance Melodrama." Paper, Melodrama Conference, Institute of Education, London, 1992.

Kirkpatrick, Jean Romig. "The Temperance Movement and Temperance Fiction, 1820–1860." Dissertation. University of Pennsylvania, 1970.

Mason, Louise Cheryl. "The Fight to be an American Woman and a Playwright: A Critical History from 1773 to the Present." Dissertation: University of California – Berkeley, 1983.

Leighton, Judith. "An Analysis of the Life and Work of Emma Cons (1838–1912), Manager of the Old Vic Theatre, London." M. Phil. thesis, Middlesex University, 1996.

Lyttle, Thomas J. "An Examination of Poetic Justice in Three Selected Types of Nineteenth Century Melodrama: The Indian Play, The Temperance Play, and the Civil War Play." Dissertation. Bowling Green State University, 1974.

Pagel, Carol Ryan. "A History and Analysis of Representative American Dramatizations from American Novels, 1800–1860." Dissertation. University of Denver, 1970.

Ravitz, Abe C. "John Pierpont: Portrait of a Nineteenth Century Reformer." Dissertation. New York Unversity, 1955.

Silverman, Joan L. "'I'll Never touch Another Drop': Images of Alcoholism and Temperance in American Popular Culture, 1874–1920." Dissertation. New York University, 1979.

Newspapers

The Baltimore American
The Boston Herald
The Clipper
Douglas Jerrold's Weekly Newspaper
The Era (London)
The Examiner (London)
The Herald Tribune
The Illustrated London News
The New York Evening Journal
The New York Herald
The New York Tribune
The New York Sun
The New York Times
The Spirit of the Times
The Times (London)
The Weekly Telegraph (London)

Index

246